DEMON HUNT

A Caine Brothers Novel

Christine Ashworth

www.crescentmoonpress.com

Demon Hunt
Christine Ashworth

ISBN: 978-1-937254-73-5
E-ISBN: 978-1-937254-74-2

© Copyright Christine Ashworth 2012. All rights reserved
Cover Art: Tara Reed
Editor: Lin Browne
Layout/Typesetting: jimandzetta.com

Crescent Moon Press
1385 Highway 35
Box 269
Middletown, NJ 07748

Ebooks/Books are not transferable. They cannot be sold, shared or given away as it is an infringement on the copyright of this work.

All Rights Are Reserved. No part of this book may be used or reproduced in any manner whatsoever without written permission, except in the case of brief quotations embodied in critical articles and reviews.

This book is a work of fiction. The names, characters, places and incidents are products of the writer's imagination or have been used fictitiously and are not to be construed as real. Any resemblance to persons, living or dead, actual events, locale or organizations is entirely coincidental.

Crescent Moon Press electronic publication/print publication: July 2012 www.crescentmoonpress.com

DEDICATION

To my mother, Rosie Cunningham, the strongest spirit I've ever known. And to my brother, Scott Cunningham, my very first, long-ago fan. I miss you both. Thanks for cheering me on from the other side.

CHAPTER ONE

The Passageway to the Human Plane gleamed silver in the night heat. Coldness from the other side seeped out and curled around Serra. "It's time." She faced her sire and ignored the sweat running down her back.

"You are weary. Still healing. Stay, Serra. We can send someone else." A muscle in Yur's jaw clenched. His body held a powerful strength despite his great age. "Your brother is gone. Stop trying to take his place." His gaze lingered on the battle scar at her throat.

She gripped her hands together to keep from touching the reminder. A night bird twittered softly in the treetops. "It is my right," she said, her voice sharp. "He was my twin. It is fitting that I take his place." She searched his stony face for understanding and saw none. "I am going, with the blessing of the Council."

His thick brows came together. "Safe travels, my daughter. Remember to tell Gideon Caine everything. You are prepared?"

"Yes. The car and the apartment are ready and waiting for me." Urgency clenched her stomach. "Something's happening. I need to go. *Now*. Farewell the Fae." She gave a brisk nod to her father and, taking a deep breath, stepped into the Passageway. A glance back at him showed her he'd already left.

But his voice lingered in her ear. "The Light go with you."

No two journeys between the Planes were the same, and even the Fae Passages held some danger for the unwary. Serra refused to be intimidated as she moved through the chill nothingness. Focused on her destination, the dark beach in Santa Monica, she counted a thousand heartbeats and a thousand more as she walked, before the roar of the ocean filled her ears. Relief had her running toward the Human

~ ☾ ~

Plane, the scent of the sea tickling her nose. The Passage's hard floor gave way to unsteadiness beneath her shoes and she stumbled, landing on her knees on cold sand in a world far from her own.

A fierce wind tumbled her hair about her face and sent chills across her skin, a shock after the humid heat of home. She stood, pushing weariness aside, and brushed her hands and knees free of sand as she did a quick recon of the area.

The wide beach lay pale in the darkness. Thick clouds overhead partially obscured the almost full moon, but she could make out the boardwalk, a mile or so distant, that would take her to the stairs and to her car. She headed toward the walkway at an easy jog, enjoying the stretch and pull of her muscles.

A scent crossed her path and she breathed it in as she jogged. Someone else was on the beach that early December morning and he smelled—arresting, alluring. Dangerous. He'd gone the other way not half an hour before.

A cry split the night. Lightning illuminated the beach and thunder cracked, hard and close, overhead. Her skin chilled anew at the hallmarks of death, but she resisted the urge to investigate and kept moving forward. There was nothing she could do. Not yet.

She zipped up the thin hoody and regretted her choice of shorts. The brisk wind spattered stinging sand on her bare legs as she jogged. Finally reaching the cement walkway, she picked up her pace, anxious now to get to her car.

She hadn't come all this way to merely kill demons. She'd come here to help gather an army to stop a madman. Tomorrow, after she talked to Gideon Caine, everything else would fall into place.

The staircase loomed in front of her, rising the hundred feet to the bluffs and neighborhood above. She paused at the bottom of the stairs to stretch her legs. She loved running, but running on sand was much different than running in the treetops of home.

His footsteps registered not far behind, just before she caught his scent. She whirled around in shock. He hadn't been there a minute ago. The male with the sexy scent. How

~ ☾ ~

could she be so careless as to not be aware?

He stopped a few feet from her and stared. She had to look up to see his eyes. Considered tall in her world, he was much taller. His skin shone as black as hers shimmered white. His jogging suit looked immaculate even in the wind and hugged his muscled body in all the right places, as if he'd been conjured up by her most secret night fantasies. She swallowed hard. Those fantasies had died years ago.

He cleared his throat, and she quickly brought her gaze back up to meet his.

"Excuse me, miss. Didn't mean to startle you, but haven't you seen the news this week? There's a serial killer on the loose." His voice, smooth and deep, rang with concern. "You shouldn't be out here, not this late."

"Yes, and the serial killer is killing homeless men. I'm not homeless, and I'm not a man, so I think I'll be safe enough." Serra cocked an eyebrow even as her shoulders tightened. "Thank you, but I'm just going up to my car."

She caught his scowl out of the corner of her eye as she turned to go up the steps. The heat of his gaze brushed her back. She sighed and shook her head as he followed, checking the pocket of her hoody for her can of pepper spray, just in case. Human irritations were best taken care of using human methods. Though she had to admit her first thought of him was *not* as an irritation.

The wall of mist that had hung back on the ocean began its rush toward land, filling the air around her with a salty gray and somehow unfriendly density. She rubbed her arms against the chill, aware of the man climbing up the stairs behind her.

As she reached the top of the long staircase, a noxious odor drifted toward her, a remnant of death on a finger of wind. Demon stink? Dismayed, Serra followed it toward a small side street, in the opposite direction of her car. The stranger topped the staircase and came behind, his footsteps crunching through the dry leaves littering the ground. The wind had lessened up here on the bluff, and the night was oddly quiet.

She didn't want an audience when she dealt with the

~ ☾ ~

demon. The sexy stranger behind her would either freak out, or he'd rush to protect her. Either one would end in his death. Caught between doubt and duty, she slowed her steps as she rounded another corner.

The stench hit her harder and closer this time, one of moldy socks and copper, with an aftertaste of an electrical fire. She sneezed and her stomach twisted. Definitely demon, and it was definitely close. She backed up the way she came, still sneezing, and bumped into a hard, warm body.

His arms came around her, steadying her even as he cursed all demonkind, his words low and bitter. In the next breath, he swept her off her feet, leaving her gasping at the sensation. He ran back the way they'd come, holding her high and hard against his chest.

Her heart thrummed faster than hummingbird wings. He'd known the danger, too. He'd known the scent. He'd *known*. "I can run."

"Shut up." The snap of command rang in his voice.

A crack behind him had him running faster. Wind tore at her eyes. She turned her face to his chest and breathed him in. He smelled like dark resins and crisp pine. *Dangerous. Enticing.*

"Hang on tight. We're going into the bushes."

Serra made herself as small as possible in his arms and kept her face buried against his wide chest. A crack and a wail had him cursing as they crashed through a hedge and into the bushes behind it, and only then did she realize they were being chased by a demon wielding a whip.

Her rescuer dropped to his knees and rolled onto his back, keeping her protected from the ground. She scrambled to get her mouth as close to his ear as possible.

"You know demon stench. *How?*"

His arms tightened around her, one big hand cradling her head, the other firm on her ass. She was sprawled over him. Heat sparked deep inside her. She could feel her breasts flattened against his broad chest, his knee possessive between her legs. Desire, long-forgotten, flooded her body and became a tart flavor on her tongue.

"Leave it alone." His words were a thread of sound.

~ ☾ ~

Silence fell around them, not a bird or an insect to be heard. The demonic scent grew stronger, and Serra's stomach revolted. She pressed her nose into her stranger's chest and took a tentative breath. His hand gentled on her head.

A loud whip-crack shattered the silence, the sound so near her ears rang with it. The man beneath her jerked.

He rolled her off him. "Stay here," he muttered as he grabbed onto a sturdy trunk with both hands.

"I can help." Her hand touched his cheek, lingered there. All she had to do was push slightly, and she could give him her energy, her strength. She gave a tentative push but was met with solid mental resistance.

"No. Stay hidden." His deep blue eyes met hers. "I'm Gregor Caine. When the time comes, run like hell for your car."

"I'm Serra Willows," she said, her voice barely a whisper as shock reverberated through her. A *Caine?*

"Once you're safe, find my brother Justin. Tell him everything." The Caine's body jerked, loosening his hold on the trunk. "Sorry."

She watched regret flash across his face just before he let go, the whip dragging him along through the bushes and out of her sight toward the street. Serra crept toward the edge of her hiding place and peered out. She couldn't remember the last time someone had gone into the fight before her.

The streetlights were all out, and the dirty mist masked the houses nearby. A dark form loomed tall in the street, the source of the stench. Serra bit her tongue to keep from crying out. The Caine was being pulled toward the dark shape at a leisurely pace, the whip curled tight around one of his ankles.

Serra raised a hand above her and, in a whisper, called for the wind lingering out over the ocean. It came with vengeance over the bluff and battered at the demon, who staggered and roared and bent into the wind. The demon set its feet and continued to drag Gregor Caine through the street.

Even as horror speared through her, Gregor rolled and tugged hard on the whip with both hands, pulling the demon off balance. He sprang up and head-butted it in the stomach.

The demon howled, a high-pitched keening that set the

~ ☾ ~

neighborhood dogs to barking. Serra clutched her ears as pain splintered into her head.

As quickly as it had started the cry stopped, but the neighborhood dogs continued to bark. Her heart racing, Serra focused again on the fight and the demon in front of her. The crescent of white that curled around its left eye told her this one was young, and hungry, not yet fully mature, and so slightly less deadly.

Still, she had her doubts about Gregor and held herself ready to help him out.

Leaves and street debris, lifted by the wind, filled the air. Gregor kicked at the demon and spun away. The demon held its throat, stumbling backward. Gregor kicked again, this time at the thing's knee, and brought it down. The demon's eyes widened and one huge hand thumped its chest as it fell exactly the way a huge fruitwood tree fell when lightning struck it back home.

But when the demon should have hit the pavement, it dissolved into air. No hard thud of body against ground, no nothing. Serra stared as the implications of that trick reverberated through her mind. Not just a demon, then. This was a Hjurlt, a hunting demon, and where there was one, there were two. Always. *Leaves and berries!* Was she already too late?

Gregor swore and turned around, his face set and his body tensed. "Where are you, bastard? Get back here. I'm not finished with you." His voice fell flat.

The wind hadn't dissipated the thick, unfriendly mist. Dogs barked. Serra glanced at where the homes across from them should be, but they stayed dark. No one heard. No one came to investigate.

He turned around again just as the demon reappeared behind him. Serra's mind shouted an incoherent warning, her tongue unable to react fast enough. Gregor danced away from the demon and turned just as a vicious set of claws originally aiming for his head swiped down his shoulder to his belly, shredding his clothing and spilling his blood.

Her protector went down hard. The demon seemed to smile and took two steps toward him.

~ ☾ ~

White-hot rage burst through Serra. She rolled from her hiding place and ran full tilt at the demon. At the last minute, she jumped and struck out with her feet, targeting hip and knee. The demon staggered sideways but before it could regain its footing, she'd whipped out the pepper spray she'd been fiddling with and blasted the demon in the eyes. It wasn't as good as her Daggers of Atalon, but it would do.

Skipping back from it as it howled and clawed at its face, she stopped in front of Gregor Caine and began the protection. As she chanted, she prayed the earth would continue to respond to her here the way it did in Faeland.

CHAPTER TWO

To Serra's satisfaction, a shimmering dome of greenish-brown light rose to encompass both of them.

The demon had recovered from her pepper spray attack and now snarled, focused on her. Chanting still, the earth's power flooded into her, power so rarely tapped by anyone now. No wonder the demons wanted the Human Plane for their own. She reached into the sky and drew down a firebolt, shot it at the demon, straight into its belly. Her own stomach clenched in protest as she did what had to be done.

The firebolt cut the demon in two before burning all the pieces. Lightning flashed and thunder rumbled. She looked upward and rain hurtled down in response, washing away all evidence of the demon that had threatened them. Her barrier between them and danger lifted.

She'd gotten lucky. A fully-grown Hjurlt wouldn't have been dispatched so easily.

Moving to Gregor's side, she sat abruptly.

No matter how long she'd been killing, no matter that she felt it her duty, she hated it. She had hated it when Terrell did it, and she hated it now. This would be her last mission, her last fight. There had to be more than death for her in the world. It was past time she sought it out.

Lifting her face to the welcome rain, she allowed herself the joy of it against her skin. It smelled of the ocean and electricity. Caine's hand twitched against her hip, and she turned a frown toward him, but he didn't move again. Not even the rain soaking him caused him to stir. Now that she focused, she could smell his lifeblood emptying into the ground.

Dread made her stomach clench again. He'd fought *for her*. She was honor-bound to Heal, no matter what. No matter that it had been ages. She knelt at his side and pushed

~ ☾ ~

her hands against the three thick rips in his flesh, shoulder to waist, his blood still warm against her cooling skin. Memories of the very last time she'd Healed intruded, and Terrell's pale face imposed itself on Gregor's. Her heart stopped and her breath caught in her throat.

But Gregor was not her brother. They weren't on the Fae battlefield right now, and the demon—this time, anyway—had been vanquished. Blinking away those thoughts, Serra dug deep for her Healer instincts, gone mainly unused in the last decade.

She pulled the waiting energy from the very earth and layered it, piece by piece, into Gregor's torn body, painstakingly healing the internal wounds, becoming breathless with the effort. She'd forgotten. She'd been a Warrior for so long now that she'd forgotten how much it took out of her to heal.

The rain drenched them both as time passed in uncounted heartbeats while she used both mental and physical abilities to reconnect what the demon had so casually torn apart.

Her head and back both ached and her focus wavered as, finally, she eased the last of the rips in his skin back together. The very last of the Healing. The squall had lightened, turned to mist before she finished and sat back, dazed. She wiped the rain out of her eyes and sneezed.

He murmured something under his breath. She looked at him to give him comfort, but his eyes weren't blazing at her.

He was still out cold.

Checking his stomach, she smoothed the tattered microfiber jacket across his now-whole body and leaned over him, her hands searching for a heartbeat in his throat.

The beat was sluggish. *Light*! She needed to get him moving again somehow, but the memory of him towering over her made her put aside any thoughts of muscling him to his feet. She looked at his face, so peaceful, and her steady hands trembled.

So she'd Healed him, as she hadn't Healed anyone for years, as she hadn't been able to Heal Terrell. It didn't, it *wouldn't* mean anything. Still, she couldn't prevent her fingers from moving lightly over the sculpted line of his jaw

~ ☾ ~

and up to his sharp cheekbones. Serra scooted forward, her knees by his shoulder, and bent low. She'd been a Warrior for so long that at times it was hard to remember she was also female. Now, her blood heated and her body craved. With his face cradled in her hands, she followed impulse and kissed him.

His lips were warm against hers and tasted of rain. She nipped at his bottom lip then soothed it with her tongue. Kissing along his jawbone, she nuzzled his ear, wishing briefly they were anywhere other than the middle of the road in a rainstorm. Rather, make that a thunderstorm. Lightning flashed overhead and thunder accompanied it, the ground trembling in response, and the raindrops grew fat once again.

"Wake up, Gregor. I need to get you home, and I can't exactly carry you," she murmured, putting heavy suggestion into the words. It might take awhile, but he'd wake up. When he did, she'd be Warrior once more.

In the meantime, she may as well kiss him again. Straddling him, she bent to her task with enthusiasm.

~~~

The most talented mouth in the world pressed against his. Gregor breathed in her scent, one of green and growing things, and moved his lips under hers. Before she could leave him, he wrapped his arms around her and deepened their kiss, exploring her mouth much more fully.

Springtime. She tasted of spring, and of growth. Fresh and necessary. He groaned as she wiggled on top of him, her lean muscles and soft curves throwing his body into a maelstrom of need. His hands tightened on the woman's truly excellent ass as he gave himself up to her, while one part of his mind processed his last couple of hours.

The demon. He went utterly still. She stilled, too, and moved to sit up. Her legs were on either side of him, her hands pressed against his chest. The heat of her pressed right across his groin. Rain spattered his face.

He opened his eyes.

She peered down at him, her purple and silver eyes

~ ☾ ~

distinctive even in the depths of night. "Do you remember what happened?"

He searched his mind for her name. "Serra."

"Yes."

"You're Fae. Fae? Damn it. There was a demon?"

"It's dead."

Which had to mean she killed it. Nice of her not to rub it in. "You're okay though?"

"I am fine."

"Would you let me up?"

He watched as she scrambled off and leaned down to offer a hand. With a strength that didn't show on the outside, she drew him easily to his feet. He stared down at his tattered clothing in disbelief.

"Are you all right? Do you hurt anywhere?" The top of her blonde head came to about his chin. Her hands smoothed his ruined jacket and t-shirt, touching his skin as often as not. "I Healed you. It's been awhile since I've done any Healing on a regular basis though, so you might be a little sore for a few days."

Curses he didn't want to utter in front of her flew through his mind. He'd almost let her walk right into a demon, and all she could talk about was how she healed him? Was she crazy? No. No, she was Fae, damn it to hell.

He had to get to Justin. He took a couple steps away from her then headed east, the ocean at his back, his legs rubbery beneath him. The dirty mist deadened all sound and made seeing difficult.

"Caine?"

"I'm fine." He willed his body back to its normal state, while his mind still reeled. She was Fae. They'd been attacked by a demon. Now her energy brushed up against his as they walked, helping him to stay upright but also tempting him to toss out all his rules. *She was Fae.* He was *human.* As good as she felt splayed on top of him, it was a non-starter from his point of view.

His eye twitched and he wrenched his focus away from sex. "What happened to the demon?"

"Firebolt," she said, and shrugged. "He got in the way."

~ ☾ ~

"Right." Hell. She wasn't any old Fae. She was a Warrior Fae if she could call firebolts. She threw him off his stride, and he didn't appreciate it.

"Why can't I reach your mind?"

And there she was, still at his shoulder, her scent pulling at him, her energies flirting with his and her mind questing. He sighed and scanned the streets and the wind, preparing for another attack. Just in case.

"Caine?"

"No one reaches my mind." He shrugged, his gaze sharp on the shadows around them. He knew she, too, was watching the streets.

"Your barriers are strong. Why?"

"Because they are."

"But why? You're a Caine. You have Fae and demon blood inside you. We should be able to communicate mind-to-mind with no problem. A big help when things go wrong."

Gregor stopped abruptly. He stared into her purple eyes. "I'm *human*. Human, and nothing else." The words felt thick in his mouth, almost wrong, for the very first time. He continued walking, aware that now she was full of more questions than ever.

She gave what sounded like a sniff. "I did kill the demon, and I did heal you. So you owe me some answers."

"Did it look like I needed help with the demon?" he demanded.

"Well." She bit her lip, and he scowled.

"I had it under control. If you hadn't distracted me with your warning, I doubt I would have been injured, you wouldn't have had to heal me, and you wouldn't be trotting at my heels like a puppy waiting for a bone from its owner." To his surprise, it rankled, being saved by a girl.

It was Serra's turn to stop. "I *didn't* call to you. I didn't warn you, not verbally. My English deserted me and I couldn't speak."

He turned back to her. "You did, too. I heard you clearly."

Her pale eyebrows rose. "What did I say? Exactly?"

Gregor opened his mouth but nothing came out. She *had* called out to him. He'd heard her. What had she said? Watch

~ ☾ ~

out? *Behind you? Something* had made him turn around and he'd have sworn it was her voice, shouting at him.

But the words she'd used didn't come to mind. Unable to find the right ones, he walked away. "Enough. I've had enough." He wiped rain off his face again as a sliver of doubt slipped down his spine. What had she *done*?

He heard Serra sigh behind him. "I'm sure you have. So just point me in the direction of Gideon Caine, and I'll leave you alone. I've got a portal to close and more demons to kill, and I really need to speak with Gideon."

Gregor turned at the corner, his eyes on a brightly-lit house a third of the way up the street. "I haven't seen or spoken with Gideon in ten years, so either you're late, or you know more than I do. You'll just have to deal with me instead of Gideon." The demon, the girl, and now his long-gone father. What else could possibly happen that night?

Gregor approached Justin's house with caution. All the lights inside were blazing, and at a time of night his brother was usually sound asleep. "What the hell?"

"Were you expecting company?" She sidled up next to him.

"Stay behind me until we know what we're dealing with." He moved slowly up the walk, checking the wind, but only his brother's scent rode it.

Serra hovered at Gregor's right shoulder. "This is the best I can do. I don't hide well anymore."

Before they could reach the front door, Justin opened it, half-naked in gray pajama pants. "I'll call you back." He hung up his cell, tossed it on the hallway table and crossed his arms, his green eyes blazing and dreadlocks quivering. "You look terrible. What the hell is going on?"

"You good? The lights had me concerned." Gregor prayed he'd be able to stay upright until the Fae was gone. "This is Serra. She's here to see Dad, but obviously that's not going to happen. We've got demons. Oh, and she's Fae."

Serra pointed at Justin. "You are his brother. Tell him to sleep. The Caine needs to rest. A demon tried to gut him."

Justin stifled his laughter. "Well, I've never been able to force him to sleep."

Gregor glared equally at both. "I'm fine. Just tired. In the morning, we'll need to call Maggie, have her meet us. We'll see you then, Serra." He turned to face her and took a step backward, into the house, leaving her on the porch.

"I'll accept your thanks for killing the demon now."

Gregor stared. Tall for a woman, with generous curves and skin that radiated faint light, she stood there with clenched fists and a tired, sad, and angry look in her eyes. Warrior. Female. *Fae.*

He almost heard it, that click of recognition, that wary knowledge unlocking inside him, telling him to step carefully. He took a breath and bowed his head to her.

"Thank you, so much, for killing the demon."

He shut the door in her face, heard her stifled annoyance, and waited for the sound of her footsteps on the path. He leaned against the door and shut his eyes.

"Do you even want to know why I am so frantic?" Justin's tone was barely even.

Gregor jerked, annoyed that he'd almost fallen asleep, and stumbled to the couch. "Why are you so frantic? Rose? Gabriel?"

"They're fine. Enjoying their vacation up in Cambria. You *idiot.* What did you think it would do to me to feel you slip out of my head that way?"

Gregor gaped at him. "Excuse me?"

Justin moved to the chair opposite the couch and sat, dangling his hands between his knees. "You're always in my head. Always. Only tonight, all of a sudden you weren't. You woke me out of a sound sleep because *you weren't there.* You weren't where you've been since I was born. Would you mind telling me just what the hell happened?"

Gregor straightened. "I couldn't sleep. Anniversary of dad leaving, I haven't had a date in months, and the damned serial killer all jumbled in my head, so I got up and went for a run. And then, boom. Demon. I could smell it, but I couldn't find it. Serra and I met at the stairs by the beach, you know where."

Justin listened as Gregor laid out the events of the night.

"So, he got me, slightly." Gregor gestured to the tattered clothes he still wore. "Serra healed me. She's Warrior Fae.

~ ☾ ~

Pulled down a firebolt, no problem, and sliced the demon in two."

"Hell," Justin said, and leaned back in the chair. "You know what this means?"

Gregor winced. "Open portal to the Chaos Plane."

"Which means we go into battle, again." Justin rubbed at his eyes.

Gregor rolled his shoulders. He had a sinking feeling that his life path was about to undergo a sea change.

~ ☾ ~

CHAPTER THREE

Fran stared at the glowing portal in the corner of the vast, empty warehouse and swallowed hard. "I thought you said nothing bad was going to come out of there." She sent a fearful glance at Bryce, standing in front of the computer and tapping. "Those were demons that escaped, weren't they? Did Kendall send them through?"

"I've told you before. Kendall knows what he's doing, Frannie. Now shut up while I think." He rested his hands on his hips and stared at the screen.

Fran struggled to keep her panic in check. Kendall Sorbis had been bad news in college, and the years between hadn't changed him. Bryce was younger, so maybe he didn't know just how bad Kendall could get. "I know you're cousins and all," she began.

"Shut *up*, Frannie."

She shivered at the darkness in his voice and shrank into herself. She'd been so sure Bryce was the only guy for her. Just her luck he was joined at the hip with Kendall, who had disappeared a few months ago. Taking, rumor had it, most of his new wife's fortune with him.

Now Kendall was back in an undercover way, spreading the cash around, and Bryce had fallen hard into hero-worship. Frannie blinked back tears. At least Bryce hadn't thrown her out of the apartment yet. She would put up with a lot before she'd go back to her stepfather's house. She was over thirty, for Pete's sake, not a child. She could handle this. She could handle demons. Hadn't she even been a Wiccan in college?

"There." Satisfaction oozed from him as he reached an arm out and snagged her around the waist. "I've got everything set up. You're putting together a party, baby. A big, fancy party. Champagne and appetizers. A new dress. Now give me a kiss."

~ ☾ ~

She emerged from his embrace mussed and happy, willing to push aside her uneasiness. "When's the party?"

"Four days. Friday, December twenty-first."

"The winter solstice." Fran nodded. "There's an eclipse that night, too. What are we celebrating?"

"The winter solstice," he said, and let out a chuckle. "Endings and beginnings. It's what Kendall wants, okay baby? And we'll be having some more guests coming through the portal. We need to be respectful."

"How many for the party? A hundred, two hundred?" She nuzzled his neck and did her best to ignore her growing panic. "That's going to be a lot of champagne."

"We're aiming bigger. You're the only one I can trust. I need you to work with me here."

She tightened her arms around him. "I don't have to actually talk to any of the demons, do I? They scare me."

"You'll deal with the illegals who'll decorate this place for you. Leave the demons to me."

The portal glowed a sickly green and Kendall stepped through, his gaze zeroing in on the two of them on the other side of the big room.

He smiled and Fran's heart skipped a beat in fear.

"Bryce. He's here."

"Hmm? Oh, hey Kendall." Bryce pulled away from Fran's clinging arms and went to meet his cousin halfway across the room.

Fran shut her eyes tightly, wishing she could do the same for her ears. She didn't want to know what they were planning. She just wanted to keep her thoughts on cheddar puffs and champagne and festive winter decorations, and not think about the demon Bryce gutted earlier that night, nor how it went up in flames at the touch of a match.

"As for my Francie." Kendall's voice was so close that it was no surprise to find him standing in front of her. "My dear. The whole Goth vibe works on you. And I can see that sex with my cousin works, as well."

She flushed with pleasure and embarrassment. He'd been the only one to call her Francie. "Um. You look terrific, Kendall." It was true. Kendall's golden hair was artfully mussed, his ice-blue eyes as bright as ever. If perhaps his skin stretched a bit too tightly over his bones, few if any would comment.

His gaze caught hers and she knew again the deep yearning of her college days. "You won't tell anyone you saw me, will you?" He cupped her cheek and hummed a sweet folk song under his breath.

She blinked as his form grew foggy and wavered in front of her. She steadied herself with one hand on his shoulder. "Of course I won't tell. Of course not. I pledged my soul to you, don't you remember? I would never betray you."

A deep, satisfied chuckle filled her ears. "I do remember. Now I know you remember, too. I wonder who else from the coven will come out and play? Never mind. Go over there and sit until Bryce is ready for you."

Fran floated to the chair in the corner. Kendall had returned. Kendall said she looked good. Kendall had searched her out, and now she would be doing work for him. Maybe, if she were very good, she'd get to talk to him again. She watched as the two men conversed, the sweet folk song running through her head, soothing as a lullaby.

~ ☾ ~

CHAPTER FOUR

Gregor walked to Justin's house at dawn, once again immaculate and in control in a gray three-piece suit. Fog still blanketed the streets in Santa Monica. The threat of more rain hung in the air.

He let himself in and heard the rush of the shower. Instead of bugging Justin, he went to the kitchen and poured himself a cup of coffee, then drifted toward the wide picture window framing the tropical backyard.

The pool in the corner of the yard gleamed. Mist rose from it. A pale form cut through the water, swimming steadily. He was out the door and striding across the lawn before he realized he'd decided to move.

Serra stopped swimming to tread water. Invitation shone from her. "Join me."

"No." He hadn't remembered her voice as being sultry. Now the sound of it curled deep inside him, set him aching. That there was even a question in his mind about her, about the two of them, pissed him off.

She was Fae. Off limits. End of story.

Right?

The neat pile of her clothes on the chaise caught his eye. "I'll get you a towel." He turned on one heel and headed back into the house. Made his way blindly into the guest bathroom and stood, his mind blank.

She shook his control, and he didn't like it. He reached for his customary imperturbability and caught sight of himself in the mirror, coffee cup suspended half way to his mouth, his reason for being in the bathroom escaping him for the moment.

"I'm drawn to water. It soothes me. It always has." Coffee spilled over his hand at the sound of her behind him. He turned and blinked, and remembered why he had gone into

~ ☾ ~

the bathroom.

She stood there, naked, pool water beading on skin that gleamed like a pearl. He looked his fill, helpless to do otherwise. An inch- thick scar ran down her throat to the top of her breasts, which were plump and tipped with pink nipples that tightened as his gaze brushed them. Her waist dented in and her hips curved out, making his hands itch, and the sparse curls between her legs were as pale a blonde as the hair on her head. Her eyes, those amethyst jewels, watched him with unnerving intensity.

He yanked the towel off the rail and thrust it at her while he passed her on his way out of the suddenly too-small room. He'd almost made it to the living room when she spoke again.

"I want you."

A straightforward declaration, not a whine nor an invitation. A muscle in his cheek twitched. "We've got a portal to close and demons to kill. There's no time for sex."

"There's always time for sex," she said, shocked. "I'm quite good at it. I know you'll enjoy yourself."

"I'm sure I would. Get dressed," he said, and taking a deep breath, headed into the kitchen for more coffee. If the demons didn't kill him, dealing with her just might do the job.

~~~

Serra wiped her sweaty palms on her new jeans and stared out the car window. In many ways, killing on the battlefield was easier than dealing with humans. Caine tugged at her, and it wasn't just the bond of Healing between them. He had been surprised at her wanting to have sex with him, which didn't make any sense. The human women weren't usually stupid when it came to attractive men.

Of course, she'd been pretty surprised by it, too. Since taking up the mantle of Warrior, there hadn't been a lot of sex in her life. Oh, there had been release mating—of a sort— rough, tumble, in the dark and not sure who was doing what, but that's what came with Warrior territory.

Gregor Caine, on the other hand, was someone she'd

prefer to *see* while they had sex. Slowly, in daylight, eyes wide open and preferably on thick, soft bedding. She'd want to see her hands roam over his muscles. Watch his eyes blur as she touched him. Revel in the look of his night-dark skin within her pale body as they finally came together.

But he'd been right. They had work to do. She resisted the urge to squirm in her seat and turned to look at him.

"Tell me about the wolves." Her lips twitched. He looked so serious as he maneuvered his car smoothly through the early morning traffic. So constrained in his formal suit, when she'd much rather see him naked. She wrenched her mind to the coming meeting. "Your alliance is an unusual one."

"I don't know them very well. They worked this past summer with my brother Gabriel. Helped take down a nest of vampires."

"How many of them are there?"

"I don't know that, either." He turned into a parking garage and went up a level before parking near a staircase. "Like I said, I don't know them."

"No one expects you to know everything," she replied mildly.

He just got out of the car. She followed him down the flight of stairs, across an alley, and into the open-air mall.

"This is a shopping mall, right?" Avid to take in all the sights, Serra tried to look everywhere all at once. "So many choices."

Still early, the scent of coffee and fresh breads hung in the air. The dirty mist of the night before had gone, but the clouds hung low overhead and sounds were muted. Knots of people, in twos and threes, walked vigorously up and down the tree-filled mall. The clothing stores and bigger restaurants wouldn't open for hours, but the coffee shops seemed to be doing great business.

She breathed it all in. "What a nice place."

"This is the Third Street Promenade. Dad rented office space here years ago, and we've managed to hang onto it through all the renovations. This way."

His hand on her back burned through her sweater. As if he felt the heat too, he released her quickly and opened a glass door set beside an imports shop. A narrow staircase faced the door.

They went upstairs. Serra sneezed twice. "I forgot about the Were smell."

He sniffed the air. "Animal, and something else, something basically human."

"Human animal, and of the earth. Animals are different here, and the human-wolf scent different yet again. Not bad, just distinctive." She shrugged. "I'll get used to it."

Gregor waved her through the door to the office.

The reception area was warm and inviting, painted a pale yellow with soothing green accents dotting the room. A green carpet, a huge *ficus benjamina* tree in one corner and a row of ivy curling down a half-wall added freshness.

"This is nice." She looked around in delight. "Like being in a small, sunny garden."

He shrugged. "It's not bad. Come on."

His hand landed in the small of her back again, and she moved forward at his unspoken urging, peeking into open doors along the way. The rest of the place had a sterile feel with white paint on the walls and charcoal carpeting. They went down the long hallway to the last room on the left.

As they entered, emotional currents from those in the room bombarded her. Serra worked fast to strengthen her inner shields, mentally cursing for having forgotten to be on guard. Gregor took her focus, which left her vulnerable.

That wasn't acceptable.

The mood was tense, a question of leadership from what she could tell from her brief scan. Well, she'd take care of that. Serra concentrated as Gregor introduced them.

Justin leaned against the windowsill, unsmiling. Serra noticed his tension eased into a calming influence that spread through the room.

A tall woman named Magdalena de la Cruz, Maggie, stood at his side, arms tightly crossed, her wild black hair pulled up into a ponytail that still skimmed her waist. She had a figure to rival the great Ulandia herself, and her aura pulsed, pale blue with a hint of orange around the edges. Interesting. A witch.

~ ☾ ~

The Weres stood on the opposite side of the table. The woman had eyes that flashed golden as she gazed at Serra. The mate to the Alpha, Serra could feel the woman's strength. She would not want to count her as an enemy for any reason.

Serra's gaze moved to the man next to her. His hands were fisted at his side, and the look in his eyes held a pain she knew all too well. She skimmed his public mind. He had lost a brother. Compassion welled and she bowed her head to him.

"I am Serra Willows, a Fae. I am sorry for your loss."

"Danny Roush, of the Santa Monica Mountains Preserve Wolf Pack. My mate, Chandra." Danny's yellow eyes searched hers. "You suffered a loss, too?"

"My twin brother. Yes." Serra moved to sit at the head of the table. "Please sit, and tell us your tale."

The rest of them took their seats, the witch pulling out a yellow pad and a pen from a purse Serra coveted.

"First, thank you for allowing us to crash your meeting. As you came to us in time of need during the summer, so now we return the favor." Danny's gaze turned inward. "My brother James went out to pick up pizza, around ten last night. He and his wife were celebrating their baby turning five months old. Ciro's, the pizza place, backs onto an alley. It's about three miles from our compound. James smelled demon, and blood, so he called me. Told me he could hear the demon eating. I told him to wait for me, but by the time I got there, he was already dead. And in wolf form. We buried him early this morning up in the mountains."

"Were there any demons left when you arrived?" Serra kept her voice cool against the heat of his grief.

"Not alive. Bits. Pieces. We gathered everything together and burned it up in the mountain. Some of the bits and pieces were human, but I don't know how many it killed." Danny scanned the others, and came back to her. "Do you know what's going on?"

"I know some of it." Serra glanced around the table. "Has anything else been happening that I should know?"

Maggie frowned. "I've been having dreams for the past couple of weeks. They involve someone I used to know, years ago. The dreams are splashed with blood, and there's a full moon in the sky. Lots of people die."

Justin put a hand on her shoulder. "Why didn't you tell me?"

She inched her chair further away from his and crossed her arms. "I told Gregor."

Serra cleared her throat. "Dreams. Demons. And the dead. Not to mention the serial killer on the news lately. I believe they're all connected. The Fae have learned that a human mage has been going back and forth to the Chaos Plane for the last several years. The Fae Council has been watching him from afar, not willing to interfere without good reason."

When Maggie would have interrupted, she held up a hand for silence.

"However, not long ago we saw him bring demons to the Human Plane through a portal. I have been sent here to help gather an army for the purpose of killing the mage and cleaning up the demons littering this world."

Maggie spoke then. "Why didn't *you* bring an army?"

Serra skewered her with a look. "Our world has been at war with those on the Chaos Plane for one of your decades, but time is different, slower, in our land. We have lost over half our population, and our political structure has collapsed. We are doing our best." She looked to Gregor and Justin. "Our ties with the Caines, and our mutual pledge of support, bring me here now." Serra heard the pain in her voice and took a breath before continuing.

"I was supposed to meet with Gideon Caine, as he had been our liaison. When we couldn't make contact, the Fae Council gave me leave to come anyway, in the hope that Gideon could be found." She glanced at Gregor. "Gideon's son Gregor happened to meet me. So it was destined that we work together."

"We killed a demon last night. Rather, she killed a demon last night, one that stood what, eight, nine feet tall?" Gregor looked to Serra, who nodded.

She pushed at her hair. "That demon is one of the problems. It was a Hjurlt demon; its claws carry poison, it has two mouths in demon form, it can go invisible when attacked, and can shape shift to the native species on whatever Plane it finds itself. Worse than all of that? They usually travel in pairs. Which means there's at least one more out there, and they are always hungry for meat. The one I killed was a youngling. Its brother-pair, if it still lives, will be wary on its own. It will gain in strength with every meal. I cannot guarantee that I will be able to kill it when it reaches full strength, though I will try."

Silence held them all as they took that in.

Danny put his hands over his eyes. "Then the other one might have been what killed James."

Serra kept her face impassive. "Maybe. Or maybe it was a different type of demon. We'll know more once we start the hunt."

Justin spoke then. "Do you know the man's name? The one handing out passports to demons?"

"No. But he is white-skinned, blond and blue-eyed. Approximately six feet tall, slender, in his early thirties. He could be considered good looking." Serra's gaze strayed to Gregor again, who was frowning.

Justin thumped the table. "Damn it. Kendall Sorbis. I'll bet a million dollars."

"Don't jump to conclusions, surfer boy." Maggie sniffed and turned to Serra. "What do we do now?"

"We hunt. We search for the demons undoubtedly in your community. Since most of your society doesn't believe that demons exist, we can't exactly raise a city-wide alarm. We need to mobilize those you can trust." She glanced around those seated at the table. "How many can we count on?"

"The wolves." Danny reached for Chandra's hand. "I can gather twenty, maybe more." At Chandra's glare, he relented. "Definitely more, including our women."

Chandra burst into speech. "No one should go hunting alone. That's what got James killed, his damned cocky attitude that he could handle demons and vampires and everything else by himself. He was still angry that Danny kept him from the battle this past summer. He didn't get a chance to cover himself with vampire blood, ashes and glory." Chandra looked to the others and shook her head. "I'm sorry. But it's true. *Don't* hunt alone."

~ ☾ ~

"What was I supposed to do? His wife had just given birth. I was supposed to let him go into battle with a mind divided?" Danny glared at his mate.

Serra interrupted the tensions simmering between the two. "You did what you had to do. And now we will do what we must do to keep others safe. Chandra is correct, though. No one should hunt alone."

Maggie looked up from the notes she'd taken. "I can call on the witches from my old coven. It's been a long time since we held Circle together, but I'm sure some of my sisters will come to our aid." Maggie's eyes burned with fervor as her gaze met Serra's. "That's nine, total. How many should we put on a team?"

Gregor answered before Serra could. "Two, minimum. This is a big city and we don't have much time."

"Right. Who else can we get to help?" Maggie went back to her lists.

Justin cleared his throat. "This might be a long shot, but what about asking Little Harry at the Nine Hells? He might know people with the right qualifications."

Serra's eyebrows rose. "And what are the right qualifications?"

"Demon blood. There's a lot of it running around in this town. Very diluted at this point, but folks with scent capabilities do exist. Not to mention, some are of the criminal element. Good with killing first and looking innocent afterwards." Justin spread his hands. "Any port in a storm, right?"

"There are more like your family?" Danny looked to Justin then Gregor, his surprise clear.

Gregor and Justin exchanged a glance. "Not on this coast," Gregor said. "No, the Caines are the only tribreds around the greater Los Angeles area that we know of, and we settled here well over a hundred years ago."

"Demon, human and Fae blood. Maybe your family is something new, something we don't have a name for yet?" Chandra tilted her head and contemplated the Caines. "I'll have to think about that. And I'll want your family history. How you all came to be tribreds."

~ ☾ ~

Danny covered her hand with his. "Chandra is big on bloodlines and family trees."

"They're important," she insisted.

"We'll be happy to talk to you. In the meantime, I'll bring Little Harry online," Gregor offered.

"Okay." Serra pointed at Justin. "I'd like you to work with Maggie and the witches. Gregor will handle the part demons, and of course Danny has the wolves."

"What about you?" Gregor's blue gaze trapped hers.

"What?" Startled, she blinked.

"No one hunts alone. Who will you hunt with?"

"I will hunt with you." She shot him a challenging look. "If you don't mind."

"What about the portal?" Justin broke in on their private duel. "We don't know where it is, or how to close it. If we don't close it, we'll be hunting demons for the rest of our lives." Justin's voice was brisk, but his distaste clear.

"We know it's here, somewhere close. We will find it, and we will close it. I understand, theoretically, how it is done." Serra heard the hard edge to her voice but didn't bother to soften it. "No other outcome is acceptable."

"Theoretically?" Justin tapped a pen against the table. "That doesn't sound good."

Serra ignored him. "Something else to keep in mind is that the winter solstice is a mere four days away. It is a night for magicks, when the natural walls between the Planes grow thin. Many of the Fae, and humans as well as demons, hold rituals on the longest night of the year. For demons, many of those rituals are bloody ones. We must find and close the portal before the solstice, or there will be a great loss of life."

"There's a full moon on the night of the winter solstice. A full moon and an eclipse." Horror edged Maggie's voice. "The last eclipse on a winter solstice night was over three hundred and fifty years ago."

Danny let out a groan. "Well. That's the cherry on top. If we're going to save lives, we'll need to divide up the city so we can let the hunt begin."

"I'll get a map." Justin left the room and returned a minute later, holding a large, rolled-up map of the area. He spread it out across the table and everyone gathered around. "We'll need to dole out areas of the city so we're not doubling up our efforts or leaving any section unattended."

Danny spoke first. "The wolves will take the Hollywood Hills. From Griffith Park to Point Mugu, from the hills to the south to the 101 Freeway to the North."

"You can cover that large an area?" Gregor pursed his lips. "I'm impressed."

"It'll take a couple of days, but yes. We should be able to handle that." Chandra smiled at both men.

"The witches will take the Brentwood/Westwood/Wilshire area, from the Hollywood Hills on the north to the Santa Monica border to the south, from Laurel Canyon on the east, including Beverly Hills, to the pier on the west." Maggie glanced around the table. "It will depend on how many of us there are, and what spells we can use to eliminate some areas without actually needing to search."

"Good," approved Serra. "Gregor?"

He pointed to the Santa Monica airport. "The demon-bloods will take it from Santa Monica to the north, down to L.A. International Airport to the south, and from the ocean to the 110 Freeway." He frowned. "If any demons escape us, I'm sure we'll hear about it."

"Excellent. Start in as soon as you can. Use what weapons you have. Stealth is good. Anonymity is better. If you can, burn the corpses. Most are highly flammable in this world and shouldn't cause a problem." Serra paced the room as they worked.

Gregor took over. "Remember if you get caught, you're on your own. Call a member of your team and get someone to take your place. If you or any on your team gets hurt, go to Megan Cavanaugh. She'll take care of you."

They splintered off into groups. Maggie and Chandra made lists of who to talk to and how fast they could get a team together. The two Caines and Danny huddled in one corner, talking tactics.

Serra moved to the window. The ocean pulled at her, the rhythm and flow of it. Just like the rhythm and flow of the life that swirled in the room behind her. But out there in the

~ ☾ ~

world the blight continued, dark spots that resonated in her soul. The sickness infecting the land would surely infect her were it not contained soon.

This, after all, was why she'd demanded to come in Terrell's place. If the humans didn't crush the second Hjurlt and the darkness he represented, then it would fall to her to destroy that darkness, to take it inside her, just like Terrell had done. She knew better than to believe the second Hjurlt would be an easy kill. A death that mirrored her twin's would at least be an honorable death.

Gregor moved to her side. "What are you thinking?"

Serra focused on the positive. "I think this will work. They seem dedicated. I'm even getting used to the wolves' scent." She eased the tension in her shoulders. "This is the easy part, though. Leading is much harder in the field."

"You're not going to be leading in the field. I'm in charge."

She stared at him, at the stubborn set of his chin. Well, she could be just as stubborn. "No, you're not. This is my fight, not yours." A chill crept up her spine and into her voice. "It is my job to destroy the Hjurlt and the other demons who pollute this world. It is my job to annihilate this mage that would help the demons plunder the gifts of the Human Plane. My honor, respect for my dead, demands my leadership."

His eyes narrowed on her. "Everyone has their dead. These are my people. It's my job to protect them, and that means I lead, period."

The two of them, gazes locked, were mere inches apart. The air between them vibrated, and for one moment, Serra's only thought was to drag him to the nearest private room and get him naked.

"I've got a thought. Why don't you both lead?" The amusement in Justin's voice had them breaking their staring contest. The rest of them had stopped talking to watch, Maggie and Chandra doing their best to hide their grins.

Serra, appalled that her mind had strayed so far from the mission, straightened to her full height and checked the clock on the wall. "If we're done, it's time to disperse. We need to begin the hunt as quickly as possible."

"May I ask a question?" Maggie's gaze darted from Serra to

Gregor, and returned to Serra.

"Of course."

"I thought demons were night creatures. Shouldn't we wait until tonight before we start hunting?"

Grateful for the diversion, Serra moved into teaching mode, scanning all the people in the room as she talked. "Demons are like we are. Their sun doesn't shine quite so brightly in their world, but they crave the light as much as they revel in the dark. No two demons have the same likes and dislikes, much like no two humans are the same. The fact is, the demons are out there. The longer they are, the hungrier they will get, and more humans will die. The faster we kill the demons, the more humans we save. It's a simple equation."

Maggie sighed. "I suppose. I'll get started calling my list as soon as it's a decent hour. Not even eight a.m. I'm starving."

Justin stopped her with a hand on her arm. "Breakfast?"

"No."

"Fine. But Maggie, as soon as you've got an idea of who we're working with, call me. We'll all meet up."

She frowned and edged away from him. "All right."

"I'd like to start hunting no later than ten," he added, following her out the door.

Serra watched as they all left until it was just Gregor and herself in the room. Her conscience nagged at her. How many of these humans would survive the coming days? Could she live with herself if any of them died? Justin, or Maggie, Danny or Chandra?

Could she live with herself if Gregor died while they got this portal closed? She shivered and turned to the window, looking out with eyes focused on battlefields of the past.

"We should get something to eat. You do eat, don't you?"

Serra heard the uncertainty in Gregor's voice. "Yes, I eat." She turned to see him standing a good six feet from her. She gave him a measured smile. He didn't want to get close to her, fine. She'd be an ice queen from now on. "Let's go forage for our morning meal."

~ ☾ ~

CHAPTER FIVE

"Shut up, Frannie. You're fine." Bryce sprinkled lighter fluid on the corpse and lit a match. The demon went up in quick, bright flame.

Frannie stifled her low moans with an effort. She refused to look at the glow pulsing at the far end of the room. "You said they'd be easy to control. You said we had nothing to worry about. You said all I had to do was set up a party." She wiped her runny nose on her sleeve and shivered in the cold. The fire in the corner stank and she sneezed, her eyes tearing up at the smell.

"That is all you have to do. Set up a party," Bryce said. He threw the lighter down on the table. It skipped across and landed on the floor against the wall.

Frannie threw him a nervous glance. Whenever he talked like that, biting the words as he said them, that was bad. She knew better than to upset him. She did, she did.

She pulled herself together and stood, wiping her nose again. She needed him. They had plans. Frannie steadied herself with another breath. "Then I guess I'll go make some phone calls. We need this party, right? And we need it soon."

"In four days."

"Right, four days. How did you want me to set this up? There's only one credit card. I'm not sure if you need it or not," she pointed out. "If you do, then I'll set everything up and have you call the number in to the vendors. If that sounds good."

Frannie watched as Bryce visibly relaxed. As long as she did the bulk of the work, he'd be fine as usual.

"No. That's okay. I trust you, baby." He turned and smiled at her and her heart melted.

Frannie went to him and slipped her arms around him, snugging her head on his shoulder. "This is going to be

~ ☾ ~

some party, I promise," she said, and kissed his throat. He smelled like demon, sweat and lighter fluid.

"You'd better buy yourself a pretty dress then." He patted her on the back and pushed her away. "Get going. I'll be late getting home tonight, so don't wait up."

Frannie tapped his shoulder. "The credit card, remember?"

Bryce blinked. "Right. The credit card." He dug in his back pocket for it and handed it over.

"It's heavy," she said, surprised.

"Those black credit cards don't have a limit. I guess they have to be heavy. Now remember, everything in white and gold, with champagne to get a few hundred people drunk. Don't forget to open new Facebook and Twitter accounts and push this with all you've got."

"I promise." She darted in and gave him a quick kiss. "See you soon."

"Yeah." Bryce turned back to the fire now dwindling in the corner of the room.

Frannie shivered and hurried out of the building. A party for a few hundred people. Where to begin? They'd need tables, the kind you stand at and talk to people while you sip your champagne. Waiters, of course. Where would she get waiters? A party rental place would have referrals for caterers and everything, wouldn't they?

An unusual north wind cut right through her sweaters and leggings, and she shivered despite all her layers.

Her cell phone jingled. She answered it without looking at the caller. "Yeah."

"Fran, Fran Thomas? It's Maggie de la Cruz. From college. Remember?"

Frannie stopped cold. "Yeah. Hi Maggie. Been a long time."

"I know and I apologize. I guess my breakup with Kendall years ago broke everything up. That wasn't my intention."

Frannie's heart pounded hard in her chest. "Um. Okay." This couldn't possibly be a coincidence. Her stomach cramped with panic.

"Look, would you be available to meet me this morning? I

~ ☾ ~

want to get a few of the coven together. Something's come up and I need the support." Maggie's sincerity came through loud and clear. "I wouldn't ask you if it wasn't really important."

"Sure. No!" Horrified, Frannie looked at the phone. She rushed into speech. "My bad. Sorry, but I'm putting together a last minute party. An, um, industry party, you know, and there'll be hundreds of guests. There's just no way I'll have even a second for you. Thanks so much for calling. Now I have your number I'll call you back and we'll get together soon. Bye." Shocked at the words that came out of her mouth, Frannie disconnected the call and ran for her car, locked herself in, and huddled in the front seat.

The coven hadn't been together since Maggie had tossed Kendall aside, over eleven years ago. Why had Maggie sought her out now, after all this time? Now, when Kendall had come slithering back into her life?

Kendall owned her soul. She hadn't forgotten that. She hadn't forgotten anything from her time with him, and seeing him last night had made it all real again. She'd loved Kendall once. She loved Bryce now. Didn't she?

She shuddered at the memory of the glee she had seen in Bryce's eyes while burning the demon. The scent had sunk into her clothes. She started the engine and pushed in the CD Bryce had given her. She'd need a shower before she did anything else that day.

A low melody filled the car and she relaxed back into her seat. Of course. A shower, and a load of laundry, and she'd be a new woman.

Humming, Frannie headed north to Westwood, her conversation with Maggie already forgotten.

~~~

Gregor took Serra to CafeGo, the Caine boys' favorite coffee shop. The two of them chose a corner without any nearby tables, their fruit cups and bagels between them. A stiff awkwardness had settled over them that Gregor didn't know how to erase.

~ ☾ ~

"A lot of emotion in that room." Serra bit into a blueberry bagel. "They'd better learn how to rein it in. Control is the ultimate weapon when dealing with demons."

He twisted the sleeve on his cup around. "Control is always important. How is your world handling the aftermath of the war?"

"It is still difficult in many places, while in others life goes on as it always has. We believe we have finally sealed all the portals that had been opened between us and the Chaos Plane." Her gaze lifted to meet his. "We also believe this same mage was instrumental in our war with the Chaos Plane. His first attempts at opening portals were weak but caused us problems. He has grown stronger over the years."

Gregor sat back in his chair. Her white-blonde hair seemed to dance around her head like dandelion fluff, and her skin gleamed pale against the bright blue of her sweater. He hated the thought of her fighting demons. He wanted to lead and keep her safe.

Her eyes held a distant look, her chin set at a stubborn angle, and he knew she wouldn't back down. He narrowed his eyes. "Tell me why you need to lead this fight. And don't spout honor or any high-mindedness at me, either."

"Revenge. I will see the mage dead. We believe he was behind the beginning of the demon infestation in our land." The words burst out of her, startling them both. Her lips twisted. "Have you ever been so bonded with another person that you felt their pain, their joy?"

Gregor remembered his mother and winced. "To an extent."

"Then maybe you can understand. My twin and I shared that bond. We went into the wars, him as Warrior and me as Healer, to win honor for our family. We were among the youngest and therefore the most expendable."

Her face still had the blush of youth on it, but her eyes held memories of times long past. He found himself wondering about her age. "What happened?"

"We fought. He killed, I Healed, and we went with our army from one corner of our land to the other. We saw the very best of the land destroyed. We saw the very best of our

~ ☾ ~

young brutalized." She stopped.

He reached for her hand, helpless in the face of her pain and not knowing what else to do. "What *happened?*" he prodded.

She took a shuddering breath. "The worst of their demons – the Hjurlt - had just come through. They were starving, so they'd left a path of destruction through the eastern verge. This breed destroys and spawns, seeding the barely living with their progeny to hold the land for their future. Killing them all was painstaking work. But once the leader had been killed, the rest of them were easy prey."

The look on her face made him pause. She obviously didn't like talking about it, but he needed to know. "How do you kill the leader?"

Her eyes flickered over him. "The only sure way is to have a Warrior take the Hjurlt leader's darkness into themselves." Her voice had gone curiously blank and she glanced out the window. "Terrell did what had to be done, but destroying the dark destroyed him, too. He didn't have the resources to win. The demon this morning was a youngling, and in a strange land. Not yet desperate for food. I got lucky. Terrell didn't."

The Fae's purple gaze swung back to him. "That's why I need to lead."

The starkness of her voice shook his truth out of him. "My mother was attacked by a demon that impregnated her. She died giving birth." Saying the words chilled him. He released her hand. "She died too soon."

He could see sympathy in her eyes, mingled with her pain.

She reached out and touched the back of his hand. "Like you said earlier, we all have our dead."

The scent of coffee rose in the air. The cheerful pop music mingled with the chatter of voices that surrounded them, a surreal backdrop to the topic of death.

They sat there, not talking. Gregor didn't want memories of his mother cluttering up his mind, not now. They needed to focus on the living. "This human mage. Is there any way we could get a picture of him? It would help if we could pin down his identity."

She met his gaze, cool once more. "Of course. I have no

~ ☾ ~

great artistic talent, but if you get me a pencil and some paper, I'll do my best."

"Back to the office, then. Are you done? We have a refrigerator if you need to save the fruit." He waved at her untouched fruit cup.

"I'll eat on the way."

They left the coffee house and walked the short way back to Caine Investigations. He noticed the way she looked at everything, her expression calculating, and had to wonder.

"Planning on doing some shopping later?" He manufactured a chuckle to ease the stiffness between them.

She raised an eyebrow. "Looking for hiding places. Lesser demons will hide and lure their prey to them. Only the most bold will do what the one did last night."

"Of course. Anything else you can tell me about the habits of demons would be greatly appreciated." She had knowledge he didn't. It was stupid not to take advantage of it.

"They are as varied as humans."

She didn't say any more, and Gregor found his need for answers dimmed. He didn't ask more questions, just pushed the door open to the stairwell and let her go first.

Upstairs in the office, he found a couple of pencils and a stack of copier paper and handed them over to Serra in the conference room. "I'll be in my office when you're done."

"We need to start the hunt as soon as possible. When will you call Little Harry?"

Gregor stared at her, her head bent diligently over the paper as her hand moved the pencil swiftly across it, laying down lines that would become a face. He didn't understand her and sure wouldn't figure her out by staring at her. "I'll call him right now. After you're finished, we'll go see him and start our hunt."

"Gregor? If you've got a weapon, you should carry it."

He went back to his office, frustrated by her coolness. What had happened to the warm, squirming female splayed across his body? Where did the wanton go who had kissed him as he lay in the middle of the street, getting rained on? One he'd entertained some pretty salacious thoughts about before he opened his eyes.

~ ☾ ~

Gregor went to a file cabinet where he kept small weapons. He found the long dagger he was looking for and slipped it, safe in its sheath, into his inner jacket pocket, still fuming.

He slammed the file drawer shut. She assumed she was in charge, which never sat well with him. It was his job to protect women, not have them protect him. On the other hand, she was *Fae*. Warrior Fae, to boot. So did he want her warm and squirming on top of him? Did he want her kissing him? Which made him angrier, her expecting to be in charge, or the memory of her lips on his?

He scowled at the phone and punched in Little Harry's number.

Serra stared at the face she'd drawn from memory. They'd never met, yet she'd know him anywhere. The Fae labeled him "death bringer", and not even the lowest of the Dark Fae honored him.

Yet they knew so little of how he worked. How he managed to slip into Fae territory with few if any alarms being raised. How he managed to control the demons, manipulate them into doing what he wanted. The Dark Fae had been working on that for eons and still hadn't had success on the scale that this human had managed.

Not since the Divide, the thousand-year War of Ages between Fae and the Dark Fae, had their world been so damaged.

Deliberately, she put down her pencil and stretched out her cramped hand. Emotions had their place, but not here and not now. Control was important.

Control was everything.

She stood, rolled the drawing into a tube, and went to find Gregor.

Gregor Caine. Capable. Deadly. And so not what she had expected. If the demon hadn't disappeared on him, she now had no doubt that he'd have killed it. He was as much a warrior as she, if perhaps not as seasoned.

He stood looking out his window at the mall below, a pensive bent to his head. She cleared her throat and he turned, came toward her, all emotion gone from his face.

~ ☾ ~

"You've finished it already?"

She handed the drawing to him. "We've tried to put our mark on him, but we haven't managed to get close enough. He prefers to use others rather than do any of the fighting himself."

"Your basic coward."

Serra watched as he studied the face she'd recreated. Caine had reverted to being reserved, his gaze cool and unreadable. Which was a good thing, she assured herself.

Minutes ticked past before he spoke again.

"He looks familiar."

"Is it this Kendall person that Justin mentioned?"

"I'm not sure. I'll look him up. He used to be in the local press all the time." Gregor sat at his desk and keyed in some words. Serra moved to stand behind him as a list of articles came up.

"He called himself the 'Sorcerer to the Stars'? Not too vain, is he?"

"You should ask Maggie about him some time. There," he said, and leaned back.

A photo filled the screen of a blond man with piercing blue eyes. Serra, her eyes narrowed, looked from the screen to her drawing. "That's him. Justin was right. Do you know where he resides?"

"As far as we know, he left the country a few months ago just ahead of the law. Wanted for white-collar crime. He managed to bilk a few celebrities in his time, but most of them were too embarrassed to come forward even after he left town."

Chagrin flooded her. "Of course he left. Otherwise it would be too easy, right?"

"We'll get him."

Serra headed to the door. "We need to focus on the demons. What did Little Harry say?" She waited there impatiently until he stood, straightened two papers on his desk, and headed toward her. Once he did, she took off again, down the hallway to the main door.

She heard a sigh behind her but didn't stop.

"Little Harry wasn't in. I left a message on his answering

~ ☾ ~

machine, but he might not call back right away. We're not exactly the best of friends."

"So for now, it's you and me. Where do you want to start?"

She headed down the staircase and waited again for him to lock up the office behind them before he followed.

"Our area is from the Santa Monica airport to L.A. International, from the ocean to the I-110. But..."

His big hand came out and caught her arm when she would have walked out the door to the mall. Reluctantly, she turned to face him and looked up into his eyes. This close, his strength, his masculinity, was mesmerizing. Almost overwhelming. "Yes?"

"We need to check the mall first, and the nearby parking lots. This is my neighborhood. All of us will be hanging out here. I need to see it safe."

"That's sensible." Her heart warmed. He wanted to see to his own. Keep them safe. She knew that feeling, knew what it was like to live with people who didn't understand. Who took safety for granted. Damn it, she really didn't want to like the man.

"I lead this time."

His voice deepened, and she realized there was a bit of compulsion in his words. She guessed he didn't know and fought to keep her mouth straight.

"This time," she echoed, and held the door open for him.

They bumped into an annoyed Maggie and an amused Justin just outside.

"Glad we caught you. Maggie's got news." Justin shoved his hands into his coat pockets.

The four huddled together as the wind tugged at their clothes.

"I'm meeting my coven in fifteen minutes. I got the brush-off from one person, another is living in Bolivia, one is dead, and the last one is Kendall, but he left town months ago. So I've got Aubrey, Cait, Ursula and Hayden. Better than nothing."

Justin sent a sharp look to Maggie before facing Gregor. "There's nothing that says Kendall isn't a part of this. He opened a portal last summer."

~ ☾ ~

"True. But we've got no proof that he *is* behind this," argued Maggie.

To Serra's ears, it sounded like they'd hashed this out before.

Gregor laid a hand on Maggie's shoulder. "I'm sorry. Serra did a sketch of the mage, and it is a dead ringer for a photo off the Internet of Kendall. It's on my desk if you want to check."

"Now we just have to find him," Serra added.

Maggie paled, leaving an ashen tone to her olive skin. "If Kendall doesn't want to be found, you won't find him. He excels at hiding in plain sight."

"I'll do some quick checks. His ex-wife, in-laws, that sort of thing," Justin offered. "If Sorbis is anywhere within a hundred miles of Shannon Sorbis, then Craig Hamilton will know. The man has more eyes on the ground than Trump has in his casinos, and he adores his only daughter."

Justin gripped Maggie's elbow when she swayed. "Let's go upstairs. I've got a few things to say to you."

Maggie tossed her head. "I'm sure you do." She turned on her heel, neatly dislodging Justin's hand, and left him to follow, cursing in her wake.

Serra watched them go. "They're in a relationship?"

"Yes. But they don't believe they are. It's a strange thing. You ready?"

"Of course." Serra strode at his side, the two of them not speaking as they walked the mall. They followed short walkways that lead to the alley behind the mall, checked behind dumpsters and in dark corners. They walked up one stairwell and down another, searching the mall and the connecting parking garages thoroughly.

"What was your childhood like?" Serra peeked behind a dumpster. A rat scuttled away from the wall.

"Normal. Justin and I did everything together. We learned how to surf together, how to get around town before we knew how to drive, and how to charm our teachers when necessary. It was a good childhood. Once we hit puberty, our speed kicked in. Running fast was a pleasure that we kept for ourselves, though I'm pretty sure Mom and Dad knew. Justin found he could heal, and he and I always had this mental

~ ☾ ~

connection. Soon, Mom and Dad were talking to us about who and what we were. Until then, we were just regular kids, you know?

"We spent a lot of time on our own after that point, since Mom and Dad were doing much of what we do now, patrolling, keeping people safe, healing when needed."

Serra watched as he stopped to think.

"I guess I forgot about that. How they were available to anyone who needed them." Gregor checked a stairwell. "I started working in the business when my mother became pregnant and my cousin Kellan moved in." He paused, tossed her a smile, and headed onto the next alleyway. "What about your childhood?"

Serra followed him, letting her memory run backwards to when time seemed new. "I ran wild, learning about our world, about our abilities and always with Terrell. When the border wars began and Terrell decided to fight, I couldn't bear to let him have adventures without me. So I tagged along, as I had done so often in the past." She bit her lip.

"Now you're here, without Terrell, having your own adventures."

"Oh yes, quite the grownup." Serra rolled her eyes. "And we're finding nothing here. Yet another absolutely boring alley."

"You're right. Nothing. Come on."

Over an hour had passed. They made their way back to where they had started, standing in front of the door to Caine Investigations. Serra sighed. "I don't know whether to be relieved or angry that we didn't find any demons."

"Not even any signs of demons."

"Let's go see this Little Harry person and get the part-demon front working." She caught Gregor's eye. "What do you think?"

He checked his watch. "Yeah. We can try the bar. He should be doing paperwork and restocking. Let's go."

~ ☾ ~

CHAPTER SIX

As he drove to Mar Vista, Gregor's sense of awkwardness between them grew. He hadn't liked that she'd sketched Kendall so accurately; he liked even less that he'd talked about his childhood to her at the smallest of prompts.

The fact that he was beginning to enjoy her company worried him. At least she couldn't talk in his head. He preferred to keep his mind free of other voices, hence the barriers that protected him. Memories of his mother soothing him to sleep at night, humming lightly in his mind, shimmered through him, along with a wondrous, safe sense of being loved.

No. He couldn't handle having, then losing, that intimacy. Not again.

Almost on autopilot, Gregor pulled up to the curb and got out of his car without speaking. He surveyed the building in front of them.

The outside didn't look like a place called the Nine Hells. A front deck held empty tables, the chairs all stacked and locked up against the wooden-sided building. It stood quiet in the chilly morning. Only a coffee shop down the street seemed open for business. As Serra came around the car to stand at his side, Gregor headed to the front door.

"There have been demons here."

Gregor gave her a sharp look, saw her sniffing the air, and did as she did. Faintly, the scent came to his nose. "I agree, hours ago. Damn it. Come on." He covered the last few feet to the front door and knocked heavily on the wooden panels. Without waiting, he tugged on the wrought iron handle, pleased when it opened outward. The lights were on. Gregor stepped into the bar, keeping Serra behind him. He ignored her snort of annoyance.

"Little Harry? It's Gregor Caine. I have some questions to ask."

~ ☾ ~

Silence reigned. Fear hung heavy in the air and the scent of it mingled with that of old grease. Gregor lifted an eyebrow to Serra. "Smell that?" He kept his voice low.

"I do. Something happened here last night."

The room was neat. It had been mopped, the tables wiped down and the chairs stacked on top, the trash taken out. Dusty plastic plants hung down over the wood paneling. The large flat screen TV opposite the big wooden bar had been turned off. Everything looked the way it should look, and yet something was off.

"Stay here," Gregor said. "I'm going to look around in the kitchen and the office."

Serra shrugged.

He crossed the floor to the bar and sniffed. Stale beer and the scent of unwashed human came to his nose. Whatever had happened with a demon hadn't happened in here. He glanced behind the bar as he moved to the kitchen door, but it was empty.

Gregor put one hand on the cold steel of the swinging door that led to the kitchen and paused to look behind him. Serra was moving from wall to wall, checking out the pictures of celebrities that hung there. Good. At least she wasn't following him.

He pushed the door open and jumped backward as a high pitch scream sounded and a blast of flame came rushing at him. He flattened himself against the wall as the door swung shut again.

"What the hell? Harry! It's Gregor Caine," he shouted. "It's Caine!" The low roar of the blowtorch shut off abruptly.

The steel door opened. The short, round figure on the other end of the butane torch gave Gregor a weak smile. His face, usually ruddy, was paper white. Sour sweat emanated from him. "Sorry."

"Point that thing at the floor," Gregor ordered. He felt Serra's hand on his shoulder and eased out to put himself between her and Harry.

Harry lowered the torch. "I'm really sorry, Gregor."

He studied the bar owner. "Why don't you disarm, pour yourself a beer, and tell me all about it? You look like you

~ ☾ ~

could use one." He pulled down a couple of chairs at a four-top. Serra did the same with the other two.

Little Harry didn't need any more encouragement. He set the torch on the bar before pulling out a bottle of beer from the fridge. He twisted off the top. "I really am sorry. I didn't know it was you. I heard you walking out here, and I just reacted."

He sat heavily, took a pull at the beer, and wiped his mouth. "I swear I aged ten years."

"Can you describe the demon that attacked you last night?" Serra's voice came low and gentle, but still Harry jumped.

"Sorry. Demons? Don't know what you're talking about." Fresh sweat beaded his forehead.

"Spill it. Nothing but the truth." Gregor laid his palms flat on the table. "This is Serra Willows. She's a Fae, and she's here to help us contain the mess that Kendall Sorbis has created. He opened a portal to the Chaos Plane and demons are pouring through. We need to find the demons and eliminate them, but even more important, we need to close that portal. Do you understand?"

Harry leaned back in his chair, trembling. "Yeah. I get it."

"So tell us what happened last night. Describe the demon to us." Gregor lifted the bottle of beer out of Harry's reach. "Or no more beer."

A ghost of a grin flickered across Harry's face. "Like I don't got a whole bar fulla beer," he said with a snort, but a little color came back into his face. "Okay. By the time everyone had left and I'd cleaned up, it was close to three in the morning. I'd let the wife and my daughters go earlier, and Sammy was off last night."

Gregor set the bottle down in front of Harry, who grabbed it and took a swig. "I was taking out the trash. Big bags full of it, plus a heavy one of bottles and cans, you know? I've got a couple of 3-yard dumpsters in the alley. Me and a couple other places share them, cheaper that way. Anyway, I was headed out there through the back, you know, across the deck and down the stairs?"

Gregor narrowed his eyes as he sorted out his memory.

~ ☾ ~

"You put the deck in early last summer, right?"

"Right. It's great in the summer and fall, doubles my nightly take. Anyway, all the tables and chairs are chained up against the wall and under plastic back there, so the deck is clear. Wide open. I go across like I always do, dragging the trash with me. But when I get to the stairs, I have to take one bag at a time cause otherwise, the bags'll rip open and I'll spend hours cleaning up that crap and washing it down with a hose, or I'll hear about it from Rosita, she'll go nag nag, clean the trash up Harry."

He took another swig at the bottle and wiped his mouth with his wrist. "So I'm taking the first bag down, you know, and I notice the alley lights are off. The fog has moved in, and it's fucking cold. I've got the bag over my shoulder. I'm halfway down the stairs, cursing at the dark, when I smell this gawdawful smell. I thought it was the trash, but it wasn't. By the time I get to the dumpster, I'm heaving and trying to hold my breath."

Harry finished off the beer in one long pull. With a wild look in his eyes, he glanced from Gregor to Serra and swallowed hard. "The dumpster'd been rolled away from the wall a little. I hear this snuffling sound. I think it's a dog, so I look around the edge and I see this thing." He shuddered. "It was...it had its head buried in some guy's stomach. Blood everywhere. I screamed I think, and the thing looked up at me, its teeth sharp and wet with blood, and it was chewing on something pinkish dangling from its mouth. Then the sky opened and it started raining and thundering and lightning. Before it could come after me, I threw the bag of trash at it and ran like hell back to the bar and locked the back door. I've been hiding in the kitchen ever since."

Harry stood up so fast his chair overturned with a crash. "Sorry." He picked it up and went to the bar for another beer. "I swear it's all true." He twisted off the top and took another long pull, his other hand lying possessively on the blowtorch.

Serra cleared her throat. "We believe you. We fought and killed a demon last night, at about the same time. Different neighborhood, though."

Gregor shared a glance with Serra and added, "You left the

front door unlocked. I say you're lucky the demon already had a good-sized meal in front of it."

Relief mixed with fear crossed Little Harry's face. "Aw hell. What do we do now?"

Gregor leaned forward. "Do you still have that list of people in the neighborhood who have demon blood in them?"

"Yeah. Funny you should ask about that. Samael, my Sammy, he met up with this guy who wanted a peek at the list. I told Sammy no, but he keeps nagging."

"Do you have it here?"

"No. It's back at home, in the safe. You need it?"

Gregor considered, and discarded, the idea. "Let's leave my involvement out of it. For now, just gather the older ones you think have a good head on their shoulders, ones who can sniff out a demon like you did. We need to find these things and eliminate them before they take over our city."

Harry's eyes sharpened. "How quickly do you need a team on the ground?"

"Truthfully? Hours ago. So as fast as you can and as many of you as possible. Go quietly, go in teams of twos and threes, use lighters and any weapons you think won't be noticeable by the normal citizen, and take these guys down."

"What's our territory?"

Gregor filled him in and Harry took notes. It all took a rather long time. Harry made coffee and brought out some bar nuts and pretzels. By the time they were through, his color was back to normal and purpose infused him. The three of them walked to the front door.

Harry hesitated. "I don't suppose you want to see the steps, the dumpster?"

"It rained hard last night." Serra's voice rang clear. "There wouldn't be anything to see."

Gregor's eyebrows lifted, but he didn't reply. He turned to Harry. "She's right. We've lost the chance. If you can think of anything else, though, give me a call. Keep me updated, too. I want to know what you find, where, if it's a kill, and whether or not anyone is injured. You know Megan Cavanaugh?" At Harry's nod, Gregor continued. "She'll have a heads up on this one, so send any of the injured to her."

~ ☾ ~

"You got it, Gregor."

"Oh, and Harry, you did good. But don't carry the torch in the open."

"Right. I'll be in touch. Thanks again."

Gregor lifted a hand in farewell as he and Serra walked outside into the bitter morning.

Pale sunlight filtered down through the clouds, but the wind stole any warmth the sun might have given. Gregor stopped on the front decking and looked out over the city. The ocean was behind him, too many people were in front, and the demons could be anywhere. He didn't like the odds.

"Where do we start now? If we're not going with Harry's people, I mean?" Serra stood at his shoulder. Having her there was a bit of a jolt. Usually it was Justin who had his back, who asked the questions. But Justin was looking after his witch.

"We go look at Harry's back decking and the dumpsters." He caught Serra's look of shock out of the corner of his eye as he headed to his car.

"But I thought you agreed it was a waste of time," she protested.

"I didn't want Harry watching us. He needs to focus on getting his team together, not on body parts."

"Oh."

Gregor drove around the block and down the alley behind the bar. Not far from The Nine Hells was an empty parking space. He pulled into it. "Come on."

They headed down the alley to the bar. Gregor glanced up the stairs and saw the two bags waiting at the top, one of them tilted over as if Harry had stumbled over it. Water pooled in the plastic. Stopping at the foot of the steps, he looked toward the dumpster. It still canted out slightly into the alley.

Moving slowly, Gregor searched the ground for blood and body parts through the trash strewn about. Serra saw it first.

"There. In the corner, a pile of clothes and a pair of shoes."

They'd been tossed there in a jumble and were wet through with the rain. He surveyed the area. "Damn. It's a demon killing the homeless, not a serial killer. Things were

~ ☾ ~

looking that way last week, but this clinches it." They hadn't even begun, and already too many people had died. His hands bunched into fists and he made a vow. Whatever it took, he would scour the city clean. "Come on. Let's go."

"I've been thinking," Serra said as they reached his car. "If there's just an open portal for any demon to come through, then we're going to get a mixture. If there's a gatekeeper, then my guess is the more deadly demons will be allowed through."

"So I should stop and ask what kind of demon it is before I kill it? Won't happen." He steered easily in and out of the morning traffic.

"No. I wouldn't, either. I just thought you should know." She turned to stare out the window.

"I'll just assume they're all lethal. We'll check the Santa Monica Airport area. There are a lot of empty warehouses and buildings."

"Someone should check the sewers. Many demons prefer the underground. In London in the nineteen eighties, the Underground was also a breeding ground for demons. It took a team of specialists almost twenty days to find and kill them all. Funny, though. Not a bit of it was on the nightly news. But there was a lot about bombings in trash cans."

Gregor felt his jaw drop. He spared her a glance as he turned south onto Bundy. "How do you know about the nightly news?"

She met his gaze and grinned, the first real smile he could remember from her. "I watch TV. Fascinating stuff, what you humans find entertaining."

"I don't have a response to that." The Fae watched TV? He didn't know what it was like in her world, but somehow he didn't expect them to have broadcast or cable television.

"It was part of my training before coming here. Boning up on the human culture. TV seemed the easiest way to do it. I can't believe I managed to surprise you."

"Trust me, Serra. Everything about you is a surprise." The memory of her naked in front of him came back to mind and he blew out a breath. Had that really happened just this morning? "Damn traffic," he muttered.

~ ☾ ~

Serra's scent drifted to him whenever she shifted positions to look out the window, and the warmth of her next to him had his mind wandering down paths better left alone.

"Talk to me," he said.

"You get your way a lot, don't you?" She had shifted again and now he could feel the heat of her gaze on him.

He frowned. "I don't understand the question."

"You 'nudge' people to do what you want them to do. I could feel it, back at Little Harry's. It was your 'nudge' that made him lower the torch. He wasn't in any state to merely listen to you."

Denial rose inside him. "Don't be ridiculous."

She let out a little sigh. "Yeah, I didn't think you knew about it. You are going to have to deal with your gifts sooner or later. Don't think you can just ignore them."

He wasn't going to be drawn into this discussion. His decisions about his bloodlines had been set in stone years ago, and she had no right to go rummaging around in them now.

But her air of expectation bugged him. "It's none of your damned business."

"It's very much my business. You are going to be dealing with demons. You're keeping company with a Fae. What do you think is going to happen to you when your body, obeying what is encoded inside it, does something you don't expect?"

"Like what? I doubt I'm going to become my demon. I sure as hell won't be able to call to the elements like you do." He shifted in his seat, tense now and unhappy at the drift of the conversation. Damn it. He didn't want to discuss it.

She continued to poke at him. "You might see with demonic eyes, more than you currently do. Your voice may contain powers you are unaware of, and you may inadvertently hurt someone. Your strength may manifest itself in a completely new and different way, which could hurt you and any human around you. Do you want me to go on?"

"No. Not particularly."

He pulled off Bundy with relief, onto a side street south of the airport, and noticed what had once been a thriving business district now stood empty due to the poor economy.

~ ☾ ~

Buildings were shut up, parking lots were cracked and weeds grew with abandon. "We'll park here and start snooping around."

Gregor stretched and shut his car door, grateful for the chill in the air. Serra came around the car and put a hand on his chest. She looked up at him, her purple eyes solemn.

"When you are ready, I'll be there to help. Don't think your talents won't manifest themselves, Gregor, because they will. The only question is, will you be prepared enough to handle what will happen, or will you neglect your talents and damn the consequences?"

Gregor took a slow step back and her hand fell from his chest. "Let's go that way," he said, pointing off to the maze of warehouses on his left. He turned on his heel and made for the nearest one, almost bursting with the need to pound on something. "Let there please be demons," he muttered. "Let something go right this day."

~ ☾ ~

CHAPTER SEVEN

Justin looked from Maggie to the other witches in front of him. The tension weaving between the five of them made his neck ache. "So everyone knows what we're looking for, and how to kill them?"

The tall blonde gave Justin a pitying glance. "You've only gone over it a dozen times. Aubrey and I will take the pier site and move north and east. Come on, Aub. Let's go." With barely a glance at Maggie, she turned on her heel and walked smartly away from the others.

Aubrey, a Halle Berry look-alike, shrugged. "I can handle Cait. We'll call in later." She waved and headed after Cait with long-legged strides.

Maggie turned to the others. "Hayden, are you sure you and Ursula are up to this?"

Justin gauged the women, sisters slight in stature, who looked almost identical.

"We're sure. Right?" Hayden looked to Ursula, who nodded vigorously.

"We've got this, Maggie. We've kept up our training." Ursula's eyes gleamed in the morning light. "You might say we've been hoping something like this would come along. It validates our suspicion of more out there, you know? The texts are so nebulous in the details of the origins, so it'll be nice to actually talk to a demon."

Justin cut in before Maggie could object. "This isn't a research project, Ursula. You don't talk to these demons for one reason. They're much more interested in having you for dinner. And I'm not talking about a date, either."

The two women blanched, but Ursula got a stubborn set to her mouth.

"Don't argue," warned Maggie. She looked sternly from one sister to the other. "If you want to question a demon you

~ ☾ ~

find, then good luck and try not to get yourselves killed. But know, going in, that unless you kill the demons you find, those demons will kill innocent people. Strike before the demon strikes and you'll have a good chance."

"Got it, Mags." Hayden grinned. "We've got the eastern side, so we'll head there now."

They turned and walked toward their car, almost in lockstep, their heads close together. Justin could tell they were arguing. "What do you think? Are they going to make it?"

Maggie sighed. "I hope so. Ursula feels stronger than she used to, but I'm worried about her. She's always had an unhealthy fixation on Kendall. If she finds out he's involved, I think we'll lose her. Gods, I hope we're not sending them to their deaths."

Justin touched her shoulder in sympathy, only to feel her slip sideways out from under his hand. He stuffed his hands in his pockets. "Well then, it's time we started our route. Wilshire Boulevard first? I'll drive."

"That sounds like a plan."

Justin reined in his surprise. He'd been certain she'd fight to drive. They got into his dark green Jag, and he headed toward Wilshire Boulevard.

"Tell me about the coven. Aubrey and Cait. They are friends?"

"They were roommates in college for awhile. They aren't exactly friends, but that's because Cait is impossible. She's bossy, prissy, always in charge even when no one wanted her to be. A predator when it came to men. She took who she wanted and damned the consequences."

"What was her friendship with Kendall like?"

"Really? You're really going there? What is with you and this stick you have up your butt about Kendall?" Fury laced her words.

Justin forced his hands to relax on the steering wheel. He kept his tone even with difficulty. "The Fae identified Kendall, remember? That picture she drew could have been a photograph, and you know it. Why are you protecting him?"

"I'm not."

~ ☾ ~

"It feels like it."

Silence settled between them. Justin drew deeply within for peace, picturing himself riding the waves at dawn. He hadn't had a chance to do that in a while. He cracked his window, and the cool air rushed in, bringing the scent of rain.

"So I thought we'd drive the streets and get out for alleys and parking lots. Does that sound okay to you?" Justin risked a glance at Maggie.

Her arms were folded tightly across her chest.

"Maggie? Are you okay?"

"Yeah. I'm fine. Your idea is fine. Beats the hell out of walking a couple dozen miles." Her arms relaxed and she sighed. "Cait and I don't get along. We never have."

"Why?"

"I'm not entirely sure."

Justin tapped the steering wheel as he waited for a light to change. She was lying. He knew it as he knew it would rain again before dark. She didn't fully trust him, not even after everything they'd been through. Her walls were thick and high, and he was having a hell of a time scaling them. Every time he thought he was getting close, she'd shut him down, and he'd find himself at the bottom of the wall again.

Most men would have given up months ago. It was a good thing Justin had an abundance of patience. He stifled a sigh and kept driving.

~~~

Gregor found his patience hanging by a thread. Serra seriously drove him crazy with her curvy body and straightforward gaze, and her scent that dug into his guts and made him crave. She blazed through his walls and obliterated his objections without even trying.

They'd toured dozens of abandoned or unfinished buildings next to residential areas without finding a thing. The entire time they hunted, he knew her location. When she'd close her eyes and lift her face to the wind, he knew she was scenting the air. If he was near, she'd point the way, and he followed. They never found anything; only felt the vague sense something *other* had passed that way.

It was stupid to be so shaken, seeing her sniff out demons. He did it himself after all; it was a part of him he'd never been able to turn off. But to see it demonstrated in her wound him up. Reminded him of his past, dead and gone, back when he thought his bloodline made him something more, something special. Now he knew he was a mere accident of birth, which made spending time with her a peculiar type of torture. He'd never be the hero he'd always dreamed of being.

He certainly hadn't been able to save his mother. Or his father, if it came to that. At least Dad had fought to keep them both in college when the debts mounted and their options narrowed. Fought to keep Justin in school when Kellan had disappeared. When Dad, too had fled, Gregor and Justin had somehow held it together during the leanest years.

But those years had passed. They were doing fine now, due to his human work ethic and Justin's way with investments. So why, now of all times, had *she* come along to stir up trouble? Force him to face the parts of himself he'd shut down years ago?

They were deep in the interior of a maze of industrial buildings, only half of which were occupied, when Gregor spied a scuttling out of the corner of his eye, pulling him out of his thoughts.

"Did you see that?"

Serra's head snapped around and she sniffed the air. "Stay behind me," she ordered, her voice low. She lifted her head to the sky and let out an ululating call, urgent on the wind. She spread her arms wide. Lightning flashed and the clouds grew dark. She called again, more seductively this time.

Instinctively, Gregor stepped back and away, keeping his eyes on the surrounding buildings.

It darted for him, giving her a wide berth. No higher than his knees, Gregor instinctively booted it away as he would have a soccer ball. It rolled and bounced and keened to the sky.

"Serra! Get to the car!"

"Are you kidding me?" She shot him a glare of disbelief before returning to the attack as more of the small demons came toward them. "They're C'dak. Tricky. Be careful."

They were gray and moved faster than his eye could track. Gregor used both feet to kick the creatures away as he slashed out with his dagger. The dog-like things had big eyes that dripped what looked like tears, but when they splashed on his skin, the liquid burned like acid.

He kept an eye on Serra, watched as she wielded a pair of knives that had come out of nowhere and dispatched demon after demon. She tripped once, fell heavily and his heart stopped. But before he could take a step toward her, Serra was up again and plunging a knife in the eye of the demon that had jumped her.

Reassured, he threw one of the mini-demons against the nearest wall. It splatted and fell lifeless.

Serra gave another cry, different this time, and thrust her hand up to the sky. Lightning shot down. Gregor watched in disbelief as gleaming bolts left her hand and incinerated the demon horde around them.

As the numbers lessened, he was able to slash and fling more and more of them against the wall, doing his best to land them head first for maximum damage.

The demons around her eradicated, Serra moved to the wall and shot a firebolt into the heap of demons he'd collected. A last, lone wail went up before the flash of fire turned the dead to ash, scattered by the winds. Pride in her skills flared within him. She turned his way and stashed her knives in her boots.

Electricity rode the air as silence settled between them. Tendrils of Serra's hair had escaped the knot she'd put it in. Now they blew about her face, and her eyes gleamed almost silver as sweat sheened her pale skin. Her sweater had rips in it, and there was a scratch on one cheekbone. She held her left hand cradled in her right. There was dirt on her face and ichor down one leg of her jeans, and he thought she looked like a gorgeous badass demon fighter.

He stalked toward her, obeying the wild impulse inside him. Her eyes widened and her hands fell. She came toward him, her intent as clear to him as his had to be to her.

They came together with an almost audible clash. Gregor

~ ☾ ~

knew only that he'd die if he didn't have her in his arms; if he couldn't taste her lips, bury his face in her hair, her neck.

Her lips against his were plush, her taste fresh as the cleanest water, necessary and life-giving. He pulled her tighter into his arms, one hand firmly between her shoulder blades and the other on her ass, holding her to him. If she struggled, he wasn't aware, so taken was he by the feel of her body against his. He couldn't for the life of him let her go, not at that moment.

But her hands were as greedy as his, her mouth as hungry, her body pressed eagerly and restlessly against him. Their tongues danced together, both struggling for supremacy, one leading and the other following until it switched again and Gregor no longer knew nor cared who led.

Her hand skimmed his cheekbone. He leaned into her touch, finding it just as necessary as her lips. She wriggled against him. His body grew even harder. He couldn't breathe and he pulled his mouth from hers, only to press kisses along the line of her jaw to where her sweater guarded her throat.

With a growl, he stripped her sweater up and off her, tossed it to one side, struck once again by her skin gleaming like a pearl in the winter light. Her breasts were encased in a dark blue fantasy of silk and lace, lifting them up almost as if for his inspection. Her scar caught his gaze and he pressed kisses there.

Flashes of knowledge stunned him, made his head spin. He saw the battlefield in a parched and desolate land far away, smoke-filled and swarming with Fae and demons. Watched as the demon, twice her size and wielding a wicked weapon, aimed at her for the killing blow. With every kiss, he saw more. Her throat had already been torn open by a thick claw, dropping her like a stone, spilling her blood into the thirsty ground. She'd watched the demon's every move and had prepared herself for death.

And then...she hadn't died. He lifted his lips from her skin and his eyes sought hers, shocked at what he'd seen. She watched him steadily.

Pain flashed through Gregor, but he couldn't tell where it came from.

~ ☾ ~

"You're hurt." Serra lifted his hand and chanted under her breath.

Gregor blinked. "You're half naked." The pain from the acids drifted away.

Her lips twitched into a smile. "You stripped me of my sweater."

He stepped back, swiped up the sweater from the ground, and thrust it at her. "Put it on." He turned away. His body throbbed with need and his mind boiled with confusion. "What did you do to me?"

"I didn't do anything to you." She stepped up to his side and slid a hand through his arm, her sweater in place. "We did good work here. My guess is we got about forty of those little bastards."

"I almost ravaged you. In the middle of the parking lot. It's barely fifty degrees out here, and I'm not counting the wind chill factor." Stunned didn't begin to describe his state of mind.

"It was a mutual almost-ravaged. I could definitely pick this up where we left off." She looked around and sighed. "But it looks like our work is done. Let's get out of here."

Gregor frowned. "I know how you got that scar."

Serra stared at him, one brow lifted. "Oh?"

His anger built. "You didn't have to prove to me that you are a Warrior Fae. I believed you the first time. I didn't need you putting pictures in my head. Damn you for doing it."

"I didn't put any pictures in your head." She spoke quietly, but the purple had overtaken the silver in her eyes. "Whatever you saw, that was a gift of your very own. I would never push such visions on other people." She hugged herself and looked away from him. "I need to change clothes. So do you, by the way. We both stink."

He started and looked down. His suit looked worse than she did. Damn it. "That's the second time in less than twenty-four hours my clothes got ruined. Hell. Let's get out of here." He strode back to where they'd left the car, knowing she'd follow.

"If you truly don't want to accept your gifts, you need to stop hanging around me, and you need to stop fighting

~ ☾ ~

demons. These things that bother you, these gifts, will go dormant again. Eventually."

He scowled and unlocked her door. "Get in and shut up, would you?"

Gregor drove on autopilot. He had two overwhelming needs and only one of them had an easy remedy. Her taste lingered in his mouth. If he didn't concentrate, he felt her body beneath his hands instead of the steering wheel.

"Are you mad?" Her quiet voice reached him as he finally turned onto his street, on the bluffs above Santa Monica.

"No. Not mad. Unless you count needing you as madness." His cell phone shrilled between them as he drove.

He answered. "Caine."

"Gregor, it's Justin. Two of the witches, sisters, had a problem and one of us should be there. Can you meet them at Doc Cavanaugh's right away? We've got our hands full here."

"Got it. We're on it. Use fire," he cautioned.

Justin didn't bother answering, just hung up. Inwardly swearing, Gregor pocketed his phone and swung his car back toward the freeway.

"Trouble?"

He glanced briefly at Serra. "Two of the witches got injured. They're at the Doc's. About twenty minutes from here."

"We can get checked out too while we're there. Maybe I can help. Your healer, she's good?"

Gregor frowned. "She's very good." He didn't get it. How could she go from such passion in the parking lot to acting so cool? What made her so different, and yet so much like him?

"You're thinking too hard." She sounded amused.

He loosened his grip on the steering wheel. "It's hard not to. I've been prepared for this type of fight, but I've never actually fought demons before. None of us had until last summer. Plus, you're...I don't know what you are. I can't figure it out."

"I am as you see me."

"You are a deeper well, my Fae. The human eye cannot fathom the depths within you, nor can the human mind easily encompass them. Plus hello, you're female, which just throws

~ ☾ ~

everything into confusion."

"This is all about sex, isn't it? Please. Just relax. I can feel your...reluctance. So forget it. I won't mention it again."

"That doesn't mean it won't come up again." Her taste made him hungry for more. If he were honest with himself, he'd wanted her the minute he saw her. Having had her in his arms, having seen both her warrior side and her passionate side, had only made the wanting worse.

"Don't worry. In four days or so it'll all be over, and I'll be gone. Problem solved," she added lightly.

Gregor scowled out the windshield. Four days was both a blessing and a curse. How could he really get to know her in the next four days? By the same token, how could he keep her from learning too much about his life in the next four days?

He chewed on the conundrum the rest of the drive to Doc Megan's.

CHAPTER EIGHT

"Behind you, Maggie!" Justin watched, his heart in his throat, as Maggie whirled and sent a fireball toward the last dog-like thing racing for her. The fireball hit it dead-on in the chest. The thing flamed and quickly went to ash.

"Is that all of them?" Maggie looked around, panting. "I can't believe how fast those creatures are."

"I think that's it. There were, what, ten of them?" Justin glanced around the small alleyway and mentally blessed the weather for being so cold. Many of the homeless were in shelters.

"About that." She shook her head, her dark eyes still wide with shock. "How many of them do you think got through?"

"I don't even want to guess. We got all that came our way, and that's what's important. Come on, let's get some food, and get back to the car."

She frowned at him. "You don't think we should just, you know, camp out here?"

"Wait for more of them? It's not going to happen. My guess is it was a random hiding place. When we came into the alley, we disturbed them, and they converged on us."

Maggie shivered. "I wonder if they got anyone else."

"Don't think about it," he advised. "Great work with those fireballs, by the way." He slid his short swords into the special hilt on his back and put his jacket on. "Come on, let's get some lunch."

She stumbled as they headed out of the alley. When he put out a hand to steady her, she pulled away. "I'm fine."

Justin bit back the hot words that came to his tongue and shoved his hands into the pockets of his board shorts. It was becoming a habit around her. "Where do you want to eat?"

"I'm not that hungry." She sniffed the air and made a face. "I smell awful."

~ ☾ ~

"Like toasted demon-dog." Justin sniffed his jacket sleeve and sighed. "Okay. I'll take you back to your car. I can't stand myself, either." He checked his watch. "It's almost three. I don't know if working tonight is such a great idea."

"I'm beat," she confessed. "But we don't have a lot of time. Can we afford to not go out tonight? Will we be the only ones who don't?"

They rounded the front of his Jag and Justin unlocked her door. "I don't know. Tell you what, let's take a break, regroup, and see how we're doing. If we go out and get ourselves killed because we're exhausted, that's not going to help our cause."

She slid into the passenger seat with a sigh. Justin came around and got in, started the engine, and turned the heat up.

"You're right, of course. I need a deep, hot bath and a glass of wine. No, make that tea. That'll go a long way to smoothing out my edges." She nestled deeper into the leather seat. "Why does life have to be so freaking complicated?"

He turned to answer her and noticed her eyes were shut. Her face was drawn tight, her forehead puckered with pain. "How much are you hurting?" he demanded.

"Don't start with me," she pleaded. "I can't."

"Damn it, Magdalena." He remembered her collapse after the fight with the vampires that previous summer, and he cursed the traffic around them. She needed warmth, water, food and rest. And damned if he wasn't the one who would supply it all, whether she wanted him around or not.

"Just drop me off at my car and go surfing, Justin. You need the ocean. I can tell."

His fury vibrated between them. "I'll damned well do what I want to do, when I want to do it. You almost used yourself up. Didn't you learn anything last summer? Never mind. My house or yours?"

When she didn't answer, he cast a quick glance her way. Her head lolled to one side; she was out. Whether she'd passed out or fallen asleep, he didn't know. Resisting the urge to stomp on the gas pedal, Justin drove as fast as practical to his house on the bluffs.

Once there, he carried Maggie inside through the garage and straight into the guest bedroom. She lay on the bed, so pale. She'd complained about being dirty. They both were. Going on instinct, Justin raced to his room, stripped off his jacket and Hawaiian shirt, toed off his shoes but left his board shorts on. Detouring into his bathroom with the big tub for two, he set the water running to full blast and checked the temperature before returning to his room. He grabbed one of his extra large black t-shirts and a pair of boxers, then returned to Maggie, where she lay looking beautiful, all curly black hair and goddess body.

Justin set his teeth and, gently, removed Maggie's layers. Jacket, sweater, thin t-shirt, bra. All had demon-stink soaked in them. Carefully, he pulled his shirt on over her head, got her arms through the armholes and tugged it down over her torso, the image of her full breasts with their puckered brown nipples staying with him even after he had her decently covered.

Focus, he chided. Focus, man! He unzipped her jeans and pulled them down with some difficulty. When he reached her feet, he cursed and removed her boots and socks, then finished with her pants. Working quickly now, he pulled the boxers up over her long legs and rolled them at the waist, ignoring the softness of the skin on her stomach. Even though she was covered, her legs drove him crazy, as did the unconscious pout her lips made.

"You'll do," he muttered. He bent and lifted her into his arms again. "Don't get used to this, man. It sure as hell won't last."

She murmured and turned her face into his chest, her breath on his body a new delight. Grimly, Justin carried her into his bathroom and walked into the tub with her. Sighing at the warmth, he sank down into the water and just held her close to him.

Her eyelids fluttered. "What...? Am I wet?" She peered up at him and blinked. "Justin? We're in the bathtub?"

"You fainted. In the car. We both stank, so I thought a bath was appropriate." He released her, making sure she was steady. "I'll leave if you want me to."

She scooted to the far side of the big tub and drew her knees up, her gaze wary. The water splashed down around

~ ☾ ~

her and Justin thought he'd never seen a more beautiful sight. She licked her lips and frowned.

"We're both dressed." Her hands plucked at the t-shirt, now plastered to her body.

"Yes. I figured you'd scream bloody murder if I put you in a bath, naked and unconscious." He rubbed both hands over his face. "I'd better leave you in peace. Don't hurry. It'll take time for your clothes to wash and dry." He levered himself up and stood, reached for a towel and dried off his chest. Wrapping the towel around his waist and dripping shorts, he stepped out of the tub and headed to the door. "I'll get your tea."

"Justin. I don't know what to say. Thank you." She sounded lost, scared.

He glanced back, giving her a wicked grin. "Holler if you need me."

Maggie's eyes turned hot. "Get out."

"Gone." He shut the bathroom door behind him and headed for the guest room. At least he'd gotten her out of self-pity mode. Tea, laundry, and a cold shower. His smile faded. He'd gotten real used to taking cold showers after spending time with Magdalena.

~~~

Frannie poured champagne for Bryce and walked carefully to where he hunched over the computer. "Try this one. It's French."

Bryce didn't even look at her. "I'm sure its fine. Pick whichever one you want, I really don't care."

Frannie sipped the wine. It fizzed deliciously in her mouth, making her nose twitch. She wandered away from Bryce but kept her distance from the portal, pulsing with light in a dark corner. It made her jumpy. This whole party-slash-demon business niggled at her. She took another sip.

"Oh, hey. I just remembered." She whirled about and champagne splashed on her hand. "Whoops. Anyway, I almost ran into Maggie de la Cruz this afternoon, as I came out of the party store. She looked out of it and smelled rank, but she didn't even notice me."

She noticed Bryce's head jerk around and turned to face him. "Yeah, it was strange. They didn't see me. She had Justin Caine with her. He put her into his car and they drove off. They both looked a little worse for wear, though." She sipped again. Bryce muttered under his breath and turned back to the computer.

The door flew open and a bitter wind swirled in.

"Shut the damn door, Cait." Bryce scowled and looked up. "What do you have for me?"

Cait strode in, almost vibrating with anger. "I had to spend the entire day with Aubrey. The woman drives me completely insane, and she always has. She's gung-ho, ready to go again later on tonight. I can't do this, Bryce. Not even for Kendall."

"What did you learn of their plans?"

She shrugged. "They weren't too specific. We were given our coordinates of the city, so I've got some safe spots for you to hide demons in if you need to." She passed over a piece of paper.

"You don't know how many people are involved?" Bryce pressed. He tossed the paper aside.

"The only people I saw were the old coven crowd, and Justin Caine."

"He's a cutie," Frannie said without thinking. Cait sent her a withering glare, and Bryce ignored her. Frannie's cheeks burned. She withdrew into a darker corner. She had a way of disappearing, of not being seen when she didn't want to be. She knew if she just kept her mouth shut long enough, the other two would forget she was even there. Then she'd be able to relax. She sipped and watched from her spot in the dark.

Cait put her hand on Bryce's shoulder. "News filtered back to me and Aubrey, news you need. Justin and Maggie killed about a dozen demons, Justin's brother Gregor took out even more. Ursula and Hayden were attacked, or something. If you need more demons, you'll need me to keep them safe. I can point the others in different directions, so on and so forth."

Cursing, Bryce sat back in his chair and looked up at Cait. "You may be right. What do you get out of helping?"

"I've always been a fan of Kendall's." She shrugged and sat

on the desk, facing Bryce. She crossed her arms. "I'm no fan of Maggie's. By extension, I'm no fan of the Caines."

"So...?"

She smiled. "If I can help you hurt them, then I'm a happy woman."

Frannie's stomach knotted. She'd never in a million years wanted to hurt any of her old friends. Not even Cait, the original bitch on wheels. She waited tensely for Bryce's response.

"That's not the goal." Bryce paced, agitated. "Yes, people will die, but for an amazing reason, and at the time of Kendall's choosing. It's an honor, actually. Though the victims won't realize that."

"But if Maggie or the Caines get hurt in the process, you're not going to cry about it. Well, neither will I. Who knows? Kendall may even reward me if I take care of them." Cait stood and slicked her hair back. "I've got to go."

"Keep me informed."

"Of course." She headed toward the door. "Goodbye, Mouse." A swirl of wind, and she was gone.

Frannie finished off her glass of champagne and poured herself another, her indignation growing. Mouse, indeed. It's what Cait had always called her in college, and she'd allowed it. But now, maybe she should rethink her position in this enterprise. Maybe the Mouse would remember how to roar, before people she'd once called friends got hurt. Lost in thought, Frannie slid down the wall, sat on the cold cement floor, sipped and thought, and totally forgot about the portal pulsing in the corner.

~~~

Serra looked into Ursula's eyes, going deeper than the woman knew. There was darkness, a shadow that warred with the light in Ursula's soul. Serra did what she could on a meta-level to put a barrier around the shadow, but as she pulled out of the other woman's mind, she remained troubled by what she'd seen.

She caught Megan's unspoken question and shook her

head. She brushed the hair out of Ursula's eyes. "You're feeling better?"

Ursula let out a sigh. "Much. I don't know why I got so dizzy. A man brushed against me, and I almost fell. He apologized, took my hand, and I got so dizzy. I think he said something, but I don't remember what." She blinked a few times and looked toward her sister. "Then Hayden came. The man was really very nice," she added. "He helped me sit down."

Hayden broke in. "The man's name started with a D. Damon, or Dillon, maybe. Something unusual. He stopped to speak with me while we waited for a cab. A compelling guy."

"Dalton." Ursula sat up straighter. "His name is Dalton. Can I go now? I'm feeling fine, I swear."

"I'll take care of her," promised Hayden.

Megan sighed. "It's against my better judgment, but if you insist. I have some papers for you to sign before you're free to go. The nurse will be back in a moment. Serra, I'd like to speak with you, if you don't mind?"

"Of course."

"Let's go into my office." They left the exam room and walked down the corridor to the office in silence.

Megan waved to the couch taking up most of the space in the tiny room. "Sit. Tell me what's wrong with Ursula."

Serra sank down with relief. "First off, thanks for the shower and the scrubs." She waved at the dark blue clothes covering her.

"You're welcome. I couldn't have you wandering around the place all smelly."

"Second, you're Fae. The others don't know, do they?"

Megan sighed. "No. Is there any reason they should know?"

"Your surgical techniques?" Serra tilted her head to one side.

"Are augmented by my *other* abilities. Granted. But I was born here, I busted my ass in med school, in my intern days, in residency." Megan eyed Serra. "I may be a full-blooded Fae, but I'm more American than anything else, raised by humans. What are you getting at?"

~ ☾ ~

"I'm just thinking over options." Serra stretched her arms over her head. "We'll talk after all this is over."

"If it's ever over." Megan yawned widely. "Sorry. Now. Ursula?" She raised her eyebrows. "Spill it."

"There's a shadow on her soul. Hayden seemed untouched. You didn't sense the shadow?"

"No, damn it." Megan's teeth worried her lower lip. "You think something's really wrong?"

Serra met the other woman's gaze. "I think something's really wrong. I don't know why the shadow is there, if it is self-inflicted, or if she's been tainted somehow. I did my best to contain it, but there is only so much I can do."

"Yeah, I know the feeling." Megan massaged her temples with a groan. "I don't remember anything like it, so tell me. What could this shadow do to her?"

"Lots, and all of it bad. Where I come from, a shadow like that would have her closely watched. One sign of evil, and she'd be purged."

"Killed?" Megan shot a shocked look at Serra. "Holy crap. What about the man who bumped into her? Could he have caused it?"

"It would be a long coincidence." The masculine drawl had both women looking toward the doorway. Gregor stood there, his suit torn and spattered with ichor, looking like a well-attired street bum. "Possible, but not probable."

"Hello, handsome." Megan stood and reached up to give him a kiss on the cheek. "No offense, but you reek."

"Nice to see you, too," he said, returning her hug.

Serra noted he kept his gaze on her, rather than Megan. His blue eyes burned, and heat swept her body. Ruthlessly, she leashed her libido and managed to keep her eyes cool as she returned his assessing gaze.

"Do you need Serra any longer? We've got more work to do."

Megan laughed and patted his arm. "From the heat you're generating, I can imagine what you two will be doing. Get out of here, both of you. Serra, don't forget your clothes in the plastic bag. And any time you want to help out around here, I'd be grateful."

~ ☾ ~

Serra rose to her feet and swept up the bag Megan had mentioned. Between herself and Gregor, they dwarfed the little doctor. She smiled. "I'll take you up on that." She turned toward Gregor. "Ready when you are."

He moved out of the doorway. Serra passed him, unsurprised when his big hand caressed her bottom, very briefly. Heat flared through her and she sucked in a breath. She heard Megan chuckle behind them. In spite of herself, Serra felt her cheeks flame.

She didn't blush. She never blushed. What the hell was wrong with her? She stalked down the corridor to the main entrance, all her senses humming. Did she want to have sex with the human? Hell, yeah. She had needs that had gone unmet for far too long.

She reached for the door, but his long arm got there first, pushing it open to the chilly night. "After you."

She didn't meet his gaze, just swept on through the door, stifling a shiver when her shoulder brushed his broad chest. She forced herself to keep her strides long and unhurried, despite how much she wanted to run. When she finally got to the vintage Mercedes, she tapped her foot impatiently. He was still halfway across the parking lot from her, and it was cold.

"Would you hurry up?" Serra caught her breath. That couldn't have been her voice. Husky, and alive with need. She hadn't heard that voice out of her mouth in years.

Gregor seemed to tune in on her frequency. His strides became more deliberate, and his focus was all on her. He practically *prowled* toward her, intent on her as his prey, caging her in by his very will.

For a brief second, she felt herself helpless, unable to move. Then she realized that was fury in his eyes. She drew herself up as he reached her, opened her mouth to speak.

"Don't," he ordered. He unlocked her door. "Get in."

Before she could say anything else, he glared. She got in, every nerve she possessed quivering.

He joined her without a word and started the car.

"I really think this has gone far enough." But at his sharp look, the words died in her throat.

~ ☾ ~

"Getting us safely home will be difficult enough without another argument."

Serra drew in a sharp breath. She'd heard the thread of need in his voice, could feel his hunger, a twin to her own. Deciding for once to obey, she turned her head and stared, sightless, out the window at the night. Urgency thrummed and the scent of desire rose between them.

Anticipation rode Serra hard. She hadn't been this needy since her first year. She could feel her sex grow plump and wet. Her nipples, puckered tight, rasped against the cotton fabric of the scrubs with her every breath. All she had to do was turn her head to look at him, see his brilliant blue eyes in his dark chiseled face, and she knew she'd start mewling with need.

The windows came down with a click and a whirr, and cold air rushed into the warmth of the car. Serra gasped in the wind buffeting her, welcomed it, let it cool the heat of her body.

She stole a quick glance at Gregor, but his profile, hard as stone, told her nothing. The windows went back up. The chill wind subsided. Serra, her mind clear once again, looked out the window and silently urged the miles to fly by.

~~~

Torture. The ride back to his house—he never even thought about taking her to her car—proved to be pure torture. Seeing her sitting on the couch wearing scrubs, her eyes, brilliant and knowing on his, had ratcheted up his need for her to painful. He'd scented her desire, knew that she knew. It had taken all his control not to toss her in his back seat and ravish her there and then.

Crossbreeding was wrong. It simply was. If his long-ago ancestors could have kept their hands off the humans, he'd be normal. His mother would be alive. His family would look much different than it did now, and they'd be happier.

But his ancestors had spread their fruitfulness far and wide. Demons, Angels, Gods and the Fae—all had taken their chances with humanity. They all contributed to the twisting of human genetics.

~ ☾ ~

How, then, could he deny the need for the Fae that pounded through him? This was beyond mere attraction. Something that had been bred deep inside him demanded Serra. He'd never felt anything like it, this primitive imperative to stake his claim.

He wasn't looking for forever. Plus, the Fae were notoriously fickle, and rarely monogamous, from what little he'd heard. He figured he'd get one night with her, maybe two, before her interest turned elsewhere. No sense in wasting time in the back seat when he had a perfectly good king-sized bed just waiting to be used. Besides, if he was kissing her, she couldn't lecture him.

Gregor realized with chagrin that in all of his life, he'd never once had to rationalize sex. Until now.

Until her.

He pulled into his garage and turned off the car. She broke the silence between them.

"If you're not planning on having sex with me, take me to my car."

The edge of irritation in her voice snapped his remaining patience. His good intentions went out the window, and he pounced.

The seatbelt restrained him. With a growl, he unsnapped it and hers at the same time, reached for her shoulders and dragged her across the space between them.

"Fast enough for you?" But before she could say a word, his lips covered hers, and he was caught up in the maelstrom that was pure them.

Her scent, her flavor sent his need soaring. Her body melted against his, her softness making him more aware of how hard he was in contrast. Her hunger fed his. Heat flared between them until the confines of the car added to his frustration.

He pulled his mouth from hers. "Upstairs. Now."

Her purple eyes blazed. "Race you."

"I've got the key." Before the words were out of his mouth, she stood at the door impatiently.

"Well?" One pale eyebrow arched and mischief gleamed in her eyes.

~ ☾ ~

He shoved out of the car and stood next to her a second later, his key in the lock and one arm wrapped around her waist. This time her mouth landed on his before they could get inside. Gregor remembered to hit the garage door button before he shut the door behind them. Turning, he pressed her back against the door while he indulged in tasting her, his big hands boosting her up by her hips.

Her mouth welcomed him. Their tongues tussled, tangled, vied for dominance over the other. Serra wrapped her legs around his waist, her moist heat pressing against him, her mouth demanding even as her hands roamed. He leaned closer, flattening her full breasts, and broke their kiss to explore her jaw line, the curve of her ear, the place where her pulse beat rapidly against the tender skin of her throat.

A part of his brain figured it was chemical, this almost constant need he had for her. And then her hands found him, and he stopped thinking entirely.

Her fingers trailed the length of him. His suit grew ever more restrictive and he pulled away from her with a gasp, lowering her to her feet.

"What is it?" She looked up at him, her eyes still hazed with desire.

"Clothes." He stripped off his suit jacket, his vest, toed off his shoes and stripped off his socks, his gaze never leaving hers. Shirt, t-shirt, and slacks were next.

She licked her lips and shook back her mane of white-blonde hair before she stripped off the scrubs she wore. "Wouldn't want you to feel strange, being the only naked one," she said, dropping the clothes on top of the pile he'd already made.

"Bed," he growled. The sight of her white skin, shimmering in the low light, had him catching his breath. Need tightened his body. Her nipples crinkled under his gaze, and her breath came quick as she took a step toward him.

"No," she answered, and took him in hand. "Now." She leaned in and gave him a kiss, one hand stroking his length. "Don't make me beg."

He took her by the waist and lifted her up. "Lean against the door again," he said. One hand beneath her ass, he used

~ ☾ ~

his other hand to guide himself into her. She shuddered in his arms as he entered her, as her heat surrounded him. He shifted his other hand to her hip and gripped her as he settled fully inside.

Her ankles locked behind him, and her hands clutched his shoulders. "Now move."

He moved. Entranced by the sight of her, pale and shimmering before him, her breasts bouncing as he slid inside her, he dipped his head to taste.

She moaned as his tongue swiped her nipple, then he settled to suckle and her moaning grew louder. Her muscles clamped down on him deep inside her, and he stopped his steady rhythm. Shifting her weight to one hand, he toyed with her other breast.

Her breath hitched and her back arched. "Gregor!" The word was a curse, a plea, a prayer.

Gregor took her mouth again, and shifted her slightly. He swallowed her gasp as his body slid deeper into hers, gave a gasp of his own as her muscles began a rhythmic clench and release that took him to the edge.

She wrenched her mouth from his and leaned back, lifted her breast to him once more. Obeying, Gregor took her nipple deep into his mouth, swirled and sucked and held her as she came, screaming his name.

He waited until her tension passed and she was limp in his arms. Moving carefully, he turned and knelt on the carpet, right there by the door, and set her down. Her eyes were closed, and as soon as her back hit the floor, her legs splayed open.

Gregor tilted her hips just a little. He gave her a kiss and plunged deeper into her body, again and again. Until his body tightened along with hers. Until his breath shortened and his heart raced. He laid his cheek against hers and they fell off the precipice into a haze of clouds and comfort and pure and total exhaustion.

~~~

Serra stretched. Every breath she took reminded her of

~ ☾ ~

Christine Ashworth

Gregor, mingled with demon and ash. She yawned. Her eyes popped open, and she let out a silent groan. No wonder! She'd been curled up around his shoulder. His very big shoulder. She stood and tapped her foot.

Right now, she barely hit five inches tall. He could capture her. Force her to obey him. Not that he would, but he could if he chose. If he thought it was a way to keep her safe.

Serra shook her shoulders and a sturdy set of wings appeared on her back. She'd really thought she'd gotten beyond her youth, but the small size and the wings had put her smack dab back in adolescence. On silent feet, she ran down the hallway and her wings fluttered, grew stronger, and provided liftoff. She flitted into the main room, sterile in shades of gray with only the occasional pop of orange to brighten things up.

But there in the corner was a large *ficus benjamina* tree, moss snuggling the roots at the top of the pot. With a sigh of relief, Serra fluttered down to the pot and looked approvingly at the springy dampness of the moss. Someone knew how to care for trees. With a regretful glance back at the hallway where she'd left Gregor, Serra settled down, covering her body with her wings. She just needed a bit of rest. Hopefully Gregor would stay asleep until she was full-sized and wingless again.

~ ☾ ~

CHAPTER NINE

The Nine Hells held a slightly oily haze from the fries churned out in the kitchen. Gregor pushed his way through the crowd to the bar in the back, wanting nothing more than a cold beer and a chance to think.

He'd woken, naked and alone in his home, and with no sign of the Fae. She didn't even bother to take her clothes when she left. Gregor didn't know whether he should be angry or worried, but after combing his house, Justin's house, and the neighborhood, he'd decided on anger, which led him to The Nine Hells.

He found room at one end of the bar and ordered his beer. At this time of the evening, most of the patrons were from the surrounding office buildings, still in their work clothes, grabbing a drink and a quick grope of a colleague before heading home. The rougher element wouldn't show up until closer to midnight.

There was an unusual intensity in the crowd tonight. He kept his head up and his eyes sharp.

It didn't take long to find it. The energy pulsed from one corner of the room. A man, a Charismatic, stood with his back to the wall and one foot on a chair, leaning forward and talking animatedly. Harry's son Samael sat in the Charismatic's circle, his eyes wide as he absorbed whatever information the Charismatic was pushing. Gregor frowned and looked to his beer, not wanting to draw the man's attention.

Not demon, but not wholly human, and without a touch of Fae, true Charismatics were rare, though they'd been around for centuries. One Charismatic in a hundred years would twist the fate of a people, a nation, or the world.

Gregor hated the thought of a Charismatic in his town, and now of all times. It would be too much to hope for, having a

~ ☾ ~

demon eat up this troublemaker.

"Caine. Here for my report?"

Gregor turned to see Little Harry behind the bar. "First, who's the preacher?" Gregor jerked a thumb toward the corner.

Harry scowled. "Goes by the name of Bryce Cannon. He's the one who wanted a peek at the list. Remember? I toldja about that this morning. He's got half the young bucks in the place fired up, including my son. Stupid sheep."

"Fired up how?"

"Samael said there were big doings going on." Harry wiped down the wooden bar, his chubby, work-worn hands moving on automatic as he spoke. "This guy is offering to train these sheep to channel their demon blood. How can we stay hidden if the town suddenly starts sprouting hotheads running around in their demon-skins?"

Gregor kept his face impassive. "We can't. But even if they have some magickal help, from what I understand, it's not that simple. How did today go?"

Harry shrugged, sent a look of dislike toward the corner of the bar. "I contacted the older ones, told them to keep their traps shut and patrol. We don't need the women and the hotheads hearing about it, or kids will be running around with guns in broad daylight, getting themselves locked up just in time for Christmas." He looked around, leaned in, and lowered his voice. "Two patrols found little demons. Dog-like creatures. Dusted about ten of them total. You?"

Gregor brought him up to speed while keeping a wary eye on the corner. "So keep an eye out, especially for full grown demons that can shift. I think this Dalton character might be Kendall Sorbis' very dangerous puppet."

"Yeah okay. I know, I remember those demons, the ones who could walk around as men. I was around the last time, you know. When your ma was attacked. We went on a hunt then, too, for demons. Your dad was righteous." Regret crossed Harry's face. "I always liked your ma," he said. "Rest her soul. But what about him?" The barkeep jerked a thumb toward Bryce Cannon. "What the hell should I do about him?"

~ ☾ ~

Gregor finished off his beer. "Keep an eye on him. Give a heads up to the cops on the beat out here, and don't hesitate to call them if you need to. As far as Sammy goes, smack some sense into his head, will you?"

"You bet. Wanna 'nother? The beer's on me. As a thanks again for this morning, you know." The round man's face flushed red. "I'd, uh, you know, appreciate if you'd keep it quiet."

"Not a word. I swear."

"Good." Harry beamed, and handed over another foaming glass. "I'll keep in touch." He moved down the bar.

Gregor brooded. The Charismatic was wringing out the crowd now, all of them pressing up toward him with their hands held out. But they weren't giving him money; instead, he was handing them paper. Tickets?

Leaving most of the second beer untouched, Gregor made his way back through to the front door, going slowly so as to overhear the Charismatic.

"It'll be the party of the year, I can guarantee that. Catered, open bar, with a band, dancing and the whole bit. Come, bring your card. You and five guests will be allowed in. Dress appropriately, though. Club wear. If you're late, you'll get locked out, so don't be late."

Gregor headed out, only slightly relieved. *This* Charismatic was pimping out a party. But he'd also been asking about residents with demon blood in them.

He stood outside the bar and considered. If he went in there and confronted this Bryce kid, he'd be tipping his hand early. On the other hand, if he didn't do anything about this, it could smack them right upside the head.

Caution prevailed. He'd keep one ear open for Bryce Cannon. If the Charismatic proved to be more than just a party promoter, then Gregor would handle him.

~~~

"I can't believe I let you talk me into coming out again. Are you sure you recovered?" Justin followed behind Maggie as she wandered down another dark alley.

~ ☾ ~

"I want these bastards dead, all of them." It was after ten. The night was cold, and any demon trail much colder. Maggie was shivering in her turtleneck and wool jacket, but she hadn't complained. He had to admire her for it.

"Let's eat." The words came out abruptly, and he frowned at himself.

Maggie turned around to stare at him. "What?" Her disbelief rang in the air.

Justin shrugged. "I'm starving. Let's get something to eat and come back in the morning. We're both tired and no longer at our best. The rest of the coven has gone to sleep, perchance to dream. Or maybe you just don't want to eat a meal with me?"

"We ate a late lunch together. I'm not tired, and I'm not hungry," she protested.

He chuckled. "You're tripping over your own feet and smothering yawns. It's cold out here. We should quit for the night."

Maggie stumbled and hopped over a lump in front of her. "What the hell was that?"

Justin stopped and stared at the ground between them.

An arm, ripped off from the shoulder, bloody and missing its fingers, stretched out on the ground between them. Maggie clapped a hand to her mouth and turned hastily away.

Justin narrowed his eyes. "It looks human." He sniffed the air. "The demon is long gone. Let's walk the area together, merging."

Maggie swiveled around and stared at him for the millionth time that night. "Are you crazy?"

He sighed. "If we merge and walk the scene, we might be able to tell what happened. Who the victim is, and what type of demon. Important information, Magdalena." He watched her. Maggie preferred being in charge. They'd always done crime scenes her way, up until tonight.

Maggie glared at him. "We've never done a merge. We've only discussed it as being a possibility. You walk it your way, I'll walk it mine, and we'll compare notes, the way we usually do."

"Waste of time. Come on, doll face. Lean on me for a

while. Let's do it together, call it in, and hightail it out of here." Justin moved to her side and held out his hand. "Or are you afraid of getting too close to me?"

"Of course I'm not." Maggie sniffed. "I suppose you bathed recently?"

"Besides the cold shower I took earlier today? Every Saturday night, whether I need it or not," he said cheerfully. "Not counting surfing in the Pacific. Come on. I won't bite unless you want me to."

With obvious reluctance, Maggie put her hand in his. "Where should we start?"

"At the back of the alley. There are a couple of dumpsters there, a good place for demons to hide out in daylight." Justin led the way to the far end of the alley. "This once, let's do it my way." He let go of her hand and slipped his arm around her waist. "Safer," he clarified.

She slid her left arm around his waist, held his free hand with hers, and took a breath. "Ready when you are."

Justin closed his eyes, opened up all his senses, and felt Maggie do the same, merging her soul with his. As one, they opened their eyes and looked toward the alley opening. They took a few steps forward and terror flashed through them.

They looked to the right, where a man had stumbled out of a doorway into the bright daylight. His eyes scanned the alleyway wildly and his heart thumped hard.

A whip flashed, slashed his back. He screamed as he fell, struggled to rise. The whip flashed again. Black ooze seeped into the wounds on his back. The demon came through the door then.

Both Justin and Maggie backed up but the demon saw only its prey. Satisfied that it wasn't going anywhere, it hunkered down behind a dumpster and dragged the man by the foot.

It tore off the shoe and sock, and one by one, delicately, the demon ate the toes off the man.

Justin felt Maggie shudder in his arms and his awareness of her drained out of his mind as she broke their merge.

"How awful." She turned into him, buried her face in his chest. He held her close. "Did you get a good look at him?"

~ ☾ ~

Justin rested his cheek against the top of her head. "I did. Nasty bugger. Two mouths. Four arms. A Hjurlt, just like Serra said." Energy pumped through him. "Let's get you out of here."

Maggie kept her arm around him as they hurried to the street. "Everything was so clear. Did you feel the sun on your face? I did. It happened this morning, before we ever started looking. God, I feel...too much."

Their bodies humming with built-up energy, Justin worked on keeping his focus. "We need to get to the car. Just let us get to the car, and we'll be better."

"Maybe we should stop touching." Maggie released his waist. "Or not," she said, wrapping her arm around him again. "Wow, what an energy overload. Did you know this would happen?"

Justin breathed deeply of her scent, enjoyed her arms around his waist. Too bad it couldn't last. "No. You're the only one I've ever merged with. Even when we walked scenes by ourselves, Maggie, you were the only one."

They reached Justin's dark green Jag. Before he could open the passenger door, Maggie had him pressed against the car, his face in her hands. "I may regret this in the morning, but right now it's all I can think about. You're all I can think about." She looked at his lips.

Justin felt that look down to his bones. "I want to warn you about one thing, Magdalena." She burned up against him, and he yearned to sink into her heat.

Her gaze flickered up to meet his, her brown eyes fierce with need and wariness. "What?"

"I won't regret anything in the morning." One hand on the back of her head, he bent to kiss her.

~~~

Someone was hammering at his front door at nearly midnight. Clad for once in jeans and a white t-shirt, Gregor put his beer down and went to answer it.

Serra stood there, wearing a clean pair of jeans and a fluffy yellow sweater. She gleamed in the night. "You left."

~ ☾ ~

"You left first." Gregor walked away, leaving the choice to come in or not up to her. He didn't hear her move, didn't hear the door close. When she spoke right behind him, he jumped, just a little.

"Have you any honey mead?"

"Honey what?"

"Never mind. Have any white wine?"

Gregor headed to the kitchen, bent to the fridge and dug out a bottle. "You're in luck." He opened the wine and poured her a glass. "Though I'm surprised you want to spend time with me."

Serra threw her hands up in frustration and went into the living room. Gregor followed her, intrigued. She wasn't running on the normal female lines, and he didn't quite know how to react.

She settled on the couch with a sigh. "I feel like yelling at you. But I don't want to yell. What I want is an accounting. What happened today? How many demons were caught and destroyed? Why is this room so sterile?"

Gregor shrugged. "The wolves have brought down three fairly big demons that had made it all the way to the Santa Monica Mountains. Much more dangerous than the dog-like things we've seen. They'll be sending us sketches of them as soon as they're done."

"Three. Well that's good, I suppose." She sipped her wine. "Those dog-like things are called the C'dak. They breed like rabbits."

"Justin and Maggie took out ten of the C'dak. Maggie needed a rest, but they went back out tonight. He'll call later." Gregor kept his focus on his beer bottle.

"What about Harry?"

"Their team ran into the same creatures that we did. They dispatched about ten of them, as well."

"A good beginning for the first day of the hunt."

"Why did you leave? I was hoping for an encore." The words burst out of Gregor without plan.

Everything about her softened. Her eyes turned a milder shade of purple, and her smile flashed. "You woke up too soon. And I'm apparently having a second adolescence."

~ ☾ ~

"Explain." He watched, fascinated, as a flush spread under her fine skin. She poured herself more wine.

"Well. The Fae don't sleep, per se. We rest, of course, but the only thing that drops us into a real sleep is extraordinary sex, and that only happens during our adolescence, or rather our sexual awakening. Changes occur to our bodies during this sleep time, and because of it, we get small. Fairy-like, you might say. But we eventually outgrow it. The only other thing that can make us go small is a spell. Magicks." She shrugged. "I haven't been that small in years. It was interesting."

Gregor wanted to believe. He wanted more than anything to think that it had been nature's funny games that took her away from him, and nothing else. "How small?"

"Five inches, give or take an eighth of an inch." She tilted her head. "If you need proof, I slept in your *Ficus Benjamina* pot, and I believe my old wings are still there. They fall off when we get big again. Anyway, your slamming the front door as you left woke me up. A few minutes later, I was full sized again."

He looked to the tree.

"Go ahead. Check. You know you want to."

He didn't move. "Why didn't you wake me up when you first noticed how small you were?"

"I was five inches tall, Gregor. Afraid."

Understanding flooded him. "You thought I'd trap you."

"Or step on me." She shrugged. "It's been known to happen. I didn't want that protective streak of yours to get the better of your common sense. You need me in this fight almost as much as I need to be here."

He remembered the way she fought that day, her knives flashing, her feet kicking out, and knew she was right. "I agree. Does that mean you'll stay with me tonight?"

Regret shimmered in her eyes. "I can't. I have things to attend to at my apartment. But I want to."

"Why did you come by? You could have called. Or waited until the morning. It could have waited."

She put her wineglass on the low coffee table and moved in to him. "I won't stay the night, but I would like that encore. In a bed, this time, as you wish." She held out a hand. "Okay?"

~ ☾ ~

Gregor felt the smile take over his face even as his body tightened in anticipation. "That's the best offer I've had all day."

CHAPTER TEN

At barely six am, Serra waited outside the Caine offices and watched the mall come alive. She'd left Gregor's arms three hours earlier, feeling loose and relaxed. She'd spent the time since talking to the Fae Council, bringing them up to date on the situation. They'd reminded her of her duties back home and handed her a timeline.

Amazing how fast her good mood had evaporated.

She had a mere handful of days, three, maybe four, before she had to return to her homeland. So she'd come to the mall early, wanting to immerse herself in the cheery decorations for the winter holiday, in the mouthwatering wares in the shops. She so loved the human clothes.

The small cafes in the area were now open and doing brisk business, scenting the winter air with coffee. Today she wore a pair of black jeans and a thick, bright red turtleneck. Her tennis shoes were the same ones from the day before. Shoes did not interest her nearly as much as the clothing.

A tall man with cropped blond hair caught her eye. Kendall. The mage. She scanned the area, but he was alone, coming down the mall toward the coffee shop. He slowed when he neared her, just as a few mall walkers passed on the other side of the mall. She cursed silently at the timing.

"What are you doing here so early in the morning, and without a cup of coffee?" He gave her a smile that invited confidence.

Her heart hammered. Surprised that the mage had come to her so openly, she marshaled her resources. Felt the power gathering within her. "I'm waiting for my job to start, and I don't drink coffee."

His eyes blazed blue at her answer, a smile curling itself on his mouth. "Interesting. Very interesting. Where do you work, my dear?"

~ ☾ ~

Serra shrugged. "It's of absolutely no interest to you." She skimmed his public mind and found nothing but a void, a blackness where something should be.

Warning bells rang in her mind as he stepped closer. She scanned the mall quickly, but there were still pedestrians out and about. She wouldn't be able to kill him here, not where there were so many witnesses.

He took another step, and now she could smell death on him. Amusement at his tactics warred with irritation. Did he think she was powerless, or did he not understand?

"You have such unusual eyes. A lovely amethyst color. Would you care to walk with me? To the cafe. For tea, perhaps, on this chilly morning." He put compulsion into his voice, but it merely pushed at her. She flicked it back at him and watched as he recoiled.

"No thanks."

His eyes narrowed and his voice grew deeper. "Would you like to work for me, then? I could pay you more than you currently make."

She raised an eyebrow. "I'm happy. Not willing to make a change."

He reached for her arm, pressing his thumb into her elbow, numbing the nerves there. "I think you'd love to work for me, sweet Fae." An ugly tone edged his voice.

Swiftly, she pushed the power she'd gathered deep beneath them and jolted the earth under the man's feet. She bent and shoved her shoulder into his stomach. He loosened his grip, and she shook the earth again. She let her eyes widen and clutched the side of the building as he fell into a heap at her feet, his face now wearing a slight greenish tinge. "My goodness. Was that an earthquake?"

People poured out of CafeGo just two doors down, all of them chattering excitedly. The blond man stood slowly, brushing off his black pants and suede jacket. "I think you know exactly what that was." With one eye on the crowd, he gave her a brief bow. "Tell Justin Caine I will find him, and I will end him, and nothing he can do will stop me. I have sworn an oath."

Serra lunged toward him and grabbed the man's bare

~ ☾ ~

wrist, rendering him immobile. Despite the shock of death on his skin, she held on, secure in her own power. "I am a protector and a fighter, and the Caines are now my own. I protect my own more fiercely than any others. You have no hope of winning against me."

Unable to move, he paled at her words. She leaned in closer and whispered in his ear. "Those who take on Death's mantle tend to lose themselves completely. But you are not Death himself. You are just an errand boy. So remember, even the trees have eyes, and as far as you're concerned, they'll always be able to find you."

The man gritted his teeth as her hand tightened on his. When she finally let go, her family's sigil had burned into his skin, a tree spreading its boughs and a pair of eyes glinting through the branches.

He stumbled back. "Bitch," he spat, his good hand covering her mark on his skin. "You're dead. You're all dead."

Serra drew herself up to her full height and stared scornfully. "It is time you left, errand boy."

Gregor and Justin came toward them from the far end of the mall. Gregor wore a dark gray suit today, Justin easily seen in his brightly colored Hawaiian shirt and board shorts. The man turned to stare at them and anger twisted his face. He turned back to her, malice in his eyes, his voice.

"The day is not far off. I will be at full strength and where will you be?" He made a quick gesture with his hands.

Serra jolted as a burst of his power slammed into her body. *Gregor!* She crumpled to the ground.

"Nowhere, I'm thinking." He smirked, turned on his heel, and slipped into the crowd still milling in front of CafeGo.

Gregor started running toward her even as she lost the blond in the crowd. Fear made his voice harsh. "What in all of Hades have you done?"

"I've done nothing," she snapped, her head whirling with pain. "Help me stand and get me to a tree for the love of the Light."

Gregor put an arm around her, helping her up. He walked her to a tree nearby. She leaned against it gratefully, her feet wedged into the tiny circle of dirt showing.

~ ☾ ~

Justin came up. "You don't look so good." His concern reached out and soothed her. Her lips trembled but she smiled.

"I've had better mornings," she said. Breathing deeply, she drew in the healthy green energies from the tree.

"Who was that with you?" Gregor demanded, his hands fisted at his side.

"Kendall Sorbis. He wanted to know who I was and what I had to do with you."

Justin leaned in and sniffed the air around her. "Faugh! He needs a new aftershave."

"He's a Death Bringer, a Death Mage. He's trolling for more power. Justin, he's aiming for you." She struggled to shove out the tendrils of death the mage had thrust into her.

Justin's eyes flickered. "Kendall Sorbis hates my guts. He always has. It was a total misunderstanding, but did he allow me to apologize?"

"Don't make light of it, Justin. How much danger is he in?" Gregor turned back to Serra.

"As much as the rest of us. Times a hatred factor." She closed her eyes, thankful for her returning energies. "Sorbis is a glorified errand boy, but the scent of death clings to him. Just seeing him can kill, if you can see beneath his masks." She sent a bright look to Gregor and took a step away from the tree. "Let's get inside."

Gregor offered her his arm, which she took with gratitude. "Did you feel the earthquake?"

"Yes. Not too strong," she said. "Made everyone at the cafe nervous, though."

"Us, too." Justin unlocked the office door.

"How did you and Maggie do last night?"

Justin shrugged as he went into his office. "We found part of a man that a demon had eaten. Maggie and I merged and walked the scene. It was pretty intense."

Serra frowned. "Can you give me an idea of what it looked like?"

"Long tail that looked like a whip. He used it like one, too. It was big, easily a foot taller than us." Justin gestured to Gregor and himself. "A bluish gray, with dark markings down

~ ☾ ~

its arms. Lots of teeth and wicked claws. We found an arm torn out of its socket. No fingers." Justin shuddered. "Not a pretty memory."

"How many mouths did it have?" Serra leaned forward, urgency shaking her body. "How many, Justin? Could you see?"

"Two. He was eating his victim's toes."

"Hjurlt. Like the one we killed that first night." Serra sank into a chair. "I could really use an apple or a banana or something right now." She reached out for the plant on the desk, fingering its green leaves.

Surprise had Justin leaping to his feet. "Of course. I'll go get you some fruit. Is that what you eat?"

"Fruit of the soil, the tree or the vine. Vegetables, grains, wine, honey from the bees. No meat, of any kind. I'm not used to dairy, but I can eat it. Eggs, too, though don't ask me why."

"I'm gone." Justin sent her a wink and he left.

Gregor stood just inside Justin's office, leaning against the wall. "Are you sure you're all right?"

"I will be. Come, sit. Let me lean against your shoulder." She patted the couch invitingly.

He moved to her side and settled next to her. "Tell me why I shouldn't send you home."

She poked her finger in the soil of the pot and rubbed it between thumb and forefinger. "Because I have a job to do. I thought we settled this last night. I'm here to fight, and trust me, what he did to me would have taken you out for a week or more. I underestimated him, but I'm resilient. Besides, now we know he's targeting Justin."

"It's not that I'm not glad you're here," he began.

"You just want to be the hero. I understand. As for Kendall, I have marked him. It should make it easier for me to find him. Plus my family's sigil will cause him pain. He has sworn an oath to kill Justin. I have sworn an oath, too. At the end, he said we were all dead." She shivered and leaned into him, grateful when he moved his arm up and gathered her close. "I know death will come eventually. But for the Fae, it is a blessing when nature takes us, almost another kind of

~ ☾ ~

birth. I could not stand to die a messy, bloody, human death."

"Tell me about the Fae death."

"I can't explain, not now. I am sick for my home." She gasped for breath and her vision wavered. "His energies hit me hard. He did his best to suck life out of me."

Gregor bit off an oath. "You need a park, something more than that houseplant you're fondling."

"I'll be fine, in time."

"Look at me. Damn it, Serra. Look at me!"

Schooling her features to show nothing of importance, Serra looked into his bright blue eyes, such a contrast with his dark skin. She saw concern and anger there, mingled with confusion and desire.

"You have been protecting me since we first met," she reminded him, and her heart ached, leaving her confused. She summoned up a smile. "It does any Fae good to have a protector, even when they feel they are the ones doing the protecting. I accept your offer to be my champion, if you accept my right to do the same by you."

She held out a hand and willed it not to tremble. "Please."

He took her hand in his, kissed it, and touched his forehead to the back of her hand. "As you wish it, so it will be." He rose then and turned away from her, clearing his throat. "You need to eat. What's taking Justin so long?"

"Can we sit beside the sea? It's still soil, rock that has been worn down through the millennia to become sand. I should like to touch the water."

"That can be arranged. Maybe you'll tell me stories of your homeland."

"Maybe." Serra closed her eyes. She hadn't felt this fragile since picking up the Warrior mantle. She knew what she needed, but after yesterday, or rather, this morning, she would not use him again. Already she felt herself wanting him, wanting to rest on his strength. She took a breath to steady herself. The source of her strength was inner control. It always had been. She would not lean on another to provide that strength.

"Why did you run to me? Did you see me fall?" She looked at him then.

~ ☾ ~

"I heard you call my name. You sounded scared, desperate." He took a step backward. "I heard you in my mind again, didn't I?"

Her heart ached at the faint distrust in his eyes. "Did it hurt you? Hearing me, I mean. Did it cause you pain?"

Justin burst in then. "Hey. Sorry. I got you a banana and an apple, and this little bag of trail mix. Dried fruit, and nuts and stuff." He shoved everything into her lap and eyed her nervously. "Feeling better?"

"Your plant needs better soil. All the nutrients are leached out of it," she said, and smiled at Justin. "Thank you so much for the food. May the Light shine upon you. Shall we go?" This last she directed to Gregor.

Gregor held out a hand and looked to Justin. "She needs land. Growing things. I'll be taking her to the park by the beach and eventually," he said, forestalling her with a glance, "I'll take her to the beach itself. She needs to heal."

"I'll write up my notes from last night and then the Wiccan crowd is gathering again for more hunting. Take care of her," he said to Gregor, and gave Serra's cheek a quick kiss.

~ ☾ ~

CHAPTER ELEVEN

"We're going to focus on the Wilshire Center today, between Western and Vermont, all the north/south streets. Any questions?"

The women just looked at him. They were not a friendly group. Justin suppressed a sigh. "Stay in pairs, please. In your cars. Call nine-one-one if you have to. Don't be a hero, and if you make a kill, let me know."

"You want pictures?" Aubrey waggled her cell phone.

"If you please, Aubrey," Maggie answered. "The more we know about the threat, the safer we'll be in the long run."

"Remember to take breaks. If you have to stop searching, let Maggie know."

The women dispersed, some giving the two of them sidelong glances.

Maggie dropped her head into her hands and groaned. "Everyone knows."

"No, they don't. They won't know unless you tell them about it." Justin took her by the elbow and steered her across the street. "You might also want to stop blushing every time you look at me. It's a dead giveaway."

"I don't blush," she retorted. "I wouldn't tell a soul. And let go of me."

"Nice." Justin dropped her arm and faced her. Took in her antagonistic stance, the uncertainty behind her eyes. It was the uncertainty he aimed for. "Let's get something straight. I thoroughly enjoyed myself. You did, too. I expect we'll enjoy each other more in the future. I'm all for it. I don't regret what happened last night between us because, as far as I'm concerned, there's nothing to regret."

"Regrets are nature's way of making sure you don't make the same mistake more than once," she bit out. "Trust me, I'm not about to make this mistake again."

~ ☾ ~

Abruptly, Justin's patience gave out. "I'm calling Aubrey." He pulled out his cell phone. "We'll change partners."

"Why?"

"Obviously you can't concentrate on what we need to do here, since you're so worried about making love with me again."

"We had sex. It wasn't lovemaking," Maggie hissed, blushing. She averted her face and glared at a passerby.

Justin raised an eyebrow. "Aubrey, hi. I'd like to work with you today, give you some pointers. Can you and Cait return to our original meeting place? We'll just give it a switch. Great, see you in five."

"There," he said, shutting his phone and slipping it into his shorts pocket. "You'll be safe with Cait, and I'll get some work done with Aubrey."

"Don't try to pretty up what happened last night, Justin." Maggie crossed her arms, her chin lifted. "I remember quite well."

He cupped her face in his hands and gazed into her wide brown eyes. "Then you remember how we felt together. How amazing we were together, and how the energy rode us as surely as you rode me." As the blush rose again in her cheeks, Justin knew a small measure of satisfaction. "You also remember that last time, when we were sleepy, and our coming together was slow and sweet, and it felt like home. That was lovemaking, Maggie." His thumbs caressed her cheeks before he let her go.

Aubrey strode up to them, a sour-faced Cait stalking behind her. "So we're switching partners? Is everything all right?"

"It's fine," Justin said smoothly, taking Aubrey's arm. "Thanks for coming so quickly."

"We weren't far." Aubrey looked from Maggie to Justin. "As a matter of fact, we ran into Fran Thomas. She was coming out of that fancy party store on Wilshire. You remember the one, right?" She appealed to Maggie. "I asked Fran why she wasn't working with us, and she said she had too much to do. She's been hired to plan some big party for the solstice. I told her to keep her radar up for any demons."

~ ☾ ~

Maggie raised an eyebrow. "Is she still in the area, do you think?"

Cait shrugged. "Don't know. She was on foot, juggling a phone and a list as she walked. Why?"

"I'd like to talk to her myself. We did speak on the phone, but face to face can give more satisfactory answers. Since we're going in that direction anyway, why don't we see if we can catch up with her?"

"Good plan. Aubrey, you ready to get these monsters?"

Aubrey grinned up at Justin. "Let's go, handsome."

Justin tipped his imaginary hat to the other two women. "We'll see you later. Keep in touch." His gaze lingered on Maggie, and she flushed again.

With a hand on Aubrey's back, Justin turned her, and they walked north.

Aubrey blew out a breath and laughed. "Wow. Now that's what I call chemistry. So much for my chances with you, beautiful man. You only have eyes for her."

"Try telling her that." Disgruntled, Justin shoved his hands in his pockets.

"And have her hand me my head on a platter? Thanks, but I don't think so. We've never been that close. I was surprised she called me after all these years."

"What was it like, your coven in school?" Justin figured he needed to learn all he could about the witch that had caught his attention.

"Mmm. Powerful. Few of us actually had that something extra, but we learned the rituals. We studied and grew to be proper little Wiccans. Maggie did have that extra kick, though. So did Cait, a little, and Kendall, or Ken Doll as we called him then." She laughed again. "Ken cut quite a swathe through our group. Maggie was the holdout, until she, too, finally fell under his spell. I always wondered if it was an actual spell," she mused.

"What kind of man was Kendall? Maggie doesn't talk about him much." He shortened his stride to match hers.

"You know, we'd make a stunning couple, you and me. No? Ah well." Aubrey put her arm through Justin's in a friendly fashion and squeezed a little. "It was worth a shot.

~ ☾ ~

Kendall was dark emotionally, and blond physically. He wanted to know how things worked by taking them apart. Apparently, he'd always been that way. The family goldfish first, then the family rat. His mom stopped buying him animals after she found the hamsters eviscerated. He was nine," she added.

"You're joking."

"I'm not. I'm not talking out of school, either. He used to tell us all about it, but then he'd swear he'd seen the light and was no longer the dark person he'd been as a young boy."

"You didn't believe him." Justin didn't like the picture of Kendall Sorbis forming in his head.

"No. None of us did. He and I were only together for a couple of weeks. Maggie had gone away for spring break, and he was waiting for her. He saw things that no one else saw."

"In what way?" He looked down at her, her short brown curls barely hitting him at his shoulder. She walked along easily, her athletic shape one that would normally call to him. To his surprise, he realized she was beautiful but held absolutely no attraction for him. He stared ahead and focused on their conversation.

"How do I explain it? It was like he knew when someone would get sick. Or he could tell when a teacher was dying. He surprised us a couple of times with predictions, as though he could see into the future."

"But he couldn't see into the future?"

"A part of me always wondered if perhaps he foretold the things that he knew would happen because he'd made them happen. Whether through magicks or regular means." She heaved a sigh. "And I know how stupid that sounds. We didn't gossip much about Kendall. The few girls who did talk? They ended up dropping out of school. One committed suicide."

Justin patted her hand and kept his face easy. Kendall Sorbis was sounding more and more deadly.

Aubrey frowned. "You know, now that I think about it, Maggie is the only one of us who broke it off with him. Kendall was always the dumper, until Maggie. Then he became the dumpee less than a week after they got together."

~ ☾ ~

We never got the full story out of her. Understandable, I guess, but soon after they broke up Kendall disappeared. He left L.A. without graduating. Then whoosh, seven years later he's back and engaged to one of the Hamilton girls. Old L.A. money, you know. Suddenly, he was golden, and everywhere. He sent all of us invitations to the wedding."

"Did you go?"

"Nah. It had been over and done with for years, and I never cared that much to begin with. I think Maggie went though, and that surprised me when I heard. I guess I thought she'd have been happy to see him safely married to someone else. I'll tell you, it was a shock to everyone when he disappeared under such a cloud last summer."

Justin didn't say anything, his thoughts in turmoil with the information she'd given him.

~~~

Serra dug her toes into the sand and smiled with delight. The wind whipped her ponytail about, and the waves crashed to the shore. The moving, pulsing water caught her up in its rhythm, made her feel as one with the universe.

Gregor dropped down and wrapped an arm around her. "Better?"

"Mmm. Much." She breathed in the salty air. She'd spent close to an hour with trees and bushes on the bluff, but down here she felt her strength returning with every wave.

"Explain it to me. How you were able to brand him, basically, but had no defense against his attack? I don't understand."

"Hubris," she said. "I forgot basic protection. That simple, and that stupid." She sighed and leaned into him. "I had to lower it to mark him. I didn't raise it fast enough. Like I said, stupid."

"What does the mark do?"

"It will help me find him. He'll set off alarms if he shows up in Faeland again, and if I try, I can locate him by what he sees."

"Move in with me."

She tilted her head and looked up at him. "Why?"

His eyes grew stormy as he searched the horizon. "Because."

"That's not an answer." But her heart beat just a little faster, and she curled her knees up toward him, drawing comfort from his warmth.

He huffed out a breath. "Because I want to know where you are. Because I need to keep you safe. Because you are unlike anyone I've ever known."

"I have my orders. I'm supposed to wrap this up by the solstice and then go home."

"Please. Allow me to do my best to protect you for the time you are here."

She didn't respond, and the only sounds between them were the cry of gulls overhead and the crashing of the waves.

"Gregor." She searched for the right words. For the first time she could remember, a lover mattered. But she would be leaving his world in a very few days. Would it be selfish to keep him close for the time they had together? "For the rest of my time here, I would love to stay with you." She'd deal with the subsequent fallout.

The tension flowed out of him. "Thank you."

"It's going to be a busy few days. We don't have much time for sleep, if any time at all," she warned.

"That's okay. As long as I know where you are, I'm good." He turned his head and kissed her.

Serra responded, surprised at how cherished his kiss made her feel. She sank into him, into the comfort, the slow-rising passion, so different from their heat the night before. Finally, she pulled away and rested her head on his shoulder. "We should go. Head back to where we were yesterday, when we took out the C'dak."

"You're better."

"I'm better." She picked up her shoes. "Come on, Caine. Let's get back to work."

He stood and picked her up, cradling her in his arms. "Back to the office first, then to the airport area."

Serra wrapped her hands around his neck and grinned. "That works for me."

~ ☾ ~

As he headed to the car, she rested in his care and concern, something she never got from home. As long as she didn't come to depend on it, count on it, the very least she could do was savor it. Savor him.

She'd be leaving all too soon.

They were both content to keep silent on the drive back to the office. Once there, they walked through the bustle of the morning crowd. More shops in the mall had opened, and some buskers were out. Singers, guitar players, and jugglers were entertaining the passersby.

"After you, my Fae," Gregor said, and opened the door to the stairway.

"Thank you, kind sir." Serra headed up the stairs.

The smell of unwashed flesh wafted down the stairwell toward them as a body hurtled at her, shoved past them both, and flew out the door.

Serra moved but Gregor was faster, racing after the intruder.

~ ~ ~

Gregor caught the man with a flying tackle, bringing them both down hard on the cement outside. Someone screamed, there was a shout or two. Gregor got to his feet, keeping the man's arms tight behind his back.

"Everything is fine, folks. The cops are on the way. You, my friend," he said, lowering his voice, "will come along with me. Or you will be handed over to the police."

"Fuck it, man. I ain't done nuthin wrong. You got the wrong guy, see?" The kid whined as Gregor forced him back up the steps and into the office. He shut the door behind them and tossed the kid onto a chair in the lobby, aware of Serra, perched on the reception desk.

Gregor stood over the smaller man. "Who are you working for?"

"Nabuddy, man. I tol' ya. You got the wrong guy." He wiped his wrist under his nose, his eyes darting from Gregor to the door to Serra and back to the door.

He upped the menace in his voice. "You were up here. You

stink of sweat, alcohol and drugs and you were in our private rooms. I'll be happy to press charges. Breaking and entering, and assault since you knocked the lady down. What's your name?"

"Cash." He grinned then, a cocky grin showing two missing teeth. "'Cause I never have any."

Gregor gripped the man's upper arm. "Cash. Who sent you?"

He whistled tunelessly, his eyes scanning, scanning. His fingers twitched and he tucked them under his thighs while the rest of his body bopped to a tune only he could hear.

"What are you going to do, Gregor? Beat him?" Serra slid off the desk and came to his side. "What a pathetic human. But he stinks of demon."

"Hmm. I'd rather not beat him in front of you."

"Nice, that bending to my sensibilities. Very good. I could always leave you two alone," she said, and looked up at him. They ignored Cash's sudden start, the babble that fell from his mouth.

"Na. Please. Live and let live. Tell and be told," he pleaded.

"Of course, I could always have a go at him. Since you don't do the mind thing," she added.

Gregor gestured. "Be my guest."

Cash's eyes got wide. "Wha? Keep her away from me, filthy Fae. Filthy," he spat.

"Be easy, Cash." She stepped toward him, keeping out of his reach. "Be easy."

Gregor watched as a blank stare came over Cash's face. The kid was more like in his twenties. Hard living would account for the stench of an unwashed alcoholic. But Gregor could smell demon stink under the body odor, too.

How did Cash fit in? They had a lot of questions but no answers yet, and time flew. If, as Serra suspected, something big was planned for the solstice—coincidentally falling on a full moon, a rarity—then they had work to do and no time to screw around.

Cash's lips moved and his eyes shut tight. Serra swayed where she stood and Gregor put a steadying hand on her shoulder. If this worked, if Serra could get to the root of the

~ ☾ ~

issue with Cash, then maybe they had another weapon they could use.

Serra released his mind. Cash sprang up, his fists flying like a wild thing. "You can't keep me! You can't, you can't!"

"Restrain him, but don't hurt him," she said to Gregor.

He held the wiry man, with his arms once again behind his back, and looked to Serra. "Well? Now what do we do with him?"

"He needs food, and sleep. And a bath."

"Food?" Cash's ears pricked up. "You want to feed me? Feed Cash?"

"Yes. We want to feed you. You need rest. Food and rest." She looked up at Gregor. "Can we take him to your place? I'll explain everything, I promise."

"This had better be good," he said.

She ignored him and turned to Cash once more. "Gregor is going to release you. You are in no danger from us. We will give you food, and a bath, and a place to sleep for a few hours. Once you've slept, we have a proposition for you."

Gregor balked. It was one thing having Serra as a temporary roommate, and quite another having this hooligan at his place. "If he's not becoming a permanent guest, why don't we keep him here? There's a bathroom, a big sink, towels and soap. While he's washing up, I'll get food and maybe a set of sweats."

Serra beamed at him. "Perfect solution. Show him the bathroom, and then get the food and clothing if you don't mind. I can watch him until you get back."

Gregor left on his errand, feeling somehow like he'd just won a contest he didn't know he'd even entered.

~ ☾ ~

CHAPTER TWELVE

Frannie paced, her mind in turmoil. Why, today of all days, did she have to run into the coven? Seeing Cait with Aubrey had almost made her blurt out everything. A shiver ran down her spine. It had all the hallmarks of a bad omen. A really, really bad omen. She looked around the space to distract herself.

The hangar was slowly getting transformed. She had organized the men Bryce found for her. They stood on big ladders hanging poofs of netting from the ceiling. White fabric already covered the bare cement walls.

Now, though, horror speared through her as, with a shout, a man plunged from a ladder twenty feet to the hard floor below. The dull thud of his head against the concrete set her own head throbbing.

Death. Another bad omen.

Men rushed down from their ladders and ran to their *compadre,* chattering rapidly in Spanish. One, a big, meaty man, bent to search for a pulse. After a moment, he straightened and shook his head. As the others fell silent, his gaze met Frannie's.

She froze. They were going to walk away. Just...walk away. She knew it, knew by the way they'd all turned to look at her. She hadn't moved, hadn't cried out, hadn't even rushed to the fallen man to see if he was okay. She'd done nothing, and they damned her for it. She could see it in their set faces, feel it in the heat of hate streaming toward her.

They wouldn't come for her now, but she'd just made their list. She lifted her cell phone and dialed, but before she could complete the call the phone was snatched from her.

"You will do nothing." Bryce's voice cut her like a whip, and she jerked with it.

"Thank God you're back. What about the workers?" She

~ ☾ ~

turned to him, brushing her hand across his chest, taking comfort from him. "What about the dead man?"

"We'll chuck him through the portal," he decided. "The rest of them will get a bump in pay."

"How? We don't have that kind of cash." But her words trailed off as he pulled a fat wallet from his pocket.

"I picked up some, in case of emergencies. This is a fucking emergency." Bryce scowled and moved toward the men, shouting in Spanish.

Frannie watched as he cowed them all into getting back to work, all except the big one. They argued, and finally Bryce opened his wallet, counted out ten hundred dollar bills.

The men climbed the ladders then, armfuls of netting shrouding them. Frannie shuddered at the imagery. Too much death, too much of the past haunting her. Doubts crowded into her brain.

She'd escaped talking to Maggie that morning by a hair. She'd hid in a dermatologist's office until she saw Maggie and Cait finally giving up the search. At the time, she'd only known relief at dodging the confrontation, but maybe she should talk to Maggie? Just in case?

Frannie glanced over at the workers, suddenly aware that while they were working, they continued to shoot her piercing, hate-filled glares. She shivered again and wished, heartily, that she'd never met Bryce, never joined the coven, and never gotten mixed up with Kendall Sorbis again. Twice in a lifetime was two times too many.

~~~

"Well, he's clean at least," Serra observed as they watched their captive devour the sub sandwich.

Cash ate with the single-minded concentration of a person who never knew where his next meal was coming from.

They'd moved to the conference room, where there was nothing to steal but whiteboard markers and blank notepads. Cash sat the farthest away from the door.

"Can you tell me, please, what you learned?" Gregor leaned against the door, keeping an eye on both of them. "I've been incredibly patient, you know."

Serra gave a dainty snort. "He's being used. He isn't adverse to it, either." She studied him. "We have two choices. We can either send him far, far away, which will undoubtedly save his life, or we can use him, too."

He wondered where her thoughts were headed. "What aren't you saying?"

She leaned her chin on her hand. "If we send him away, they will just use someone else. Someone who may not be as controllable."

"And we'd have no way of knowing who that person would be."

"Correct."

Gregor's hands fisted at his sides. "I don't like that option. What does using him involve?"

"A mental tag, so I can keep track of him." She shrugged. "Plus some subconscious suggestions that may save his life. We need to know what's being planned."

"What did you get so far? Surely more than he's being used," he pointed out.

"There's someone he answers to nicknamed B. They're putting together some sort of party, and it's happening soon."

"The solstice." Gregor sighed heavily. "Bryce. The Charismatic. Damn it." He glared down the room at Cash, who seemed to have eyes only for the shreds of lettuce and bits of tomato and onion left on the wrapping from his sandwich.

"We have to assume that's the target date. As far as why he smells like demons, he was in the same room as the portal. Some of that stench stuck with him, I'm afraid."

"Did you get the location?"

"Someplace big. I'm sorry, Gregor. The last time he was there, he was flying high. His hallucinations mingled with reality, and while I know which is which, his focus remained on the beings he saw and not his location." She spread her hands, a sympathetic look in her eyes. "I'll know more once he's back in that environment."

Gregor studied her. She seemed to have rebounded from the early morning encounter with Kendall, but he didn't want to take any risks. "Can we send him back in new clothes?"

"I think so. I'll implant a memory of him stealing them from the store. The cleanliness we'll just ignore, and hopefully, so will his friends." She rubbed her arms and frowned. "We have three days. Only three days, Gregor. That's not enough time to find them all."

"We have three days until something big happens. After that? We'll still hunt the remaining demons. As long as it takes, we'll cleanse the city." He hesitated. "Why did Cash call you a 'filthy Fae'?"

Serra wrinkled her nose. "Just as there are good humans and bad humans, there are good and bad Fae. The Dark Fae have gone underground, literally. They have taken to the caverns and the dark spaces beneath the mountains of our land. They seek more. Always more."

Another ideal smashed. Gregor sighed. "Like humanity, then. I had so hoped the Fae were different."

"There is light and dark in every sentient being. It is what we decide to do with it that matters," she said. "Even you. You have your Fae side, and your Demon side. Both are light, both are dark. As is the human within." Her voice deepened with intensity. "You need to learn your abilities, Gregor. Walk with the Fae, walk in your Demon-skin. If you never feel the tug of the dark, how can you possibly keep your face toward the Light?"

"The Light is a lie," spat Cash.

"Be easy," Serra said, turning toward him. He ducked his head, flinching when she moved to him and put her hands on his shoulders.

Gregor saw her lips move, saw Cash answer, but couldn't hear what they said. Restless and unhappy about being out of the loop, Gregor pushed away from the door and took a couple steps toward them.

Light gleamed from her hands and slid under Cash's hunched shoulders. Cash's mouth opened in shock or pain, Gregor couldn't tell which, but no sound came out. The light traveled across his collarbone and rested in the hollow of his throat. It winked once then went out.

Serra backed away and Cash was out of his chair like a

~ ☾ ~

shot. "Let him go, Gregor."

Gregor opened the door and let Cash speed out of there without stopping him. He sent her a thoughtful look. "Was that wise?"

She shrugged. "It was necessary. He agreed to it, mentally, and I'll be able to monitor what's happening to him."

"A spy in the enemy's camp. I like it." He smiled.

"I finally had a good idea?" Amused, she crossed her arms. "Shall we go out and hunt demons, or do you want to face your own, here and now?"

"I'm ready to hunt demons when you are." Gregor held the door open and raised an eyebrow.

~~~

"On your left!" Justin hissed the words, his eyes darting around the daytime quiet of the neighborhood. The stink of demon drifted to them.

"I see it," Aubrey muttered. She shifted slightly behind Justin and hefted her cop-style flashlight.

It came at them in a blur, no higher than their knees. Justin dropped to its level and led with his shoulder, meeting it in a crash of bone.

The demon howled as it somersaulted backwards. Dogs all over the neighborhood responded, raising their voices in sympathy. Justin blinked as the demon came up on its hind feet and snarled at him.

It looked like a dog. Could pass for a dog, except for its almost-human hands that ended in wicked claws. This demon looked like a variant of the ones he and Maggie had killed the day before.

The demon snarled again and leaped. It chose Aubrey this time, grabbing her by the shoulders.

She shrieked and hit it on the head. It howled and bit at her face but caught only air in its teeth as Justin plucked it off Aubrey and slammed it full force into the cement, falling to one knee as he did so.

The demon didn't move. Justin looked around and lifted it into his arms. "Come on." He moved to the backside of the house, glad there wasn't a gate to keep them out. The yard was mostly cement and swimming pool. Justin set the demon down and struck a match. Soon the demon was nothing but a stinking pile of ash.

Aubrey, looking as gray as the demon, found a broom and swept the ashes into the bushes crowding the house.

"You okay?"

Aubrey gulped. "Justin, this isn't the first time I've seen demons like this. I just didn't know they were demons."

Justin's eyes sharpened. "Let's get out of here, then you can tell me all about it." He took her by the elbow and hurried her back out into the street, looking carefully both ways. Nothing stirred in either direction. He slung his arm around Aubrey's waist and kept them both to a saunter as they headed back to the main drag.

"Tell me about it."

"Yesterday. I was with Cait, and we passed a house that seemed off, somehow. It smelled like that thing smelled." Her body shook, and Justin hugged her closer to him. "Cait said they were just dogs. A friend of hers lived there, she said, and he raised this weird breed of dogs. But that wasn't a dog, was it?"

"No. It didn't hurt you, did it? I thought I got to you in time. Your face."

"My face is fine. But my arms."

Justin stopped them at the corner of a busy intersection and pulled away from her, holding her gently by the elbows. Her coat had puncture holes in the shoulder area. Beneath her coat, her beige sweater showed six droplets of blood on both shoulders. Justin remembered the claws on the demon and scowled. "Hell. I'm so sorry." He looked up and down the streets until he spotted a coffee shop. "Come on."

He steered her toward the coffee shop and got them a booth inside, crowding her into a corner as he sat beside her. When the waitress came by, he spared her a quick glance.

"Two coffees, two danish, whatever's the freshest. Add a side of scrambled eggs to that," he said.

"Coming right up." She sashayed away.

"Danish? Scrambled eggs?" Aubrey leaned against the wall

and stared at him. "What are you doing?"

"You're in a bit of shock. I'm going to heal you, and we'll both need the sugar and the protein. The coffee is because it's been a couple hours since my last cup. Now let me see." He pulled back her coat and moved her sweater off one shoulder.

Angry red rips, darkening to black, marred skin the color of cream-laced coffee. Justin sucked in a breath. Even as he watched, the dark spots grew. Slowly, but definitely, they crept toward each other. "You feel okay?" he demanded, peering into her glazed eyes. "Aubrey?"

"I can't move my arms." Only a hint of panic threaded her voice.

Justin swore and pulled out his cell. He punched in a number while watching Aubrey through narrowed eyes. He could almost see the poison at work in her. "Doc Cavanaugh? Justin Caine. I've got an emergency."

Within ten minutes, a van pulled up and Justin had Aubrey safely stowed in the back, along with their breakfast order to go. He kept one cup of coffee for himself and let the driver have the other. He'd done a cursory healing that would keep the poison from spreading, but she needed more help than he could give her.

He wrapped Aubrey in a blanket and cinched the seatbelt around her. "Be safe. Be careful. I'll see you soon."

Panic flared in Aubrey's eyes. "Hey. Find Cait. She's with Maggie. Cait hates Maggie, she always has. If she's on the other side of this fight, that would be bad."

Justin's blood ran cold. "I'll find her. I promise." He watched the van pull away, grim. If Cait, or any other of Maggie's old coven, sought to hurt her, they'd have to go through him first.

If he could find her in time. He sent a tendril of thought her way, more familiar now with her mind after their night together. How could he have left her in someone else's hands? Damn it, he knew better. He knew she belonged at his side. *Magdalena. Damn it all, where are you?*

He heard her exasperated sigh. *Can't you use a cell phone like everyone else?*

Relief filled him at her acerbic response. She was fine,

then. Fine. *Shut up and listen, woman. I need you. Aubrey's been hurt. Meet me at the car, fast.*

Aubrey's been hurt?

Come fast, Magdalena. As fast as you can move. He broke their connection and headed for his car, several blocks away. He hadn't wanted to tip her off to Cait, not yet. Not until he had her near him again. He didn't want her going head to head with Cait without him.

Heaving a sigh, he pulled out his cell phone. Talking to Gregor the old fashioned way sucked, he decided for the millionth time as Gregor's phone went straight to voicemail.

"Hey bro, listen up. Cait Lanyon is going to be a problem. Keep it quiet for now, but dig up everything you can on her. Aubrey is hurt and on the way to Doc Cavanaugh. I'm out looking for Maggie now. Call me when you get this message." He shoved his phone into his pocket and walked faster.

~ ☾ ~

CHAPTER THIRTEEN

Gregor did a fast sweep of the garage, but it was empty of dog-like demons. Serra stood in the stairwell, her arms crossed and her face intent.

"What is it?" He paused in front of her. "What do you see?"

She shook her head. "It's not a seeing so much as a knowing. And I can't explain it any other way. Someone died here, not long ago." Her gaze caught him, her purple eyes glowing with sympathy. "It was a simple death."

He snorted. "Simple. Right. How many more people will die a simple death while we try to round up all the demons?" Frustrated, he kicked a soda can. It bounced along the ground, hit the far wall, and came to a rest. "All this death is getting to me."

"We might not get them all. Still, we will do what we can." She seemed to look through and beyond him.

He bashed the wall of the alley and cursed silently as his hand throbbed from the force of the hit. He hadn't felt this out of control in years. If he let his anger rip free, his demon could take over and then where would he be? Gregor took a deep breath and carefully wrapped his emotions up into a tiny square and locked it away. Becoming emotional rarely solved any problems. He looked up to find Serra studying him intently.

"Anger is normal and healthy. It actually crosses sentient species. The Fae can feel anger, as do demon-kind." She brushed his shoulder with her hand. "Do not be upset with yourself for doing what is normal." She sucked in a breath. "Cash."

"What about him?"

"He has some talent. He got in touch with me." She put a hand out as her eyes went glassy. "He's showing me where he is by looking around, taking note of landmarks. The area is

~ ☾ ~

run down, weeds and graffiti. There's an empty parking lot, and lots of big warehouse buildings. He's stopping at one six six three—that's the number on the side of the building."

"The streets he's on. Which streets?" Urgency had him taking her shoulders in his hands. "Which streets, Serra?"

"I can't... I can't see. He's gone inside and it's dark. I can't see." Abruptly, she sagged in his arms. "I'm sorry. I haven't merged with someone like that in a long time. It's draining. Surprising. I didn't think he'd initiate contact."

"You need food." He slid his arm around her and bolstered her as he headed to CafeGo.

She stumbled. "I'm so sorry. I hate feeling helpless. You're right, we should have gone to the airport area where we were yesterday."

"In which case, we might be fighting, and you might be down for the count. Just slide your arm around me and hang on."

They made it into the shop, the warm aroma of roasting coffee welcome after the cold of outside. The place bustled. Gregor sighed, knowing he'd have a wait. He found her a cozy armchair and settled her there. After an intense look at her, he nodded. "I'll get you the food. Don't go anywhere."

"I'll stay put. I promise." Her purple eyes creased at the corners as she smiled at him, and his breath caught. He went to stand in line, a frown pulling down his thoughts. She really was too lovely. Far too lovely for someone like him.

"Gregor Caine. Since when do you buy your own coffee? Where is the luscious Gabriel?" Carmen's rich, warm voice rolled over him. There were five people in front of him, and he was taller than all of them.

"My younger brother is enjoying Cambria with Rose. Remember? He's married, Carmen," Gregor retorted with a smile.

"I was at the wedding, wasn't I?" She made change and handed out coffee, took the next order. "No harm in looking."

Carmen was fifty if a day, and almost as tall as she was wide. Her heart was as warm as the caramel color of her skin, and she'd never met a man she didn't like. All the Caines adored her like a big sister.

~ ☾ ~

"You've got a good crowd here," he said as she took care of the remaining two customers in front of him.

"I do," she acknowledged, but her smile looked strained. "What can I get you?"

Gregor handed her the two fruit cups. "Plus give me an apple juice and a large French roast."

Carmen totaled his order, took his money, and gave him his change. Handing over both the coffee and the apple juice, she called to her co-worker. "Betty, can you take over here?"

Betty looked up from her conversation with a customer and frowned. "I'm still on break, Car."

"Break's over. You'll get another one. Now, please," Carmen said firmly.

Betty came around to take Carmen's place and ignored Gregor. "Next customer in line," she said, a sulky look in her eyes.

Gregor took the fruit cups and his coffee. Carmen grabbed the apple juice and motioned to a corner near the door.

Concerned, he followed her. "What's happening? You look tense."

"I am," she said, and handed over his juice. She stood in front of him, giving him the view of the entire store. "You see the dark man in the corner? The one that Betty was flirting with?"

A man sat there, his face in shadow. Gregor didn't recognize him, so he looked back down at Carmen. "Yeah, I see him. What's going on?"

"He's been here every day and every night. Keeps chatting up my staff, my customers. Flirting outrageously."

Gregor waited. "Nothing else?"

"You think I'm a fool, don't you?" Carmen shook her head. "Maybe I am. But I've never seen him walk in here. He's always got a cup of coffee, and whenever Betty goes over to give him a refill, he hands her a five-dollar bill. A five-dollar bill, Gregor. For a refill. Of a cup of coffee he didn't pay for to begin with." Her voice rose and she clapped her hand over her mouth.

Gregor frowned and looked over at the corner again. The man had left, however. Curious, he scanned the room and saw him crouched down at Serra's side. Cold fear drenched common sense. Power began to build inside him, power he'd never learned to control. The room trembled in response.

Serra!

Her head swiveled toward him, her mouth open in surprise. *Gregor?*

He got lost a moment in the feel of her in his mind, him in her mind. At Carmen's impatient voice, he looked down at her and broke the link. "What is it, Carmen?"

"I hate earthquakes. You looked spooked. You okay?" She peered up at him, suspicious.

Gregor looked toward Serra and noted with relief that she was alone, her attention on him. "Yeah, I'm okay." He smiled down at Carmen. "Your dark man is gone now. Do you want me to put some sort of warding on the place? I know someone who could take care of that for you."

"Magdalena's a friend of mine too, you know. I'll have a word with her." Carmen followed Gregor's gaze to where Serra sat. "She's a pretty one. But can you keep up with her? That's the question." She chuckled and patted his arm. "You go, take her the fruit and the juice. She'll feel better soon."

Gregor felt his eyes widen. "Are you a witch, too?"

"No, dearie. I just pay attention to who walks in through my door." She headed back to the counter. "Betty. Wake up, child, and get moving. The display case needs sorting out again."

Gregor went to Serra and sat in the chair next to hers. He handed her the fruit cup and the apple juice. "Here's another one, if you need it," he said, and set it on the table between them.

She smiled her thanks and opened the container of fruit.

"Who was that man that stopped to talk to you?" Gregor asked the question idly. At her flush, something grew cold in him, and he knew whatever came out of her mouth next would be a lie.

"He was no one. Nobody." Her flush spread and she bent her head. "But look at you, reaching out to me," she said. "I'm so proud. Why, though? What happened?"

Gregor shrugged. "I thought you were in danger."

~ ☾ ~

She put a strawberry in her mouth. He watched her think but couldn't follow where her mind went.

"That may be the trigger for you," she said, her brows drawn together. "Either anger, or fear for another. The blocks you've put on your talents seem unmovable. Your own anger or fear could rip them right away from you."

"I like my blocks just the way they are," he said. "Eat your fruit and drink your juice. Do you need anything else?"

"A bagel?" She batted her eyelashes at him, and he blinked.

"Right. I'll get you a bagel right away, no problem." He stood. "Again, don't go anywhere."

She grinned. "I'm unmovable," she said. "As unmovable as the blocks on your talent."

Grumbling a bit at that, Gregor went to get her a bagel.

~~~

Serra rubbed her face. What happened to her? She'd been sitting here, then suddenly it was as if every stitch of clothing she'd worn was gone, and it was her and the man in the corner. He'd searched every part of her, sniffing at her, and finally proclaimed her worthy.

Worthy for what, she had no idea. Fretful, she picked up her apple juice and gasped when the cold glass touched her palm. Carefully, she put the rounded bottle down and opened her left hand.

There, in the center of her palm, was an almost perfect round spot, red with white splotches in it, delicately rendered. It throbbed as though she'd been branded.

Terrified, Serra closed her hand over her secret and opened the second container of fruit. Marked, damn it, by a Hjurlt. How could she not have sensed him? They couldn't have fought here, though, in so public an arena. He must have been warded to an extent, since she didn't even smell him. Damn that Death Mage.

Gregor came back with the bagel in a bag, a concerned look on his face. "Are you okay?"

"Yeah. I'm fine." She tightened up her shields and polished

off the last of the fruit. "Let's go back to the office, check in with everyone." Nerves such as she hadn't felt since her first battlefields skittered down her spine as she stood. She gathered the containers and headed to the trashcan. A push against her mind had her faltering.

The thing that put his mark on her drained her. Not much, not a lot, but she could feel her strength ebb.

She would need warding. She would need healing. This was not what she had come to Earth for. Sticks and berries!

~~~

Gregor half-carried Serra back to the office. She seemed so self-contained, so strong, that to see her weak startled him.

"I'm fine, really," she said firmly, and waved him away. "No need to hover." They were in his office and she had curled up in the corner of his small sofa. Gregor leaned against the arm of the couch, watching her closely.

"Why don't I believe you?"

"I haven't a clue," she said, and leaned her head back on the sofa.

Gregor frowned. "What did the dark man say to you?"

"The who?" She paled.

Gregor pushed. "In CafeGo. Who was the man who stopped to talk to you, and what did he say? What did he do to you? No more lies. Tell me." Gregor held his breath. She'd either trust him now, or not.

She smiled, her eyes clear. "I need Maggie. Could you find her for me? Please? It's important."

"When Maggie is here, you'll tell me what happened with him? You promise." His gaze held hers.

Her chin lifted and her eyes grew bright. "You demand promises from me? I give no promises. That is not my way. If I see fit to tell you, then you will know. Now go, and find me Maggie. Hurry." She closed her eyes.

Gregor left the room, frustration riding him. She didn't have to go all high and mighty with him. He was just trying to keep her safe. Why didn't she see that? He pulled out his cell phone and noted the message from Justin. After listening to it, he swore and put in a call to Maggie.

No answer. "Damn it, Maggie, we need you. I'll work with Justin to find you." He shoved his phone in his pocket and left the office without talking to Serra, locking the door to the hallway. Locked her in to keep her safe. "You'd better stay there, you stubborn Fae, if you know what's good for you."

With worry dogging his steps, Gregor headed for the parking garage.

~~~

"You sanctimonious bitch," spat Cait as she swung a baseball bat at Maggie, who dodged it. They'd gone in an alleyway with dumpsters and a dead end when Cait took her first swing at Maggie, taking her by surprise and knocking her sideways. Maggie had darted in and slugged Cait on the jaw, turned her around, and slammed her into the wall. But Cait recovered before Maggie could run.

Dizzy from the hit, Maggie went the wrong way in the alley and cursed at the wall in front of her, too high to climb.

Breathing heavily, confused and disoriented, Maggie looked around wildly for something to use as a weapon. She darted behind a dumpster and pushed it into the middle of the alley, hoping to grab a few seconds of cover.

Spying a paper bag with a bottle sticking out of the opening, Maggie swooped and hefted it, tearing off the bag. An empty bottle of cheap vodka. Perfect. She grabbed it by the neck and brandished it toward Cait with her left hand. The other woman stalked toward her, eyes red with the madness of hate and something else.

"What's going on, Cait? Why the attack?" Her right shoulder throbbed where the bat had hit.

"Who told you it was okay to kill demons?" Cait demanded. "I suppose next you'll want to kill the Fae that come through, too. Damn you and your purebred kind."

Understanding trickled through Maggie's panic. "My God. This isn't still about college, is it? Cait, it doesn't matter that you aren't a hereditary witch. I'm pretty sure your ancestors had it in them. They just didn't practice or recognize it. That's not your fault, nor is it any reflection on you. You're an exceptional witch."

"Damn straight I am, no thanks to you," snarled Cait. "Kendall was the only one in our coven who believed in me. The only one who truly loved me."

"Kendall loved all the girls." Maggie's response was automatic, and she bit her tongue for it. "But I know he loved you the most," she added, jumping back just in time as Cait swung for her waist. The bat caught the end of the vodka bottle and flung it out of Maggie's hand.

She cursed as she heard it shatter against the alley wall. "You want me to stop hunting demons? Fine. I'll stop hunting demons. Just stop this, Cait. Stop trying to beat the shit out of me."

"Kendall loved me. He truly loved me," Cait insisted. "Not you. Never you."

"But he married Shannon Hamilton, remember? He ditched both of us." Maggie's heart pounded as her strength waned. Keeping her eyes on Cait, she anchored herself to the ground and connected with the power there. *Northern winds come to my call. Fling the bat against the wall. Bind her hands against her face, allow me to escape with grace. With gesture meek that she'll not see, as I will so mote it be.* Maggie made a graceful gesture to the winds.

Within seconds, they swirled into the alley. Cait struggled to keep the bat in her hands. "What did you do? What did you do?" she screamed.

The bat wrenched away from Cait and flew against the far wall. As Cait wailed, her hands went to her face. "You bitch! I will not forget this insult, not if it takes a hundred years times a hundred to avenge it, this I vow."

"If Aubrey got hurt because of you, a hundred years will be too short for any punishment the Universe may have in mind for you," Maggie said, grabbing the other woman's shoulders.

Cait raged on as the winds calmed. Maggie steered Cait in front of her as they stumbled along the alleyway to the busy street.

Justin? Come get us, please? Maggie leaned against the corner of the brick building, envisioning their location for

~ ☾ ~

Justin, one hand firmly locked on Cait's belt.

Almost there. I've been tracking you two. Almost there, woman. Almost there, he crooned.

Maggie closed her eyes. She could relax. Justin was coming. Justin was almost there.

A head butt to her stomach stole her breath and her voice. Another to her face crunched her nose and had her head slamming back against the brick. Reality wavered as Maggie opened her eyes.

"Stupid bitch." Maggie felt big hands pulling her up from where she'd crumpled to the ground. She heard the pounding of running feet getting closer, and knew it was Justin.

"Hey, scumbag! Drop her!" Justin's voice seemed to come from far away.

Maggie fell heavily to the sidewalk. All sense of her attackers drained away. *Hang on, Maggie. Just hang on. Justin is coming. Justin is almost there. Justin is coming...*

~~~

Gregor watched as Justin paced the tiny waiting room. The planned expansion had just begun and construction plastic taped from ceiling to floor shrouded the waiting area from the drifting plaster dust on the other side.

"Two. Two of them down. Damn it. Damn it, Gregor. That's not the way this is supposed to go." Justin rapped his fist against one thigh as he moved.

"I know." Uneasy, he wondered about Serra, still in the offices. "Aubrey. Will she recover?"

"Yeah. Doc Cavanaugh said she'd have scars on her shoulders, but she'll pull through. She said Maggie was refreshing, being a human. Except even when she's under, she keeps trying spells to feel better. They had to give her a super dose to totally knock her out."

"I need her. Something's wrong with Serra, and she's asking for Maggie." Gregor brought Justin up to speed on what happened in CafeGo, and what Carmen had said about the dark man. "I don't know what to think," he concluded.

"Hopefully, it's nothing more than some gigolo putting the

moves on all the pretty girls."

"I don't know. The solstice is almost on top of us. Two of us are down, and Cait Lanyon is a nutcase. We've eliminated some demons, sure, but how many are still out there?" Gregor leaned against the hard back of the couch and rubbed the space between his eyes. "Did we take on more than we can achieve?"

"Don't even think that. Once we shut down the portal, the number of demons will diminish with each kill. If Maggie and Serra both focus on the portal's location, we should be able to get to it and turn it off. Or whatever it is we'll need to do." Justin resumed his pacing.

The doors swung open and Maggie stood there, swaying slightly. "Can I hitch a ride with someone? Anyone?" Her nose was still swollen, but the bruising around her eyes had already faded to a yellow-green. Her brown eyes were dull with pain and medication.

Justin strode to her side and had an arm around her before she finished talking. "There you are," he crooned and hugged her to his side. "There you are. I'll take you home now, let's go."

"No." Maggie's eyes sought out Gregor. "I need to see Serra. I need to talk to her. It's really important."

"The office, it is." Gregor stood. "I need to get back to Serra. You two come along as you can. I'm sure there will be doctor's instructions before you can sneak away."

Doc Cavanaugh came out then, her eyes hot with frustration. "Damn it, Maggie. I should have tied you to the bed."

"So she's not discharged, then?" Justin frowned down at Maggie.

"No, she's not. But she really wants to go, so I have to tell you I'm worried about concussion. She'll need someone with her for the next twenty-four hours at least. Justin, I swear if she comes back to me in worse shape, I'll blame you."

"I promise I'll take care of her. She'll be good as new in no time," he added. He winked at Maggie, who just shook her head and closed her eyes. "See? She's speechless in my devotion to her."

~ ☾ ~

Doc Cavanaugh brushed hair out of her eyes and sighed. "At least she's not yelling at me. Speechless can be quite nice."

"And on that note, I'm out of here. Thank you, Megan. See you two at the office." Gregor dropped a kiss on each woman's cheek, and took off, eager to get back to Serra.

As he drove the freeway down to Santa Monica, Gregor continued to worry the issue he'd brought up to Justin. Too many of their number had been hit all in the same day, and they'd all been women. Either they had a misogynist behind the scenes, or there was another significance he'd missed. Either way, his protective instincts were screaming.

There would be more mayhem to come. He'd bet his no-iron shirt on it.

~~~

Serra thumped the locked door. The brute had just left, without a word to her, and he locked her in? She'd never been locked in *anywhere*. She didn't like it, not one bit. True, once she'd gotten lost in a Dark cave, but that had been her own fault. Ever since that experience, not having an exit, not being able to feel the wind in her face any time she wanted, made her anxious.

She went back to Gregor's office and breathed in his scent. It calmed her, somehow, made her think of home. Moving to the wide bank of windows, she curled up in the deep sill there and stared out at the glimpse of ocean, the same gray as the sky.

Truth was uncomfortable. Yes, she provoked him by pushing him away. But did he have to be so cavalier in his treatment of her?

She should call fleas to plague him. Mosquitoes to bite. Planning revenge sent a sweet peace through her body as she considered him sprawled out on his bed, swatting at unseen insects biting him in some very sensitive places. Of course, finding any mosquitoes at this time of year was bound to be difficult. Rain, however, would be no problem for her.

Sniffing, she moved to the couch and huddled down.

~ ☾ ~

When she heard the front door open, she didn't move. She was not about to run to him like a child. She had more dignity than that. She turned her back to the door and looked out the nearest window. Her disinterest would perhaps be a spur to his side.

Though, they were fighting the same battles. And she'd been attacked. He'd only been trying to protect her, said her inner voice of reason. She squirmed at the reminder. The problem was she'd become used to being the protector, rather than the one who others protected.

A footstep in the hallway had her halfway turning toward the door when a hand covered her mouth. Instinct had her holding her breath. She struggled against the hard arms holding her still and a low chant filled the air.

Magicks were being used. Serra's sense of reality, of size, wavered.

Oh no. Gregor. Gregor, help!

CHAPTER FOURTEEN

Serra came to awareness slowly. Her head throbbed, and her body felt strange. She took a breath and almost choked. The air was saturated with coffee and the sticky scent of bastardized magicks. Plus her ass was damp. What in the Light had happened?

She opened her eyes and shut them immediately at the brightness of the light around her.

Caught like a fly in a web. Or, more accurately, like a Fae in a coffee cup. Her eyebrows drew together. Her captors had known what she was, had known how to capture her, had known the magicks to contain her size. And now, feeling the slick walls of her prison, they knew enough, too, to enclose her in something not made of the natural world.

A clear plastic Starbucks coffee cup, with residue in the bottom and a handy hole in the lid. She wouldn't suffocate, nor could she destroy the cup. The Fae did not control plastics. Serra made a face. Plastics. An abomination.

She couldn't tap into the earth's energy to heal herself, either, not surrounded by plastic. But what she could do to them, once she was free... Burning them would be too good, too quick. Demonspawn. Darklovers. Light help her! If her stubborn pride hadn't kept her face turned away from the door, she'd have seen her attacker. She could have taken evasive action, could have brought him down with the power of a thousand suns, or at least a well-placed kick.

Gregor. At the thought of him, she paused. Was he all right? Were the rest of them? Light, she hoped so. She truly hoped so.

Serra opened her eyes again and stared at her prison. The cup was one of the bigger sizes. Even standing up, she was still a good half-body from reaching the top. She had no idea of how long she'd been out. What would happen if she

~ ☾ ~

changed shape while trapped in the cup?

She forced herself to think in practicalities. If she did change shape while in the cup, either she'd shatter it completely, or she'd run out of air before the change was complete and she'd die.

Not that she had any way of knowing. Trapped Fae didn't exactly talk about their entrapment. She assumed she could keep her small size for longer than three hours. After all, their children stayed small for long periods of time when first born. But trapped... No. She refused to think about it.

To take her mind off the looming dilemma, Serra stood and put her hands up to her prison, to see where she'd been taken. High windows let in the afternoon sun. She was in a corner, on a table. A computer rested near by. As she traversed the circle of the cup, she took note of everything she could see. Finally, there was only a dark corner left.

She focused on the corner and on the shape she saw hiding in the shadows. As if in response to her gaze, the opening began to glow. She cursed under her breath. She'd found the damned portal and couldn't do anything about it. Sinking once again to the bottom of the cup, Serra dropped below sight of the portal but the glow remained.

Time to push Gregor again. He didn't want to communicate mind to mind, but that was her only weapon right now. She had to trust in him.

Serra closed her eyes and sought for Gregor in the pathways of her mind.

~~~

Gregor felt the lack of air in his lungs even as he heard Serra call for him, her voice panicked. He cursed the traffic as it crawled south on the 405 due to two lanes shut for construction. Keeping his mind wide open took some effort. He searched for her mind, strained to find her as he inched closer to the Santa Monica Boulevard off-ramp, but his sense of her was lost.

Gone.

What could have happened to her? Who could he call?

~ ☾ ~

Christine Ashworth

Justin was back at the hospital with Maggie and Aubrey, and he hadn't met the sisters when Serra did. Fear settled around him, a bright, strangling cloud of half-remembered regrets and stupid indecision.

It didn't matter any more that genetics had him panting after a full-blooded Fae. Keeping her safe mattered, damn it. Why did he think leaving her behind had been a good idea?

Minutes stretched to what felt like hours until he could finally swing off the freeway. Controlling his wild need to gun the engine, Gregor drove as quickly as he could to the Promenade.

He pulled into a parking space in garage four and set the brake. He tore out of the car, into the freshening breeze, grateful for the air.

"Serra!" He ran then, across the parking lot, through the alley and into the mall itself. It teemed with people going to and from restaurants, others with shopping bags full of gifts. A Santa Claus with his bell and kettle added to the cacophony. The noise made his head throb.

Gregor pushed through bigger than usual crowds. Cops stood outside the imports shop next to the stairwell. The front window had been smashed. Patricia, the blood running down her cheek mingling with tears, gave her statement in a low, gasping voice to a detective.

His heart sank even as a curse rose up inside him, aching to be spilled into the air already polluted with the stench of violence. Syed, Patricia's husband, now dead. Grief for the gentle man swamped him as he thought of Patricia, her life forever changed now.

The Singhs had opened their shop just as Gregor and Justin had moved in upstairs. They'd been good people. Neither one of them deserved what had happened here today.

He caught Patricia's gaze and nodded, just once. She nodded back, her eyes swimming with tears. Gregor would pursue Syed's attacker. They'd been through a lot in the ten years they'd been neighbors, and Patricia and Syed had helped him more than once. He intended to repay that debt.

Pushing through the door, he stopped with one foot on the stair and sniffed. Strangers had been here. His pulse kicked up to a gallop and, taking the steps two at a time, he rushed for his office.

It was empty. Violence filled the air here, too, and he sneezed. A trickle of magicks and an oily stench lingered, mingled with the violence. A desperate need to know what had happened opened something inside him, and suddenly it was as if he were in the room with her.

Serra had sat on the couch, turned away from the door. Her face held stormy thoughts, and Gregor had no doubt she was angry with him for locking her in.

He heard the front door at the same time she did; but her chin went into the air. So only he saw the two masked men in nondescript sweatsuits, one of them hefting a baseball bat and the other carrying a damp washcloth.

Both wore gloves. The taller of the two covered Serra's face with the washcloth while intoning some ugly spell that Gregor couldn't hear. She'd fought briefly before going limp. The tall one forced something into her mouth. His mouth moved, but again Gregor couldn't hear. Then Serra's body shimmered, tilted oddly, and shrunk into itself.

The taller man pulled off his mask. Satisfaction oozed from him. He picked up the small, doll-like Warrior Fae and put her into his pocket. The two men left Gregor's office after a last quick look around.

Kendall Sorbis' blue eyes gleamed as he looked toward the corner where Gregor now stood. The light of madness shone there.

Gregor staggered to the sofa. So that was what Justin could do? His head ached and his stomach twisted. How long had it taken? It had felt like being in the same place at two different times, and his system now vibrated with energy.

Full realization of what he'd seen confirmed his worst fears. Kendall had Serra. Time. Time, damn it, how much time had passed? What could he have done to her with the time he'd had?

Gregor stood, the room a hazy red. His lips firmed and he grappled with his control. Acting like a hothead wouldn't do anything but get them both killed. He'd be cool, controlled, and he'd get her back. One way or another, he'd get her back

~ ☾ ~

even if he had to go through Sorbis to do so.

Moving quickly, he went to his weapons cabinet, unlocked it and wrenched it open, fury still dictating his movements despite his struggle for calm.

Gregor.

Shock held him still. The voice was faint, and for a minute, he couldn't tell if he'd heard it with his ears or with his mind.

Gregor, please listen to me. Please.

Serra! Relief swept him. *You're alive. Where are you?*

Her hesitation was brief. *I'm not sure of my physical location, but I'm with the portal.*

His heart pounded as his fists clenched. *Are you all right? Damn Kendall Sorbis. Are you hurt?*

Slow down, Gregor. Breathe. So Sorbis is my kidnapper?

Her calm eased him a little. He took a breath, then another. *Okay, fine. I breathed. Yes, it was Sorbis. Now tell me what I need to know.*

Serra took a breath. *He knew the magick to make me small. Now listen. I'm trapped in one of those clear plastic coffee cups. What I can see around me includes...*

Gregor grabbed for a pen and paper and took notes.

...and there's a sense of space, as though it's bigger than what I can see. I haven't seen any people or demons yet, though I can smell both. It might be the same area that I saw Cash go into, but I don't know.

What's your escape plan?

Her snort of disgust trickled in his mind. *I don't have one, yet. But when I'm free, I'll shut the portal down and get back to you as soon as I can, I swear it.*

Gregor felt her determination and knew she'd do everything in her power to keep her promise. *Okay. Is there anything else? Or should I let you get to it?*

The dark man, this morning. Reluctance dragged at her words.

Gregor could feel the force she put behind saying them. *Go on.*

He marked me. A red full moon on my left palm. It's like a tattoo but not one, and it's slowly turning black.

Gregor sucked in a breath. *Confession time. Another one*

of my gifts kicked in, and I saw what had happened to you. Freaked me out.

She sighed. *See what happens when you hang around with a Fae? As far as Sorbis goes, I'm beyond loathing that mage.*

Abruptly, their communication cut off. Gregor groped for the awareness of her in his mind, but she was gone.

How could he find her? Grateful for their communication, for her relative health, he stood in the room and closed his eyes. Searched for her scent.

Found it. She smelled like the sharp green of vetiver and the soothing brown of rich loam, plus an intoxicating femaleness that was hers alone. He followed the scent into the hallway, where it died.

Okay. So he couldn't track her that way, but perhaps Danny could loan him someone? A Were would come in handy.

Gregor gave Danny a call and left a message. Back to square one. He could, and would, go looking again down in the airport area where they'd run up against so many of the C'dak. If her scent was out there, he'd find her. But in the meantime, they needed more firepower.

Gabriel and Rose were celebrating Yule in Cambria, and he wasn't about to bust in on their newlywed happiness. Justin was already stretched thin between wanting to hunt with him and needing to keep close to Maggie.

Which left... Gregor sighed, leaned against the wall, and frowned.

Kellan Caine was their cousin. More than a little bomb-happy, Kellan was as wild as he was urbane. His ties to the rest of them were long but securely bonded. If he were to ask Kellan for help, Kellan would give it. He may crow about it the rest of their naturally long lives, but he'd be there. Hadn't he killed vampires that past summer for Gabriel and Rose?

Gregor spent the next several minutes searching for another way, but each time he came back to Kellan. Finally, he pulled out his cell phone and punched in the number. When the beep sounded for a message, Gregor grimaced.

"Kel. It's Gregor. Call me."

~ ☾ ~

~~~

Justin cast a sidelong glance at Maggie. Her olive skin looked pale against the vibrant red sweater she wore. She'd huddled into herself, her chin touching her chest and her shoulders hunched around her ears.

They were almost to Santa Monica, the freeway gods had been good to them, but still Maggie didn't speak.

He cleared his throat. "Do you want something to eat?"

Silence met his query. He sighed and changed lanes in time to hit the I10 West onramp. "You're going to have to talk to me at some point. You're far too polite not to answer me." He caught the ghost of a frown on her face and pressed. "Except, of course, when you're damning me as the devil's own and suggesting lifetime accommodations in Hell. Come on, Maggie. Talk to me, for pity's sake." He took the first off-ramp and turned north at the light, cruising along Cloverfield and up to 26th street.

"You...came."

"Did you think I wouldn't?" He brought the car to a stop at the light. A broken sob, quickly stifled, had him thinking fast. When the light turned green, he made a right turn and parked. Flicking his seatbelt off, he turned to her.

She flung herself into his arms before he could glimpse more than big brown eyes damp with emotion. He soothed her, rocking her awkwardly in the small front seat, rubbing her back in a circular motion. Like a mother with a baby, he murmured nonsense words, cooing and kissing the top of her head now and then while the storm inside her raged.

Finally, her tears stopped. She pulled herself out of his embrace and bent her head, searched in her purse for a tissue.

Justin pulled a clean handkerchief out of his pocket. "Here."

"Thank you," she mumbled. Her nose was red, her eyes too, and there was a droop to her luscious mouth as she wiped her face. He thought he'd never seen her more vulnerable, nor more beautiful.

~ ☾ ~

He brushed her hair back over her shoulder. "You're welcome."

"Hell," she said and slumped further into the seat. "The thank you was for more than the handkerchief. It was for the rescue. They were going to kill me. I totally believe it."

Justin winced. "Yeah. I don't want to think about that part, if you don't mind."

Her head came up. "No one has ever come to my rescue. I've always, always had to rescue myself." She wiped her nose again and sniffled. "So thank you."

The words sounded fierce and mad, as though she'd rather be dragged through mud than make that confession. Her walls were back up, too. He could tell by that wariness in her eyes and the slight stiffness in her body.

He stifled a sigh. Close, but no cigar. One day she'd trust him enough to tell him all her secrets. He wanted the keeping of them, and that still surprised him more than anything else he'd learned.

"You're welcome." He buckled himself in and started the car. "Let's go talk with Gregor."

"We're no further than we were, are we?" After buckling up, she wrapped her arms around her shoulders. "Once again, we're behind the eight ball but don't know where the cue ball is, damn it all to hell."

Justin grinned. "You play pool."

She shifted in her seat. "My dad. Long time ago, but some things you don't forget."

Prickly about it. Hmm. Justin coughed and turned into the parking garage. "Okay. Still, you're right on. We don't know what direction to look in. We don't know who's behind it all. The coven somehow got corrupted, and I'd love to know who's behind that. Do you have any idea?" He parked the car and they got out.

"I've been wracking my brain. I can't come up with anything. At least, not anything that makes sense." Her sigh drifted between them.

Justin put a friendly arm around her shoulders. "Keep turning it over in your mind. You never know what you'll come up with, but if anyone can make a connection, you can."

~ ☾ ~

They walked through the garage to the short alley leading to the mall. It was crowded with people, more so than usual, even considering the upcoming holiday. "I don't like this," Maggie said, her voice soft. "There's something wrong here. The air feels wrong."

Justin quickened his steps and resisted the urge to look behind them. "I know what you mean." It was like a coating of slime, unseen but making him reluctant to walk through it. He pressed on through the thick air and the people that crowded the mall.

The cops at the imports shop gave him pause, the shattered window almost stopped his heart. Maggie gave a soft cry and clutched at his hand.

"Oh no. No. Syed. Patricia will be devastated. I should go to her."

But at her convulsive attempt to leave his side, Justin tightened his grip on her shoulder. "Not right now. She's still with the police. She'll come up and talk to us when she can."

Patricia's dark eyes met his across the crowded area, her despair palpable. Justin banished his grief for her husband. There would be time later to pay his respects to the dead.

His heart heavy, Justin and Maggie went up the stairs to the offices of Caine Investigations.

~~~

Serra had tried to knock over the cup. On one side lay a book, but on the other side of the cup, the desk was empty. Throwing her body against the smooth plastic just gave her bruises and aggravated her headache. No amount of wishing would get her out of there.

Frowning, she pushed her nose against the plastic. There had to be something she could use to get out of the damned cup.

A door crashed open and the cup wobbled a bit. Serra threw herself against the side one more time and the cup crashed down and rolled to a stop against a stapler. The fall knocked the wind out of her. She didn't move but kept one eye partially open.

~ ☾ ~

Two voices were raised in anger, each overlapping the other. Serra sharpened her hearing and lay very still.

"You let her go. You fool! We'll never get another chance at her. The damned Caines will see to that," the female raged.

"Caitlyn, take an aspirin and chill. So we didn't get the infamous Magdalena. We'll deal. We've got options."

The male's voice was cool. Serra shivered. She was undoubtedly one of his options.

"Options," Cait sniffed. "Will Dalton heel? We haven't seen Damon since their first night here, so he's either dead or he slipped his leash. I don't think Dalton will tamely obey us. We've got very little time left."

"There's enough time. Frannie has everything handled. The rest of the building is just about ready for the party." Satisfaction oozed from his voice. "Relax. You'll be here, won't you? Friday night? I'd love to toast our triumph with you."

"Of course I'll be here. Someone needs to act as hostess, and you can't believe that Mouse could possibly handle the stress. Show me what she's done so far."

Their voices became muted before fading away entirely. Serra ground her teeth. If she had her way, that Caitlyn would be stifled for good, as well as this Fran person. If they were in any way responsible for that portal...

Serra inched her way up to the lid of the cup, going slowly so her movements didn't rock the cup from side to side. She put her hands on the top and struggled to twist it open. The cup rocked but the lid didn't move.

The door to the outside opened and closed quietly. Serra stilled and listened. It was a woman. She came to the desk and sat at the computer.

Serra heard a sigh as the woman tapped away. Without warning, Serra sneezed three times in quick succession.

"What? Oh no. No, they didn't!" The woman picked up the cup Serra was in and lifted it to peer in. Serra tumbled with a shriek to the floor of the cup.

"I am so sorry. So sorry." Hurriedly, the woman looked around and unscrewed the top. "Do you need help out?" The words came out in a whisper.

~ ☾ ~

Serra smiled up at those anxious eyes. "If you could put the cup on its side on the desk, that would help."

The woman rushed to do so. Serra tried to go with the angle but still experienced a bit of a bounce. She'd crawled half way out of the cup when it was snatched back up into the air. Serra balanced on the edge, her eyes wide on the woman.

"There's someone here. I'll free you, I promise, just not now," she whispered urgently, and waggled the cup, loosening Serra's hold on the edge and sliding her back inside. She capped the cup and laid it back on its side, just the way she'd found it.

A wide denim purse abruptly blocked Serra's view of the woman. The handles sagged over the other side of the cup, providing a bit of cover. Serra crawled as close to the air hole as she could get and listened hard.

"Fran. You did an acceptable job with the room." The praise was grudging and Serra felt sorry for Fran.

"Thank you, Cait. It was fun." Fran seemed to sink inside herself. Serra frowned. Cait had styled Fran a mouse. Perhaps she was a mouse forced to act a rat?

"Do you have an update for me, Frannie?" That was the man's voice.

"Bryce. Yes, the caterers are all set. They'll start service at eight sharp. The DJ will bring his equipment and set up at seven, and he's promised the sound will be louder than the airplanes. We'll open the doors at seven forty-five. You'll give your speech at half past eight, and the champagne will pop right afterwards. Dancing will last until midnight." Fran recited the facts cool enough, but Serra detected a tremor of uncertainty.

Apparently, so did Bryce. "Are you concerned about the arrangements?" His voice was smooth. "Is there any reason I should be worried?"

"The caterer was confused about the hundred pounds of fresh, uncooked beef you wanted. She just wanted me to be sure about the storage. You want it on ice?" Fran sounded apologetic.

"I want it cool, not frozen. If she needs to rent a refrigerator to give me what I want, then she'll have to do so.

~ ☾ ~

Do I make myself clear?" Bryce's voice had gone cold. Serra shivered.

"Absolutely. I'm, uh, just double checking the invitations and prepping another round of tweets for Twitter. I'll be done here in, oh, about half an hour, if that's okay."

Bryce just grunted. "Cait, let's talk strategy. About this Magdalena chick. Can you deal with the necessary magicks without her? Kendall says you can, but I just want to make sure." Their voices faded away. Serra heard a door shut.

"Oh God, oh God, oh God," Fran's voice came to Serra in a whisper. "I'll hurry, I promise. I've just got to get this done or I'm dead, I swear."

Serra turned over on her back and stared up at the ceiling, distorted through the double layer of plastic. She reached for Gregor.

Are you there?

Serra? I'm here. Are you still okay?

She could feel the relief pouring from him. *I'm fine. I've got some names for you. Bryce, Fran and Caitlyn have all been here where I am. Fran says she'll let me go. I don't know if Bryce or Caitlyn know I'm here.*

Damn it. Bryce keeps coming up. That damned Charismatic! What else?

Dalton and Damon. Damon hasn't been seen since their first night, and I'm thinking that's the one we killed. Which most likely means Dalton is the one who marked me in CafeGo. Unfortunately, I don't know any more than that.

The burn in her palm throbbed. She took a quick peek at it and stared. The creeping darkness over the red now encompassed almost a half of the disc.

Whatever it meant, it couldn't be anything good.

Her cup was swept up and shoved into the denim bag. The stifling sense of darkness didn't make her feel any safer. She looked up to find big eyes looking down at her.

"Okay, we're going. Just, you know, keep quiet, and we'll be safe before you know it."

Serra heaved a sigh. This had to be the strangest day of her life. The cup bumped and rolled. Serra sat cross-legged, her chin in her hands, and squeezed her eyes shut. If she ever got

~ ☾ ~

out of her plastic prison, she'd be one happy Fae.

The swing of the purse stopped and the light from the opening cut off. Serra sat up, alert.

A low voice rumbled. Fran answered smoothly, no hint of uncertainty in her tone. There was another rumble, and a door opened and shut. The bag around the cup compressed, as if it were being clutched tightly, and there was a sense of speed.

Serra gripped her sides and held on. Something had happened to panic Fran. She heard a frantic fumbling and two beeps. A car door opened and the bag was tossed inside. Serra landed hard. The engine gunned and they were off.

"I am so over being five inches tall," she grumbled to herself. "I can see why some Fae never allow themselves this size. One bad experience is all it takes." Disgusted, she pulled herself up to a sitting position. "Hey, Fran. Let me out now, okay?"

The car swerved wildly. A hand, huge to her in her present size, reached down and grabbed for the cup. "I'm sorry, I'm so sorry," Fran babbled.

She put the cup into a cup holder next to her and unscrewed the cap. "There. That should work. Can you climb out?"

Serra just looked at the girl in disgust. As she jumped for the rim, Fran screamed.

"No. Kendall, no. I swear I'll be good. Kendall, no, don't shoot! Don't shoot!"

The car jolted from one side to the other before the sound of brakes and a crunching of metal filled the air. Grimly, Serra hung on, her feet swinging free. The car shuddered and came to a stop. Serra pulled herself up and over the rim of the cup and landed on the fabric passenger seat. It smelled of cigarettes and dogs. Serra sneezed, and with little warning, her body stretched to its full size.

She blinked once, disoriented.

Fran leaned against the steering wheel, blood trickling down her head, her eyes open yet already filming over. Serra put a hand out, but Fran's spirit had fled. She was safe, now, from whatever evil had ensnared her.

~ ☾ ~

Fear clutched her and Serra fumbled for the car door, her eyes blurry with tears. If Kendall Sorbis had hung around, she'd get a chance to kill him. Once in the street, she looked around wildly, expecting to see his figure coming toward her with a gun aimed straight at her.

There was no one about. The car's trajectory could be clearly seen, with skid marks on both sides of the road before the car had nose-dived into a tree, the front of the compact car crumpled almost to the driver; but Serra couldn't scent Kendall Sorbis.

Fran had been tricked with illusion, and because of it, she had died.

Serra stood in the middle of the road, barefoot but clad in her jeans and sweater, and mourned her rescuer as the sound of a siren reached her ears.

Gregor. Come and get me. I'm... Oh, never mind. The police are here. I'll be with you soon. She cut the connection, his voice pulling her to him. She had work to do before she could return to him. He might not appreciate it, but Fran certainly would.

Serra straightened her shoulders and turned to the officers who approached her warily. The mist fell heavily, and her grief surprised her more than anything else that had happened that day.

~ ☾ ~

CHAPTER FIFTEEN

Justin took the remains of the tiny metallic receivers from Gregor and frowned. "You found them *where*?"

"One of them was tucked in my office plant. The other was attached to the underside of your office phone. We're a fine pair of investigators, Justin." Disgusted with both of them, Gregor leaned back in his desk chair. "My guess is it was Cash, which means Kendall. Do you disagree?"

"No." His face grim, Justin handed the pieces back to Gregor. "But I don't like it. This, plus the attacks on the women? It's starting to feel personal. You know what I mean?"

"I do." Gregor drummed his fingers against his thigh. "I wish Serra was here."

"She's okay though, right?" Maggie spoke from where she'd curled herself into the couch. "She'll be fine?"

"She said she would. Fran didn't survive the car accident. Serra told the cops that she'd been asleep in the passenger seat and didn't see what had happened."

"Fran." Maggie's voice held shock. "I still can't believe she and Cait were working together. I wish I knew who the hell Bryce is."

"Bryce Cannon. He's the Charismatic I saw at The Nine Hells. I've already started the investigation, which so far has turned up only his address and nothing else. No job, even. Regarding Fran, without police approval, I can't do much to dig into her personal life. To be frank, I don't believe we'd find anything shocking, anyway." Gregor rolled his head to loosen his neck muscles. It felt like years since morning. "Oh, and I might as well tell you. I've called Kellan, left a message. I felt we needed more power here."

Maggie rubbed her eyes. "I so thought the coven would be a good idea. I can't believe any of them would turn on any of us."

~ ☾ ~

"Yeah, about that." Justin leaned back in his chair, his hands clasped behind his head. "I had an interesting talk with Aubrey this morning. She said the coven pretty much became Kendall's private harem. True? And if so, wouldn't that be enough for some women? Jealousy is a primal emotion."

"True," she admitted slowly. "But it never seemed like that big a deal." She shrugged and winced. "It wasn't an obvious thing. He wasn't splashy or overly demonstrative in public."

"Aubrey said you were the only one who broke off the relationship, and the entire coven heard about it. That soon afterwards he left school without graduating. True?"

Frowning mentally, Gregor watched his brother. "What are you getting at, Justin?"

"Last summer, the Wolf Pack said they heard Kendall had opened a portal somewhere here in the southland, but we figured it was the vamps behind it. In retrospect, that dog doesn't bark. So if we assume that Kendall opened the portal, and I for one don't believe that's much of a stretch, we have to consider that Kendall's a lot more powerful than we suspected."

"It makes sense." Gregor steepled his fingers together and tapped them against his lips. "It goes along with what Serra said, that he's been opening portals for years, harassing the Fae."

"He doesn't have the power," Maggie protested. She turned to Gregor. "I've been telling the surfer kid here that Kendall had very little natural power. There is no way he could open a portal by himself."

"If he was playing with portals eleven years ago, I'm guessing you never knew the extent of his power. It's not beyond the realm of imagination," Justin added. "From what I've heard, Kendall was power-mad. Didn't he marry the youngest daughter of one of the wealthiest families in California? Plus, he disappeared just before graduating. Where's he been? What has he learned?"

"Hmm. Let's go through it." Gregor shot Maggie a conciliatory glance. "So far, we see him as the bad guy. Power hungry loner, statistical weirdo cutting up his childhood pets, and ready to kill humans if need be. Not to mention, he gave

~ ☾ ~

his best power punch to Serra this morning. Do we have the wrong impression of Kendall? If so, now's your chance to set us right."

Maggie bit her bottom lip. "No," she admitted. "Your read on his character is accurate. He never talked about his family. Always dressed well, always seemed to have money, and I don't know how he managed to pass any of his classes.

"Now that I think about it, spending time with him totally wore me out. And there's not an ounce of sexual innuendo in that statement," she added ruefully.

"Pulling on your power. Maybe he used *your* mojo to open the first portal, all those years ago." At Maggie's snort, Justin shrugged. "Something to consider. Did he live on campus?"

"No. He shared a house with two other guys who also went to UCLA, but they never seemed to be home." Maggie wrapped her arms around her knees. "I don't know. It all seemed perfectly normal at the time. We all lived in our cars, at each other's houses, or in our dorm rooms. We were all over the place. We were kids." Frustration edged her voice, lingered in her dark eyes.

"We'll figure it out, Maggie." The words were barely out of Gregor's mouth when a knock came on the front door. Gregor jumped up to answer it.

Serra stood there, battered and bruised and in quite a temper with the cop hovering behind her.

"Gregor!" She flung herself into his arms and he closed his around her, grateful to have her safe. He pressed a kiss on the top of her head.

"Thank you, officer. I appreciate you bringing her back." Gregor's obvious sincerity seemed to ease the young man's apprehension.

"Officer Tibbs," he said. "So, she does belong here?" He tapped his notepad anxiously. "She couldn't give me this address, so I was concerned."

Gregor smiled. "I couldn't give you this address, Officer Tibbs, and I've had my business here for the past ten years. This is Serra Willows, and she's my fiancée, so you can be sure she's in good hands now."

"Well, take care of her. The crash beat her up some," he

~ ☾ ~

said, casting an eye over her.

"I'll be sure to do so. Thank you so much." Gregor had one hand on the door and, smiling, closed it in the surprised cop's face. He locked it and hugged Serra to him again, breathed in her scent, and allowed himself to relax.

"I've got Maggie and Justin in my office," he murmured into her hair. "Do you have the energy to tell us everything that happened, or do you need to rest? Eat? Bathe?"

Serra smiled and cupped his face in her hands. "I'll rest, eat, and bathe later, when I can have you to myself. Right now it's important for us to share stories." She hooked arms with him and turned him toward the inner office.

"Maggie could use some healing, if you've got any energy at all. Concussion, a girl fight. It got kind of ugly." Gregor whispered in her ear, enjoying the way her hair waved out of the way with his breath.

"I'll take care of her." When they stepped into the office, Serra headed straight for Maggie. She sat on the couch. "You're hurt," she said, and Maggie burrowed into Serra's arms. Surprised, Serra shot a look at Gregor while she patted Maggie's back a bit awkwardly.

Gregor stood beside Justin. "She'll be fine. Serra is going to heal her."

"It doesn't matter," Justin growled low. "I promised to watch her for the next twenty-four hours, and I'm going to keep my promise."

The two men watched as the clean green light of Serra's healing spread over Maggie, who stiffened in shock. When Serra was done, all signs of weakness had washed away and Maggie once again looked like the hard-ass witch they'd come to know and appreciate.

"Better?"

Maggie sent her a fierce look. "Much better. Thank you."

"You're welcome." Serra moved gracefully to Gregor's side. "So you told them the players?" At Gregor's confirmation, she held out her left hand. "Here's what you need to see."

They crowded around and watched as the blood red moon ever-so-slowly got devoured by the blackness. Serra held out her hand to Maggie. "You've got one, too. Show it."

~ ☾ ~

Her eyes wild, Maggie reluctantly held out her left hand. The moon was in the same phase as it was on Serra's palm. Justin grabbed her hand with a stifled exclamation, closing his own about it. Pain came and went across his face.

Gregor rubbed his chest to ease the tightness there. "It looks like we won't have much time until this marker is called in." At the others' sharp inhalations, Gregor sighed. "I've seen it before, yes. Mom had one on her hand. I overheard her and Dad arguing about it. He wanted her to go see someone, and she just laughed at him, said she was powerful enough to handle it." He drew Serra close against him and after clearing his throat, he continued.

"On the night of the full moon, we'd gone out to the grocery store. We weren't supposed to leave the house, but Mom thought Dad was being overprotective. The man jumped her as she opened the back of the car to take groceries in. Changed into a demon in front of my eyes. She barely survived that, and she didn't survive Gabriel's birth. But from what I remember of that demon, and what Maggie saw of the digit-eating demon, they weren't the same. So we're still dealing with an unknown of sorts."

Justin turned Maggie's hand over to check out the spot. "It's... Can it be dug out? Surgically, I mean?"

"I don't know. I don't think so. Otherwise you know Dad would have done it in a heartbeat."

Serra looked up from studying her palm. "It's our link to whatever will happen on the solstice. What I wonder is, how many other women have that same mark in their palm? How many other women are marked for rape, or worse?"

To that, Gregor had no answer.

~~~

"How did you know?" Maggie's voice was low.

Serra leaned back in the desk chair and surveyed the other woman. Maggie was still hunched in a corner of Gregor's couch. Her olive skin looked pale and sweat beaded on her forehead. "I could sense it. Plus, I could sense how it bothered you. You want it out."

~ ☾ ~

"It feels like it's inside me." She rubbed and rubbed at the mark. "It's a demon thing. It's evil."

"Yes. And no. In and of itself, it is no more evil than a chair. It just is. What is drawn to it, however, is what you may consider evil." Serra tapped her fingers together. "I cannot put up protections here. Not where so much of the building is man-made and not natural. You, however, can do wardings. Keep the men safe and us, too, while we're here. Or am I wrong in this assumption?"

Maggie's head came up at that, and her eyes flashed. "I can do wardings."

"Do you need any supplies? Herbs, things like that?" Serra leaned forward, interested. "Or can you go without the trappings?"

"I researched wards and safety bubbles a few months ago. I prefer using tangibles, but I can do the wards without them. It seemed prudent to learn, after last summer."

Serra pursed her lips and gave Maggie a considering look. "Are you sure you're up to it? The protection would be welcome, but if you can't sustain a spell, perhaps it is wiser to wait until you're stronger."

Maggie stood up straight, her eyes flashing fire. "I can do it." She tilted her head, as if daring the other woman to tell her she couldn't.

"Good," Serra said. "Then do it."

Maggie muttered and left the office in a huff, passing Justin in the doorway. His eyebrows raised, he looked after her before looking toward Serra.

"What did I miss?"

"Maggie is going to put some basic protection around the offices. No one who plans harm on any of us will get in or out. At least, that's what I think she's planning."

Justin frowned. "You shouldn't have suggested she do that. Maggie's not strong enough. She took a couple bad hits. You didn't see her when I...you didn't see her."

Serra sent him a level gaze. "She was healed at the hospital, correct?"

"Yes, but..."

"And you did some healing too, as did I. Maggie is fine.

~ ☾ ~

She is now mad enough to do her job. She is not the weakling who whimpered into the couch this past hour. Don't baby her, Justin. She won't love you for it."

Justin, startled, shook his head. "She's not weak."

"That's what I said." Serra stood and stretched. "I haven't had the easiest day myself. Maggie needed to remember her strengths, not relive a moment of weakness over and over."

"Oh. I see." He shoved his hands into his pockets and rocked back on his heels. "What are you going to do now?"

"I don't know. I'm wiped out, and so is everyone else, I think." She looked at Justin, considering the options. "You should have Maggie put wards around your house. I can handle Gregor's."

"What do you mean, you can handle Gregor's? You do witchcraft too?"

Serra huffed out a breath. Humans were invariably curious, but this did give her the opportunity to stretch his thinking. "I work within the natural world. Just as you do," she said. "You feel the living and growing things easily. You feel the death of those things easily, too, and it hurts you."

"No."

Serra raised her eyebrows. Justin coughed.

"Not exactly. It doesn't hurt, okay?" He walked to the window, irritation showing in the line of his back.

"At any rate," she continued, "I work within the things of nature. I can manipulate the weave of life to heal. I can also manipulate it to harm, or protect. It is similar, but not the same, and I pay for doing such things, just as you do."

"Everything comes with a price," Justin said, turning away from the view and meeting her gaze straight on. "Doesn't it?"

Sorrow caught at her heart and then was gone. "Yes," she said. "Everything comes with a price. What will matter is if what is done is worth the price that will be paid."

His face cleared. "You're not just talking about us, are you?"

"No." It was Serra's turn to look out to the sea. "Someone is manipulating earth's forces, creating portals. The creature who created these—"she gestured to the mark on her palm, "—who put these on our hands, this was a human using demon power, or perhaps the demon doing its own work. It's a type of spell, but I didn't want to tell Maggie. There is nothing she can do to reverse it."

"This human will pay?"

Serra lifted her palm and traced the blood red moon, slowly being covered in black. "He will pay. It is partly the way of the demon. The human thinks he's in charge, but in reality, the demon is the puppet master. The human is merely his pawn. And if he's got other witches with him besides Cait, then the demon has more power to draw upon. More puppets to manipulate."

Justin wiped his face. "Why did I ever think that demons were stupid?"

She sighed and cradled her marked hand against her chest. "It's easy to equate ugly with stupidity. Most of them are smart. They've had to be. Every two-bit sorcerer since the beginning of time has called out to them for help, for money, for revenge. Demons have been slaves, over and over again, eon after eon. It is partially their own warring nature that keeps them from reaching anything like civilization, making them perfect slave material."

"I could almost feel sorry for them."

"Don't waste the emotion on them. They wouldn't do the same for you."

Justin narrowed his eyes. "Perhaps not. But I am human. Emotion is both a strength and a weakness of ours. Or didn't you know that?"

"Maggie is in the other room, remembering her strength. I'd say I'm pretty aware of humans and their emotions." Serra held his eyes, keeping all warmth from hers.

Justin's gaze moved from cool to cautious. He turned on his heel and left her alone. Serra leaned back in Gregor's chair with a sigh. She'd done it. She'd manipulated Maggie to working with her strengths, and she gave vital information to Justin about his own powers. Whether he understood enough in time was still to be seen.

As the sounds of Justin and Maggie quarreling drifted down the hallway, she sighed again. Life was so much simpler around the Fae. The outer door slammed and the office quieted.

~ ☾ ~

Serra closed her eyes and drifted toward more pleasant thoughts. Tonight she would stay with Gregor. Warmth suffused her body, and she knew keen anticipation. How interesting, that he'd taken her back to her adolescence. Maybe because he was a true mate?

Bah. Being bonded to a mate wasn't her idea of a good time. By the same token, going from partner to partner paled after a few decades. Humans were a good substitute for the men at home. But as far as she knew, they couldn't be bonded to a Fae.

"Knock knock."

Serra came fully aware and to her feet in a flash..

A man stood in front of the desk, arms akimbo, eyes coolly appraising. "You're a hell of a lot prettier than Gregor."

Serra sent a searching look into those wary eyes the color of caramel. His quick intake of breath had her relaxing back into the chair. "You're not so bad yourself."

His brown hair had been cut military short. The sun had left white creases around his eyes where he smiled, and the desert khaki clothing told its own story. "Where's the big guy?"

Serra smiled. "He's out. He'll be back. I'm Serra Willows." She was pleased to note she was only a few inches shorter than him. His broad shoulders and the planes of his face proved he was a Caine. "You're a relation?"

"Cousin. Kellan Caine." He held out a big hand. "So you're the Fae come to pull our asses out of the fire?"

She put her hand in his and was pleasantly surprised at his gentle touch. She gestured to the guest chair. "Please, sit. I'm here to help close the portal and get rid of the demons. Why have you come?"

Kellan sprawled out in the chair. "Gregor called. Simple."

"He only called you a couple hours ago. How did you get here so fast?"

"Plane," he said laconically. "Friend of mine. Santa Monica airport." He wrinkled his nose at a memory. "Smelled terrible, too. Something big died on the beach nearby, I imagine. It happens sometimes."

"Airport." A memory niggled. "Fran said something about

the band being loud enough to drown out the airplanes. The accident took place on Howard. That's near an airport, right?"

"Near Santa Monica airport. It's private, but they rent out buildings now and then."

Serra's warrior senses sharpened. "Cait was talking about a party being set up in the next room. We have to go there, later tonight when the world sleeps. I'm fairly sure I can find the place if we start with the scene of the accident. That portal must be closed before the full moon."

Gregor stood in the doorway. "You've got a game plan? Care to share?"

Serra looked up and her smile took over her face. "Hi. I think the portal is near the Santa Monica airport. Maybe in one of the hangars or warehouses they rent out. What did you discover?"

"Fran moved out about six months ago and never left a forwarding address. Cait's apartment was stripped clean before I got there, and is her landlady pissed. She owes three months' rent. Aubrey is doing better, but since Fran's death, she's afraid and constantly looking over her shoulder. She wants to help." Gregor looked to Kellan. "You could go pick her up from Doc Cavanaugh's, since you know the way."

Kellan raised his eyebrows. "You called me all the way out here from my cozy shack in Arizona to be your errand boy?"

"There'll be plenty of time for killing," Serra interrupted smoothly. Both men looked at her in surprise. "They fired the first shot, so to speak, with the attacks today. With Fran's death, plus the death of who knows how many innocent people, there will be plenty of deaths to come."

"I suppose we'll camp at the homestead?" Kellan shot a glance from Gregor to Serra. "That's what we did last summer. It kept us all in the same place. Safer somehow." He shrugged. "But you know, whatever you want."

"I have no problem with that. The house is warded, and with Rose and Gabriel out of town, we won't be stumbling over the lovebirds. I'll let you tell Justin and Maggie though." Gregor grinned at Kellan's expression.

"I'm glad you came, Kellan. Do you know anything about

portals?" Serra gently filched the reins of the conversation. If she hadn't been watching him so closely, she would have missed the knowing deep inside his caramel eyes.

"More than most," he said, his gaze flickering between Serra and Gregor. "You said you could find it."

"Yes. I'm pretty sure. You said you smelled something that died on the beach when your plane landed. Did it have a demon scent at all, do you think?" This time her probe was less delicate and she got the response she wanted.

Awareness, and a dark fury, glowed in Kellan's eyes. His face slowly emptied of all emotion and even his eyes dulled in color. Serra made a mental note. Kellan was utterly lethal. What's more, he didn't mind being that way. Good to know, all things considered.

"Right, then. Kellan, I think you should come with us." She turned to Gregor. "Have Justin and Maggie pick up Aubrey and take her to the, what did you call it? Homestead? The three of us will search for the portal. Between us, we should be able to find it, shut it down, and take care of anyone who might be guarding the place."

"Maggie won't like that," Gregor said, clearing his throat. Serra raised an eyebrow and he continued. "If Cait is there, Maggie's going to want a piece of her."

Serra waved his concern away. "Maggie will just have to put her revenge fantasies on hold. Getting her and Aubrey somewhere safe is the important part." Another piece of the puzzle fell into place and her eyes widened. "I remember. Bryce asked Cait what they would do if they didn't have Magdalena's help with the spells. We have to protect her, and any of the rest of the coven."

Gregor's thin lips tightened. "We'll keep them safe." He turned to Kellan. "Either one of us stays at the homestead, or we get the wolves."

"I need both of you with me." Serra kept her voice calm. These alpha males needed to know what it was like to be led by an alpha female Fae. And they'd better remember it.

Kellan bared his teeth in something resembling a grin. "The wolves it is, bro. You making the phone call, or am I?"

Gregor waggled his cell phone and walked out of the office,

~ ☾ ~

the number already connecting.

Serra took the opening. "You didn't want to talk about the portals. You've been through them?"

Kellan's gaze turned wary. "How did you know?"

Serra just waited.

"Yes," he growled. The emptiness was back. "I've been through them. So?"

"You know how to shut them down. I need you to tell me."

"It'll kill you." He stood, hands on his hips, his eyes edging toward angry. "If any shutting down is needed, I'll do it."

She cocked her head. "Why? My father opens the Fae Passageway to Earth for me."

"And he closed it behind you. But that's a Fae Passageway, not a Chaos Plane portal. It's a different process. I've been lucky so far."

Abruptly he left, passing Gregor in the doorway. "Tell her to stay away from portals. I'm going for coffee."

Gregor shifted his gaze from Kellan to Serra and raised an eyebrow. "You do have a way of making men uncomfortable."

Serra opened her eyes wide. "Who, me?"

CHAPTER SIXTEEN

Gregor met up with Kellan at CafeGo. Serra was safe with Justin and Maggie, and he wanted to get this interview over with in private.

Kellan, a large cup in his hand, stopped short at the sight of Gregor standing in line. "Are you getting coffee?"

"Yeah."

"I'll wait for you there." He indicated a corner of the crowded shop with his cup. Gregor watched as Kellan took charge of the area. The two tables closest to the one he sat at emptied before Gregor got his coffee.

He sat across from Kel. "That was impressive."

Kellan shrugged. "What's up?"

"You came without me asking you to. Why?"

"You haven't called me since I left fifteen years ago. I keep hearing rumors. Plus, had a friend flying this way."

"Coincidence, then?"

"You want me to leave? I'll leave."

As Kellan stood, Gregor held out a hand. "No. Stay." Gregor met Kellan's cool gaze and his lips quirked. "Please."

Kellan sat back down. "You're worried."

"Too many people getting hurt or dying. I'd like to minimize the human damage. It sounds like Maggie is targeted, along with Serra."

"The Fae may be a problem."

Gregor sent him a hard look. "Why?"

"Have you ever known them to do anything from an altruistic standpoint?"

"I've never known full-blooded Fae."

"I have." Discontent sat on Kellan's face. "They're sneaky. Manipulative. And not necessarily always on our side."

"What are you talking about?" Gregor sat back and stared. "You can't be serious."

~ ☾ ~

"Deadly." Kellan's gaze didn't waver. "You've got to be ready to cut her loose. You do not want a Dark Fae standing against you."

"She's not a Dark Fae," Gregor protested. "Can you prove she is?"

"Can you prove she isn't?" Kellan countered.

Gregor stared at him. "Hell." They needed Kellan. With Gabriel gone, and Justin's attention divided, Kellan was his next logical choice. "I don't believe you. I *know* her. But, hell. Keep your eyes open. Tell me everything that transpires, and I'll do the same with you."

"Start at the beginning, and don't leave anything out."

Gregor hit the highlights of the past two days, including the Charismatic at The Nine Hells, and the dark man he'd seen earlier that day near Serra.

Kellan kept his eyes closed while Gregor talked. They emptied their cups and still Gregor talked.

When he finally ran dry, Kellan opened his eyes. "Tell me about this Bryce guy. He's encouraging partial demonspawn to embrace their demon side?"

"Apparently. The blood connection is so weak at this point though. I don't understand why he's going down that path."

"Is there any obvious connection to the portal? Anything at all that you can think of?"

Gregor thought back. "Just what I've already told you. Serra saw Bryce and Cait at the same place where she saw the portal, and Fran was putting together a big party for the solstice."

"Let's talk it out," Kellan muttered. "When they make that much noise, they're looking for power. Harnessing that power would make someone hard to kill. These nitwits can't be asking a bunch of half-breeds to learn how to become their demon for nothing. They can't be thinking of trying to take over, can they? Suicide."

"Serra is afraid of a widespread killing spree on the night of the solstice slash full moon." Gregor brooded into his empty cup. "I'm starting to believe she's right. If you gather together a bunch of half-breeds, and toss in some witches of indeterminate power, add mood music and alcohol, then let loose a, oh, let's say a demon who hasn't fed properly, what does that all add up to? Or to put it another way, add Bryce the Charismatic plus half-breeds plus Fran's party plus Cait plus the Portal plus a demon, toss in a Death Mage, the winter solstice and an eclipse and you get?"

"A killing spree."

"And who wins?"

Kellan frowned. "What do you mean?"

"The partygoers don't win, because they die in the feeding frenzy." Gregor crumpled the top of his cup.

"Keep going."

"The demon who gets to eat all those lovely people wins. And…so does the person who called out the portal. As the demon eats the people, the mage or witch can choose to let the corpses pass, or take their power from them before they depart, whatever that power may be."

"So if you've got someone like Kendall Sorbis hanging around the party site," Kellan began.

"He's most likely stealing power as the demon steals life. It wouldn't surprise me if he'd been there last summer with you, hiding in the shadows, stealing what he could from the dying vampires. Hell." Gregor rubbed his eyes.

"It was crazy, that fight. Lots of smoke, Rose disappearing, Gabriel going nuts, vampires everywhere." Kellan's eyes narrowed. "I can easily believe we didn't notice him there."

"If Serra can lead us to the portal, if we can get it shut, that would be huge."

"Or." Kellan's gaze met Gregor's. "If the portal is closed, more may die in order to reopen it."

"Either way we go, people will die and there's not a hell of a lot we can do about it. You know how to close the portal?"

Kellan nodded but shifted in his chair. "It can be a brutal process. Part blood and part sheer force. At least, that's how I've done it in the past." He grinned, a bleak stretching of his lips.

Gregor just watched him. What evil had he seen in the past? What demons were riding Kellan, and how did he get such a deadly aura about him? Finally, Gregor shook his head. "I trust you. You're family. You knew Mom and Dad. We've been fighting each other since you first came all those years ago, but I'm okay with that now."

Kellan held out his hand. "I've got your back, Gregor. Swear."

They shook on it. "Good. Okay. Let's go back to the office and get our Fae to find this damned portal."

They rose, picked up their empty cups and headed toward the door. "You gonna change first before we go out?"

Gregor turned to Kellan, surprised. "No. Why?"

Kellan eyed his cousin's business suit and smiled, a much more natural smile, as they pushed out into the chilly dark. "Oh, no reason. No reason at all."

~~~

"Here," Serra said, tapping Gregor on the thigh. "Pull over here."

Gregor spied a parking spot across the street, pulled an illegal U turn to get to it, and shut off the ignition.

Serra and Kellan were out of the car before he finished. Gregor sighed and joined them on the street, locking the car and pocketing the keys. "Where?"

Serra pointed. The wide boulevard had a median. A tree had been hit and leaned at a drunken angle, caution tape staked around it. "There. That's where Fran died." She looked up the street. "Do you want to try to piece together the scene?" She tipped her head up to Gregor.

He shuddered. "No thanks."

"Then let's walk."

Gregor took the street side while Kellan flanked Serra on her other side. After midnight, not many people wandered the streets, and never in this part of town.

Serra led them across and down a side street. The lights were dim here, the buildings clustered together. Dry weeds poked through cracks in empty parking lots, giving the whole area an abandoned feeling.

She stopped and lifted her head. "Do you hear that?"

Gregor and Kellan both looked around. "Hear what?"

"Hush. Listen. Tune in." She lifted an eyebrow at Kellan. "I know you can do that."

Irritated, Gregor closed his eyes and listened hard. The usual night sounds were absent here. No ocean waves, no cars. The whooshing of the distant freeway was subdued, barely audible. As he identified each sound, it seemed to disappear leaving only a humming noise.

Like overhead wires, maybe. Gregor looked up, but they weren't around any power lines that he could see. "Humming. Where's it coming from?"

Serra smiled. "That's what we're looking for. It's a portal. Right?" She sent a challenging look to Kellan.

"Yeah. It sounds right." He jerked his head toward the right. "That way."

"Following you." Gregor slipped an arm around Serra's waist. The deeper they went down the street, the darker it seemed to get. Thick clouds obscured the fat moon above them, and the knife-edge of the wind made it feel even darker.

Kellan slipped off to the left through a maze of buildings. Gregor and Serra followed until they stopped in front of a huge parking lot, with a building off to their right. It had high clerestory windows that glowed with light, but otherwise the building was cement block front and a big double-door entryway. No name anywhere, just a number. 1663.

Serra looked around. "This is the place." She shivered, as if finally feeling the cold. Kellan signaled them to stay there while he did a quick tour of the building. "Remember? Cash saw 1663."

It stood big as an airplane hangar, but completely out of place in the maze of smaller buildings. It looked to be a warehouse of some sort, and long disused.

Gregor really didn't like the feel of the place. "You're sure?"

"I can smell Fran here." She pointed to the front doors. "We came out from there, and she went through the lot to the middle." Tracing their path, Serra pointed to where the car had been parked. Not a single car remained in the dark lot.

Kellan rejoined them. "The back door isn't locked. Interesting, don't you think?"

~ ☾ ~

"If they've got demons in there guarding the place, I wouldn't lock the back door, either. Would you?"

Kellan answered his cousin's question with a shrug. "We going in, or not?"

"Of course." Serra slipped from Gregor's side and skipped ahead. "Come on. Let's check it out." She waited at the corner of the building until she saw them heading her way before disappearing around the corner.

"Damn it." Gregor stepped up his walk to a run as Kellan chuckled.

"She's certainly enthusiastic."

"Shut up. Serra," called Gregor, catching sight of her as she hesitated at the far end of the building. "Do not go in there without us." He caught a glimmer of her smile before she disappeared again.

"You can't clip a Fae's wings, whether she follows the Light or the Dark," murmured Kellan.

"Thank you for your words of wisdom." Gregor flipped his cousin off as they rounded the back of the building.

The single door stood open. Little light came from inside. Kellan caught Gregor's arm before he could walk through. "Wait. It could be a trap."

"Serra's already in there. If it's a trap, she'll need help."

"She might be behind the trap, idiot. Go cautiously, that's all I'm saying."

Gregor reached under his suit coat and pulled out his hunting knife. At nine inches long, an inch wide and with a wicked set of half-inch sharp barbs on the top, it was a knife to make even the angriest demon think twice about attacking. "Good enough?"

"Good enough." Kellan pulled out a knife with similar power. "Got your back."

They stepped through the door.

~~~

"Sit down, relax. This is home sweet home," Justin said as he moved ahead of the women and turned on lights. They'd made it to the homestead in the San Fernando Valley with a minimum of angst. He went to the fireplace and set a match to the kindling laid ready.

The great room glowed in welcome, the old wood furniture polished to a honeyed gleam. Greens, reds and golds gave it a warm and luxurious feel. Aubrey gnawed on her lower lip. "It's a nice place," she said, looking around.

"Rose and Gabriel have been slowly fixing it up." Maggie collapsed into the depths of the couch.

Justin straightened and turned toward them. "May I get you ladies anything? Beer, wine, tea, crumpets, anything?"

"Crumpets? You've got crumpets?" Aubrey's face fell as Justin shot her a guilty look.

"No. Sorry. I'm sure there are munchies in the kitchen, though. I know I'm hungry, and I won't sleep until the others are back."

"I won't either," confessed Aubrey. She curled up next to Maggie. "I'd love a glass of wine, if you don't mind. Maggie?"

"What? No, nothing," she said, and yawned. "I might turn in, though."

"Stay down here. I want to keep an eye on you. The couch is comfy and you've slept there before," he added, and lifting an afghan off the chair nearest him, he shook it out and draped it around her.

She sighed and punched a throw pillow. "I guess I will." Putting her head down she yawned again. "Sorry, Aub."

"Not a problem." Aubrey tucked the afghan around her and stood. "I'll follow you for that glass."

Justin led the way into the kitchen. "Did you have something to say?"

Aubrey grimaced. "Be nice to her, okay? Her parents died in the Tuscan witch riots in the 1980's. She was sent out here to live with a relative, who died when she turned seventeen. She's been alone a lot. She deserves more."

Justin paused in the act of pouring out a Pinot Noir and stared at her. "Seriously?" He handed her the glass, poured his own, and hustled them both back to the hearth room. They settled in a couple club chairs pulled up to the fire opposite the couch where Maggie slept.

"Tell me everything," he demanded.

~ ☾ ~

Aubrey shook her head. "I don't know much more. Maggie is very private, if you hadn't noticed. She doesn't trust easily."

"I've noticed." He had believed her reticence meant indifference. "How badly did Sorbis screw with her head?"

Aubrey pursed her lips. "I don't really know. She stayed intensely private about that aspect of her life, too. But she saw what the rest of us went through. It wasn't like we didn't talk about it, you know. We were just very careful. Subtext was king."

"But you got close enough to know what happened to her parents."

"She got drunk one night. The anniversary of the night her life changed, she called it, and she wasn't talking about getting her period or losing her virginity, either. When she finally told me, she was plastered on shots of tequila and swore me to secrecy. I haven't told anyone until now."

"Why did you tell me?"

Aubrey looked at him over the rim of her glass. Her eyes, honey-gold, seemed to bore into him. "You'll need to know. It'll be important that you know, when the time comes. She carries their blood. They'll respond to her call."

Justin sat back in his chair and frowned. "Is this going to happen soon?"

"Spring. What?" Aubrey blinked and rubbed her eyes. "I'm sorry. I hate when that happens."

"You're a foreseer." He let out a bark of surprised laughter. "I don't know why that startles me."

She grinned, looking like a sexy pixie curled up in the chair opposite him. "It makes it easier, doesn't it, when you realize you're not the only weirdo in the neighborhood? It did for me, once I found the coven in college. God bless UCLA," she added fervently.

"I don't suppose you saw exactly what we'd be up against?"

"I'm sorry. It's not exact. And what I see is subject to change. But when the time comes, have her reach out to the family that has gone before her. They will help her as her last resort. They died to save her, and they will protect her again, save her from death once more." She shrugged. "That's the best sense I can make of it."

~ ☾ ~

Justin rubbed his hands together, suddenly chilled despite the warmth of the fire. "Well, I'm going to hang my hat on us clearing up this portal business, and the mark on her hand, within the next couple of days. By springtime, we'll all have a new lease on life."

Doubt flickered across her face and was quickly banished. "I hope you're right. In the meantime, cheers." She lifted her glass to him. "May the new year bring all of us good things."

~~~

Serra stared at the portal, sweat beading on her forehead. It pulsed in front of her, energy humming through it. With a part of her mind, she knew Gregor and Kellan had followed her.

"Kellan, keep him away," she ordered.

"Don't even try it," Gregor growled and started forward.

"Leave her. If too many of us get near the thing, it could suck us through to the other side. Trust me, it's not a pleasant trip," Kellan said.

Gregor stopped two yards away from her. "Are you all right?"

She raised her arms up over her head, grabbing at something she could feel but couldn't see. It must be the portal's earth-energy. She pulled on it, hard, like stretching a huge piece of plastic wrap. Inch by inch she pulled it, until she knelt down and sealed one side to the ground, sweat snaking down her back from the effort. A hand came out of the opposite side of the portal and tugged at her ankle.

She screamed. Gregor sprang to her side and grabbed for her, yanking hard. Kellan was there at her feet, jabbing at the hand with his knife. With a yowl, the hand disappeared and the unseen door slipped open again with a rush of hot air that blew in their faces.

Serra and Gregor scrambled back from the opening. The light from it pulsed an angry orange.

"Further back," gasped Serra, and getting on their hands and knees, they crawled to the far wall.

Kellan stepped inside the portal. He slashed the fleshy part

~ ☾ ~

of both thumbs, a slight cut that still bled. With both hands, he marked a circle in blood against the unseen barrier that had opened.

Slowly the barrier, rolled up at the top of the opening, became clearer, pulsing red with the blood he'd fed it.

Kellan stepped back out of the portal and with muscles straining, he began folding it in on itself, over and over, reopening his wound and feeding it blood when it showed signs of returning to full size. Eventually, with enough blood and enough of Kellan's strength, the portal hit a tipping point and, small enough, devoured itself with a last spattering of blood on the cement floor.

The humming sound, the orange light, disappeared. The room was empty of all except the three of them.

Serra stood, ashamed. "I should have listened to you. I was wrong. And I apologize."

Kellan merely held his hands out, his eyes hard, wary as he looked at her. Serra put her hands over his and a green light pulsed, swirling between them. Without warning, the light ran over his body, hovered around a knee, raced around his torso. Kellan stiffened. Serra grabbed his hands and kept her eyes on his.

When the light finally died out, Kellan took a staggering step. "Gregor."

"I've got you." He put an arm under Kellan's shoulder. "Let's get back to the homestead. After that, I need a beer. Maybe some pizza."

"We'll have to get that on the way home. No one delivers after midnight on a Wednesday."

Serra followed the two men as they stumbled back down the dark street. "Really? We're just leaving?"

Gregor turned to her. "What did you expect? There's no one else here. Aren't you exhausted?"

As if him saying the words made it true, Serra reeled. "Yes. I'm tired. I need food. And time to think. At least we know where they are now. We can come back tomorrow and wrap this all up. Right?"

Gregor and Kellan shared a look and a grin.

"What's so funny?"

~ ☾ ~

"We'll come back tomorrow," promised Gregor. "I just can't guarantee we'll have everything wrapped up before the winter solstice. It's just not the way things seem to go with us Caines," he added apologetically.

Serra harrumphed as she followed them to the car. "Men just make things so complicated."

Kellan slumped in the back seat. Serra sent a swift glance to Gregor. "He'll be fine. He had some internal injuries that needed tending. It was a bit of a shock to him."

Kellan muttered something under his breath but Serra ignored him. Gregor shook his head and pulled out into the street.

"We got out of there too easily." Gregor drummed his fingers on the steering wheel.

"Anticlimactic." Kellan shifted, stretching his legs out on the back seat. "I expected a fight."

"I'm just as glad we didn't have one," Serra said tartly.

Gregor had pulled up to a red light. She glanced out the window at shadows that seemed to fly in the dark night. A shape landed on the hood of the car and a face pressed leeringly to the windshield.

"Hell. Looks like you get your wish, Kel."

Another thud, and the car rocked. Thick fingers scrabbled at Gregor's partially open window. "It's on the roof." He glanced toward Serra. "You ready, Warrior?"

"Always," she said, her grin matching his. Her blood pumped faster. "Let's go!"

As one, the two men leaped out of the car and pulled their weapons.

Serra, watching her chance, slammed the door open right into the path of an oncoming demon. It crumpled, and she jumped out of the car to join the men, but the street was crawling with the C'dak. Serra used them like stepping-stones as they snapped at her, leaping lightly across them to a cement light pole on the corner. She crawled high up it to get a look at the fight.

The intersection was eerily empty and the streetlights dead. The clouds remained thick overhead.

The two men had managed to clear a circle around

themselves, their knives gleaming dully, dripping now with demon blood. She counted. Ten dead, and ten times that coming from the shadows, carpeted the ground beneath her. She really didn't like the odds. Jumping down there, even with her knives, would be just short of suicide.

And because she wasn't connected to the earth, she couldn't access the fires of the sky.

She scanned the area, aware that her window of opportunity was narrowing. If she moved from pole to building to pole, she could get far enough away to touch earth. If she could touch earth, she could call the fires and do away with the demons.

The noise of the battle increased below her. The C'dak had set up quite a howl, and dogs from around the area lifted their voices in protest. She glanced quickly at Gregor. His suit jacket had been shredded front and back, but she didn't see any blood. If she were to be of any use at all, she needed to move. *Now.*

Her heart in her throat, Serra leaped for the building six feet away. It was just like tree running back home, she reminded herself. Just like tree running.

At Kellan's enraged bellow and Gregor's anxious call, Serra swallowed hard and moved faster.

~ ☾ ~

CHAPTER SEVENTEEN

"Son of a bitch." Gregor wrenched his focus back on the creatures snarling in front of him, but the sight of Serra running across rooftops seared itself in his mind, his heart.

"Dark Fae," Kellan shouted as he fought.

"I don't believe you." Gregor renewed his attack on the dog-demons snapping and snarling around him. Using his feet as much as his knife, he took down four more of the things.

Dodging the thick claws had him sweating even as the fog rolled in. Below his feet the earth trembled, the demons yowled, and Gregor swore as he adjusted to the movement. This was not your typical earthquake weather.

Noise from the neighbor dogs increased.

Lightning streaked from the sky, pinpointing the demon at his feet. It burned to a crisp in front of him. Jumping back from the flames, he stumbled over a demon body behind him and went down hard.

A dog-like creature jumped him, its hands—it was hard to call them anything else—pressing him down as it snarled right in his face. Breath more foul than any restaurant dumpster choked him. Before he could head-butt the ugly thing, it was plucked off his chest. Ichor sprayed as Kellan took it out with a knife across its throat.

Gregor got back to his feet and swayed with fatigue. Lightning bolts were heading their way through the thick fog. With pinpoint accuracy, the demons they hadn't killed yet went up in flame and burned quickly to ash.

Serra came striding toward them, a cluster of lightning bolts in one hand. With the other, she tossed them, one at a time, toward a pack of demons who had turned on each other, sending them all up in flames. Hope and a wild joy blazed through him at the sight of her moving toward him,

~ ☾ ~

strong and confident.

"If you manly men could pile the bodies up, it'll be easier to dispose of them." Serra gestured.

Energized, Gregor and Kellan hauled dead demons away from the car and into the middle of the street. The neighborhood remained quiet, no signs of any activity from the warehouses and boarded-up storefronts in the area.

Gregor watched her flame the rest of the demons, her eyes cool and her hand steady. Once the last spark went out, she surveyed the surroundings. Piles of ash here and there made it look like there'd been a fire.

"A sea breeze, I think," she said, and lifting her face to the sky, muttered words he didn't catch.

Gregor glanced at his cousin who leaned against the car, his arms folded and a stern look in his eye as he took in Serra's actions. He felt impelled to defend her. "She needed the strategic positioning, Kel. Plus, she kicked demon ass. It's good enough for me."

"I know. Doesn't mean I fully trust her yet."

Kellan had never been one to trust quickly, even as a kid. Gregor nodded. "Understood."

A breeze came up, cooling the sweat on his body. Serra moved her hands gracefully in the air and it responded, the ash rising off the pavement and swirling about to be scattered by the winds. Nothing was left behind for anyone to get too curious about.

Gregor went to his battered and dented car and got in, too tired to worry about how much the bodywork would cost him. Still too revved about Serra's return.

"Let's go," he called to Serra, who remained in the street. She looked his way and joined them in the car without saying anything. She touched Gregor lightly on the back of his hand before pulling away.

"Get us out of this neighborhood." Kellan sprawled out on the back seat and put his head back.

Gregor took off. The further north they went, the lighter the fog until it was gone completely. He slanted a look at Serra. "The fog your work?"

"Yes." She stifled a yawn. "I decided to use the enemy's

trick. Sorry about taking off that way, but I didn't see the advantage of three of us being surrounded by demons. By running to safe ground, I was able to reconnect with the earth. Call the firebolts."

"And if you'd done that where we were," Gregor said, "you'd have..."

"I'd have been attacked and way too busy trying to stay alive to call anything. This morning there were, what? Almost forty of them? Tonight there were at least five times that amount. Getting to the ground safely was paramount. As it was, I took out half of them."

Kellan sniffed in disbelief. "A third, maybe."

"You are both well?"

Gregor merged onto the northbound freeway. "We're fine. Or we will be, once we get to the homestead." Not that he'd needed it, but her explanation made perfect sense. Plastic, cement, these were things she couldn't draw energy from, as they'd never truly been alive. A grin he couldn't stop took over his face.

"Food and beer and sleep will go a long way to curing what ails me," Kellan declared. "Wake me when we get there."

Gregor drove as swiftly as possible through the empty streets. He glanced at the woman—Fae—beside him. Her eyes were closed, her face paler than usual. "You're okay?"

"I am tired." Her tone was distant, cool.

"Of course." Immediately, he became professional. "The homestead has many bedrooms. My half-brother and his wife have parties now and then. Invariably, we end up spending the night. You'll find it comfortable there."

"Good."

"What's wrong?"

"Nothing." But Serra had stiffened a bit and turned her head to face the window.

Gregor knew what that meant. He'd stepped in it, somehow. But a car, with his cousin in the back seat, was not the place to dig deeper. They finished the drive in thoughtful silence.

None too soon he turned into the long driveway. The gate slid open and he drove in, parking next to Justin's Jag. He surveyed the house. Porch light and hearth room lights were on. One bedroom light on the second floor shone. The rest of the house remained dark.

He shut off the engine, and before he could pull the key out, Kellan had left the car, his long legs taking him to the front door before the other two could stir.

Serra looked at Gregor. "You thought I'd deserted you," she reproached.

"It crossed my mind, very quickly, and left again. I trust you, Serra."

"I am *not* Dark Fae," she insisted. "I know what your cousin is thinking, and he's wrong."

"Is he?" Gregor got out of the car, circled around to her door and opened it for her. "Is he wrong to be careful of whom to trust?"

She stood and looked him in the eye. "If you believe he's correct, and I am one of the Dark ones, what are you doing with me?"

Gregor caught back the flip response and looked closely at her. Exhaustion had darkened the skin under her eyes. Her hands gripped the door between them, knuckles showing white. If she was Dark Fae, and he couldn't believe that she was, he'd still offer her a place to sleep. If it rebounded on him, he'd deal.

He leaned his forehead against hers and just breathed her in, his head clearing as her scent sank into him. How had she come to mean so much, in such a short time?

"I like to believe I'm taking care of you," he answered, and taking her hand, he led her away from the car, closing the door behind them. "Let's go inside, find some food, and get some rest." As she came even with him, he slipped an arm around her waist.

She sighed and leaned her head on his shoulder. "By the looks of the welcoming committee, it'll be awhile before we get rest."

Gregor saw what she meant. The doorway was crowded. Justin and Maggie were there, plus two women he assumed were part of Maggie's coven. "There'd better be food," he grumbled.

~ ☾ ~

It took some time, but finally they were settled around the kitchen table. Submarine sandwiches had been set out, plus a big green salad. Wine was poured, beer bottles opened. Between bites, Kellan and Gregor told their story.

The women regarded Serra in awe as she ate her salad.

Aubrey put her hand up in a high five. "Way to go!" Serra looked to Gregor, one eyebrow raised.

"Give it here, girl," he said, and slapped Aubrey's hand. "It's a congratulatory thing," he explained to Serra.

"Of course. Everyone's been assigned a room?"

"All taken care of," Justin answered. "Ursula and Hayden even stopped for food, as you can see. It's not pizza, but it did the trick."

"The house is warded?" Ursula had her arms wrapped around herself. Deep circles shadowed her eyes.

Hayden hugged her sister. "We're safe here." She flashed a grateful look around the table. "I can't tell you how much this means to us."

"Hands." Serra said the word abruptly and everyone stared. "Ladies, please show your hands." Aubrey promptly put out her hand, palm up. It was clean. Reluctantly, the other two did as well.

Serra looked from one woman to the other. "Both hands."

Slower this time, the three put their left hand on the table. In the middle of their palms sat the same blot that was on Serra's hand. She and Maggie showed their palms as well, and the three witches gasped. The men shared a grim glance.

Gregor stood. "So now we know what we're dealing with."

"Nothing will get through my protections, I swear it. Serra?" Maggie stared at the Fae.

"I will add my own layer, of course."

Tears ran down Ursula's face. Hayden cleared her throat. "But what does it mean? We don't understand."

"Maggie, Serra, take them to their rooms and brief them on what we know so far," Gregor said. "Let's all get some sleep. We'll figure out what comes next in the morning."

The women left without another word, Hayden murmuring softly to a still-weeping Ursula. Justin, Kellan and Gregor remained behind.

~ ☾ ~

"This has all the marks of a bad slasher movie." Justin swirled the wine left in his glass.

Kellan grunted. "We don't have a basement. And I don't think anyone's planning on having sex tonight, despite the several attractive women who will be sleeping under this roof."

Gregor shifted in his chair. "The house is warded."

"Of course. Maggie worked on it again after she took a nap, and Serra will do her mojo." Justin's face split open with his yawn. "I don't know about you guys, but I need sleep."

"I'll take the couch in the hearth room." Kellan rose. "I'm so tired it won't matter where I fall asleep."

"I'm in the den. Gregor, we've put you in the master bedroom."

The brothers rose as their cousin left the kitchen. Justin gripped Gregor's arm. "How bad was it, really?"

Gregor gave a mental look back at the battle in the street, the lights out, the neighborhood empty. The C'dak demons coming for them, seemingly without end.

He shrugged. "We were lucky. We had a Warrior Fae on our side."

~~~

Gregor stepped into his parents' bedroom with mixed emotions. He noticed with relief that the bedding had been updated and the room painted a soft blue. It had been streamlined, and little of his mother was left except for the marvelous, painted medallion in the center of the ceiling, a sophisticated intertwining of vines and letters, pulsing with love and urging to fertility. She'd been a master at painted spiral spells, scattering them throughout the house. Perhaps she'd had the foreknowledge she wouldn't be there to see all her children grow to manhood.

He stumbled to the bathroom and turned the shower on to hot, shrugging out of the now-useless suit. Stripped down, he stepped under the spray and sighed with delight as the heat eased tight muscles. Soap washed away any demon residue.

Propping himself up with a hand against the shower wall,

he let the water flow over his head and down his body, his mind finally quiet. He jerked himself awake before he fell and turned the water off, dried off, and went back into the bedroom, half-expecting to find Serra in his bed.

The bed was empty. Stifling regret, he crawled under the thick country quilt. His great-grandmother had pieced it together. A hazy memory of her smiling at him over her quilting hoop slid across his mind before he tumbled into sleep.

~~~

Serra had made a nest for herself on the floor in a corner of the master bedroom with a t-shirt she'd found in a drawer. She had just settled herself to meditate when Gregor had come into the room.

She couldn't help herself, she stared. Especially when he came back from the shower, naked and damp and oh, so tired.

So sexy.

Unfortunately, the effort she'd expended had flung her back, once again, into adolescence, and she'd found herself the wrong size to placate her libido. She stretched out her wings and squirmed around until she got the t-shirt just right, then drew a corner of it up and over herself. When would this end? When would she regain control of her size?

Grumbling a bit, she set herself to a meditative state. Three hours. That was all she needed, just three hours of solid rest, and then she could pounce on him. If she had to go back home in two days, she wanted to leave behind some wonderful memories.

~~~

Bryce slapped Cait hard across the face. She recovered from the blow and stared, face stony, straight ahead.

"You left the place unguarded? They shut the portal. They *shut* the *portal*, you witch whore!"

Her eyes glittered with hate. "I was running your stupid

errands. You were supposed to be here. Where were *you*?"

"Dalton and I had work to do." They'd gone to the beach to try to get Bryce's demon to appear. His failure to change stung, brought out his cruelty. He slapped Cait again.

"You also put an illusion spell on my girlfriend. You killed her. Not only did you kill her, you allowed the Fae to escape. Are you terminally stupid or just having a bad day?"

When she didn't respond, Bryce shouted in her face. "Answer me!"

She jumped, her eyes wide. "Sorry. I didn't know about the Fae. You didn't tell me." She clasped her hands together tightly.

"You didn't ask." Bryce kept his voice dry, devoid of expression now. She needed to learn that he held power such as she wished she had. She needed to learn fear.

"Dalton," he snapped. From the depths of the big hangar something stirred.

"What?" The voice was deep, bored.

"I need to mark her. Come to the edge of the light." Inside, Bryce quailed. Whenever Dalton gave him the power to mark someone, it jolted through him, tearing pieces of his personality away. He focused on the main goal and braced himself.

When the dark hand appeared in the light, Bryce gripped it. Power stronger than a current shook him. His vision blurred and his hunger grew.

He turned to stare at Cait.

She shook under his glare. "Don't, please. I swear I'll be good. I'm sorry about Frannie, I really am. I didn't realize the illusion would make her crash into something. I'm so sorry."

The energy holding him in place cut off. Bryce held out his hand to Cait, his eyes dry and burning. "I usually have time to calm down before doing this. But it must be done. You must be marked. Come to me, Caitlyn."

She shuffled toward him unwillingly, her hand stretching out to him.

"That's right. Another step." Once her hand was within reach, he grasped it, opened it palm up and traced a burning circle there.

Cait fell to her knees, her eyes going blank with shock.

~ ☾ ~

When he released her, she tumbled to the polished cement floor and didn't move.

Bryce surveyed her. "Sure you won't just take her, have done with all the mating business?"

Dalton's voice came from the darkness. "I want the Fae. I crave her. She is the one I will mate with. The rest are food, that is all."

"I'm meeting up with other demonbloods tonight. I'll get them to be guards, ensure no one leaves once the party starts." Bryce buzzed with the demonic energy. He reached for his own demon, but it receded, eluding him.

"Damn it." Perspiration dotted his forehead. "I still can't change."

"Hmm." Dalton's rumble sounded.

"What am I doing wrong?"

"I've told you how it should work."

"Reach for your demon. Use rage. Force it out while chanting the spell. Well, it doesn't work." Bryce took a deep breath. It wouldn't do to get agitated, not now. He needed to keep a cool head. Running those bloodlings would take all his considerable control.

"I'm gone. Do you need anything?"

"I'm hungry." Dalton's hunger pulsed in the air, and Bryce shivered against the beat of it.

"If you must, grab someone walking past." He made it to the door. "You knew they would close the portal, didn't you?" The words burst out of him.

"There was a good chance, yes." Satisfaction oozed in the words.

"You have no intention of going back to your world, do you?" Bryce looked over his shoulder.

The demon shifter came into the light. Skin the color of polished oak threw his orange eyes into high relief. His dark hair flowed down his back, and his face, while bony, could pass for attractive to some people. When he grinned, white teeth gleaming, Bryce stifled a shudder.

"Why should I go back to hell, when this world waits for me to conquer it?" Power curled lazily around him in visible eddies.

~ ☾ ~

Caution crept through Bryce. He forced an admiring smile. "I live to serve." He gave a brief bow before making his escape.

~~~

All the way to The Nine Hells, Bryce shook with fear. He was doing the right thing, he knew he was. People like him, who had *other* abilities, kept themselves safely underground. If the general public knew, demon-hunting would become a new sport. It was time his people were revered, feared. Got the recognition they deserved by claiming the power of their blood.

By the time he parked, his fear had dissolved into a stronger determination. He would see his people to freedom. It was time for the whole demon world to come into the open and lead the lesser humans. It was past time for the humans to learn their place.

The bar had closed for the night, but that didn't bother Bryce. He walked around to the back and climbed the steps to the outdoor patio. A bunch of men milled around, young men mostly in their early twenties. The scent of beer hung on the air. Good, Samael had followed orders.

The younger and drunker they were, the easier it should be to train them.

He jumped onto a chair. "Listen up." Faces turned to look at him and the crowd quieted.

"The training I've received worked. I've shifted into my demonskin, and I can show you how!" He shouted the lies, as if volume would make them truth.

Cheers erupted. Lots of back thumping and beer cans waving in the air. "Shift for us now! Show us what to do!"

Bryce made a damping motion with his hands. "Keep it down. We don't want anyone calling the cops on us. Shane, I can't shift now. To do it too often is hard on the body. I don't want to collapse on you all, not this close to our grand unveiling. Did you all get your invitations?"

Another cheer went up. "Good. So be on time if not early. Dress in tuxes or at least a suit. We want the world to take note of us, to remember us."

~ ☾ ~

"Can we bring a date?" a voice called out.

"Leave your womenfolk at home. It might get dangerous, and you don't want them to get hurt. Besides, some of you will be acting as guards, keeping out those who haven't been invited." There were some mutterings at that. "Don't worry, the press will be there, and we'll have plenty of sexy women there, too." Bryce wiped his forehead. Despite the chill of the night, he burned, but whether from the lies or from his contact with Dalton, he didn't know. "Any other questions? No? Good. Who wants to go first? Shane. You're up."

The other men backed to the edge of the wooden patio. They'd never seen a man shift into a demon, but they didn't want to get too close to the action just in case.

Shane swaggered forward, a burning joint in one hand. Bryce had chosen him for several reasons. If he managed the change, then he'd have a strong second-in-command. If he didn't make the change, he could mark Shane and tell him he'd made the next step. A definite win/win for him.

"What am I supposed to do?"

Bryce jumped down from the chair and focused on Shane. "Stand in the center of the pentagram. Here, put this charm around your neck. Now, close your eyes. Reach for your rage. Embody it. Then search within for your demon, the part of yourself that you know isn't human. Give life to that part of you. Feel it inside you, accept it, and allow it to dominate you. The demon is you, and you are the demon."

Shane grinned. "Let me just take one more hit before I do that." He took a deep inhale of the joint. He tossed the tiny bit of glowing paper to the ground and let his breath out in a fragrant cloud. "Okay. I'm ready." The men jeered at him.

"Quiet!" Bryce held back his irritation. "Close your eyes. Reach for your rage. Embody it." He chanted the spell Cait had given him, his hands spread wide.

Shane stiffened. "Oh holy shit." His body trembled and jerked.

Bryce backed away now, too, still chanting, as Shane's hands twitched, the fingers elongating. His white skin turned deep green, and the color flowed up his arms. He howled, an inhuman sound.

~ ☾ ~

Bryce held his breath, watching as Shane made the change. It was real. They *did* have demon blood in them, hot damn! They could make the change, and they would rule now. Power was theirs for the taking.

Excitement held him as Shane writhed in front of them all. His hands were now changing back and forth, human to demon and back fast as thought.

"Hang onto your rage," Bryce commanded. "Dig deep for your demon roots. You are master of your fate. You are in charge."

Shane threw his head back and screamed, a high-pitched sound that had the rest of them clapping their hands over their ears. His arms spread wide, his body now flickered between shapes as he writhed in pain.

Without warning, Shane exploded. Blood and viscera spattered the onlookers, Shane's torso now stuck in bits and pieces all over the men and the deck of The Nine Hells. His legs and arms had shot off; his arms landed in the alley by the garbage bin, and one of his legs was on top of chairs stacked eight feet high beside the wall. Shane's head rolled, coming finally to a stop at Bryce's feet, his blank eyes still somehow staring accusingly up at Bryce.

Silence held them all and Bryce knew he had seconds to act before mayhem resulted.

"Do you see what happens when you use drugs to control who you really are?" His voice thundered out over the group. "Do you see how hubris affects your life? Come to me, and I will give you protection. Then go home and speak to no one about this, or your life is *forfeit*."

They filed past him, shocked and fearful. He took each by the hand and marked them without them being aware. They'd see it in the morning and would either take it as a good sign, or take it as a sign to be extremely careful. He didn't much care which. The marking would force them to the party tomorrow night and that was all that truly mattered.

As Samael, Little Harry's son, tried to slip past him behind someone else, Bryce gripped his arm. "You weren't going to say goodbye?"

Samael licked his lips. "Sorry. This was intense. Do you

know what drug he took beside the weed?"

Bryce let him go, his mind now on the new problem. "Not a clue."

"Bryce, dude. I'm seriously freaked out." Another young man crowded the two of them and Samael took off.

Bryce watched him go and shrugged. There would be plenty of time to reel him in. He turned to the next in line. "Aaron." He clasped the man's hand. "I'm so glad you were here. It's at least proof that we can change. We can do it, if we try."

"If you say so, man. I just want to light out of here, you know? Take a shower and drink another beer."

Bryce clapped him on the back. "Go do that. Just keep it quiet." He turned to the next man. "Josh."

When everyone had gone, Bryce looked around at the mess and sighed. He could bury the arms, legs and head, and hose off the patio. What he really wanted to know, though, was what had happened and why. If he'd succeeded in tapping into his own demon, would he have exploded the same way?

Sobering thought.

It occupied his mind as he cleaned up the mess that had been Shane Eck.

By the time he got home, exhausted and smelling like shit, Bryce could barely stand. He wasn't the action hero type, and digging graves for the arms and legs had worn him out. He'd finally tossed the head into a garbage bin, too tired to find the right spot to bury it.

In the heat of the shower, he relaxed as the last bits of Shane went down the drain. He rubbed his hair and his left hand prickled with heat. He looked at it, impatient, and stared in shock.

There, in the center of his left palm, was a perfect red circle, almost completely covered in black.

The solstice was tomorrow night, and he was now compelled to be there. Food for the demon he'd borrowed power from.

Curses flew out of his mouth even as fear clutched his bowels.

~ ☾ ~

CHAPTER EIGHTEEN

Serra slid under the covers and wrapped herself around Gregor, pressing kisses across his broad back. It wouldn't be light for another hour or so, and she needed this contact more than she wanted to admit.

He turned to her, rolled her so he surrounded her with his big body, one of his muscled legs thrown on top both of hers. One arm guarded her head, the other nestled between her breasts until slowly his breathing evened out again.

Gregor slept. Slept! She didn't know whether to be insulted or amused. He hadn't kicked her out, but did he know she was even there?

His warmth seeped into her. His scent surrounded her, those dark resins that made her think of the forests of home. She found herself lulled by his breath fanning her hair, by the beat of his heart against her back. As her own breath slowed, she drifted. Time seemed suspended.

She'd love to take him to her home. No. No! What was she thinking? Her eyes shot open and she stared into the dark. He wouldn't fit in. His suits would look ridiculous in her world. He wouldn't be able to tree walk.

Besides, he belonged *here*. Taking care of *this* world. As soon as they wrapped up this anomaly, she'd be gone and he'd carry on.

Except...the Caines needed a Fae ambassador as much as the Fae world needed the Caines. It would mean staying here. Serra frowned as a thrill of uncertainty went through her. Stay here? Unconsciously, she moved against Gregor, seeking reassurance.

"Stop thinking so loud," Gregor murmured against her hair. He brought her closer to him. She could feel him growing hard.

"Mmm." She rolled her hips, causing both of them to revel

in the sensations. "Are you finally awake?"

"If I'm having a dream, I'd like to stay asleep for a very long time," he answered. His hand cupped her breast possessively. "This is the best wakeup call I've had in forever." His thumb flicked at her nipple. It tightened under his teasing.

Need flooded her and she pressed back against his groin. "I can't believe you're not mated for life. What are the women here thinking?" She turned in his arms to face him, her pale breasts brushing against his dark, smooth chest. She lifted a hand to his face and cupped his cheek, looking deep into his blue eyes, hazy now with desire.

Serra nipped at his mobile lips before capturing them in a long lazy kiss. Her blood heated even more as he shifted her, making room for his erection, now pressing against her stomach. He'd reclaimed her breast, flicking at her nipple, pinching it when she least expected. She let out a long, luxurious sigh and arched against him.

In one smooth move, Gregor rolled on his back and kept her on top of him, one of his big hands splayed on her ass holding her firmly in place against him.

She grinned as he captured her mouth in a long, slow, deeply intimate kiss. Her amusement turned into greed and she kissed him back for all she was worth.

He cared for her. She knew he did. It was in the way he looked at her when he thought she wasn't looking. It was in how they talked to each other, a sort of shorthand that excluded other people. It was in the absent way he'd touch her, as if to reassure himself that she was still there.

Living on Earth as an ambassador wouldn't be bad, not if Gregor was around to be her consort. If she stayed, she'd eventually have to find a mate. But she could put that off until Gregor tired of her.

He moved from her lips and pressed kisses down her scar until he reached her nipple and suckled. Serra let out a cry, pleasure coursing through her at his touch. Her head fell forward, her downy hair drifting around them. Gregor went from one nipple to another, suckling, teasing and nipping lightly.

~ ☾ ~

"Mine," he growled, and twirled his tongue between her breasts. "While you are here, you are mine. Period. I don't sleep around indiscriminately. I know the Fae are fickle, but I'd prefer you stick to my bed."

Serra stiffened. "Fickle? Ahh!" She let out a cry as he tugged hard on one breast, sensation streaking through her body. Before she could catch her breath, he flipped her beneath him. His legs spread her knees and one hand circled her entrance already wet with need. He slipped two fingers inside, and she found herself clenching around them in desperation.

"I like finding you wet and ready for me. I like watching your eyes glaze over when I pinch your nipples. I like watching you watch me enter you."

His erection replaced his fingers, dipping into her wetness without penetrating. "Gregor," she pleaded. "Now."

"Watch," he commanded.

She kept her gaze on where he hovered over her, and watched as he pushed gently into her body. Slowly. Until he was firmly seated, all the way inside.

Serra sobbed in relief as she lifted her legs and tilted her hips to take even more of him into her. She looked up, up his dark body to where his eyes were steadily watching her, his arms locked on either side of her, his body still.

She'd never seen anything, anyone quite so magnificent between her legs. They looked like the yin and yang symbol, purest white against darkest black. The thought tightened her body as she ran her hands down his sides.

"You are exquisite." He pulled out, then pushed in again, slowly as she moaned low, clenching around him. "You are like a drug. I'm not an addict, but I promise you, I will indulge in this drug as often as possible while you are still around."

"The Fae love sex, we're not fickle. You're killing me here. Gods!"

"I'll be damned if I'll have you pining for any of your other lovers," he growled. His head dipped low as he captured her nipple between his teeth and tugged even as he kept up the slow torture.

~ ☾ ~

The pain morphed into pleasure, ratcheting her higher. Her legs tightened around his back. "Gregor, please. Please!" Her need shimmered over her and she gripped his hips. "Let go," she pleaded. "Let us both go."

He moved faster then, stroking her deeply, his mouth on her breast, his tongue swirling, swirling around her nipple. Without warning her orgasm took her, shook her. She cried out and clamped her legs and arms around him.

Her body shuddered and bucked beneath him as he plunged even faster into her depths. A cry escaped him as he emptied himself into her, a curse or a prayer, she couldn't tell which.

Gregor slumped against her, his heart beating a crazy rhythm that matched her own. A few long minutes slipped by as they both got their breath back, before Gregor moved to one side and cuddled her against him.

"Mine," he said once more.

Even as panic zinged through her, as she searched for something to say, Gregor fell asleep.

~~~

Justin brooded in the corner, fully dressed except for shoes. Cold moonlight illuminated the room. Maggie had finally fallen asleep, but it was a restless one. She allowed him in the same room with her, but only because it had twin beds.

He didn't get it. Their one night together had been glorious. One of the best nights of his life. He'd have bet the moon that she'd felt the same. How could she not want him and what they'd shared?

Her arms flung out, as if to stop something, then they sagged to the bed. He stared at the black circle almost completely covering her left palm and scowled. He'd kill anything that even tried to get to her. But how to keep her safe and away from Kendall? That was the big question.

Maggie moaned and Justin gave in to impulse. He moved quietly to her side and stroked a finger down her arm. Her eyes opened wide.

"Justin? What's wrong?"

~ ☾ ~

"You are. You're moaning, and thrashing about, and I can't sleep with all the noise. Let me get beside the wall." Before she could wake up fully, he slid under the covers, taking the wall side. Wrapping an arm around her, he brought her fully against him, and pulled the heavy quilts up over both of them. "Rest now."

"I was cold. So cold. Dreaming." She shuddered and dropped her forehead against his shoulder. "You shouldn't. I shouldn't let you."

He stroked her head, allowing his hand to follow down the length of her body. "Just sleep."

"I don't think I can, not right away. Talk to me instead."

"About what?" He felt her shrug.

"I've been thinking. The only way to keep us safe is by locking us in somewhere, with guards."

"I really don't think prison is the answer."

She stifled a startled chuckle and thumped his arm. "No, stupid. Like, have the werewolves guard us. Or something."

"And when you, or one of your witchy friends, decides they really have to leave? You'll be flinging spells left and right. You could kill people, Magdalena."

Her heavy sigh reassured him. "Oh hell. I'd forgotten about that."

It felt so right, talking to her this way. Quietly in the dark, as if they did it every night of their lives. "There is a solution. I'm surprised you haven't thought of it. You're slipping, de la Cruz."

"I am not. Let me think." She snuggled into him, resting her cheek against his chest. "Just let me think for a bit, would you?"

He smiled into the dark. "Take all the time you need. I'm not going anywhere."

"I'm not going to have sex with you," she warned. "Don't even think about it."

"Until you mentioned it, that was the farthest thing from my mind," he said truthfully. "Now, however..."

She laughed. "No."

"It'll be okay, M. We'll figure this out."

She didn't reply for the longest time. He hoped she'd fallen

~ ☾ ~

asleep again, but her breathing told him she remained awake. A gulping sound sent fear through his body.

"You're not crying, are you?" He could handle her anger, her being sick, even her haughtiness, but the thought of her in tears again just wrenched his guts.

"Hell no," she snapped, but her breath caught.

He resumed his stroking of her hair, her back, his thoughts frantic. "Because, you know, I just can't abide a crying woman. Makes them weak, you know."

"Shut up, Justin." She sniffed, a little of her usual feisty attitude in her voice.

He stroked her head again. "It's okay, Maggie. I'm not going to let anything hurt you. I swear it, by my mother's bones. Go to sleep. If you haven't figured out a solution in the morning, I've got one."

"I won't like it," she warned.

"That's to be expected."

"You won't leave me?"

"Not for a second. I told you the other night. You're mine, Magdalena. I won't stand aside for any man, much less a demon."

"I should be mad at you."

"Why?"

"You make it easy to feel safe." Her hand crept up and curled into his shirt, hanging on. "I'm not used to it. Besides, all that macho crap of saying I'm yours. You know."

"I know." Justin brushed the hair away from her face and traced her jaw line with one finger. "I know you're beautiful." He hated that she was scared enough to hang onto him.

She sniffed. "Going to sleep now."

He shifted, settling his free hand on the small of her back, under the covers. "Good. I'm right here if you need me."

She mumbled something and relaxed even further.

Justin held onto her and stared off into the dark. If they could protect these women, just these women in the house. That had to be something, right?

~ ☾ ~

CHAPTER NINETEEN

Serra came downstairs, yawning and rubbing her head. Daylight streamed inside the house. Gregor had turned to her at dawn, ravished her, and sent her into a sensual haze of completion. She never heard him get out of bed.

Now, a good two hours later, she was bemused at how easily he'd managed to lull her into a stupor. She didn't change, become small, either. Had she finally gained control over her second adolescence?

The kitchen was a hive of activity, all female. Hayden was at the stove, cooking scrambled eggs. Aubrey worked the coffee maker while Ursula sat pale and quiet in the corner, and Maggie stared out the back door.

"Morning everyone. Where are the men?" Serra moved to the table where a bowl of fruit sat, piled temptingly. She selected an apple and rubbed it on her t-shirt.

"They're outside, figuring out what to do about us." Maggie sniffed in frustration. "I got a hint of the idea from Justin, and trust me, I don't like it."

Serra only raised her eyebrows. "Do you see another way?" She crunched into the apple, savoring its sweetness.

Maggie turned to her, hands on her hips. "You mean, you know about it, too? And you're okay with it? I don't believe it."

"I know of only one solution to keeping you all safe here, and not pawns to be used by the demon that marked us all." She looked at the others, their puzzlement clear. "They don't know?"

"Not yet." Maggie took the cup of coffee passed to her by Aubrey and sat down at the big kitchen table. "Let's do our own powwow on this, shall we?"

Serra blinked, then sat. "We have a choice. We can let the demon take us, and die tonight, or we can hold fast." She

~ ☾ ~

looked at each of the women in turn. "Doc Cavanaugh can drug us until we are senseless. We will just sleep, safe, until the party is over and the demon has been destroyed."

Aubrey came to the table and sat with a thump. "Sleep?" she said doubtfully. "You want to drug us? I don't know about that."

Hayden humphed. She brought over a big bowl of scrambled eggs and a fistful of forks and plunked them down on the table. "Better to sleep than get munched." She flashed a look toward her sister, who kept her gaze firmly on the table. "It's probably the only way, Ursula," she added, her voice gentler. "You know we discussed it last night."

"Did we all come to the same conclusion, then?" Serra looked from one woman to another.

"What if the demon has humans working for him, and they track us down? What if we get found and can't fight because we're, oh, asleep?" demanded Aubrey. "I can't go along with that. I just can't." Panic edged her voice. "If I'm going to die, I want to die fighting."

"That's the problem, Aubrey. If you get near the demon, if you go to this celebration he's having tonight? You won't want to fight. You won't even totally be sure of your name. But you will die, and before you do, you'll know panic, and fear, for demons feed on those emotions. They crave them as much as vampires crave blood. You don't have the weapons to keep him out." Serra's mouth set as they sent terrified glances to each other.

"I swear everything will be done to keep us all safe. Between Maggie and I, the house is well guarded on a mystical plane. The Caines will make sure it's guarded on the physical plane. The only question is how long will we have to be out completely, in order to be safe from the demon?" Serra looked to Maggie, who shrugged.

"I don't have a clue. I'll call Doc Cavanaugh and see what she says. I'd like her to actually be here while we, you know." Maggie gestured.

Serra looked from one woman to another. "So. We're all agreed? A safe sleep, instead of sure slaughter tonight?" Slowly, one by one, the women all voiced their agreement.

~ ☾ ~

Ursula, too, though she bit her lip and refused to look at anyone else.

"Good. Now it's just a matter of logistics. Maggie, get on the phone. I'll go talk to the Caines."

~~~

They stood in the yard in front of the biggest barn, the sun shining warm down on them with just a chill of winter in the air. The perfect winter day in Southern California.

Gregor cradled a gray barn kitten, scritched it under the chin until it purred. "So we're all agreed? The women should be put into a deep sleep until the damned demon is killed?"

Justin looked to Kellan, who gave the idea two thumbs up.

"Looks like it's unanimous. Think we can get the wolves out here to play guard dogs, Justin?"

"I think so, as long as you don't put it to them in those terms." Justin sent an acerbic look toward Gregor, who just shrugged.

"I don't want anything happening to them," Kellan burst out. "How many more are marked? How many people will die tonight? Damn it. I'm so tired of being on the short end of the stick."

Gregor and Justin stared at their cousin's unusual outburst. "That bothered me, too," Gregor offered. His dreams had been filled with women screaming as they died. "We'd have to kill the demon before the party started."

Kellan stared at the ground. "I'll do a stakeout of the warehouse."

"No. Serra and I will do the stakeout." He brushed aside their exclamations, their concern. "Serra will be there whether I want her there or not. If I agree at the outset, then I can keep an eye on her. Do my best to keep her safe and alive." He refused to entertain any thought of her being hurt, much less killed.

Justin narrowed his eyes at Gregor. "You look different. Did you and the Fae get frisky?"

"Stop it."

"No, seriously. Different."

~ ☾ ~

Kellan's head snapped up and he narrowed his eyes on his cousin. A moment later, he whistled. "Oh man." Kellan and Justin exchanged a look.

Gregor shook his head, exasperated. "You are not going to get me to fall for that, guys. So just, please, stop it."

Kellan shoved his hands into his jeans pockets. "You've seen the bonding threads on Gabriel and Rose, right?"

"What's your point?" Gregor set the kitten down with a final scritch to its head. It bounced over to tackle one of its siblings, worrying at Justin's shoelaces.

"Well." Kellan brushed one hand down his cousin's suit-clad chest. "Not only am I seeing residual faerie sparkle on your clothes, but you've definitely added blue and purple to your aura. It's threaded through everything—you, your clothes, your hair—everything."

"Looks like you've caught yourself a Fae, Gregor. Should I say congratulations?" Justin's quiet voice penetrated the shock that had sunk into Gregor's bones.

"Humans can't bond to the Fae," he said, stunned.

"Aside from the fact you're not wholly human, how do you explain Gabriel and Rose? Gabe's got the Fae genes. Rose doesn't," Justin pointed out.

"She's part angel, which takes everything and twists it. This shouldn't happen to me." Gregor tried very hard not to whine. He hated whiners.

"Don't look now, but here she comes."

His heart gave a hard thump. Gregor spun around to see Serra walking toward them.

She shone in the winter sun, her hair a white-blonde riot around her face. Her sweater, an orangey-pink, clung to her figure, making Gregor ache to hold her. Purple and blue threads of color sparked in her aura, something Gregor had never seen before. Worse, they spun off her and led straight to him. His mind blurred with the implications.

Serra put her hand on Gregor's shoulder and went on tiptoe to kiss his cheek. "Good morning." Her purple eyes sparkled up at him and for the first time in his memory, Gregor felt heat in his cheeks. She turned her gaze to the other two. "Have you come to the same conclusion that we women have?"

~ ☾ ~

Justin spoke up. "Deep sleep for everyone until the demon has been killed. Stop it now, kittens," he reprimanded, and picked up both culprits. They climbed up to his shoulders and perched there.

"I knew you weren't slow," she said. "Maggie is calling Doc Cavanaugh."

Gregor shook himself out of his daze. "You and I will be the stakeout team."

"I was certain you'd want to wrap me up in cotton and keep me safely here." She slanted him a questioning look.

"It wouldn't have worked, not on a Warrior Fae. Besides, I'd rather have you with me." He looked down at her, surprised to find his arm wrapped around her waist. "There's got to be something that will keep us together when you start going crazy from the mark."

"Ask Magdalena," said Justin. "If anyone can figure out something, it would be her."

"Yeah, about that. Why don't you go in and ask her for me? Both of you?" Gregor looked from Kellan to Justin. "I need some time with Serra. Call Danny and get the werewolves' take on the situation, too."

Without another word, Justin set the kittens down and left, Kellan trailing him.

"What's going on?" Serra looked at him, amused. "What's so important that you needed to speak with me alone?"

Gregor shot a look toward the house and grimaced. "Let's go into the barn and feed the kittens." He steered her to where the barn doors stood open, out of sight of the kitchen windows. The place had once been a workshop but over the years it had become a storage pit. By dint of hard work and many hands, they'd cleared it. Now it worked once again as a tool shed, workshop, and home to the barn cats.

As he filled the bowls with food, Gregor knew uncertainty. He, who always had a focus, was decidedly unfocused, and it threw him off his game.

"You're worried. What's wrong?" Serra stopped just inside the barn doors.

"The bindings." He gestured to her, then himself. "I'm... I don't know what I am. Frustrated. Furious. Wild with

~ ☾ ~

anxiety. I'm most definitely not myself."

She stared. Took a breath, then stared again. "Oh."

"Did you know this would happen?" he demanded.

"No. I didn't have a clue." She crossed the barn to his side. "Gregor. We don't have to be bonded like this. We can fix this." Urgency thrummed through her words.

"How?" So she was eager to dissolve what was between them? That shook him almost as much as finding out about the bindings to begin with. "My parents were bonded. When my mother died, my father barely held it together. How do you dissolve something so strong?"

She gave him a sad smile. "You just need to make love to lots of women. As soon as you can. I take it you've never seen this before, with any of your other women?"

"Never."

"It happens in the Fae world. It happens." She shook her head. "But it's never happened to me before, either."

"So you need to make love to lots of men?" Saying the words left him with a bitter taste. "You could go back to Faeland today. It would at the very least keep you safe from the demon."

"The demon." She let out a mirthless chuckle. "I'd forgotten about that. No, I'm here for you, for the duration. We'll see the demon destroyed, then figure out the rest after."

He looked at her then. Shadows lingered in her eyes that hadn't been there moments earlier. How could he give her up? How could he keep her? If that were even the right way to think about it.

On a sigh, Gregor pulled her into his arms and just held her. She clung with equal fierceness to him, and a part of him settled. "You fit me, you know that? You fit, in so many ways. That kind of pisses me off right now."

"I'm not the only one who will fit you," she said in a soothing tone, her cheek resting against his chest. "Please don't worry about it. Let's just focus on getting rid of this damned demon. Okay?" Her arms tightened about him before letting him go.

As she stepped away, he knew a loss that rocked him to his soul.

~ ☾ ~

Serra gave him a crooked smile. "Come on. Let's go talk to Maggie, see if she can give us something to keep me safe tonight."

Gregor followed her back to the house. He knew they didn't need anything other than what they'd made between them. The mating bonds would hold her to him. Perhaps more than she would wish.

Give her up? Break those bonds? Fat chance. He'd thought they'd just enjoy each other while she was here, and then they'd both move on. Now that the truth had hit him between the eyes, he had no intention of letting her go.

~ ☾ ~

CHAPTER TWENTY

Cait checked the packing list, impatient at having to do the grunt work. Damn Frannie for dying. That so wasn't the plan. An accident, yes. Death? No. Damn it.

She'd just wanted Bryce for herself. Boy what a mistake. Now she was in so deep, there wasn't anywhere she could run.

Except... Cait stared at the delivery boy.

"Um, ma'am? Are the refrigerators all right?"

She shook herself. "Fine. They're fine. Everything works? They're plugged in and ready to go?"

"Yes, ma'am. If you'd just sign here for delivery." He handed her a clipboard. She signed where indicated, handed it back, and forgot he existed.

If she could just contact Maggie without anyone knowing. Without Bryce finding out. The *thing* on her hand terrified her, the black spot almost totally covering the red now. After waking up cold and scared the night before, she'd spent hours researching spells and found exactly nothing.

No answer from the rest of her old coven, though she'd left messages everywhere. And despite her determination to never come back to this warehouse, as soon as she woke up this morning she'd headed here without thought. It wasn't until she'd found herself at the computer checking the last minute to-do list for the party that she realized.

She was screwed.

"Not true, Caitlyn."

She stifled a scream at the feel of a hand brushing her neck. "Jesus, Kendall. You scared me." Her heart pounded. He couldn't read her mind. Could he?

He rounded the desk and sat on the corner. "How are preparations going?"

"Fine. Everything is just fine. The refrigerators are here

~ ☾ ~

and the meat will be delivered at noon. The champagne is coming in coolers, so we won't have to worry about keeping it cold." She took a breath. "The buzz is ferocious. We've got a Twitter hashtag going about the party. Of course, once the party actually starts, the building will be shielded, nothing in nor out electronically. I've set up feeds to automatically keep the buzz going all night."

Kendall smiled, his bright blue eyes steady on her. "Excellent. Soon they'll want one in New York. San Francisco. Seattle. Just a matter of time before we hit England, France, Spain and Germany."

A shiver went down her spine.

"Does that bother you? You, who have worked so hard with me for this day?"

"I expected to be at your side," she said, the lies coming easy. "But Bryce marked me." She thrust out her left hand. "Now I'm nothing but food."

He studied the mark on her hand with interest. "Well now, that's a complication. But one that's easily erased. Tell me. You weren't seriously thinking about throwing yourself on the mercy of Magdalena and the Caines?"

Her heart leaped with hope. "I panicked. The pain—"She choked on the memory. "Bryce left me alone, helpless, here in the warehouse. I panicked. I'm not proud of it, but I do admit it." She curled her fingers over the mark on her hand. "But no one has returned my calls, so fuck them."

"So you remain."

"I'm here. Loyal to you. Not to Bryce, no. Only to you." Inspiration struck. She moved around the desk and sank to the ground on her knees to kiss his polished loafer. "My loyalty is all to you."

"Rise, child," he said, and helped her stand. He trailed his fingers down her arm until he reached her hand. He traced the circle in her palm with his finger against her skin. As his finger lifted up and away from her, the color slowly rose in the air until her palm was as it had been, unmarked to her eyes.

Sweet relief flooded Cait and her breath caught. "Thank you. Thank you so much." She caught his hand and kissed it,

~ ☾ ~

staring at him in open adoration. "Oh Kendall," she sighed. "I have missed you."

He stood. "There will be time tomorrow to take our relationship to the next step," he promised. "Or rather, to take it back to the next step. I think finally our appetites match, as they didn't when we were in school." He kissed her cheek. "Now be a good girl and finish up your preparations for the party. You really are the only one who can do it the right way."

She walked with him to the door, reassured and accepting of her role in the events to come. "You'll be here, right?"

He slipped on sunglasses, hiding his eyes. "You will see me before the end," he promised. He drew his thumb across her cheek. "You have all my gratitude," he added, and pressed a surprisingly chaste kiss on her mouth. "Enjoy your day."

Cait didn't know how long she stood in the doorway, her hand to her lips and her mind blank. A delivery truck pulled up, and a rough-looking man got out.

"Is this where you're wanting the ten coolers of champagne?" He hitched his pants around his wide waist.

Cait, startled, gave him a broad smile. "Yes. Yes, of course. I'll show you where to store them."

Her heart light, she led him into the storeroom. She was the only person who could handle the details of this party, and she was sure it would be world-class. The Twitterverse would be tweeting about it for *hours*. Humming under her breath, she settled down to the rest of her tasks with a bubbling sense of anticipation.

~~~

"You marked her." Fury rattled the room.

Bryce set his teeth and refused to look scared. "I had to. Besides, you told me I could. Or did you forget?" Bitterness filled his voice. "It's not like I'm unmarked." He thrust out his hand, the circle there in his palm throbbing.

"You were supposed to wait. Wait. Is that such a difficult concept for you?"

"She pissed me off, man. What about my mark? Why

aren't you angry about that?"

Kendall looked at Bryce with disdain. "You will do your job and be glad about it." He waved his hand twice. "There's nothing wrong with you that you can see. You don't even know what I'm talking about. Everything on track for the party?"

Bryce stared. He'd been anxious, upset, but really. What was there to be upset about? And why was his hand sticking out like that? He shoved both hands in his pockets. "Sorry, man. Don't know what you're talking about. Of course everything's on track for the party. So far, Dalton's been the perfect guest." He frowned, something tickling the back of his mind.

"I'm so glad. There aren't many hours before the party. Go, check up on Cait and make sure she doesn't need any help. You'll need to keep an eye on the caterers and the waiters."

"Sure boss. No problem." Bryce picked up his keys and headed out of his apartment, whistling as he went. He was halfway to his car before he remembered Kendall. Had the guy actually been there? Bemused, he shook his head. Too much weed the night before, that was all. Just too much weed.

He headed out to the warehouse.

~~~

Megan Cavanaugh stared at the five women and three men like they'd all gone crazy. "You want me to do *what*?"

"Anesthesia. For four of us. We just don't know how long it'll take."

Maggie sent an outraged glare to Serra. "Make that three of us."

"Maggie," murmured Justin. "Do you really want to be demon fodder?"

"I don't have those kinds of resources." Megan looked around and spread her hands. "I've got one anesthesiologist at the moment. One. Not enough to handle four patients, not safely anyway."

Gregor gave it some thought. "What about a shot?

~ ☾ ~

Something you can just pop in to keep them senseless?"

Megan sighed. "How long do I have to do some research?"

Gregor checked his watch. "No more than a couple of hours. We're not sure when the demon will exert his pull."

"There's also the possibility that no matter how deeply they're put under, they'll still try to get to the demon." Justin took Maggie's hand. "I know this one will do her damnedest."

"So we might have to restrain them to the beds. I shall leave that in your hands," Megan said, looking from Kellan to Justin. "You know there's always a danger with sedatives. I'll need everyone to sign a release form. I'll do my best, but you all are not my patients. We don't have time to do full histories on each of you, so there is real risk involved."

"Doc? Between dying in bed here and dying at the hands of a demon, I definitely choose here, in bed, while I'm asleep," said Aubrey. "It's taken me a couple hours to get there, but now? I'll sign anything."

Kellan looked at her, speculation in his eyes.

Gregor coughed. "Magdalena, Serra needs your expertise. If you could go with her? Aubrey, you and Kellan and Justin will work out the logistics. Which rooms, what type of restraints, that sort of thing."

"Right. Come on, Serra, let's go out into the garden."

Serra, after a steely look at Gregor, followed.

"What about us?" Hayden kept her arm around her sister, who refused to look up from the floor.

He turned to Ursula and Hayden with a reassuring smile. "Do you mind if I put the two of you in charge of food? Make sure everyone is fueled up for the fight to come. Even though you'll be unconscious, that doesn't necessarily mean you won't be fighting for your lives."

Hayden grinned in relief. "We can do that. Come on, Urse. Let's make some brownies. Chocolate is a great stress reliever." The two women left the room.

Justin frowned. "I worry about Ursula. She's completely shut down. I can't get even a glimpse of her, mentally."

"I worry about all of you. Of all the totally insane plans," fumed Megan.

~ ☾ ~

"Um, I'm going to help make brownies." Aubrey made her escape.

Leaving just Gregor, Kellan and Justin to face Megan's wrath. "Could you have come up with a stupider idea? Because I really don't think so."

"Then come up with a better one. In just a couple of hours, mind you, because we don't have a lot of time." Kellan crossed his arms and narrowed his eyes at the petite blonde in front of them.

"I can't. I've been worrying about it since you told me, and I can't think of a single thing that will take care of the women without putting them, or the people around them, in greater danger." She sat abruptly on the couch and put her head in her hands. "I'm scared I won't be able to take care of them properly."

"I'd let Maggie help you, but if she's conscious at all, she'll be doing her best to get to the demon. Compulsions can override even the strongest will." Justin put a reassuring hand on Megan's shoulder. "If it helps at all, we have complete faith in you."

"Wait, wait wait. Maybe you won't have to restrain them," Megan said, her eyes wide. "And maybe I won't have to knock them out. You've got the full-blooded Fae out there. She can do all of that. Make the women unable to hear, see, feel, even move. It's most likely the only thing that will keep them safe."

Gregor looked off to where Serra had gone. "If that's true, why didn't she say so?"

"No clue. But someone should ask her. I'd much rather watch over women who're magically unable to move than ones that are chemically unable to move." Megan stared from one man to the other. "Don't you agree?"

~~~

The sun overhead warmed them as they sat in a protected corner of the yard.

Serra sent a wry glance to Maggie. "There's nothing you can do to protect me from the compulsion, you know."

Maggie frowned. "I know. But the men don't know that."

~ ☾ ~

Besides, maybe you already carry your protection with you."

"How do you mean?"

"You're bonded. To Gregor. I can see it."

Serra sighed even as warmth spread through her that had nothing to do with the sun. "Great. Does everyone know?"

"His brothers, surely. The others? Probably not. But the thing is, that bonding between you comes first over any compulsion. It will always come first, unless you deliberately break it. And since the winter solstice is tonight, my guess is there isn't time to break it beforehand, which is a good thing."

She looked down at her hands. "You're suggesting I trust those bonds to keep me safe. Use it, use Gregor, no matter what my personal feelings about the situation may be."

"Yes."

"And if the bonds fail? What then?" She looked up into Maggie's sympathetic eyes. "Am I doomed to become a demon's chew toy?"

"You don't believe in what has blossomed between the two of you?" Shock crossed Maggie's face. "A bonding is to be celebrated. It's not something that just happens all willy-nilly."

Serra jumped up and walked to the nearest tree and back, frustration dogging her. "You see, that's where you're wrong. It may be my first time, but it happens all the time with the Fae. And there are steps we take, all the time, to break those bondings. It's as normal and as irritating as the fertility cycle."

Maggie stifled a laugh. "Okay. But you're not in Faeland, and you didn't bond to another Fae, Serra. You bonded to a complex human, who happens to have Fae and demon bloodlines. You're not exactly Gregor's first love, you know. If he were meant to bond before, he would have. Don't you think?"

Scowling, Serra came back to sit beside Maggie. "I don't know what to think anymore. Except that it's becoming clear my life will be in his hands tonight."

Maggie shook her head in sympathy. "Not so, my friend. It's not his hands that will save you. It's the bonding between you, and what lies in both your hearts. That's how you will get

~ ☾ ~

through the night alive. And, I might add, you'll be protecting him just as much as he'll be protecting you. The bonding goes both ways."

"How do you know so much about a Fae custom? I don't know whether to be impressed or irritated."

"I've seen the bonds in action. Gabriel Caine is Gregor's half brother. They share a mom, but Gabriel's sperm-donor was a full demon. Still, his bloodlines held. He had enough Fae inside him that when he fell in love with Rose, they became bonded. I totally believe that's the only way he was able to find her that horrible night."

Silence fell between the women. Serra felt pulled in too many directions. There were things she could do, but would they work? Should she do them, if it meant cutting herself off from Gregor? "I'll have to think about all you have said. In the meantime, we will not lie. You have given me the only protection possible, even if it was just to remind me that it existed. We don't have to tell them exactly what you did."

"Got it."

Gregor came toward them from the house, his hands stuffed in his pockets and his tie partially undone.

Maggie smiled. "You're good for him, you know. He's nowhere near as stuffy as he used to be." She stood and squeezed Serra's shoulder. "I'll just go in, see how everyone else is doing."

Serra watched as Maggie and Gregor stopped in the middle of the yard and briefly spoke, before Gregor came on, his steps slower now.

"Hey."

She smiled. "Come sit with me."

He settled beside her and picked up her hand. "I want to get one thing clear, before we go any further."

"What?"

"I have no wish to sleep with a dozen other women. Or even one other woman. The only woman I want in my bed for any reason whatsoever is you. So if you don't want this bonding between us, you'll have to be the one to break it. Because I can't, and I won't."

Fear bubbled up inside her, mingled with a painful type of

joy. She couldn't stay here, couldn't pretend to be human. Or could she? If she could, she would want no other man than Gregor. He was her other half, her complementary half.

"Thank you for your honesty." Her hand clenched on his. "I appreciate it, more than you know. I heard from Maggie that bonding in this world doesn't happen often."

"She's right. It doesn't. I told you about my parents. My dad held it together until we were all more or less on our own, then he split." He shrugged, but it was obvious to her that he missed his father.

"It's not quite like that in the Fae world." Which gave her something else to think about.

"So, onto another subject. Megan said you could bind the women in their beds, so they couldn't hear, speak, see, or move. Is that true?"

Anger flashed through her. Serra stood, all the soft feelings burned out of her for the moment. "I can see I need to speak to the good doctor."

Gregor stood beside her. "She's waiting to speak with you as well."

Serra was halfway to the house before she took another breath. Fury all but blinded her, and when Gregor put a hand on her shoulder, she almost snarled at him. "What is it?"

He took his hand away warily. "Just wanted to remind you that Megan isn't Fae. She knows a lot, but she isn't Fae, and she may have gotten some information wrong. It's not her fault. There's not exactly a book of the Fae lying about, giving humans all the details they need about how to deal with you people."

She sent him a look that should have shriveled him where he stood. "A lot you know." Her hand on the kitchen door, she sorted rapidly through her thoughts and emotions, struggling to bring them into some semblance of order. Megan was Fae, and the Caines didn't know it, which meant she had to keep the doctor's secret. "Humans are just so much work," she said finally, before heading inside.

~~~

~ ☾ ~

"You know nothing," Serra insisted.

Gregor watched warily from the doorway into the hearth room, where the two women were verbally battling. The two blondes, one pixie-sized, the other a tall and willowy shape, stared each other down in front of the fireplace.

"I know that you can handle these women with one hand tied behind your back. That it won't hurt them, that they won't be drugged, and that they can't die from it," Megan shot back.

"I can't believe you want me to put a numbing on them. Have you no heart? Have you totally forgotten everything?" Incredulous, Serra dropped down into the couch and curled her feet underneath her.

Not even the scent of brownies stealing through the room could divert Gregor's attention.

"You want me to pump them full of drugs? What if I kill one of them? Where's your heart?" Megan, hands on her hips, faced Serra. "If what I'm asking is so wrong, why don't you explain it to me?"

"Because we don't talk about our punishments to outsiders," Serra bit out.

Silence fell in the room. The three men, lounging around the perimeter, straightened up. Megan's eyes were wide with shock. No one said a word.

Finally, Megan sighed and moved to sit beside Serra. "Tell me," she said simply. "So I, so we, can all understand."

"You are asking for all sights, sounds and movement to be taken away. How would you like it, not being able to hear, see, talk, or move? It's called 'numbing', and it's a punishment that can make the Fae go mad."

"It can't be that bad." Megan bit her lip. "Can it?"

Serra raised an eyebrow. "Let me demonstrate."

Gregor cleared his throat and took a couple steps into the room. "Demonstrate on me, then. Not Megan."

Megan waved him away. "Demonstrate on all of us. If you can."

At first Gregor thought that everyone had fallen silent. Then he spoke, and realized he couldn't hear himself. His vision blurred, went dark. And when he tried to take a step,

~ ☾ ~

he realized he'd been immobilized.

Panic gripped him. He could feel the sweat on his forehead, knew his heart tripped hard in his chest even as he struggled to breathe. Without warning, all his senses came back and he staggered in the doorway, still talking.

Everyone was talking. Megan shouting, Kellan swearing, Maggie with her hands tight over her mouth, and Justin doing his calming mantra.

"Stop it, everyone. Stop!" He had to raise his voice loud enough to cut through, but they heard and looked toward him. Megan's eyes were haunted. Kellan and Justin both had a spooked look about them.

Finally, he looked at Serra, her chin lifted in defiance, her mouth set in a thin line. Shame radiated from her, and she refused to meet anyone's gaze. He went to her, brushed her shoulder with his fingertips.

"I understand now. I'm sorry we pushed you. I understand."

She didn't look at him, but her breath shuddered out of her and she gripped his hand. "Thank you."

"How...how did you do that?" Megan's eyes were wide with both fear and awe. "I couldn't move. How?"

"It's a weaving. The Fae use their knowledge of the natural world. Of air, fire, water, earth and all the energies that naturally reside here. The numbing can be done in whole or parts, using weaves of air." She looked from person to person. "It's complicated and takes time to learn, but it can be done. You can see why I refuse to use it on those women. The stress alone could cause them to have a heart attack."

Megan tapped her fingers on her leg. "Okay. So maybe we don't use the whole enchilada. Maybe we only use it to keep them still. Weaves of air around their legs, say. Which would prevent them from moving. That, plus a sedative, that could work."

"And if I'm captured, or die? If I can't come back to undo the weave, what then? Would you really subject these women to that kind of torture? I'm sorry. I won't do it, not even to keep them safe. We'll have to think of something else."

Maggie cleared her throat. "If you die or are captured,

won't the spell just dissipate? I mean, when I do something very intensive, I need to keep a mental eye on it. Check it every few minutes or so to keep it strong. If I were to die with that kind of spell going on, the spell would just stop."

Serra sighed. "What I do isn't a spell. It's an actual weave. The Fae don't do spells, not in the way you think. We call, and the elements answer."

"It's back to the drugs then." Resigned, Megan stood. "I'll go do some research, bring what I need." She held out a hand to Serra. "I'm sorry I pushed you, but thank you for the explanation and the demonstration. Sometimes I'm pigheaded and need to be forced to see all sides." A muffled snort from one of the men had her glaring about suspiciously.

Serra took her hand. "I understand. We all have a common goal, and that's the important thing to remember."

Megan grimaced at her and left.

Kellan stood and stretched. "I think I'll hit up the Hustler store in Hollywood."

Justin snickered. "Need some porn?"

"For your information, they have handcuffs. Fur lined. Plus ropes that can be used to tie people up, ropes that won't leave a nasty rope burn on delicate skin." Kellan headed to the door, only to run into Aubrey.

"Can I go with you? I'm desperate to get out of here," she said, casting an anxious look over her shoulder. "Ursula is angry and scared and Hayden is being all Disney cheerful. It's driving me demented."

"You got it. Let's go." He slung an arm around a surprised Aubrey and waved at the rest of them as they went.

"Be back here by two, kids," called Gregor. The front door slammed.

~ ☾ ~

CHAPTER TWENTY-ONE

Gregor perched on the roof of the building across the parking lot from where they'd shut the portal and scanned the area, Serra at his side.

Winter dark had come quickly and with it, a frigid wind. Across from them, a red carpet had been unrolled. Workers had been coming and going for hours, but there'd been no sign or scent of the demon.

Serra moved, restless. "I still think I should go to the party. Do an up close and personal recon and kill."

"No."

"Be reasonable. He's not going to come out here, not when his dinner is going to him. Why should he? He's probably been inside there since we closed the portal."

"You're not going inside." He'd sworn to keep her safe. How could he do that if he couldn't even see her?

"Not even with you as my escort?" She leaned her head against his shoulder. "I figure if we go in together, toward the end of the night, we might actually have a chance."

"No." But his resolve weakened in the face of her arguments. Why should the demon come outside? He lowered his binoculars. "If we go in together, we'll be trapped together. The likelihood of both of us getting out of there alive is slim to none."

"Then I'll go. I've got the invite, after all, and you don't," she said. "But you are going to have to let me in, mentally."

She'd been patient with him, so he lifted his shields on purpose. *I don't want to lose you.* Reaching out to her mentally felt awkward, like his first time on a skateboard.

Her arms went around him. *I'm very hard to lose, and I'm as protected as I can be. If we don't do this, how many will die?*

How many will die, even if we do?

~ ☾ ~

"You cannot think that way. If we can prevent that demon from finishing the breeding cycle, then we have saved thousands. Tens of thousands."

She was right. He knew it, but it went against his grain to just allow her to walk right into danger. "Serra..."

"Let's get off this roof, go to my apartment. I need to change for the party."

They scooted around the air-conditioning unit, shielding themselves from the building opposite before they stood and made their way to the far side where they'd left the rope ladder.

Once back on the ground, he brushed her cheek with his knuckles. "I don't want anything to happen to you."

She lifted a brow. "Gregor. We must put what's between us aside, or we'll never get through this night. Terrell taught me that." She coiled the rope and hung it on one arm. "Come on.

"I know you're right." He frowned, searching for the right words as they walked the dark streets. "I'm not used to caring, I guess."

"Not even for your brothers?" They reached his car and got in.

Gregor ignored her question as he moved them into sluggish traffic. "Which way to your apartment?"

She directed him there. While she got ready, he roamed the sterile environment. White walls, a bed, a couch. Nothing else except a bowl of fruit in the kitchen. "It looks like you're not planning to stay long." It looked a lot like his house, he admitted.

"Did you look in my closet?"

Gregor moved to the bedroom closet. It was jammed with clothes. Dresses, skirts, jeans, pants, boots, shoes of all sorts. "What did you do, rob Macy's?" He shoved his hands into his pockets, astounded and not sure what to think.

"I like human clothes." Serra came out in a simple white, floor-length sheath dress. It had a high neckline and long sleeves, and a slit up one side to mid-thigh. It clung to her every curve, leaving nothing to the imagination. "What do you think?" She turned around, slowly, until she faced him again.

His jaw dropped. "There's no back to that dress."

~ ☾ ~

She smiled. "I know. I love this dress."

"I wish I could undress you. I wish I could—" He stopped when she put a finger across his lips, her eyes steady on his.

"Gregor. I know. This will not be our last day together, I promise you."

"How can you—?" This time, she stopped his mouth with her own.

~~~

"Music will help." They'd moved a second bed into the master bedroom in order to keep better watch over the women. Now Megan put soothing chants on the iPod. The sound filled the room.

Maggie looked over at Justin, hovering near by. "You'd better not let me out of this bed, Justin." Her hands were handcuffed to the headboard and a blanket covered her body.

He grinned. "I've been waiting for you to say that for months, woman."

At her snort of annoyance, he moved to her side and sat beside her. Brushed her hair out of her eyes. "Don't worry. I'm right here. I'm not going to let anything happen to you."

"So you'll let the bad guys get us and not Maggie?" Aubrey snorted. She lay next to Maggie. "Gee, thanks for that."

Kellan shot a glare at her. "Nothing's going to happen to you. To any of you. Trust me, you're not going anywhere. Not if we have anything to say about it."

"Hey, where's Ursula?" Hayden lifted her head. "She should be back from the bathroom by now."

Megan bolted for the bedroom door and dashed down the hall.

"Justin?" Maggie's worried gaze met his, and he sent a reassuring smile.

"It'll be okay, Maggie. We can't protect someone if they don't want to be protected."

"Who says she doesn't want to be protected? Damn you, Kellan, stay away from me." Her face red with rage, Hayden kicked out at him. Justin noticed that Kellan dodged her kick and moved out of range, keeping a close eye on her.

~ ☾ ~

Megan returned, her brow furrowed and her shoulders slumped. "I'm sorry, Hayden. Your car is gone. Ursula is gone."

Justin stood and reached for his cell phone. "I'll warn Gregor. Maybe he can intercept her."

Hayden just stared at him, all the angry color gone from her face. "She's gone? Oh, Justin."

His heart aching for her, he went to stand at one side of her bed. "Do you want to be freed? Do you want to go to her? I'll loan you my car. It's totally your call. We're not keeping anyone here that doesn't want to be here."

Indecision fluttered across her face. "I don't know. I don't know what to do. She's always been there. We've always been there for each other. What would you do? If it were Gregor?"

"I'd go. I'd risk it. Family is everything."

She stared at him wonderingly. "And people think you're shallow."

He gave a brief laugh at that. "What do you want to do? Stay or go?"

Hayden squeezed her eyes shut. A tear trickled out of the corner of one eye. "I'd better go. Ursula isn't the best driver. She panics, you know? She gets lost and scared."

Justin fished the keys to the handcuffs out of his pocket. He released her wrists and helped her to stand, handing her the keys to his Jaguar at the same time.

"Hayden. Are you sure?" Maggie's voice, sharp with anxiety, seemed to stiffen Hayden's resolve.

"I'm sure, Maggie." She went swiftly to her friend and kissed her cheek. "Blessed be, sister." She repeated the same with Aubrey, and looked around the room. With a wry smile, she shook her head. "It's been interesting, Justin. Kellan. Blessed be."

Without glancing at Megan, Hayden left.

Justin moved to Megan's side. "You have the happy juice?"

Megan gestured to the syringes on the dresser. "Right there." She checked her watch. "It's almost seven. If Ursula already felt the call to go, perhaps we should get this sleepover started?" She slanted a glance toward Justin, who frowned.

"I don't know. How long will it last?"

~ ☾ ~

"The good thing is we now have twice what we had originally. If we have to, we can hit them up again," Megan said briskly.

Grateful for her no-nonsense approach, Justin looked to Kellan but his cousin was watching Aubrey. He turned back to Megan. "Let's get it done. It'll be easier on them, I think, if they're as insensible as possible."

"Right." Megan picked up a syringe and took a deep breath. "Here goes," she said, and walked over to Maggie.

Justin looked at the phone still in his hand. "I'll call Gregor now, have him keep an eye out for the girls." Saying a brief prayer for humanity, Justin placed the call.

~~~

"Give me a thirty-minute head start, Gregor. Promise me." Serra stood with her hand on her front door. "I'm going to need a little time to lure him outside. Plus I want to see if I can find Ursula and Hayden."

"I don't like it."

"I know. But you'll give me the time." Pictures floated in her mind then, and she gasped. "It's Cash. Oh no."

Gregor reached out to steady her as she swayed on her pencil-thin heels. "Is he still alive?"

"He may as well not be." She pressed a hand to her chest. "He's working the party, opening bottles of champagne. Not many people are there yet. I can try to get him out of there, but unfortunately, my powers won't countermand a direct order if he's been marked like me. Oh. He's there, too," she said, and wondered.

"He? He who?" Gregor's hands tightened on her shoulders.

"The death mage. Kendall Sorbis." She shuddered, remembering the emptiness in the man's eyes.

"If you can, kill him."

"That's the plan. You're not coming with me." Serra used all the suggestive power she had. "Whether Kendall is there or not doesn't change anything. You're giving me half an hour head start."

~ ☾ ~

She eased from his grip and opened her front door. Giving him a last look, she tapped his chest. "We're connected. If you need to find me, search for the bondings."

"Gabriel said we can travel them if we need to." Urgency thrummed through him, transmitted itself to her.

"Emergencies only. I'm serious, Gregor. Reach to my mind first. If I don't respond, then." She pressed herself against him one more time, refusing to think why she might not be able to respond. "Half an hour. I'm counting on you." She kissed his cheek and left, closing the door behind her, not wanting to hear goodbye.

The night pressed close, the fog closer. She got into her car and headed out, the way seemingly clear in front of her. Behind her, the fog gathered in.

The drive didn't take long. Serra was drawn to the place. It didn't feel like a semi-abandoned airport hangar; the outside now had the looks of a fancy nightclub. Trees in huge wooden boxes surrounded the doorway, where two bouncers in tuxes waited and a red carpet emerged.

White twinkle lights were wrapped in the trees, and the light from the doorway held a shimmer.

The welcome was about as subtle as a sledgehammer. Serra parked and grimaced. She'd have to go in there in order to bring the demon back outside. Maggie had better be right. The connection between her and Gregor had better be enough to keep her from the thrall.

She got out of the car and smoothed her dress. She could feel the urgency of the demon. It was hungry, anxious. Searching. For her? Probably. If there were another full Fae wandering around with a mark on its palm, she'd be very surprised.

Her pulse pounded in her temples. The saving grace in all this was that he'd be too busy gorging himself before he got around to killing her. Technically, that should give her a few hours to figure out how to beat him.

She crossed the parking lot to the doors streaming out their welcome. One burly man blocked her entrance.

"Hand," he barked.

Serra lifted up her left hand and dazzled him with a smile.

~ ☾ ~

He smiled back and let her pass.

The cold, joyless hangar had been transformed into a cozy nightclub setting. What looked like puffy clouds hung from the high ceiling, dotted with twinkle lights. Amy Winehouse's smoky soul voice added even more atmosphere.

The room was already crowded. Lots of women, yes, but some men were there, too. Tuxedo-clad waiters carried around trays full of brimming champagne glasses, while girls in French maid uniforms handed out appetizers.

Serra searched but couldn't see the blond man or the dark one. Spotting Cash at a bar in a distant corner, she reached to him. *Cash. Go now, while you still can. Go while you still live.*

Across the distance she saw him clutch his head and look about wildly. *Show me your hands, Cash.*

He lifted them off his head, palms out. She couldn't see any mark and knew a measure of relief. He was one person she could save. *Go. Now. Without making a scene. Make an excuse to go to the bathroom or something, and leave. Don't turn back, no matter what.* The compulsion she added to her voice was stronger than most humans could resist.

Cash scratched his head, made what looked like a joking remark to the waiter who'd come up to the bar, and vanished through a door hidden amongst the fabric draping the cement walls.

A waiter thrust a glass of champagne in her hand as he passed. Serra sipped, then twisted her lips. Something about the champagne was slightly off. Or maybe it was her?

Keeping the glass in her hand, Serra moved about, searching, searching for the dark one. She saw Kendall and ducked her head, moving into a crowd of people. The last thing she needed was him noticing her, hanging onto her.

She couldn't see the demon Dalton anywhere.

Serra walked the edges of the room, skirting clumps of potted trees tucked in corners, gently touching the fabric that fell from the ceiling to cover the walls and pool on the floor. On two sides, the fabric touched the edge of the actual walls. Spying a slit in the fabric on the third wall, Serra poked through and took a peek.

~ ☾ ~

Four feet of space between the fabric and the wall. Looking swiftly in both directions, she didn't see any other doors, but it looked like the corridor continued around the corner to the left. A serving hallway, perhaps?

She returned to the room just as a romantic waltz filled the air. Nerves fluttered in her stomach.

Serra. See anything useful?

She grimaced. *No sign of the big bad.* She sent a mental picture of what she had seen so far. *I think there might be dancing.*

Gregor chuckled. *Oh, horrors. Just keep your eyes open. If you need to, hide.*

Hide? Please. There's got to be close to a thousand people in here.

Just trying to keep you safe.

A tap on her shoulder had her whirling around, champagne spilling out all over the person behind her.

"Oh gosh, I'm so sorry," she gushed, and looked up at the man in front of her. Shock lanced through her even as she smiled. *Target acquired, Gregor. Currently in human form.* She felt him acknowledge it even as the demon's scent crashed over her. She sneezed twice.

A waiter stood there with a cloth, brushing at the champagne dripping from the man's tuxedo. "It is no matter." His dark voice rumbled through her. "May I have this dance?" He waited, the jutting bones of his face and jaw combined with the look of the hunter in his eyes to send a chill down her spine.

"Of course." Serra handed her glass to the waiter and tested her mental bond to Gregor. Still there, still strong.

Simpering slightly, she even gave a little curtsey to the demon in front of her. "I'd love to dance, though I'm not very good at the waltz."

"I will lead. I am a good leader." He swept her into his arms and onto the dance floor, where other couples circled around. His hand on her bare back burned. "I am Dalton." He bent his head to her neck and breathed in her scent. "You are Fae."

Serra blinked. She hadn't expected such a direct attack.

~ ☾ ~

Maybe he thought she was too...infected? She twittered. "How clever you are. Not many humans know what I am, and even when I tell them, they don't believe me." She looked around. "Wonderful party," she added brightly.

"I am glad you approve." The sincerity in his voice rang true. "I will do everything in my power to please you."

Again, Serra felt the incongruity of his words. Nothing was matching up the way she had expected. He was ugly, yes, but his voice soothing, his words nothing she could possibly take exception to.

His touch, however, made her skin crawl and the sigil on her hand burn. She wrapped the bonding light with Gregor around her skin as tightly as she could and the feel of the beast surrounding her lessened.

Serra needed to breathe. His stench made her head whirl, and she desperately needed fresh air. "My, I am out of shape." She laughed as he whirled her around the floor. "Shall we get some fresh air? It's awfully stuffy in here."

"I don't find it stuffy. I'm fine. But there are windows. I will have them opened for you."

"Ah. How nice." Damn it. Casting an anxious glance around the place, she noticed the single women following their every move, some with longing in their eyes, some with the fires of jealousy. "Wow, you've got some admirers. You should probably dance with the rest of your lovely guests."

He stopped them abruptly at the edge of the dance floor. "As you wish." He released her with obvious reluctance. "We do, after all, have all night." Taking a flute from a passing waiter, he handed it to her with a slight bow before turning away.

Serra made it to the entryway but found it barred. A bouncer stood there, a different one from before. He seemed apologetic but firm.

"Sorry, miss. No one out and no one else in. The crowds out there would go crazy if I opened this door," he said.

She retreated. *Gregor. The bouncer is preventing anyone from leaving. Any line outside the building?*

I'm not there yet. Frustration simmered in his mental voice. *The damned stupid fog has me all twisted. I can't seem*

~ ☾ ~

to get there from here. It's like there's something deliberately keeping me away.

But you know which direction I'm in? You can sense me, right? Serra frowned as the beat of the music pulsed through her body.

Yes.

Keep trying. I'm counting on you.

Serra broke the mental link between them and watched as Dalton went from woman to woman, flattering them, making them blush, sweat, and giggle. She tried to blend in with the white walls, hiding behind a clump of trees. As an hour or so passed, more and more of the partygoers stumbled. From too much champagne, or something else? She couldn't tell.

A scent arose. Musty, moldy, with a whiff of stale wine and the burn of copper. Serra locked in on Dalton, who had a woman draped over him. As she watched, he calmly ripped off the woman's left ear and began munching.

~ ☾ ~

CHAPTER TWENTY-TWO

Gregor cursed the filthy fog that pressed down on him and struggled once more to head south to the Santa Monica airport. He should have been there, watching out for Serra, a full two hours ago but had been driving in circles. Traffic jams, accidents, and the damned, *unnatural* fog prevented him from going the way he needed to go.

When he turned north for the twentieth time on Lincoln Boulevard, he gave up and took the next tiny street south. He knew it was a dead end, but it would do. He parked his beloved, battered Mercedes and got out.

The fog seemed to lift, thinning in front of him as he faced north.

He could walk, or he could run. Or he could call on his demon heritage and run like the wind. He hadn't done it in years, not since his mother's death. Not since he rejected his mixed blood. Midnight grew near, though, and he didn't have time to lose.

A part of him panicked as he began jogging south, an incongruous sight in his three-piece suit and camel-hair trench coat. A breeze freshened the air, seeming to come from the sea. It blew the fog further eastward, clearing the way in front of him.

As he poured on speed, panic gave way to joy. Soon he was running too fast for human eyes to see. Miles flew under his feet within minutes until a surprising scent caught at him and he came to an abrupt stop.

Ursula's car. He walked around the battered Honda. He could smell her fear, her anxiety as she headed toward the demon that called her. Hayden had been here, too; he caught sight of Justin's Jag parked not far away. Both scents were hours old at this point.

He headed out at a jog now, feeling a subtle repellant in

~ ☾ ~

the air, turning him aside from his goal. Focusing on the bonds with Serra, he could see, faintly, the blue and purple strands going off in front of him. He kept his gaze on those bonds and ignored everything else.

He almost missed the place. The trees he'd seen with his own eyes earlier were gone, as was the red carpet. The door was tightly closed, and the whole building had an abandoned feel to it. Illusion?

Circling around the building, he was met everywhere with the same sense of abandonment. Long empty, long disused.

His blood boiled at the palpable lie. He checked once more, saw those bonding threads heading straight into the building. Straight to where Serra waited for him.

If he couldn't get in, it was glaringly apparent she couldn't get out. Rage roared through him at being kept from her, and he shook from the fear shredding his control.

While he could still think straight, he stripped off his coat and clothes, down to his t-shirt and boxers, and stuffed them behind a bush at the corner of the building. Focusing on his demon side, he called it forth, roaring a challenge. As if in answer, the heavens opened up and rain poured down. Thick clouds carried thunder and lightning in them as well as the rain.

Gregor roared again and jumped to the fire escape at one side of the building. Climbing quickly, his form changed as he moved. He convulsed, the pain catching him off guard, but he forced himself to keep climbing. Once on the roof, he took stock.

His feet had grown to almost twice their normal size, and his hands, also bigger, now ended in wicked-sharp claws, thick and unbreakable. His body gleamed like obsidian in the dark, and an otherworldly power pumped through him, giving him a rush of adrenalin.

A choking sound from one corner of the roof caught his attention and he swiveled, narrowing his gaze to see a human cowering against an air conditioning unit.

Cash.

Gregor resisted the urge to move to him. "Cash, it's Gregor Caine. Are you okay?" His voice had deepened to a guttural

~ ☾ ~

tone that reverberated in the night.

The man shivered, all the remembered bravado long gone. "She saved me. Now they're dying down there. Dying. All of them."

Gregor's eyes sharpened. "What do you mean?"

"I can smell it. Through the vents." Cash gestured to a vent large enough for a child to go through. "Is she okay? I mean, I think she is. I can't tell, but I know I'm still tied to her. I can't leave."

"Let me check." He concentrated on Serra. *Where are you? Damn it, Serra. Are you still alive?*

Gregor. Relief saturated her mental tone. *I'm coming out to you. I'm coming.*

Before he could relax, pain slashed through her. He could feel it, whip strokes across her back, filled with poison and something worse.

Serra, its okay, we can help. Just get to the door.

But she didn't answer. Her touch in his mind was gone.

~~~

The killing had started earlier. As more people dropped, some started screaming. Running. Dalton had just grinned and snatched those running, those whose adrenalin was high, and tore them apart, limb by limb, sucking the blood from them as it fountained out.

He'd changed fully into his demon self now; two mouths, four arms, just like the demon she'd killed her first night among humans. Too bad they weren't outside so she could snag a bolt from the sky.

Serra had almost managed to disappear completely into the white folds of fabric lining the walls. What she witnessed sickened her, even as she studied Dalton. He'd be a more formidable foe after he'd eaten.

Gregor had been missing from her head for hours. Cash still lingered, though, which was a surprise. She could feel him somewhere near by. Scared, but there. She checked the ceilings. There were no convenient dropped ceilings hiding duct work. It was open all the way to the soaring, three-story high roofline. No way out through the roof.

More people died. Serra shut her eyes and searched for Gregor.

When she found him, her eyes opened in shock. He'd become his demon, and he was close.

Where are you? Damn it, Serra. Are you still alive?

Gregor. Relief made her knees weak. *I'm coming out to you. I'm coming.* A sudden decision. She couldn't watch people die anymore, but she couldn't save them, either, not in here. She didn't have the weapons she needed to kill the demon. She had to go outside. She knew he'd follow.

Then the fight would begin.

She slipped through the draperies to the walkway behind it as the screaming escalated. Hesitating, she almost turned back at the sound of a whip whistling through the air.

It found its mark through the curtain, once, twice, three times, slashing her bare back and one of her arms. As poison spread through her system, she fell.

An unfamiliar mind reached for hers. *You are mine, Fae. Mine, and no other. My bride. The nurturer of my children. Mine.*

As her body drifted to the floor, her mind screamed for Gregor and she pushed what power she had toward him. *Gregor! Now!*

~~~

He caught the barest glimpse of her intentions before it roared into him, her powers filling him, his Fae blood accepting it.

Need for her, the need to find her, pulsed through him, insistent. Demanding.

Gregor stepped off the roof and landed easily on the ground. Power swelled into him with every step he took. Looking down, a tendril of a thought set the ground to shaking. Wind whipped the building as it trembled. A couple of windows, high up off the ground, popped and the illusion that had given the building an abandoned air vanished. The doors rattled and shook.

~ ☾ ~

Gregor strode to the doors and ripped them off their hinges, tossing them into the parking lot behind him. Screams filled his ears as he ducked to enter the room.

It looked like a massacre. Pools of blood surrounded piles of dead body parts. The survivors were huddled against the walls, frozen in fear. Maybe three, four hundred still left alive. As Gregor advanced and the fresh air swirled into the room, more of the humans stirred, noticing him.

After a passing glance, he didn't take further interest in them. He had eyes only for the Hjurlt, the sudden knowledge of it as an enemy from generations past blurring in his mind, beating through his blood.

The demon looked up from where it had sat on its haunches, the little mouth still nibbling on a victim's toes. At the sight of Gregor its eyes widened. Slowly it stood, dropping its food on the floor.

"You are done." Gregor put all the compulsion into his voice he could muster.

Dalton staggered back two full steps before he could catch himself. "I am not done. Feast with me, brother. For in this land of Humans, we could rule."

"We are not brothers," Gregor spat. He swiped up a table, swung it at Dalton. "Die now."

Dalton bared his teeth. "You refuse my offer of food?"

Gregor didn't answer, just swung the table again, making Dalton jump backwards. Gregor let out a cry, similar to the wind-voice he remembered Serra making, and wind and rain rushed into the room, targeting Dalton, harassing him.

The demon bellowed into the teeth of the wind, but his eyes were wide with fear.

Gregor swung again, this time catching the demon in the side and flinging him into a wall.

Before he tumbled to the ground, the demon disappeared.

Just like before. Only this time Gregor could see. His demon eyes could clearly make out the outline of the demon getting back to his feet.

Gregor hefted the table and stalked toward him. "I promise you death."

After a swift, dazed glare, Dalton ran. As fast as Gregor

could run, Dalton was faster, and out the door before Gregor realized what had happened.

The need to pursue the other demon throbbed through him. He started for the door and stopped, frowned.

Serra.

All thoughts of Dalton left him.

He raked the room with a glance. All the living had fled during the brief fight except for Cash, hovering near the entrance. "Keep watch for the demon," he said.

Cash stared at him. "Find her, and I'll keep watch."

Closing off grief, Gregor bent to the task of searching for Serra amongst all the dead. One by one he turned them over; sorrow touched his heart when he found someone he knew, or a face he recognized.

The main room took the longest. He finally found the secondary rooms. Found Cait, Ursula and Hayden sitting together on a couch, posed, and very, very dead.

Seeing them shook his resolve and he found himself human again, naked and freezing in the cold rooms. The wind inside the building died down.

A startled exclamation had Gregor turning his head.

Cash hovered nearby. Their eyes met in wordless sorrow. Gregor blinked. "Get my clothes. They're behind a bush outside."

Cash ran to do his bidding. Gregor left the secondary room and found a corridor behind the draperies just as Cash returned with his clothing.

Gregor dressed. Despair made his limbs clumsy. As he tugged on his overcoat, the blue and purple threads connecting him to Serra caught his eye and hope beat painfully through him.

He followed the threads back into the huge room, straight across it to a fabric wall. Pulling it aside, he found her stretched out on the cold cement, her back and one arm striped with black ichor.

Cash rushed by him and put a finger to her neck. "She lives." His face turned up to Gregor's. "She's still alive."

"Thank you." Gregor bent and picked her up in his arms, grateful for her weight. The power she'd loaned him drained

~ ☾ ~

out of him and sank into Serra once more. He breathed in her scent, kissed her cheek before carrying her across the cavernous room, aware of Cash practically at his heels. Serra didn't stir.

They exited the building, both of them taking a deep breath of fresh air. The wind had abated; mist fell gently to the ground. They walked in silence, Gregor wrestling with what to do about Cash.

Finally, he sighed. "I can't leave you here. Come with me. Stay the night at my house, where you'll be protected."

"Are you sure?"

"No, but I don't want you taken up by the cops, or killed, either. Please." They'd arrived at Justin's Jag. "Besides, I'll need you to take us to my car. You can bring this one back to my family home."

He juggled Serra and opened the car, put her gently on the passenger seat. Straightening, he turned to Cash. "I really need your help."

Cash nodded. "Okay then. Okay." He wiped his nose with his wrist. "I know how to drive a stick. This is a stick, isn't it? It's been a long time though."

"I have faith in you, Cash. So does Serra. Here." Gregor tossed him the Jag's engine key. "You drive."

The ride back to the San Fernando Valley was nerve-wracking. Cash handled Justin's car well enough. Gregor, in the lead, in his own car and with Serra next to him, was the one who had trouble keeping his car to a reasonable speed on the way home.

~ ☾ ~

CHAPTER TWENTY-THREE

The closer they got to the homestead, the more Gregor relaxed. Despite the odds, he had Serra back, alive. Not everyone who went to the party died, and that was a win, too.

But more people died than he'd hoped, and Serra's injuries needed tending. They had badly miscalculated.

Part of their failure had to do with misunderstanding how big the event would be. Last night needed massive quantities of food. Today, tonight, it would be an intimate killing. Just him and the demon.

I want in too, bro. Justin's weary voice filled his mind. *I owe the bastard. Kellan says he'll help. And we can't forget Kendall is still around, somewhere.*

Gregor gave a brief shake of his head. The whole talking-in-his-mind thing would take some getting used to. *Everyone still alive there?*

Yeah. But it hasn't been pretty. The women are finally asleep. How's Serra holding up?

She's wounded, in shock. We'll be there soon, and we're bringing Cash. Have breakfast ready, I'm starving, he added. Justin loved to cook.

Justin snorted but didn't reply.

Grim, Gregor glanced at the Fae next to him. The urge to protect her still surprised him. He wanted to wrap her up, keep her safe.

But Warrior Fae didn't allow that kind of behavior, not normally. Sex was one thing. Protection? Another thing, entirely. He'd just have to do something about strengthening the bonds between them. He had no intention of letting his woman get away from him, not now.

He didn't care, and it no longer mattered, that his DNA had coded him to bond to her. She was everything. Her goofiness about clothes, and her love of the water, her

~ ☾ ~

abilities with firebolts, her quick mind and clear-headedness all called to him. Seduced him, in the best possible way.

As he acknowledged their bond to himself, he felt a part of his childhood, the part he'd been clinging to like a hurt son, slip away, and he breathed easier. Until another thought crossed his mind.

She needed to understand that she wasn't going back to Faeland.

Not to stay, at any rate. Her place was with him, and his was with her. Their mating bonds were proof.

He brooded the rest of the way to the homestead, his mind exercised by how to kill the demon as much as how to keep Serra with him. He'd embraced his bloodlines, hadn't he? Learned to open his mind to communicate. Learned some of his strengths and weaknesses as his demon-self. What more could the woman want?

By the time he pulled into the long driveway leading up to the family house, he'd given himself a headache. He cut the engine and just sat there. Cash pulled up next to them in the Jag, got out, and gave them a wave before heading to the front door.

Serra stirred, her eyes opening, clear and aware. "You're exhausted."

Gregor turned to her, lifted a hand to her cheek. "You're awake. Come on, let's get you inside." He got out of the car and came around to her door. Darkness still held sway; the clouds gathered low above held the scent of rain. His bones ached and he felt every one of his forty-odd years.

Serra got out of the car. He could feel the energy surrounding her as she took a deep breath, as the strength poured into her through the earth.

Wonder stirred in him. "You are of the planet."

"Yes. So are you."

"You really were helpless inside that concrete building."

"You'd think, since concrete is made of rock and water, that it wouldn't matter. But yes, all I had were my own natural abilities."

"You pushed your strength toward me."

"Luck," she said. "Our bonds carried that, not our mental connection."

~ ☾ ~

They stared at each other. Her skin shimmered in the dark, very faintly, as the earth restored her energies.

"It's not over, Gregor. He'll come hunting for me. He wants to kill me to perpetuate his species."

Gregor held her gaze steadily. "I'll be there. We'll take him down. We will destroy him. He's not touching you."

She searched his face, nodded. "Okay."

He lifted a brow. "What, no argument? No telling me how this is your fight, not mine?"

"Why argue against my heart's desire? I want you there with me. I want you there. But right now, I need a healer," she admitted with a wince.

Gregor put an arm around her, holding her gingerly. "Let's get you inside." She nestled her head on his shoulder and they stumbled together toward the front door.

Justin stood on the porch. "About time you came in. Coffee's on." He came down the wide steps and supported Serra from the other side. "Doc is ready for you. We've got some fresh fruit and vegetable juices for you, with some honey stirred in. You'll need it to heal, the Doc said."

"She'd know. Stay here and rest." After squeezing Gregor's hand, Serra went inside with Justin.

Gregor turned and sat on the top step, grubby from the night, sweaty from dancing with his demon, and dazed with everything else that had happened in the past few hours. He longed for a shower and a clean, crisp white shirt. Somehow he felt able to take on the world in a clean white shirt. He'd packed clothes, right? Or had he? Well, at least he carried a clean suit in his car.

Justin returned with two cups of coffee. He passed one over to Gregor and sat next to him. "Cash is crashed out in the den. He looked wiped and totally sober."

"He helped out tonight. I'm glad he was there." Gregor looked at the cup in his hand, and wondered momentarily what he was supposed to do with it. "Let him sleep, let him stay. I don't know his living situation."

"We'll figure it out. By the way, I've had the radio on. Seems there were three big explosions in the Santa Monica area. The cops are thinking a terrorist attack. They've called

~ ☾ ~

the FBI."

Gregor's heart sank. "So that's how they'll explain it." He finally tasted the coffee. Strong. Good.

"It was bad out there, wasn't it?"

"Yeah. Ursula and Hayden are both dead. So is Cait." Bitterness welled up inside him. "I couldn't stop it. I thought I'd known what being powerless meant, when Mom was attacked. But tonight." He rubbed the space between his eyes. "At least we saved some people." But his heart remained heavy for the ones they hadn't saved.

"So it'll come after Serra?"

"That's what she says. I'm going to kill it."

Justin waited a beat. "The demon probably didn't set those bombs. Did you look at all the dead?"

Gregor frowned. His mind shook off fatigue. "Enough of them, looking for Serra. What are you getting at?"

"Your Charismatic, Bryce whatsisname. Is he still alive? Could he have been the one to detonate the bombs? Or perhaps it was Kendall?"

"Serra said Kendall was in attendance. My guess is that he got away before the fun and games began." But Gregor's thoughts were on Bryce Cannon. "Bryce might have been there. He might be dead, but I don't think so. He might have been the one to set off the explosives. Hell, he might have been the DJ for all I know. I wasn't in the damned room, and I should have been."

"If you had been there, you'd be dead now." Justin's voice cut into Gregor's brooding thoughts. "And I'd be very pissed off if you were dead. But if Bryce is alive, maybe we have a line to your demon. Since they blew up the building, the demon would need a place to sleep off his feeding until it's time to find Serra. My guess is, if we find your charmer, we'll find the demon."

"And if we find the demon before he wakes up, Serra won't be in any danger. I like it."

"First, we have to find Bryce. Then the demon. Then we can celebrate. You okay with that?"

"I've got his address. Haven't had time to check it before now." Gregor looked deep into his coffee cup, then up to his brother. "I'll be okay with that after some breakfast and a shower."

"I hear ya. Come on."

They went into the kitchen. Gregor sat at the big scrubbed-pine table as Justin took out a pan full of egg burritos from the oven.

"Tell me what happened here." He nodded his thanks for the plate set in front of him, and waved Justin to a chair. "I need to know."

"At first, we managed okay, the sedatives seemed to work. But as the night went on, it was like they forgot everything." Justin took a breath, his eyes dark with memory.

"Magdalena started muttering spells at me. Curses. I know she didn't know what was happening and I know she didn't mean it personally, but wow. Aubrey, too. Got Kellan good a couple of times." He rubbed his shoulder. "It was a rough and bloody night. About midnight, they both started weeping and wailing. Ten minutes later, they were out like a light. Deeply out. I couldn't tap into their minds at all."

"Midnight. That's when I finally got inside and started attacking the demon." Gregor wiped his mouth. "Burritos are good. What I don't understand is, why? Why the demon, and all the deaths? What the hell is Kendall up to?"

Justin watched his brother eat. "If we kill the demon, what will Kendall do next? That's what *I* want to know."

"A lot of blood was shed. What kind of spell takes that much blood? Surely more was spilled than the demon needed. Serra said there were close to a thousand people there, and we got maybe four hundred out still alive. Hell." Memory niggled and he tapped the table, staring intently at it.

"You've got your thinking face on, Gregor. What is it?"

"I'm forgetting something. I just can't figure out what." Gregor yawned then, his jaw cracking. "Thanks for the food. I'm going to find a bed."

Megan Cavanaugh came in and sat at the table, resting her head on her crossed arms with a groan. "Remind me to charge you guys double. No, triple."

Gregor pushed over the pan of burritos. "Here. Eat. You'll

feel better. And while you eat, tell me how Serra is."

Megan lifted her head and dragged a burrito toward her. "That wasn't a whip that scored her back, it was a tail. The demon's tail, to be exact. While I was cleaning it out, I caught a whiff of something that I can only call a pheromone."

"In layman's terms, Doc," Justin prodded.

She turned his way. "A tracking device. One that isn't electronic, can't be totally washed away, and will never be completely gone because now it's in her bloodstream." Megan looked from one brother to the other. "The Hjurlt demon will be able to find Serra, no matter how far away you take her." She bit into the breakfast burrito and let out a contented moan. "These are so much better when they're homemade. Eggs, onion, potatoes, cheesy goodness. Did I miss anything?" She arched a brow toward Justin.

"You can talk cooking later. We've got to leave." At Megan's protesting mumble, Gregor sat back and reconsidered. "Serra and I will go as soon as we're both rested. I don't want to give the demon any reason to kill more people. If we stay here, everyone around us is vulnerable."

Justin stared at his brother. "You've got a place in mind."

"The shack. It'll provide some shelter while we wait, plus the view is gorgeous."

Megan, her mouth full of burrito, waved a hand for an explanation.

Gregor rubbed his face, absently noting he needed to shave. "The shack is located up in the Santa Monica hills above Pacific Coast Highway. A getaway that's been in the family for years." He turned to Justin. "I always thought you'd live there, it being so close to the ocean."

Justin shrugged. "It's rustic. If I can get running water up there, I'll consider it, but right now, 'shack' is a good word for it."

"So that's the plan?" Megan snorted. "Wait for the demon to come to you? Why aren't you out searching for him, instead?"

Justin wiped his mouth with a napkin. "We talked about it. There's this Charismatic, the one that held the party. But you know, he probably knows the evening didn't end as planned. I doubt seriously he's just hanging out at his apartment, waiting for the demon to wake up."

"Yeah." Since it was there, Gregor reached for another burrito. "Little Harry's son Samael was practically at the Charismatic guy's feet when I saw him in the bar a couple nights ago. I've got Bryce's address, but maybe we should talk to Sammy first. Sammy might be able to give us a clue about where to look."

"If I were you guys, I'd go as soon as I was done eating. Once Little Harry gets wind of what happened, he'll send Sam away. That boy is his pride and joy. If you go very soon, you might be able to get away before Serra wakes." Megan licked her fingers and stood. "Anyone else want more coffee?"

"What are our chances of leaving Serra behind?" Justin shot a questioning glance toward Gregor.

"I can't leave her behind. I won't. Which means I get a shower and some much needed sleep. Besides—" Gregor checked the clock on the wall, "—it's not even five in the morning."

Justin raised his coffee cup. "Go. Shower, and sleep."

~~~

Serra rolled over and stretched. She was on the bed she'd shared with Gregor, the mingled scents of them from a day ago still clinging to the sheets.

Serra's left hand burned. She looked at it and frowned. Now, where there had been a black circle outlined in red, the circle had changed back to red outlined in black. The red seemed to pulse in her hand, like a heartbeat. White glimmered now and then.

The demon had changed her. Doc Cavanaugh said it was a tracking pheromone running around in her bloodstream, but there was something else there now, too. Something uniquely demonic. She could feel it. But her ties to Gregor were stronger; even now they were changing the imperative that had been slipped into her bloodstream. Maybe they were changing the mark on her hand, too?

She did feel the urge to seek and protect her mate. It

threatened to overwhelm her, the need pulsing with every beat of her heart. But the mate she needed to protect was Gregor. Whatever Dalton had done was being twisted now inside her to favor her bonded mate. Instead of a longing for Dalton, she knew a wild protectiveness for Gregor. He would be the father of her children, and the Fae didn't have children lightly. She would protect him with her life, for without him she had no life.

If what Gregor had said was true, bonded mates didn't survive well in the world without their other half. It had been bad enough, losing her twin. She had no wish to wander around, barely alive, in a world without Gregor. By the same token, she couldn't allow Dalton to take her, dooming Gregor to such a half-life.

Not that she wanted to think about how quickly her thoughts on having a mate had changed. She'd never been the clingy type. Sex was healthy and the Fae indulged frequently, with multiple partners. But if that man downstairs thought she'd share him, he'd have to adjust his thinking. If they survived, she wanted to take him home, but he'd have to pledge to her first. Without his pledge to her, showing him off at home would be tantamount to sharing him with every Fae that passed by. Not going to happen.

As if her thinking about him drew him to her, Gregor appeared in the bedroom doorway.

"Hi."

"Hi. Come, join me." She held the covers open for him. He stripped out of his soiled clothes and tossed them to the side. Slid into bed with her, and took her in his arms with a sigh.

She buried her nose in his chest, much as she had just a few days earlier. His scent was the same—pine and resins, earthy and elemental—now familiar and deeply appreciated. She relaxed against him. "I missed you."

"I'm here now. I missed you, too."

"I am tired of being alone."

"You'll never be alone again. I swear." He pressed a kiss to her hair. "Do you need something to eat? I should have brought something for you."

"Hush. I'm fine now, fine. Just rest. I can feel how tired you are."

~ ☾ ~

Before she could say anything more, Gregor dropped into sleep. His breathing evened out and his arms slackened their hold on her.

Serra, her mind still on her dilemma, rested beside him. When the Fae became a true bonded pair, which didn't often happen in her circle of friends, they were ferocious when it came to their mate's personal safety. How could she let him fight this demon that had marked her? But then, how could he let her fight the demon?

They would tackle it together. There was no other way, and a part of her rejoiced at the thought. To go into battle with those you loved kept you sharp.

To Heal those you loved kept you strong. Fighting wearied her, took a toll, demanded a price she was no longer willing to pay. This, then, would be her last battle for the Fae Council. She had more than earned her freedom.

Settled in both heart and mind, Serra draped one arm across Gregor's chest and willed herself to a meditative state. A brief rest would be enough.

~ ☾ ~

CHAPTER TWENTY-FOUR

They managed to grab a spare three hours of sleep before Gregor hit the shower and emerged, refreshed and in the clean suit from his car. Serra sat with Megan, sipping tea and nibbling at the burritos, and they discussed what more was needed for the clinic.

When Justin finally woke up, the three of them decided it was time to talk to Samael. Megan agreed to keep a watch over Aubrey and Maggie, and feed them when they woke.

Gregor drove to Little Harry's house in comfortable silence. Gregor knew Serra was adjusting to whatever the demon had put in her blood. She'd shown him how the mark in her palm had changed, and they both took it as a good sign.

Gregor pulled up to a nondescript tract home in Mar Vista and cut the engine. "I'd ask you to stay in the car, but I'd rather have you with me."

Her hand reached across the space between them to grip his. She squeezed it briefly. "I'd rather stay with you."

Justin started, yawned. "I'm awake." He got out of the car and stretched.

Gregor scrambled to follow Serra, who had already marched up to the front door. By the time he and Justin reached her, the door opened.

Little Harry stood there, his eyes wide as he saw the Caines on his doorstep. "Ah. Come in. Come on in." He stepped back and tightened the belt around the dingy green robe that concealed his bulk.

"Let's go into the kitchen," he said. "The kitchen table." He waved them down a short hall.

"We need to speak with Samael," Gregor said. "Get him up and in here, now."

Little Harry gulped. "Sure thing. Sure thing." He scurried

~ ☾ ~

down a dark hallway and the others heard him bang on the door. "Sammy. Get your ass out of bed, pronto."

Gregor followed Serra into the kitchen. Clean and bright, it was obvious no one had cooked in there for some time. They sat at the table and waited.

Little Harry took the time to slip into a pair of pants with bright red suspenders holding them up over a white t-shirt. He dragged Samael behind him, the young man yawning.

"Hey. What's up?" He caught sight of Serra and his eyes bugged out. "Wow. She's Fae. You're Fae, aren't you? Wow."

Little Harry cuffed him on the side of the head. "Sit down and answer their questions. Sorry I can't offer you all coffee."

"Yeah. Mom left us because Dad let Bryce use our bar to recruit." Samael shivered. "The guy was cool to start with, leading us all on with promises of power and demon glory. And the one time it happened, the one time a change actually took place, man."

"We need you to tell us what happened." Serra leaned forward, put her chin in her hands. "Tell us so we can see it."

"I was told to bring beer. I swiped a bunch of bottles from the bar. Sorry Dad," he said with a quick, nervous look to Little Harry. "The guys were smoking weed, drinking beer, having a good time, and then Bryce showed up, said he'd changed into his demon just fine that afternoon, which amped the guys, you know?"

"What else do you know about Bryce? What can you remember?"

"He's a cousin of that charlatan Kendall Sorbis. Anyway, so Bryce, he gave a big hoo-rah talk about believing in your inner demon. Then this guy—Shane Eck—was picked to try first." Samael turned white and swallowed hard.

"What happened?" Gregor tried to make his voice non-threatening.

Samael's head twitched. "His hands. They went from normal to bright green with claws. Back and forth, back and forth, and Bryce is muttering this spell or something, and then boom! Shane exploded into little bits. Bryce sent everyone home after that, but he was weird about it. Insisted on talking to everyone one at a time, held their hand, calming people down I guess. I just left."

"Put your hands on the table, palms up," said Gregor.

Bewildered, Samael did so. Justin grabbed his left hand and wiped a finger across the palm.

"Nothing. He's clean." He sat back with a sigh.

"You never had one of these on your palm?" Serra showed him her left palm, where the red circle pulsed.

Samael pushed back from the table, his fear souring the air in the room. "No way."

"You're lucky. Did you get an invitation to a party last night?"

Samael's head swiveled to face Gregor. "No. I mean, yes, but I didn't go to any party. I worked in the bar with Dad. We're short handed since Mom and the girls left, you know? Then we came back and had pizza for dinner."

"Did you know all the guys at the gathering the night that Shane died?"

"Hell, Gregor. Most of them, I guess. You need their names or something? You gonna talk to them?"

"Names would be helpful, but I'm afraid they're not able to talk any more." Swiftly, Gregor and Serra brought the two up to speed on what had happened at the party the previous night.

Samael lost any bit of color he had left in his face. "You mean, we were all just food? All those people died to let one demon live?"

"And that demon intends to settle down here, raise a bunch of demon kids, and take over Los Angeles." Justin leaned back in his chair.

Samael stood, tipping his chair over in a panic. "You're not going to let that happen though. Are you? You can't let that happen. Dad, tell them. They've gotta kill that stupid demon."

Little Harry had stayed in the background, leaning against the kitchen wall. Now as his son appealed to him, he nodded, a gleam in his eye. "I appreciate you guys. You know I do. My group killed another dozen of those dog-like things, you know? We didn't see many other demons, but we're still patrolling."

Samael sent a shocked look to his dad. "What? You never

told me a thing about that. You've been killing demons?"

Little Harry looked scornfully at his son. "You wanted to become a demon. We were out *hunting* them. Would you have killed something that you wanted to be like? We couldn't take our chances. Thank your lucky stars and get out of here. Get some more sleep."

Samael stumbled to the doorway. "I'm fascinated by the science of it," he said over his shoulder. "I want to learn."

"When things settle down, come and see me, Sam. It's a fascination of mine, as well." Sam acknowledged Justin's comment before disappearing deeper into the house.

Little Harry raised an eyebrow. "Kind of you. Sam's the wimp in the family, more into figuring stuff out in his head than anything else. Spends hours alone in his room."

Justin pinned him with a steely glance. "We need every weapon at our disposal. His intelligence, and basic sense of survival, is why he's still alive."

The big man shrugged. "So now what?"

"Now we go pay Bryce a visit. If he's home."

Little Harry belched. "It's still way early. If he partied hearty, he'll be asleep."

"How...?" Serra's voice trembled with rage. "How could he sleep, after leading all those people to their deaths?"

"He's related to Kendall. There's some bad blood in that family tree somewhere." Gregor stood and held out a hand to Little Harry. "Thanks for your help. If we can ever help you, just let us know."

Little Harry shook his hand. "Yeah, well. You all have grown up enough to have your heads on straight." He held out a hand to Serra. "Thank you for visiting my humble home. It is an honor to once again meet one of the Fae." His eyes flickered between Gregor and Serra. "Kind of amazing. I always thought the bonding stuff was made up." He shrugged, punched Gregor on the shoulder. "Good for you. May you make sweet babies. The light go with you," he added in Serra's direction.

Her smile turned rueful when he mentioned the bonding. "Let's go." She walked out, once again leaving Gregor and Justin to follow in her wake.

~ ☾ ~

Once free of Little Harry's house, Justin stopped Gregor on the doorstep. "You're bonded. Mated." Worry creased his forehead. "I've been ignoring that today. You okay?"

"I'm fine with it. Other than that, nothing has changed." It had, of course. Her safety now meant everything to him. He stepped off the porch. "Let it go, Justin. It'll either work out, or it won't."

Justin grumbled under his breath, but when they all got back into the car, he switched on the radio. A Saturday cooking show came on, and as they made their way to Bryce Cannon's home, the car filled with KNX 1070's own Melinda Lee discussing the trials and tribulations of getting chocolate to melt just right.

~~~

Bryce stared at the darkly glowing demon, sleeping curled up in the only dry corner of the cave. They were just north of Leo Carrillo State Beach. The ocean had carved caves deep into the cliffs and over the years, the whole area had become unstable. Now surrounded with warning tape to keep tourists away, it made the perfect spot to stash a sleeping, growing demon.

He still wasn't sure why the creature kept him alive. The night before, as he'd carried out his orders and planted the explosives that would cover their tracks, he'd been certain that when it came time to detonate them, it would be someone else's hand pushing the button because his fingers and toes would already have been eaten. Putting the detonator on a timer only partly relieved that fear.

When the other demon had blown into the building, bringing rain and wind and fresh air, panic had grabbed Bryce by the throat. He'd started the rush to the open doors, his only thought one of safety for himself. Others quickly followed his lead and fled the scene.

But it hadn't been long before Dalton found him, hiding behind a dumpster and shivering like a newborn. Forced to bring the demon to safety, Bryce chose the caves as the place the least likely to be found.

~ ☾ ~

Part of him wished with all his heart that he had been blown to bits, that he was as dead as those others. The horror of the demon had him scared shitless.

He tried to swallow, but his throat was too dry. Swigging the wine he brought didn't help, either. The spot on his hand had changed with dawn. No longer black, now it was a throbbing, pulsing red, and it had grown to take over most of his palm.

If only Cait were still alive. She'd have been able to help him contain the demon. She had told him so as they stood in a corner not ten hours ago, sipping champagne while their guests danced. But his blood was still high with Dalton's energies and he had refused to listen.

He'd done what he'd been told, he'd made sure Cait and Ursula had warded the place. The wards that would have lasted until sunrise if it hadn't been for that wild demon. Thank goodness Ursula had been willing to help. Dalton had done a huge number on her mind, and Kendall had always held Ursula's heart. Before Dalton had killed her, she'd prattled on happily about how she and Kendall would get married in the Bahamas in June.

As for Hayden, well. He regretted killing Hayden, but he couldn't risk her snapping Ursula out of her hero worship.

But when Dalton casually ripped Cait's foot off at the ankle, the better to get to her toes, Bryce had just as casually turned away and taken another glass of champagne from a waiter who'd been charmed not to see the feeding. Later, Bryce had felt compelled to give some decency to the women he'd known, putting them together on the couch in the back room.

It had taken all his strength not to vomit on them.

He shuddered and lifted the bottle to his lips again. All those halfling demons, dead. All those pretty women he'd met in the past week, dead. Hundreds of people were dead and all because of him.

No. All because of Kendall. He'd hero-worshipped his only cousin and had been ripe for anything Kendall had wanted. He'd have done anything for him, for the feeling of belonging.

He slumped against the rough rock of the cave and

~ ☾ ~

breathed in the scents of the ocean. There was no way out of this mess, short of death. He knew it. He figured Kendall knew it, too.

At least Frannie, his dear, sweet Frannie, had died cleanly. No demon had touched her soul, her body, or her blood.

Something hot dropped on his hand and, startled, Bryce lifted his fingers to touch his cheek. He was crying. For Frannie, who was gone forever.

How stupid.

Bryce wiped his face and took another pull at the bottle. If he'd had a weapon of any kind, he'd kill the demon himself. As it was, the throbbing circle on his palm gave him pause. He had no way of knowing just how connected they were.

He drank, and watched the demon sleep, and wondered just how long he'd end up surviving before he, too, was torn limb from limb, shrieking in fear and pain.

~~~

They'd gone through Bryce's small apartment room by room but found nothing except a handful of flyers advertising last night's party. The place had a neglected air. Clean, but stale, as if he'd gone on vacation for a couple of weeks. Half of his closet held women's clothes. Fran's, most likely.

Serra's shoulders twitched. They were the only ones there, but still it felt like unfriendly eyes were watching her.

"I don't like this place." She moved back to the front door, uneasy.

Justin flipped through the address book. "Gee. No entry for Kendall. If they're cousins, wouldn't he at least keep Kendall's cell in his address book?"

"Address book? People still write things down here? That's a surprise," Serra said, looking over his shoulder.

"Good point. I still have a paper address book, but he's probably got most of his contacts in his cell phone. Still, I think I'll hang onto it." Justin tucked it into a pocket in his shorts.

Gregor rejoined them from the bedroom. "I can't believe there's nothing here. Not a damned thing. What a waste of time."

~ ☾ ~

"Well, at least we know he's not here," Justin said. "He could be one of the hundreds of dead."

"If he's one of the dead, then who blew the place?" Gregor shook his head. "No. I believe he's still alive. It just doesn't make sense otherwise. There was Frannie, and then Cait, and Bryce, all working with Kendall. We know Frannie is dead. Cait, Ursula and Hayden are, too. That leaves Bryce as caretaker for the demon while he sleeps, because I can't see Kendall taking on that chore."

"Can we leave? This place. It feels like someone's watching us or something." She saw something shimmer out of the corner of her eye, but when she swung around to stare, she didn't see anything out of the ordinary. Just a mirror that quivered a little. "Please. Let's just go."

The men followed her out, Gregor locking the door behind them. "Funny about finding the door unlocked," he remarked.

"Lucky. Nothing more than that," Justin said as they headed to the car.

Serra's urgency seemed to pass to Gregor, and as he pulled the car out into the street, he hunched his shoulders. "You know, I think I'll head straight for the shack. Justin, you can take the car back and grab reinforcements."

"I'll stay with you guys. Three against one big demon is a bit fairer I think." Justin put a reassuring hand on Serra's shoulder.

She patted it. "That's nice of you," she said absently. "But we should have a few hours before he comes." She hadn't counted on Justin. A part of her mind worried about how to keep him safe in the coming fight.

Saturday morning, three days before Christmas, and the city was coming alive. The holidays were right around the corner and the malls were gearing up for shoppers. The sun shone weakly, a nice change from the clouds and fog they'd been getting. But the closer they got to the ocean, the gloomier it got as the marine layer hugged the coast. Serra didn't say anything, just stared out the window, plotted strategy, and tried not to miss the trees of her homeland.

Depending on the building, it would be prudent to get as

~ ☾ ~

high as possible. "Do you have access to any good weapons?"

Justin snapped his fingers. "Gee. Fresh out."

"Demons don't like flames," she snapped back. "I'm not sure how bullets would stop it, though I'm aware that is the human answer to conflict."

"The Fae answer is flames and arrows?" Gregor's voice carried respect, and Serra's ruffled feelings smoothed out.

"We use the elements. Fire being one of those elements," she said. "Wind helps the arrow if we must have a weapon. I have plenty in my arsenal without having a physical weapon in my hand. What do you have?"

"Speed," was Justin's prompt reply. "Strength."

"He's right. We're fast and we're strong." Gregor said.

"The Hjurlt demon is faster, stronger, and can become invisible. It's claws carry a paralyzing poison, and it has no conscience as you do. It will not hesitate to kill any of us." Serra heard herself recite the facts as though she were still in school, and she flushed. "I'm sorry. It's been drilled into me, demonology I mean."

"You're saying we need weapons." Justin leaned between the two of them from the back seat.

"Yes. That's what I'm saying."

"I could see the demon when he went invisible. A shadowy outline, but I could see him," Gregor offered. "An interesting side effect I guess."

"Why didn't you say something earlier?" Justin punched his brother on the shoulder.

"Slipped my mind. Get us weapons, Justin. Serra and I are going to hole up in the shack."

"Sounds lovely." Serra sunk into herself. Shack. Terrific.

"It's not so bad, actually." But Justin said the words absently, as if he were thinking about weapons.

They rode the rest of the way in silence.

Gregor took the off-ramp for the Pacific Coast Highway northbound. The beach on the left and rolling hills to the right bracketed the road. A couple of miles north there was a turnoff to the right. He made the turn, drove until the road ended, then made a sharp left. This second, rougher road paralleled the highway but sat lower than the hills in between

~ ☾ ~

and, so, remained hidden.

"Myrtle is gonna hate this ride," Justin observed as they went bumping along the road.

Gregor grimaced. "She'll survive."

"Your car is named Myrtle? That is too funny." Serra chuckled. "Myrtle."

Another mile, another turn to the right. This part of the road was paved. It wound around in a circle, and ended at what looked like a utility building of some sort.

Serra studied it. It didn't look too big, but the roof wasn't steep. If she had to, she could easily get up there to do her fighting.

Gregor pulled the car around to the back of the building and parked next to a purple van.

Justin groaned and got out of the car.

"This should be interesting." Serra leaned forward to peer across Gregor. Maggie had gotten out of her van and was giving an earful to Justin, who was giving an earful right back.

~ ☾ ~

CHAPTER TWENTY-FIVE

Gregor watched as Serra prowled through the three rooms. His gut churned and his temples throbbed from the stress of the night, the lack of sleep, the pure tension that still crawled through his bloodstream.

He tried not to show any of it, though, just leaned against the wall by the front door and watched Serra explore.

She finally came back into the main room and settled in a corner of the couch. "Shack is the right name for this place."

"It would be much nicer with running water. I've been thinking about drilling a well. There's an outhouse, though, if you need it while we're here. It's about a hundred yards behind the shack."

He moved to sit by her side, regret eating at him. "I'm so sorry all this happened."

She snorted. "Right, it's all your fault. I forgot. Remind me to blame you when it's over."

He picked up her hand, played with her long, pale fingers. A stray memory came into his head, and he peered closer at her fingertips. "You don't have prints, do you?"

Serra looked at her other hand. "Not in the same way you do. And they can't be dusted for, or inked either. Don't ask me why." She leaned her head against the couch and closed her eyes.

Gregor felt a measure of peace. They were together, he was touching her, and no one was trying to kill them at the moment.

The front door flew open with a crash and Maggie, looking only slightly the worse for the rough night she'd spent, stormed in with Justin hot on her heels.

"Gregor, Serra, outside. I've got weapons for you, then I'm taking this idiot home with me."

Gregor stood. "Weapons? Show me." He tugged lightly on

~ ☾ ~

Serra's hand. "Come on, woman." When she stumbled, he put his arm around her waist. With a sigh, she wrapped hers around him. Gregor tried to keep the silly grin off his face, but from Justin's smirk, he guessed he didn't quite manage it.

Maggie had thrown open the back of her van and started to remove inside panels from the walls. "I've got a bow and arrow for you, Serra. Unless you're the only Fae in the world that doesn't know how to use a bow and arrow."

"I can use it. I don't like it, but I'm not about to be picky right now." She accepted the bow and the quiver of arrows.

"What about me, Mom? Got a present for me, too?" Gregor leaned against one of the van's doors and tried to see inside the dark interior.

Maggie tossed her head, sending her curls bouncing down her back. "I've got a scythe for you."

"Not planning on doing any sharecropping, doll." Justin chuckled.

"Ha ha. That would be funny if it were funny." She scooted into the van and lifted another panel, reached in, and pulled out a heavy, shiny weapon.

"If you had a sense of humor left, it would be funny," Justin said, and backed away immediately, hands raised, when she pointed the scythe toward him. "Jeez. Just joking."

With fire in her eyes, she climbed out of the van and handed the scythe to Gregor. "It's sharp, well balanced, and deadly in six different ways. I want it back, too, so don't lose it."

"It means a lot to you, doesn't it?" Serra spoke gently, but Maggie jerked in response.

"It was my father's," she said, and slammed the van doors closed. She turned her scowl to Justin. "Get in the van, now. Or I'll turn you into a toad and drop you in the Los Angeles River."

"That would kill me," he said, horrified. "You want me to die?"

"If you don't get in the van, then homicide is totally justified. Got it?"

Serra put a soothing hand on Maggie's shoulder. "May I have a word with you?"

~ ☾ ~

Startled, Maggie looked up. "Sure."

Gregor and Justin watched the two women walk apart so they wouldn't be overheard. "I'm not sure we should like this." Gregor gestured to the women, their heads together.

Justin sighed. "Does it matter? I'm going back with her. We'll get some sleep. But I swear I'll be back before dark. If I can snag Kellan, we'll both be here." He turned to study his brother. "You should get some more sleep, too. You look like hell."

Gregor kept his gaze on the women. "Maggie looks like she's on the verge of a complete breakdown."

"I know. That's why I'm being such a brat to her. If she can keep her focus on me, stay angry at me, then her mind can work out last night without her falling apart about it. Apparently, they had dreams. And the dreams weren't good ones." Sorrow shaded Justin's eyes. "I didn't know. I couldn't help her."

"She's alive. She wouldn't be without you. You know that, right?" Gregor put a sympathetic hand on his brother's shoulder.

"Intellectually, yes. Emotionally?" He just shook his head. "Let's get this done quickly tonight. There's supposed to be a terrific football game on at seven."

Gregor saw the women coming back and grinned. "You bet. I'll want nachos, though. Lots of nachos."

Serra stopped next to him, one pale brow arched high. "What are nachos?"

"Something you eat to get fat," Maggie said with a sharp glare at Justin. "Get in the van, mister." But the edge had gone out of her voice. "You both had better get some rest."

"You, too." Gregor gave her a swift kiss. "Thank you for everything."

Maggie's eyes widened. "Um. Yeah." She sent a fleeting grin his way and got into the driver's seat.

Gregor stepped back and put his free arm around Serra. She leaned her head on his shoulder, and they watched as the purple van took off down the gravel lane.

He thought of the weapons he had in his car and decided to get them later. Serra was drooping next to him, and the air

~ ☾ ~

wasn't exactly warm outside.

They went in. Serra dropped her bow and quiver beside the door with a sigh. "I haven't used one of those in years."

Gregor laid the scythe on the table. "I've never used one of these, so we're about even." He went to a cupboard and pulled out a soft plaid blanket. "Come on. Let's sit and get warm." Toeing off his shoes, he settled on the deep couch. "There's plenty of room for two."

Serra pulled off her boots and joined him, her head on his chest and her body wrapped around his.

Gregor sighed in relief. "I'm warmer already."

"Blanket, please."

He shook the blanket out and it drifted down over them, long enough to cover them feet to chin. As they relaxed into each other, that elusive peace he'd felt earlier crept back. He wrapped his arms around Serra, knowing that in a short space of time she'd become his life.

"Stop thinking so loud."

"I'm not," he protested.

She levered up and put her hands on his chest. "If you're not thinking loudly, then why can't you go to sleep?"

He brushed the wayward, baby-fine hair from her face. "I'm basking in this. In us." He tucked hair behind her ear and traced the edge of it. "You're beautiful."

Blood rushed to her cheeks. "You're delusional." She lifted herself higher and brushed her lips against his once, then again.

"I'm not delusional. You are beautiful." He looked into her eyes, saw the pleased surprise there. "Haven't I mentioned it before?"

"No. My eyes are too round, and my nose is a bit off center. My shoulders too are broad and my feet are downright ugly, but I blame that on tree-running at home. I'm not beautiful."

"You're perfect. You're my kind of beautiful."

Gregor's heart eased as he took control of the kiss, deepening it. She opened to him, and he took what she gave while she enthusiastically responded to his every caress.

"We have time," she whispered against his lips. "Don't you

think?" Fumbling with the buttons on his shirt, she kissed him again.

He couldn't ignore the plea in her voice. He couldn't ignore the raging need that drove him, so he sat up and set her from him. Stripping off his shirt and t-shirt then his slacks and the rest, he waited while she scrambled to catch up on the getting-naked part of their day.

She pushed him back against the couch and straddled him with just enough room for her knees on either side of his hips. "I want to play. Don't touch until I say, okay?"

Gregor wasn't used to being the passive party in lovemaking. He'd never let anyone else take such control, but this was Serra. Tonight, they might die. So he grinned and clasped his hands beneath his head. "It's all right with me." She was beautiful sitting there, her breasts high and proud, their pink tips ruched, enticing his mouth. He swallowed and looked to where her sex was pressed against his lower belly, her pale curls mingling with his black ones. His cock twitched and grew harder at the sight.

Gregor closed his eyes. He'd never survive what was to come if he kept them open.

Her hands, long and capable, started at his head. She lightly stroked downward, along his forehead, eyes, nose, cheeks, throat. Her fingers walked the length of his collarbone, and danced across his upper chest before descending, one hand on either side, to his flat nipples.

Her fingernails raked them lightly, tightening them. Gregor gasped at the exquisite sensations as she played, pinching, teasing, bending down to lick them. He could see her in his mind's eye, her pale body over his dark one, her blonde hair brushing his chin as her breasts swayed, almost but not quite touching his chest.

"Don't move," she cautioned as she sat up again, her hands smoothing down his abdomen. "Mmm. I love your body."

"I'm glad." The words came out strangled. His six-pack wasn't as rock-hard as it had been in his twenties, but he'd had no reason to become complacent, no wife, no family, so had continued his workouts for strength more than vanity.

She shifted again, moving off him, and he protested.

~ ☾ ~

"No, stay there. I'm not leaving." Her hands, those wickedly confident fingers, stroked down each thigh, calf, heel, foot.

He was glad he had his eyes closed. He could only imagine how ridiculous he looked, his cock standing and waving in the breeze while the gorgeous blonde ignored it and instead traced her finger along, dear God, the back side of his knees, wringing another gasp out of him.

"Serra." It was half command, half plea.

In answer, she pushed his knees apart and cupped his balls, rolled them in one hand even as the heat of her mouth enclosed him. She took him deep, her hair brushing his belly, and he clenched his hands into fists on either side of his head, wanting nothing more than to haul her to him and lavish her with kisses.

Nothing had ever felt so good. If he'd known what giving up control could feel like, he'd have done it much earlier. *But it wouldn't be the same,* his subconscious whispered. It wouldn't, because now she was his. He was hers. And that made all the difference.

At the thought, his passion surged and he lost the war with his hands. "Up," he urged, gripping her shoulders.

His desperation got through to her. She withdrew from him slowly, giving the tip of his cock one last swipe of her tongue. She looked up, her purple eyes glowing even as she put on an innocent look.

"Did I do something wrong?"

With a growl, he had her beneath him and kissed her thoroughly, her tongue thrusting and swirling around his, their struggle one of mutual delight. She opened her thighs wide and he drove into her welcoming body.

Heat surrounded him, hotter than her mouth. Her muscles clenched him and he held there, deep inside, his arms bracing him above her. He saw the desire in her lovely eyes, her lips red and swollen from his kisses, her breasts pale and pink.

"Stop thinking," she reproved, and rolled her hips beneath him. "Start moving." And she brought his mouth down to her breast.

With a sigh, he lowered himself to her, licked the hard tip

~ ☾ ~

before suckling fiercely as he thrust into her, thrilling to her strangled cry. Here was a woman who would never be afraid of him, one who could fight alongside him. His match. He moved from one breast to the other, drinking in the scent of her skin, of their mutual passion. Her skin seemed to shimmer with it.

"Stop," she panted. "Wait a minute. I want to see."

He let go of her breast and lifted his chest high, braced himself on his hands, keeping himself firmly embedded inside her.

Serra stared down at where they joined, his dark skin between her pale thighs. She looked back up to his eyes and her hand caressed his cheek.

"I've seen many colors between my thighs," she began.

"This isn't the time to discuss your other lovers," he complained.

"Hush. It's not that. The Fae skin can change to any color in nature, and I've seen it all between my thighs. But you." Her hand trailed down his chest to where he was seated inside her. "Your skin color was taken from the night sky. I am day, you are night, and you are my other half, my complementary half. It is entirely my honor, and my joy, to take you into my body." Her eyes blazed up at him. "I am not planning on dying tonight." Her body clenched around him.

He kept his thrusts smooth and even. "Good. I'm not planning on dying tonight, either."

"We will decide what to do about the bondings later," she added on a gasp, her back arching beneath him. She relaxed back against the couch and lifted her legs to wrap them around his back, driving him even deeper within her.

"Nothing to decide. You're mine. I'm yours. Done." Any further coherent thought that may have crossed his mind evaporated as she urged him on. He lost himself, buried himself into her, dropped his face into the curve of her shoulder and, following instinct, bit her there.

Her orgasm caught him by surprise. She screamed his name, held his head to her, and shuddered in his arms, her body tightening around him like a silken fist until, with a cry of his own, released all the pent-up passion, fear and anxiety, and lifted him high as he came.

As his urgency passed, he slumped to one side, not wanting to crush Serra, and lifted her slightly. He pulled the blanket up over them from where it had fallen. Serra snuggled down into his arms.

His usually busy and orderly mind seemed strangely chaotic and at peace.

"Now sleep. I shall rest, and keep watch."

Gregor smiled, rested his cheek against the top of Serra's head, and did as she asked.

~~~

Serra stirred from her meditative state, the rhythmic thumping of Gregor's heart beneath her cheek acting like drumbeats, like a call to action.

Instead of jumping to her feet, she let herself feel. Pressed against the length of him, one of his hands had come up to cradle her head and the other rested in the small of her back. He held her to him as though she were something precious he couldn't bear to lose.

They were bound now, tighter than ever. She didn't need to see to know she had a million threads, purples and blues, tying her to him. Their bodies recognized each other, their minds met on more than a basic level, and their hearts now beat for the other person. What harmed him would harm her. What made her strong would make him strong.

Their souls had entwined.

He accepted their mated status. She believed it. But did he love her? She withdrew from his arms, settled the blanket over him. A frown tugged at his mouth before he relaxed back into sleep.

Swiftly donning her clothes, she went to the tiny fridge and pulled out a bottle of water. She shrugged into her coat, and carrying the water, let herself out of the shack.

The air had turned colder. Thick clouds gathered overhead, and the sun made a feeble attempt to show itself at the horizon.

It was almost dark. They had run out of time. She looked

~ ☾ ~

again to the sky, reassured by the electrical charge there. It was much easier to pull bolts from the clouds than it was from a clear sky.

The door opened behind her, and turning, she saw Gregor come out to stand on the porch. "It smells like rain."

He'd dressed, too, his suit jacket pulled on over a bare chest. It was beyond rumpled by this point. It didn't matter. His attitude still screamed leadership.

"I can guarantee rain before dawn. It's almost dark. I'd better get my bow." She felt funny, too formal, but didn't know how to get back to their previous easiness.

"Wait. I've got weapons, too. In the car." He had the trunk open and the rug lifted before she made it to his side. "Here. This is a small flamethrower. I have it on strong authority that many demons don't like fire." He handed it to her.

She checked it out. "I've used these before."

He reached inside and brought out another, bigger one. "I'll have big Charlie here, as well as the scythe. There's a strap you can use if you want, keep your hands relatively free." He dropped the rug, hiding the other weapons, and shut the trunk.

She slung the strap over her head and rested the flamethrower at her back. "Got it."

He grinned and gave her a hearty kiss. "Yes. Yes, you do."

Serra melted. "Stop it." But her heart wasn't in it.

He wrapped an arm around her shoulders, dragged her close in a fierce embrace. "It's us against him. A much fairer fight than last night. We're not helpless, and we're not drugged. Our eyes are wide open. We know why we're here."

"To kick its ass." She breathed in his scent, took courage from it.

"Send it back to where it came from." His voice held tenderness.

"Straight to hell. Or the Chaos Plane." She pressed a kiss against his chest and took a step back.

"You're shimmering in the dark," he said, but he didn't reach for her this time, just regarded her solemnly.

She blinked. "So are you. Shimmering."

"How's your night vision?"

~ ☾ ~

She cracked a smile at that. "Catlike. Yours?"

"Not quite that good, but pretty damned good. I'm going to turn off all the lights in the shack so my night vision can adjust."

"Hurry back."

He disappeared inside.

Alone once more, Serra stared out across the darkening landscape to the ocean, a mile or more away. The lights behind her went out, and Gregor rejoined her. "I know he's coming. You know he's coming. But do we have to wait for him out here? Can't we at least wait where it's warm?"

Serra put a hand out. "Wait. I can hear fighting. Can you hear that?"

"Something's coming toward us. Damn it." Gregor, scythe swinging in the night, ran down the road. Serra ran alongside, singing a song that reeked of death.

Kellan, Justin and Maggie raced toward them. Behind them, the werewolves held the doglike demons at bay, ranged in a semi-circle across the road. The two groups were snapping and snarling at each other, not quite into attack mode.

"What the hell are you doing here?" Gregor shouted at the three coming up.

A wild-eyed Maggie shimmered with power, her hands flexing. "We had to."

"He hasn't come alone," Kellan shouted. "He's not alone. Get ready!"

"Then it's time for some firepower." Serra stepped up, shining bright in the dark night. Raising both hands to the skies, she let out an ululating call. The clouds roiled overhead. Lightning split the sky and thunder shook the ground as rain poured down, stinging and fast.

"Justin, Kellan, rear flank. They're coming up the hill behind us. Follow me!" Maggie sprinted off to the other side of the shack. Justin, cursing, followed.

"Go after them," Gregor shouted as Kellan stood there, undecided. "Go!" Kellan took off at a run.

The road exploded then as demon-dogs attacked the werewolves. Jaws snapping in the night, the massive wolves

~ ☾ ~

made short work of the demons even as several of their number went down under acid tears or wicked claws.

Gregor stood at the ready, scythe in one hand, the flamethrower ready to go in the other. "Come on, you bastard. Come on," he muttered under his breath. His heart raced. Rain ran down his face, into his eyes, and he blinked, wishing for a hat. He glanced toward Serra, and stared, his attention caught.

She stood to one side, shining in the night, a clutch of firebolts in one hand. Her song caught at him. She sang of death, of retribution, of cleansing the land. The contrast, the fierceness of her song and the quiet resignation in her face, belied her earlier statement. She may not have intended to die this night, but from what Gregor could see, she would accept death.

Terror caught at his throat. "No." Angry, he grabbed her shoulders, shook her.

Serra stopped singing and looked up at him. "What must happen will happen."

The acceptance on her face destroyed him. "No. Don't even think about taking that thing inside you to kill it. You killed the last one with your firebolt. This one should be killed the same way, yes? Yes?" He shook her again and strained to hear her through the noise of the storm.

She wiped her face of rain. "I can't make any promises, Gregor. This one is not like its brother. After the feeding it had, it's much more powerful. It must die or mankind will not last long. You get two or three of these things feeding, laying eggs, and they'll take down a country in a matter of months. I've told you this."

A chill that had nothing to do with rain slid down his spine. "I didn't want to hear."

"I know. Hear this, though. I am not going to die this night." She smiled even as the sound of gunfire on the other side of the hill echoed toward them. "Go. I am too visible. Go!" Serra dodged off to the left.

Gregor ran to the right and set his sights on the road ahead.

~ ☾ ~

The wolves were out of sight and the demon-dogs were lying dead in the road. One by one, a firebolt came out of nowhere to dispose of the carcasses. Up the road came a creature in black, flowing over the landscape like a shadow. A firebolt aimed at it bounced harmlessly off.

Terrific. Gregor wiped his eyes. The thing had a shield of some sort. A shield that not even a fire bolt from the heavens could penetrate. He hefted his scythe and flicked off the safety on the flamethrower. Let the bloody games begin.

More demon-dogs, as if conjured out of nowhere, appeared and came running for him. Gregor braced his feet and swung the scythe.

CHAPTER TWENTY-SIX

Justin followed, cursing after Maggie as she ran. He lost her in the dark and barely stopped himself from ramming into her by sheer instinct. She'd frozen at the top of the hill, her eyes wide.

Below them, the hill swarmed with the dog-like demons, what looked like hundreds of them, all coming their way.

"Son of a bitch. We need a ditch. Damn it, we need a ditch!"

"We don't have a ditch," shouted Maggie. "Where's Kellan?"

Behind her, a demon roared and thunder cracked overhead.

"That's him. He'll handle it his way." Justin gestured to the pale-skinned demon that ran past them. Close to eight feet tall, the demon's long blond hair streamed down its back, waving and seemingly alive in the night. He cracked the whip he held in one hand, and a spray of gunfire erupted from his other hand.

"That'll get things started." Justin sent a fierce grin to Maggie. "Come on. Kellan will handle the demons. We need to aim for Sorbis."

"Got it." Maggie chanted under her breath as her hands shaped fire. She threw a fireball with the accuracy of a Major League pitcher. Justin knew a moment of pride and relief. Maggie would be okay.

He turned from her and focused on the blond man staying in the rear. "Oh no you don't, Kendall Sorbis. No setting things in motion and running away, not this time." Holding his hands out, he felt deep in the earth, searched for the natural ruptures in the hillside. A gentle nudge widened the deep rift a little; another nudge sent it rumbling down the hill toward Kendall.

~ ☾ ~

Justin felt the earth tremble beneath his feet and smiled as the blond fell where he'd stood.

Kendall saw him then. His focused hatred across the space between them grew sharp as a laser, piercing Justin's flesh. He brushed off his smoking arm and stalked forward. This had to stop. Now.

Justin kept up the small rumble of earth as he moved toward Sorbis. He dodged the energy balls Kendall tossed at him, kicked the dog-demons out of his way. His fury grew as he processed everything he'd ever learned about Kendall. The man was dirt.

"Justin, no, don't!" Maggie's scream pulled his attention away from Kendall. She ran toward him, her arms outstretched.

"Go back, Maggie, now. Please." Shoving her behind him, Justin caught sight of Kendall's satisfied smile just before an energy ball hit him in the torso.

The shock dropped Justin to his knees, stole his breath. *Get back, Maggie. Kellan!* Relieved when he saw his cousin's blond mane swivel toward him, Justin's vision grayed, went in and out. More dog-demons appeared, leaping up the hill toward them, and Justin stared in disbelief.

He struggled to his feet even as wolves burst out from behind them to charge into the demon pack. Justin searched the ground again. He didn't have time to actually dig a ditch, but damn it if he couldn't open the earth a bit.

He aimed for a dozen yards in front of Kendall, concentrated on the way the bluff jutted out. These hills had been sagging toward the ocean for decades, so it wouldn't take much to help them slip.

His energy waned and his grip on the earth eased. Damn it. He could *do* this. Reaching deep once again, Justin poured his strength into the earth, gave it a push, and visualized the hillside sliding away. He saw the twenty-foot cliff in his mind's eye and directed the earth to move.

Two more energy balls hit him, one in the chest and one in his solar plexus. Justin dropped like a stone even as the earth below began to shift toward the sea.

Out of the corner of his eye, he caught sight of Maggie. Her

~ ☾ ~

hair whipped around in the wind, and her skin glowed golden as she worked with fire, shooting ball after ball toward Kendall. His retaliation came in the form of a ball of energy. It hit her mid-chest and she shuddered, fell as electricity crackled over her body. Her eyes stared over at Justin, lifeless.

Shock reverberated through Justin's bones. Sorrow and rage warred equally in his heart, blurring his eyes for a few precious seconds.

Kendall had killed Maggie, and still came toward him. The demons were headed their way. The mountain didn't move fast enough. He'd run out of time.

Fury unleashed new energy. Justin struggled to his knees and thrust a hand up to the heavens. He'd failed Maggie, but he wouldn't fail now. Words he didn't know he knew spilled out of his mouth, ancient pleas to gods too ancient for mere history books.

Lightning flashed in the sky, blinding everyone on that side of the hill. Justin blinked, felt his hand tighten around living energy, and using all his strength he threw it at Kendall.

His face landed in the mud before he saw where the bolt hit. His last thought was of revenge.

~~~

Gregor swung the scythe and split two demons at one time. A blast with the flamethrower had them a pile of wet ash before long. He'd gotten into a rhythm—swing, flame, swing, flame until it was almost routine—even as he kept an eye on the dark demon's approach.

Another swing, another blast, and the demon-dogs were done for the moment. The air had turned foul from the smoke, and Gregor sneezed.

Light from behind him lit up the landscape, turning the sheeting rain into individual glittering drops before falling dark once more. Gregor blinked and swore. The demon he'd been tracking had disappeared, damn it.

A shimmer of light caught his attention and he whirled to

his left. There she was, standing tall on a small peak. Thick fog now enshrouded the mountainside and he knew it was her work, protecting them from those who might be too curious.

The earth shook hard beneath his feet, and he stumbled. Serra didn't waver, just stood tall as she called the fog.

He regained his balance and moved to be with her. Lightning flashed. Gregor blinked, and Serra was nowhere to be seen. Demon-dogs set up a howl, and before he could totally prepare, they were on him once more.

Swing and flame, swing and flame. Even as he worked, his back itched. As if he'd missed something. As if he were suddenly playing someone else's game.

Serra! A demon-roar burst out of him, and he changed shape as he continued to the hill where he'd last seen her.

He ran straight into nothing, and bounced off it, landing on his ass. The demon-dogs surged and nipped, grabbed, bit at him. Shaking them off, he stood once more and growled, a low, menacing growl as he made eye contact. One by one they whined and slunk away, crouched low, their noses to the ground.

A hand grabbed at his arm and, startled by the warmth of the touch, Gregor swung his head around. "What do you want?" He stared at the young Charismatic, the man who had lured a thousand people to their deaths.

"My name is Bryce. I saw... I saw you change. Teach me. Please. Teach me to be like you." The man stammered. The rain pounded down, turning the ground beneath them into mud.

Gregor shook his head. "I can't. You're either born with it, or you're not. Now get the hell out of here, before you're as damned as Sorbis."

"You've got power I want. Don't you see? You've got power I *need*." The Charismatic's voice grew stronger.

Gregor felt the pull dimly and shrugged it off. "Not something I can give to you. Sorry." He swung the scythe in a lazy circle. "Now that I think about it, though, you got people killed last night. A lot of people. People I knew."

Bryce backed away, eyeing the scythe.

~ ☾ ~

"You're not one of my favorite people right now."

Bryce looked around, apprehensive.

"As a matter of fact, you'd better start running, boy, and hope those demon-dogs don't get you."

Bryce took off at a run.

Gregor forgot about him and focused on the place he'd last seen Serra. He searched for the bonding threads connecting them. And as if someone had switched on a light, the moment he thought about them, they appeared, sparkling and glowing in the night. They went from him and disappeared into black.

He started forward, only to feel a hit against one of his massive demon-sized arms. Sighing, he turned to look.

Bryce stood there with a baseball bat at his feet and shaking his hands.

Gregor looked to where Serra waited and made a swift decision. He didn't know exactly how it would work and didn't need any interruptions. He leaned down, picked up the bat, and tapped Bryce on the head. The Charismatic went down for the count.

Gregor shifted back to his human self. Naked and shivering, he reached both inside and out for the gifts of a heritage he'd yet to embrace.

Serra. I'm coming. I'm coming to you. She didn't respond. Trusting in her, in their shared bond, Gregor grasped hold of the Fae threads. *Take me to Serra.*

~~~

The smothering blackness descended before she could blink. The air changed somewhat, grew warmer. Light brightened, and Dalton appeared.

"You think to play with me." He kept his human form, that same stark, bony face that had so charmed and repelled the night before. But the quiet thunder of his power shook the very air between them.

"Not so. I think only to destroy you. This isn't your world, Hjurlt. Go back to the Chaos Plane." Serra kept her eyes steady on him.

"It is such a delicious place. Food just comes to you,

~ ☾ ~

whenever you want it. Baby toes are so exquisite, and no two taste alike, did you know that? This world teems with magick, natural, untouched, wild magick that these clods can't see, or feel, or hear. How can I leave?" He spread his hands wide, all reasonableness. "I will share this world with you, my Fae. If you so desire."

"After you lay your eggs in my body? No thanks."

A low rumble of anger filled the enclosed space. "I will not allow this planet to be taken over by the Fae. Don't for one minute think that. I have worked hard to get here, slaughtered thousands of your people and mine to make it this far. Now, there is nothing you can do to stop me from claiming this land." He shook his head, calming himself again. "A pity, really, because the fight would have been so interesting."

A tug at her side caused Serra to stumble. A piercing cry split the night and their shelter shuddered as Gregor, his upper body down as if in tackle mode, burst the bonds of magick enclosing them.

"Serra!" His big arms caught up both Serra and Dalton, and the three of them went down in a tangle of arms and legs in the mud.

Wind poured in then, whipping the barrier aside and pelting them with rain. Serra felt Gregor's arms around her, tugging on her and pulling her to her feet, pushing her behind him. "Are you okay?"

Working faster than she'd ever had to, she built a barrier around them and the wind lessened. "Now I am," she said, and grabbing his arm, she walked backwards from the furious Dalton, struggling to reach them. "We don't have much time, Gregor. Here." She took his left hand in hers, twined her fingers with his. "Whatever you do, whatever you feel, don't let go."

She saw the understanding in his eyes as the weave of air twined around their hands, unseen, binding them tighter together. "I'm not about to lose you," she said.

"Never happen." His hand gripped hers as the shelter around them rocked.

"I can't hold it much longer. As soon as I lift the shelter,

~ ☾ ~

we hit him with everything we have. Everything you aren't even sure of yet. Grab the knowledge within you and throw it at him. Do you understand?"

At his nod, the barrier between them and Dalton dissolved. The air filled then with firebolts and the ground beneath their feet rumbled.

Mud fountained upwards to drench the demon. He lifted his arms.

"Jump!" Serra and Gregor jumped up. A crackling bolt of electricity passed harmlessly beneath their feet. Upon their landing, Gregor swung the scythe, muttering a curse under his breath.

Dalton disappeared.

"Good. That's a good sign." Serra panted out the words. "We can do this, but only if we're together."

"Unbind me, Serra. Your air thing isn't going to keep me tied to your side." Gregor motioned between the two of them with his free hand. "I'm already yours. Now and forever. Remember? You split your focus like this."

She looked down at the sparkling lights racing between them, uncertainty rocking her. "I don't know."

"Believe it. I have to. I got to you, didn't I? You're not going to lose me easily. Now let me go so we can finish it. Together."

She tipped her head, met his eyes. Everything she'd never known to want was there, waiting for her. All she had to do was have the courage, the strength, to trust in what had grown between them.

On a breath, she cut the weaving. Slowly, their hands unclasped, separated. She felt the bond between them deep inside her. Knew that her life was anchored in this man as his was anchored in her. Joy filled her.

"Okay?"

She smiled up at him. "Absolutely okay."

His eyes widened. "Serra." They glazed over, and Gregor tumbled down at her feet, a whip-slash across his back telling the tale.

Fear and fury roared through her as she sidestepped the crack of the whip's tail. The elements came to her call. Hail rattled down hard on the mountaintop. Wind circled her, kept her safe as lightning shot down from the sky.

She sought the demon, found it waiting for her. Ten feet tall, black as night, with the whip curling lazily at his side. Four arms, with four sets of venomous claws. Two mouths, one at stomach level.

This was the fight of her life. No troops had her back. Her brother had been killed, taking this manner of thing inside him to destroy it. Now it was her turn.

"It's a nice night to die," she called.

The demon's mouths opened and its teeth clashed together. The whip lashed out at her, but she'd taken the split second to move. She landed on his shoulders and jabbed a firebolt in his back before she leaped off, ending up several yards away.

He staggered forward and bellowed. The firebolt, instead of turning the demon to ash, broke off and landed in the mud, useless.

Serra ringed it with firebolts, each one crackling and blazing in the freezing cold. One by one, the demon broke them with his whip-like tail. Only the sight of the tail shriveling a little by the heat of the bolts assured her that her power still worked.

The demon came toward her, to her relief leaving Gregor untouched.

Catching sight of her glowing skin, Serra abruptly dropped and rolled in the mud. Night was called for. She needed to become black, not bright as the moon. She spread mud thick with grit over her face, around her hands, always one eye on the demon.

He cast his tail around, searching for her.

Serra wrenched the flamethrower from where it hung on her back and flipped off the safety. She knew he would lock on her as soon as she let it roar, so moving as quietly as she could, as low to the ground as she could, she crept up on her target. She'd get one chance to surprise him.

Just one.

~~~

~ ☾ ~

Gregor recognized the room with a start. It was the same way-station Rose had talked about as she watched herself in a coma that past summer.

He looked about as souls in rainbow colors zipped by him, all seemingly with a purpose.

"This is ridiculous. I need to be there, fighting with Serra. Damn it." He turned and saw what appeared to be a wide movie screen in front of him. The picture had stilled, as if someone had put it on pause. He looked at himself, facedown in the mud.

The night was dark. His scythe was still clutched in one hand, and the flamethrower still lay against his side. Rain slanted, frozen, over the screen. Across his back, the result of bloody whip-strokes could be clearly seen. The whip had cut deep but the cold night had slowed the bleeding.

"So what? I'm already dead out there?" Fury bubbled up in him. "That's just bullshit. I'm not ready to die."

"You're not ready to live, my son." Marie-Therese stood next to him and put a hand on his arm. "You stopped living fully the day I died."

"Mom." Shock and guilt rose up in him and Gregor dropped into a chair. "What the hell are you doing, butting in now? I've got it under control."

"You always did think highly of yourself," she said, amused. "My darling boy. My rape was not your failure. My decision to have Gabriel was not your fault. Therefore, my death was not your fault. It was, however, a chain of events that had to happen. Which is why I'm, um, 'butting in'."

"Why?" The cry seemed to come from deep inside him, as he stared at his beloved mother. "I needed you so much. Why did this all have to happen?"

"Not every question has an answer." She sat next to him. "But what you do now will affect your future."

He gestured savagely at the screen. "I'm dead."

Marie-Therese raised her eyebrows. "You are? You can tell this from a still image?"

"Mom. Please."

"You have come far," she said. "I am so proud of you.

~ ☾ ~

When you go back, push the poison out of your system. Envision yourself whole and healthy, and your body will do the rest. Healing is natural, once you allow it to be.

"I'll have time to do that?"

"You are already healing. Time is different here. However, there is one more thing you haven't learned, haven't needed to learn until now. One thing that two must do together."

"I don't understand."

"Do you know what happened to Terrell Willows?" Marie-Therese raised an eyebrow.

Gregor frowned. "He tried to take a demon into himself. It killed him."

"Yes. For all his valor, he was a prideful male. He stubbornly denied the chance for one he loved to help him with the demon. He died trying to shelter her, and ever since, she's thrown herself into every dangerous situation possible."

"His sister. Serra." Gregor wiped his mouth.

"Yes. You have walked alone for long enough. She is your true life partner."

"I love her, Mom. I didn't want to, but I do."

"Make sure she knows. Make sure she stands at your side, not behind you and not in front of you. Make sure you do the chant together. One alone, even if you stand at her side, will not conquer the demon."

"Chant? What chant? I don't know any chants."

"You have it in here." She tapped his forehead. "I have given it to you. You'll remember it when the time comes."

Gregor tugged at his vest. "None of this is logical."

She gave him a smile. "Very often, life isn't logical, but it usually makes sense if you're paying attention. You have a bigger job to do than you may realize. Are you really going to give up before you've begun?"

"I'm in my forties, Mom. Not exactly new at living. And I don't believe I said a thing about giving up."

"Ah. Well, you have many more years in front of you. You barely look thirty." Mischief gleamed in her eyes. "But you will learn more this night than any night you've lived through yet. If, that is, you decide to live." She took a step away from him, and something in Gregor panicked.

~ ☾ ~

"Mom." He stood and waited as she turned with a patient smile.

"Yes?"

"I love you."

Tears shimmered in her eyes as her smile grew wide and her arms opened. "Oh my boy. My first born, my eldest, my baby boy. I do love you so."

He caught her up in a hug, surprised now by how small she seemed, she who had always loomed larger than life. Her arms tightened around him, held him close. He breathed in her comforting scent and shut his eyes.

"Make the right choice, Gregor. Live. Remember the chant. Love Serra. Your father and I are counting on you."

Shock startled through him again. "Dad? Is he here?"

Marie-Therese slipped from his arms and smiled even as she faded away in front of his eyes.

~~~

The demon roared into the night as it sent its tail-whip whistling across the land, searching for her.

Serra kept down, stifled a sneeze and froze. The demon's anticipation rode the air. Serra sent an urgent call to the winds to blow in a whirl around it, confusing it. The winds kicked into gear as the hail melted into rain. Serra lifted her head and took a cautious look around.

The demon was to her left, turned away from her, his head lifted to catch the scents riding on the wind.

Now. She came up on a run, her flamethrower blazing toward the demon. On the other side of the hill she caught sight of another person, flamethrower hot and aimed toward Dalton.

Gregor.

We need to destroy it. We need to take it inside us. Both of us need to speak the chant. Now. I don't have much time.

His mental voice held pride and pain. The two of them ran for their target, their flames blending as they hit the demon. Dalton disappeared and reappeared twenty feet, away, his real form smoking.

~ ☾ ~

Fear froze her. *But Terrell couldn't do it. It killed him.*

I love you. I love you, Serra. Gregor came up next to her and dropped a brief kiss on her mouth. *Trust in us. Trust. Okay?*

Serra's heart sang. *I love you, too. Okay. Let's do it.*

Gregor held out a hand to Serra. She grasped it, twined her fingers with his, and together, they headed again toward Dalton.

Along with the flame, they poured every ounce of energy they had toward the demon to immobilize it. Serra wove air around its ankles even as Gregor wove a small pattern around its fingers, sticking them together. Helpless, it stared at them as they advanced on it.

Fire lit the whip first, raced up the leather strip toward the hand that held it. The demon shook free of it but Serra caught the whip on the wind and it wrapped around the demon's waist, burning merrily.

Dalton howled with pain and fear, a sound that wrapped around Gregor and Serra as much as their weaving wrapped him up tight.

Now.

Together, Gregor and Serra chanted the Chant of Dissolution and Redemption even as they each grasped one of the demon's hands. The three of them stood close, face to face to face, and as the chant swelled on the air, the demon seemed to shrink, his head thrown back. Out of his throat came a keening wail.

Serra took the lead, but Gregor stayed with her. Their chant changed, grew darker. The demon fell silent, became a vapor. The vapor split into two and wrapped around Serra and Gregor.

Her voice strangled with the pain. It was like being plunged in boiling water. But they both kept chanting. The demon on her skin, at first hot, turned icy. As the vapor sank down into her bloodstream, into her organs and bones, every death it had ever caused flashed through her mind, overwhelming her with sights, scents, smells and sounds as the demon's life passed through her. Though young, Dalton had been an experienced demon. The deaths he'd caused

~ ☾ ~

were counted in the thousands upon thousands.

The chant changed again, this time sending the demon-spirit out of their bodies and into the earth beneath them. Its deeds and its life, the gritty details and memories, slowly drained out of them and into the waiting ground. The driving need holding them upright dissolved. The demon was gone.

Her vision blurred and her knees gave way, the warmth of Gregor's hand in hers the only tether to reality she could count on.

She knew Gregor had landed on his knees, too, but they weren't done. The two of them finished the chant, cleansing their bodies of the demon they'd destroyed. White light streaked through them, searing their blood clean of any demonic taint left behind by the Hjurlt, the pain of it almost too much to bear on top of all the rest. Finally, it stopped, and they were alone again on the hill.

Rain fell down, a gentle, natural rain now. Serra opened her eyes and searched Gregor's face anxiously. *You are okay? You will survive? How in hell did you know what to do? How did you know the chant? I barely know it. Did you really say you loved me?*

Mom came through. Yes, I love you. Sleep now. Talk later. And he fell over and lay still in the mud.

Serra worked a protection over them, keeping them rain-free and warmer than they had been, before she checked his back. His skin there had been healed. She searched, found his steady heartbeat, felt the depth of his weariness. She rolled him over and straddled him and, as she had the first night she'd met him, she set her lips to his.

Come back to me, my love. Come back soon. She nestled her cheek against his chest, took comfort in the solid beat of his heart, and allowed herself to rest.

She'd found home.

~ ☾ ~

CHAPTER TWENTY-SEVEN

"He'll be all right." Serra slid her arm around Gregor and led him away from Justin's hospital bed. "He needs time to heal. Not even the Fae can fix some things."

Gregor held her close as they walked down the corridor, guilt over failing to protect Justin chasing the joy he felt knowing Serra was his, the light to his darkness. "Justin's never been bitter. He's the calm one, the cool surfer dude, the glass-half-full guy. Now he refuses to see Maggie, refuses to come home to recuperate, and doesn't believe the glass exists any more. How can I fix this?"

"You can't," Maggie said. She stood in the doorway to her own room, her face pale and drawn, her brown eyes dulled by pain. "You can't fix something that he feels responsible for. Stupid ass." Her voice broke slightly on the last word. "Kendall Sorbis had better run, far and fast. I want him dead so badly I can taste it."

"Maggie. You should be in bed, too. We brought you in barely alive." Serra put her arm around Maggie's shoulder and turned her back into her room.

"I wasn't strong enough. I tried to take Kendall down, and all I did was expose Justin." Maggie's face set in bitter lines. "Now Justin won't even talk to me. He thinks I'm a ghost, a spirit. He thinks I'm dead."

"He's still out of it," Gregor said. "We all need time to heal, to rest. As Serra said, there are some things that take time to heal, even after the Fae healing has been done. Both of you need that time now." He settled his hand on Maggie's shoulder. "After we're all up to speed again, we'll go after Kendall. We'll find the bastard, and we'll take him down. I swear."

"How's Kellan?"

"He was discharged a week ago, but he's staying at the

homestead for awhile. Aubrey is keeping him company."

"He got to go home a week ago?"

"He had mild acid burns, some bite marks. Nothing too serious. Nothing like what hit you and Justin," soothed Serra.

"Oh." Maggie climbed back into bed. Her eyes narrowed on Gregor. "You look different. Relaxed, not so uptight." Shock crossed her face. "You're wearing denim. Denim, a t-shirt, and a plaid flannel shirt. What happened to the dress suits? You take baths in your dress suits, for Pete's sake."

"Oh no, he's completely naked in the bath," Serra assured her. "He just discovered that sometimes jeans are more appropriate for dealing with life."

Gregor grinned at an astonished Maggie. "People do change."

She leaned back on her pillows and pulled the covers up to her neck. She glared at them, the sheen of tears in her eyes. "Maybe people do change. But do they change back in time?"

~ ☾ ~

ACKNOWLEDGEMENTS

Where to begin? My thanks and appreciation goes first to Stephanie Murray and Marlene Castricato, the fearless leaders of Crescent Moon Press. Thanks also to my editor, Lin Browne, and my cover artist, the incomparable Taria A. Reed. You ladies saved my sanity.

To New York Times Bestselling Author Maggie Shayne, who read this book and loved it, and gladly gave me a blurb. Thank you for being an inspiration to me over the years; I treasure our friendship.

To my friends and colleagues at the Los Angeles Romance Authors chapter of Romance Writers of America, my love and thanks for your never-ending support.

To my husband Tom and our two sons – my never-ending love, thanks and appreciation for making dinners and doing laundry and housecleaning when I'm on deadline. You three make life worth living.

Christine Ashworth

Christine Ashworth is a native of Southern California. The daughter of a writer and a psych major, she fell asleep to the sound of her father's Royal manual typewriter for years. In a very real way, being a writer is in her blood—her father sold his first novel before he turned forty; her brother sold his first book before he turned twenty-five.

At the tender age of seventeen, Christine fell in love with a man she met while dancing in a ballet company. She married the brilliant actor/dancer/painter/music man, and they now have two tall sons who are as brilliant as their parents, which keeps the dinner conversation lively.

Christine's two dogs rule the outside, defending her vegetable garden from the squirrels, while a polydactyl rescue cat holds court inside the house. Everything else is in a state of flux.

Christine says: I love visitors! I write a blog about wines, and cooking, gardening and sometimes writing. Please drop by and visit me at :

www.christine-ashworth.com

Twitter: https://twitter.com/#!/CCAshworth
Goodreads: http://www.goodreads.com/ChristineAshworth

Keep reading for a Sneak Peak at Demon's Rage, Book 3 in the Caine Brothers saga; finally, Justin and Maggie's story!

DEMON'S RAGE

A Caine Brothers Novel

Chapter One

Justin Caine slowly jogged from San Vicente Boulevard across Ocean Avenue to the beach side and followed the sidewalk down. The sun touched the buildings on the east side of town, but here the chill of night still clung to the bushes and the trees.

He cursed his dragging pace. The magickal nature of the injuries he'd sustained needed more time than usual to heal. After three weeks in the torture chamber that Doc Cavanaugh called a hospital, he'd finally walked out under his own steam. Vowed to take charge of his rehab.

Doggedly, he put one foot in front of the other, ignoring knotting muscles and a deep queasiness that hadn't left him, and plotted Kendall Sorbis' death. It should be slow. Methodical. The Death Mage should be unable to talk or move. And while Justin carved parts of Kendall's body away, he'd ramble about the lives of the hundreds of people Kendall had taken to slake the thirst of his own ambition.

The craving for revenge burned hot in his gut. He wouldn't soon forget the winter solstice just passed.

As he plodded, a scent tickled his nose, one that drew him out of his dark thoughts. A scent he'd grown to know all too well. He stopped, looked around, but saw nothing unusual. No other joggers, not many cars on the roads just yet.

Justin sniffed the air again, all his senses on alert. Blood. Not just any blood, either, but demon blood. It carried an acrid tinge, similar to a doused fire mixed with the scent of vomit and dried-up curses.

Following his nose, Justin turned toward the bushes between the sidewalk and the strip of grass. A park bench facing the ocean sat nearby, and an earthen jogging trail went past it. Justin followed the trail to another clump of bushes to his left. As he got closer, the blood-scent grew stronger, clogging in his throat. He hacked a cough and searched further.

A bare foot stuck out from under a Mexican sage plant. Justin crouched down, parted the cluster of tall plants, and took stock.

Demon, certainly, though he didn't look it. Short and squat, he wore surfer dude clothes, similar to those Justin himself used to prefer. He took quick mental notes about the body.

Eyes were opened wide, mouth too, showing rows of sharp teeth. One ear had been cut off, the hands and legs ritually spread wide. Cause of death, a big-ass throat slice from ear to non-existent ear.

Justin frowned and looked closer. The hands were palms up, fingers curled as though he'd been holding something. He leaned in, sniffed. Wax. Scented with nightshade. His lips set in a grim line. Aside from the fact the corpse was demon, this was no ordinary killing.

This was ritual murder, which meant he needed to contact Magdalena de la Cruz.

Justin rolled his shoulders in irritation. He'd spent much of the past month avoiding if not downright ignoring her. He couldn't call her now, not about something like this. Not after the fight that almost killed them both.

But his big brother Gregor and wife-to-be Serra were still figuring out how to merge their lives in the big old homestead where the Caine boys had grown up. It wouldn't be fair to call on them, not so soon after the mess at the solstice. His younger brother Gabriel and wife Rose were back in town, but he didn't feel right about dragging the two of them into it, either. Eventually, they'd all have to know, but until then, they deserved some down time.

Kellan. He'd moved into Gregor's house near Justin's for a while. Justin could tap Kellan for help this time around, since he came through the last fight relatively unscathed.

Justin pulled out his cell phone, texted his cousin to meet him at the office, and took a couple of pictures before leaving the corpse. He couldn't do anything to help the demon at this point. The safest thing would be to just ignore it.

He hit the sidewalk with his pathetic attempt at a jog and headed down toward the boardwalk that spanned Santa Monica and Venice Beach. So internalized was his thought process that it took him almost two blocks before he heard the rhythmic thump of feet and realized he'd been followed.

"Where's Kellan? Should you be out here alone?" The acerbic tone in her whiskey voice was nothing new.

"Magdalena." Hell. He didn't need to see the pity in her eyes.

"Of course."

He chanced a glance at her. She walked—walked! Hell, he was going old-man slow—next to him, a black jog bra and a skimpy pair of bright yellow running shorts her only clothing. Even in Los Angeles, it got chilly in January. He scowled. She was human. A witch. A very curvy, very sexy human witch. She should dress appropriate to the weather, damn it.

Maggie, interpreting his glare, sniffed. "There is nothing wrong with the way I'm dressed, which is similar, I might add, to the way you're dressed." She indicated his black running shorts and muscle shirt with a wave of her hand.

He cast another dark glance her way. "I'm not worried about *you*."

Her eyebrows rose. "You're still standing, stud. You know, I almost didn't recognize you without your dreads. Why'd you do it?"

"Because." He'd had dreadlocks since high school, and it still felt weird without them. But he'd had to do it, and "because" was his best answer.

Justin brushed a hand over his newly close-cropped head. Because he wasn't the person he'd been before the winter solstice, and all that had happened. Because hate ate at him, burned inside his soul, and he didn't want to pretend otherwise. Because being nice took work and energy he didn't have.

He heard her sigh. "Well, now that we've gotten the pleasantries out of the way, what about our corpse back there?"

"He's beyond worrying about the cold."

"Very true. I ducked in after you left but wanted to talk to you before you got too far, so I didn't have time to formulate much of a conclusion. What did you think?"

Justin frowned. "Ritual murder." His leg muscles were cramping. "Damn it." He stopped and leaned against a light pole, stretching his knotted hamstrings. Slowly, the muscle eased.

Maggie pulled her left heel to her butt, stretching her quads. "We think alike. Candle wax in his palms?" She switched legs and stretched the right one.

"Boosted with nightshade."

"That's what I thought, too. Oh, gods." Despair colored her voice.

"Exactly." Nightshade meant spells. Spells meant witchcraft, or sorcery. Add in the demon corpse, and there was a recipe for disaster. Justin closed his eyes briefly. As if they needed more disaster.

"Look, you don't need to worry about this. I'm going to talk to Kellan, and we'll start the investigation. Ow," he complained, rubbing where she punched him on the shoulder.

"Don't be stupid. I'm here. This is getting into my area of things now, not so much the demon slash Fae area. Use me, use my expertise," she demanded.

"Use you so you can get burned out again?" Justin snorted. "I don't think so."

She tugged at him but he didn't turn. She huffed out a sigh. "Look at me, Justin, for the gods sakes. You never used to be a coward. Look at me."

He turned toward her, his arms crossed defensively over his chest. His eyes met her honey-brown ones. "I'm looking." She was a very beautiful, very pissed-off witch.

"I am *fine*. I can do my own wardings, I can call up fireballs, I can protect myself and those I love. I can do everything I used to do. My heritage hasn't forsaken me, and I'm not burned out. Please. Use me." The sympathy in her voice melted away. "Or I'll investigate on my own, with my own team."

Justin turned from her and walked back the way they'd come, stifling a sigh as she followed. Who knew what kind of nutcases she'd hook up with if she investigated on her own? Hadn't her old coven proved less than reliable? Of the four that had helped at the solstice, three were dead.

He took a breath, and cursed at the waft of her perfume that came with the scent of the sea. He pushed the past away and focused on the now. "Did you notice anything about our body back there?"

Maggie shot him a swift glance. "Besides the candle wax? As a matter of fact, yes. He was missing an ear."

"Yeah. Does the ear thing have a special significance?"

She pursed her lips. "Not by itself, it doesn't. But you have to have been watching the streets."

"And what have you discovered, by watching the streets?"

She looked up at him, her dark eyes wary, as usual. He took a minute just to absorb the reality of her. While he stood over six feet, the top of her head came up to his chin. A goodly height for a woman, he'd always thought, tall enough to fit comfortably in his arms and yet not too tall.

Her black hair, only partially tamed by a ponytail, curled halfway down her back. Her full breasts strained against her exercise bra, exercising all his restraint as well as his memory. Her jogging shorts left lots of long, lovely leg exposed to the elements. But it was the look in her eyes, lost and haunted, which had always hooked him deep.

His heart caught and he glanced away. Scowled down at the cement passing too slowly beneath his feet.

She cleared her throat. "This is the third demon found murdered this week with a body part missing. Not that we can't smooth the demon part over with the local authorities," she said, waving a hand in dismissal. "We can, and have. That's the easy part."

"It's making it right with the press that's proved problematical, hasn't it?" Justin replied. "How's the reporter boyfriend? Todd, isn't it?" He hated even the thought of the guy.

"Tad, and he's not my boyfriend. He was very curious about what happened on the bluffs that night, and we've talked a bit. What's with you?" Maggie's eyes flashed hot. "Tad's completely safe. I can control him. Plus, I haven't gone spilling secrets."

"I'm not saying otherwise."

"Then what the hell are you saying?"

Good damned question. "I'm just saying that we've got to be careful. What other body parts are missing? Is there a pattern? Could it be a witch? Could it be Kendall again?"

"I don't know. Hell, with the amount of tourists we get, Harry flipping Potter could arrive in town and I wouldn't know about it. But I've got a friend in Homicide who can fill me in. As soon as I get back home, I'll make some phone calls and see what I can find out. As for Kendall? I wouldn't put it past him."

"Will your homicide buddy talk to outsiders?"

Maggie cocked her head to one side. "She might. She's scared enough."

Justin gripped her forearm, not noticing when she protested. "Why is she scared?"

She looked pointedly at her arm. Justin let go and watched as she rubbed where his hand had been.

"She's scared," Maggie said, acerbic, "because she's a tribred. Like you. Unlike you, however, she knows nothing about her own abilities. She thinks she's a freak. She's scared someone will clue in on the fact that the demon killings are happening on her turf and believe she's somehow responsible because she's part demon."

Hell. He knew there were other tribreds but didn't realize there were any in the greater Los Angeles area. He'd need to meet this one, take her measure. He'd need to tell his brothers, too. Meeting someone new, delving into a shared heritage, was not on his list of top ten fun things to do. "How soon do you think I could talk to her?"

Maggie's face froze. "Don't know. I'll call you when I do. See you around." She crossed the street at a jog and was soon out of sight.

Justin gritted his teeth against envy at her easy athleticism, and stepped up his speed. He hated being anything less than one hundred percent.

CPSIA information can be obtained at www.ICGtesting.com
Printed in the USA
LVOW081824140213

320154LV00001B/67/P

9 781937 254735